Dracula

Deathless Desire

by

Jay Palmer

Dracula - Deathless Desire
Copyright © 2017 Jay Palmer
All rights reserved.
ISBN-10: 0-9911127-7-6
ISBN-13: 978-0-9911127-7-7
Version 2

All Books by Jay Palmer

The VIKINGS! Trilogy:
    DeathQuest
    The Mourning Trail
    Quest for Valhalla

The EGYPTIANS! Trilogy:
    SoulQuest
    Song of the Sphinx
    Quest for Osiris

The Magic of Play
The Heart of Play
The Grotesquerie Games
The Grotesquerie Gambit
Souls of Steam
The Seneschal
Jeremy Wrecker – Pirate of Land and Sea
Viking Son
Viking Daughter
Dracula – Deathless Desire

Website: **JayPalmerBooks.com**

Cover Artist: Jay Palmer

*To our darkest demons,
real or imagined,
with whom only the great
shake hands ...!*

- And -

With all respects to
The Master of Terror,
Bram Stoker,
creator of the
most-legendary name
in classic horror.

Jay Palmer

Chapter 1

My Friend,
 Welcome to the Carpathians. I am anxiously expecting you. Sleep well tonight. At three o'clock tomorrow the Diligence will start for Bukovina; a place on it is kept for you. At the Borgo Pass my carriage will await you and will bring you to me. I trust your journey from London has been a happy one, and that you will enjoy your stay in my beautiful land.
 Your friend,
 DRĂCULA

The day ends. My life begins.
 Light reviles me, raising white blisters where other men darken to a smooth, dusky caramel. To those unlucky few who gaze upon me, I manifest ghastly pale, more sickly-white than a dying albino. Life itself enhances imperfection, and the greater and longer the life, the more that life is tormented by base and unwanted weaknesses. Where life extends to maddening endlessness, where consciousness revisits the same concepts century after century, all thought becomes repetition. Then even the slightest annoyance grows into a hated self-revulsion.

This is my curse, which the witless call a blessing.

I can't reveal the source of my curse, for I know not by who, how, or why I am damned. My unique torment comes of no known origin but continues eternally, as natural as waves frothing upon the sea, although nothing exists more unnatural than I.

I was born as most men are, an infant swaddled by a loving mother. I ran and played as a laughing child. I cried, although my dust-dry eyes have dripped no tears for three hundred years. I grew to a blithesome youth, fell in love, fought in petty wars, and was pledged to be married. Yet my lovely bride died in my arms, and now no child springs from my dead seed. Even my youngest nieces and nephews lie in their graves, forgotten, while I continue to infinity. Like any man, I expected to die, and many times I've come close, but Death shuns me with contempt. I've no desire to continue, but the merciless and everlasting God created my loathsome reality for a reason, and I'd know His purpose before I end my deathless Hell.

I was birthed in 1431, in a small city that now despises me: Sighişoara, Hungary. The year is now 1897; I am 466 years old ... and no mystery is greater to me than my own.

My aged bones creak and pop, stiff beyond arthritic, yet I never break. My crusty skin crackles, yet I never bleed. Pain excruciates to my very core, and the worst is that I suffer willingly, for the price of comfort scars worse than any acid, sharp blade, or animal's fang. I persevere without hope; madness is the sole fruit of eternal agony, and when existence engenders irreparable torture of the body, insanity manifests ... and then I must feed.

It is past time, but I mustn't feed yet ...

The sun set on May the 5th, 1897: St. George's Day, when local peasants fear me most. I arose with the dark, for the unseen alone comforts me. Men and women alike fear me, worse than devils from the depths of infernal nightmares, those dark dreams which frequently challenge my sanity, until I can't discern where the nightmare of my waking damnation deviates from the dementias of my cruelest sleeping fantasies. My dry, aged body ached beyond mortal comprehension, yet I forced my limbs onward. Step-by-painful-step, I ascended the dark-granite stairs of my crumbling, ancestral home.

In my beloved stable, my horses greeted me warmly, neighs of love from beasts descended many generations from sires I once purchased from the very island to which I'd soon return. Yorkshire Coach Horses: large, strong, brown horses with dark legs, thick manes, long tails, and a surprisingly noble bearing. Yorkshire Coach Horses are the longest-legged carriage-equestrians in the world, with an unmatched combination of swiftness, smooth gait, and endurance. For tall, elegant carriage horses, they are the best.

I petted them; they were my most-trusted friends, and my attentiveness to their needs endeared them to me. Yet that night, as they consumed their oats and water, I strapped on their strong harnesses, and then my deception began.

With trembling fingers, my iron will restraining the stabbing crackles as each finger joint bent, I turned the key and opened my ancient, brass-encrusted black walnut jewelry box which I kept upon the middle shelf in my stable, near to its great doors. In the box was a false beard: long, thick, curly black locks grown upon the chin of a sailor long dead. The cord binding the locks slid easily over my hairless, pale, skin-cracked scalp, and came to rest above my ears, binding the false beard over my dry chin. Around my shoulders I flung a heavy cloak to hide my pale features, and I capped myself with my tall, wide-brimmed hat to prevent the friendly moon and winking stars from revealing the truth of my disguise. I opened the great doors, and then, with faltering efforts, I climbed to the top of my sturdy, ancient coach. Sadly, I drew my weapon from its hold: I was late; *my only hope was the whip.*

    I drove my horses with a mastery no mortal can claim. Over rocks and around ditches I steered, heedless of the towering cliffs abutting the only road to my mountaintop sanctuary. My coach was of the old style, constructed of dark-stained durmast, the strongest Eurasian oak, its fully-enclosed passenger compartment supported by four large wheels. My driver's bench seat hung in front, and a folding bench extended from the back for a coachman. Downhill and through cool forests I urged my horses faster; I had a long way to go and I needed to hurry.

    I feared I'd have to pursue, but as I rounded the last bend, I sighted the rugged, boulder-strewn Borgo Pass. The four-horsed, rickety, covered carriage from Bistritz, which had outlasted three generations of owners, started to depart, but his mounts were no match for mine, and I was the better driver. Its driver would take from me that which I must have, despite that he knew I couldn't be thwarted. With the constant and eternal disgust endless predictability always engenders within me, I crossed his path and drug my stalwart steeds to a halt.

    "You're early tonight, my friend," I said to the driver.

"The English Herr was in a hurry," the driver tried to excuse himself with a lie.

Why must these foolish mortals try to deceive me? Centuries have inured me to falsehoods, experiences beyond count training me until every stretch of facial muscles, and every twitch of an eyelash, not to mention their unmistakable attempts to mask their uncalm voices, trumpeted an attempt at deception. These fools were born to lands where I once ruled, whose legends told of my residence 'ere their oldest known ancestors were born.

"You wished him to go on to Bukovina?" I replied in a whisper that stabbed every ear in the Borgo Pass. "You cannot deceive me, my friend; I know too much."

"Denn die Todten reiten schnell," came a whisper from the inside of the carriage.

I smiled, for I knew every language; the speaker had whispered: *"For the dead travel fast."*

With a haste caused only by their fear of me, their only foreign passenger, a stranger to my lands, was transferred to me, and his bags loaded aboard my coach. Then they rode off with alacrity, evidencing they regarded me as the infernal counterpart to their unjust God, who alone has the power to curse a man as I have been cursed.

Now I was alone with my guest ... who knew nothing of me.

"The night is chill, mein Herr, and my master the Count bade me take care of you," I spoke to my guest. "There's a flask of slivovitz underneath your seat, should you require it."

Without another word, I turned my horse-drawn coach around on the narrow road. I'd need my whip no longer. My friends would draw us back to my castle leisurely ... and then my plan would begin. A new chapter of my life would flourish. The promise of upcoming novelty almost made me smile; in a world of boring repetition to dull the mind of even the smartest man, novelty alone delights, offering a faint, tantalizing prayer of escape from thoughts and concepts long-ago grasped.

This man will be my novelty.

The ride back was long and relaxing, and my dearest friends, the wolves, howled as I drove my horses past them across the Mittel, the deep green hills of the Carpathians. A recent dusting of high mountain snows contrasted their chill shadows. The jarring of my wheels upon the ruts beneath us felt gentler upon my joints than my frantic ride to acquire my innocent passenger. I relaxed and inhaled to absorb the cool night air. The fragrant scents of the forest delighted me; although as frail as the rest of my ancientness, my nostrils filled with their welcoming aromas, and I appreciated their subtleties. I especially liked the trees, although only the eldest had seen more winters than I; it is a comfort to know some things lived and thrived ere I was born. Yet my nasal passages detected the endless rot suffusing them, the festering molds and slimes that hide, often unseen, in the very soil from which my companions sprouted. Someday even the eldest tree must die, and upon that day, I'll be filled with regret ... *and envy.*

"Driver ...?" cried a voice from inside my carriage. "Driver, what mountains are these?"

My passenger sought conversation. Doubtlessly he sat bored by his long ride, nervous in a new country, young, inexperienced, and uncertain. In his voice I heard his attempt to mask his timidity. I didn't reply; I'd provided him a bottle of slivovitz, an excellent plum brandy, to pass his time. I shouldn't have spoken to the driver that had delivered him to me, lest my passenger recognize my voice when I threw off this disguise. Yet I had no fear; unless he chose to leap from my carriage or risk the dangerous climb up to the gotza, the driver's bench, while countless rocks and ruts shook my carriage, he'd be helpless when I remained silent.

At one point, my brother wolves ran alongside my carriage, racing my steeds. My passenger grew alarmed, shouted, and banged his hand on the decorative woodwork of my carriage. I smiled, and at my merest gesture, my brothers fled into the frosted forest.

Night was deep as I clattered under my portcullis and drew up before the heavy doors of my keep. I hesitated just long enough for my passenger to disembark, and I lowered his baggage to him. Then, abruptly, I cracked my whip and drove my horses away. He shouted at my back, impotent, choking in the cloud of my dust. Without hesitation, I rushed my horses through both courtyards and into their stables, where I dismounted as fast as I could, and then I closed the wide doors behind me. Quickly I barred their entrance, in case my passenger should tire of knocking at my front door and come exploring.

With as much haste as I could manage, I flung my hat, cloak, and false beard onto my bench, unhitched my horses, and then hurried to my front door. Many long minutes had passed, and his knock was loud and frequent; *he was impatient.* I gathered my shaken nerves, lit a lantern, and drew back the massive iron bolts, their heavy chains clinking loudly. My door creaked long and loudly as it opened.

In the light of my lantern, held high, the stranger's eyes fully widened. He was indeed young, with pale, flawless fawn-brown skin. He had a moustache, thin and trimmed, his smooth cheeks and chin recently shaved, a high forehead, and a strong, straight nose. He was large and well-built, but despite being covered by several layers of cloth, I could tell he was no laborer, for his tall frame lacked the natural imposition of a man who works with his back. If not for his startled expression, seeing my ancient face for the first time, he might've been mistaken for a son of nobility, but he had a look of mildness, an impression of gentleness rare among the men of Transylvania.

If all of England was populated with men of his ilk, then his country would indeed be a feast.

Far stronger than his appearance arose his smell; fresh, rich, youthful blood pulsing through every artery and vein. He was full of life, on the verge of his prime, when a youth's body has grown to the limit his bones will reach and his frame and muscles harden into those of a man. The tantalizing, delicious aroma of his blood flushed my features, and the urge to surrender to violence, which would ease my unbearable agony, was almost overwhelming. To the aged, memories of energetic flexibility, of taut skin and soft bones, are taunts and torments, but the inevitability of time and death condemns mortals to accept their coming doom. Where remedy for this tragedy exists in the pulsing elixir of every human on Earth, only then is the mind tested for its moral convictions.

I hungered for him, but I must keep to my plan.

His reaction was no stranger. In the flickering lamplight, my deep-set eyes, low brows, and skeletal head was draped with skin like a horse wearing an elephant's hide, wrinkled and parched. My large, domed head, once graced with thick black hair, was as bald as a boulder. My height was taller than his, my shoulders wider; I was true royalty, and had once been a leader of armies, driving back even the mighty Turks. My frame had been the most imposing in the land, but now I appeared ghastly.

"Welcome to my house. Enter freely ... and of your own will," I said.

An uncomfortable moment passed while I sized him up even further, noticing his immaculate suit, which he must not have worn much on his travels, and shoes freshly polished, although they showed feint scuffs of having been worn for a while, and a tiny scent of brine wafted from their soles; the unmistakable smell of the sea. I wasn't surprised, for I'd received several letters from his employer informing me of his nautical route.

"Thank you," he said somewhat over-forcefully, in an attempt to hide his embarrassment at being startled. Then he swallowed hard, as if summoning a strength never before used. "I'm Jonathan Harker ..."

He held out his hand. Slowly I held out mine, and dead flesh grasped the living. He startled again, dropping his eyes to stare at my cold, hard, white, dry hand, which he longed to recoil from, but couldn't politely attempt. He seemed so perplexed I repeated my invitation.

"Welcome to my house. Come freely, go safely, and leave something of the happiness you bring."

At my words he seemed to recover. He shook himself, as if to fortify his resolve.

"Count Dracula ...?" he bowed in a courtly way, but with no forward movement.

I noted his strong English accent, and his stresses on the first sounds of my title and name, so different from the usage of my homeland. I needed to adopt his speech pattern; *my plan had begun!*

"I am Drăcula, of the royal house of Drăculeşti, Prince of Transylvania, Count of Hungary and Bulgaria, Voivode of Wallachia, Order of the Dragon," I said forcefully. "I bid you welcome, Mr. Harker, to my home. Come in; the night air is chill, and you must warm yourself, eat, and rest."

When he still took no forward step, I hung my lamp on a wall-bracket, and stepping out, I took his luggage and carried it in. He attempted to object but I shook my head.

"Nay, sir, you are my guest," I said, trying to smile without revealing the points of my teeth; *there was no sense frightening him now.* "It is late, and my people are not available. Let me see to your comfort."

Jonathan Harker entered my house as a man might enter his own crypt, knowing his demise was inevitable. To this I gave him credit; his senses understood more of his fate than his mind, which would break under the burden of countless memories I possessed. Yet he was born of a younger nation, an innocent race, and I perceived him as an adult assesses a child, blissfully ignorant of the tell-tale signs he blundered past unknowingly.

He stared with wondrous alarm at my foyer, with its tall ceiling and single iron chandelier, wrought of swords once wielded in defense of these lands, now glowing with the light of a single thickly-wicked candle, but shrouded in cobwebs and dust. The carvings upon my columns and around my doorways were intricate and fluid, of a style almost forgotten save by we who cherished the old ways. Every treasure was old, dreadful, with layers of histories unknown except to me. Dust lay thick in every crevice and upon the surfaces of every carving, and even on their rounded undersides; I'd long ago given up cleaning, and my maidens were chosen for their beauty, not their usefulness.

The next time I choose a maiden I'll choose wiser.

I watched the young man intently, discerning far more than an astute detective. Jonathan Harker walked with a stiffness that seemed unnatural to him, as if he were a free spirit being forcibly restrained for fear of revealing an unprofessional demeanor. The duration of his eyes upon certain sights identified his familiarity or interest; he barely glanced at a statue of magnificent craftsmanship, yet he gazed at an empty torch sconce intently, as if seeing one for the first time, and a portrait of a beautiful young woman mesmerized him. He was careful not to be obvious; clearly he was intelligent and educated, but neither worldly nor sophisticated in matters of art. I suspected he'd never been inside a castle before, as he glanced through my doorways and down side-passages as if confused by the labyrinthine turns of my manor.

I gestured for him to precede me up the winding stairs to the room I'd chosen for him. Forcing my creaking, aged body after him, I longed for the ease of movement he displayed with every step upon my stairs, and how his neck rotated almost effortlessly from side to side as he glanced for the first times at the numerous paintings, statues, and mosaics of my ancestral home. In his wake, the scent of him wafted even stronger, surging my hunger. Yet I had work to be done; *my entrance into a new life couldn't be heralded by news of a murder for which I'd be blamed.*

We entered his room, which was elegant but spartan; I'd specifically chosen it for its location more than its comfort, and this room I'd meticulously cleaned to insure my guest would have no objection to sleeping there. A fireplace with aged wood sat, ready to ignite, beside a wide bed, a small writing desk, many sconces with new candles, and a single window which looked down upon a cliff of unsurpassable height. Unless my guest could scale walls as I could then he couldn't escape these rooms. The thick carpets and bright tapestries made it a pleasant room, a little too boisterous for my austere tastes, yet this boy, who'd always be a child to my eyes, would doubtless find it pleasing.

"Please, rest here," I said to him. "I'll see my servants have your supper ready, and then I'll return."

I hurried as best I could to the kitchen. In my rusty oven I'd cooked paprika hendl, a traditional Hungarian recipe of chicken surrounded by vegetables, mostly red pepper. It was still warm, and looked and smelled fully-cooked, so I brought it to the small dining room, placed it before the one table setting that lay waiting, lit the candles, and then returned to fetch my guest. He greeted me rather warmly, having recovered from his initial shock at my appearance, and gladly followed me to his feast.

"I pray you, be seated and sup how you please," I said. "You will, I trust, excuse me that I do not join you, but I have dined already."

I poured for him a rare wine, Golden Mediasch, which produces a queer sting on the tongue, which is, however, not disagreeable. By smelling and carefully looking at it, he pretended to appreciate it before tasting it, although I could tell his understanding of fine wines was limited. He complimented me on the taste of both the wine and his meal, and then he fell silent. I stared at him the whole time, and he stared equally at me, as if memorizing every detail of my appearance. This bothered me, although it shouldn't, for my plans meant he'd never leave my castle alive. Yet I decided to divert his attention; I gave him the last letter his employer sent me, and he stopped eating to read it:

> *Dear Count Drăcula,*
> *I regret that an attack of gout, from which malady I am a constant sufferer, forbids absolutely any travelling on my part for some time to come; but I am happy to say I can send a sufficient substitute, one in whom I have every possible confidence. He is a young man, full of energy and talent in his own way, and of a very faithful disposition. He is discreet and silent, and has grown into manhood in my service. He shall be ready to attend on you as you will during his stay, and shall take your instructions in all matters.*
> *Respectfully,*
> *Mr. Peter Hawkins*

As he finished reading it, he looked up at me and tried to smile. I handed him a fine cigar, imported from Budapest, and excused myself, claiming I didn't smoke, before I lit his tobacco. Smoking obviously relaxed him, yet he still seemed nervous and looked about anxiously.

"Do you think broadly?" I asked, startling him from his inspection.

"Broadly ...?" Jonathan Harker asked.

"Broadly," I repeated. "A mind is evaluated not by its speed or breadth of knowledge, but by its extremes of reasoning."

"I .... I'm afraid I don't understand your meaning," Jonathan Harker said.

I frowned, and the intensity of my displeasure must've shown, for his expression paled and a sheen of concern masked his youthful features. I forced myself to remain calm; *this man was a child and I had to treat him accordingly.*

"How widely and how narrowly one thinks impresses me more than memorization," I explained. "A simple man may think about what he must do each day, while a sophisticated man ponders the nature of the universe, and the structure of the smallest leaf; it is to those who seek both extremes whom I respect."

"Ah!" the young man brightened. "Forgive my sluggishness, and thank you for making your meaning clear. I hope my slowness to understand doesn't affect your opinion of me. To answer your question: I'd say I'm somewhat in the middle, mostly because I've little time to dedicate to the fullness of the greater. I'm just starting out in life, and the countless details of improving my situation leaves me little time for personal reflection."

"You'd be wise to share your time accordingly," I said plainly, although I wasn't sure yet if he was capable of deep mental feats. "Momentary concerns create who we are. Personal reflections create who we choose to be."

"Oh, I do love discussing the breadth of the universe," Jonathan Harker said with a brief smile between bites, for he was careful to swallow before he spoke. "I spent two years at Cambridge, where I studied the planetary movements ..."

My scowl caught him by surprise, and he fell silent, fixated upon my face.

"The sciences are how men think small, not large," I said, slightly angered, for my new toy wasn't nearly as interesting as I'd hoped. "How objects in the heavens move is fascinating, but true scholars know there's more to the universe than mortals can see."

"Ah, you mean philosophy!" Jonathan Harker said, pausing before he took another bite.

"No," I said firmly, my voice deepened to a command. "Philosophy is merely a statement of beliefs; but perhaps you're too young for such subjects. My years exceed yours as a mountain does a dust-mote, and matters you would deem philosophy are to me as real as the planets."

"I beg your pardon; I'm certainly too young to know this world as well as you," Jonathan said. "But I'm eager to learn, if you'd be willing to impart any wisdom ..."

Frustrating as it might be, I can't blame a person for the recentness of their birth. His entreaty pleased me; *perhaps he wouldn't be as boring as I'd feared.*

"True wisdom comes with knowledge, experience, and deep introspection," I said. "Even the greatest teacher can only give you one of these treasures. As to the Great Mysteries of Life, even the ultimate treasures are conjectures, but ... ah! What conjectures they are! After endless introspection upon conjectures, the Great Mysteries become tangible beliefs; parts of them become certainties and the remainders become conditionals, and it is only by both of these that the true nature of man may be ascertained."

"I fear I've none of the elements required to ascertain my nature, if indeed I have one," Jonathan said. "I must apologize for being a poor guest ..."

"You are not a poor guest," I said. "But I judge you a poor man, as you are unenriched by the wealth of treasures your mind could possess. It is my hope that you, that all men, and women, for they are not reluctant to learn, given the chance, would avail yourselves of the bounty of certainty each could have ... if only they took the time to delve into their own minds."

At this, a look of unexpected excitement came upon my guest's expression.

"Master Drăcula, if I may refer to you by the title I perceive you deserve, I can't express my delight in your company, and if it's not too bold, my gratitude would be yours forever if you'd become my tutor in these matters ... and share with me even the smallest part of the vast knowledge you've amassed."

I grinned widely, finally amused, for my young guest had at last shown the novelty which alone delights me. No man born in the Carpathians would entreat to prolong my company. However, in my excitement, I forgot myself; Jonathan Harker's smile froze and his face paled, and a look of abject horror superimposed his taut, unwrinkled features. I quickly closed my mouth; *I'd shown him my teeth ...!*

No time to contemplate; I had to distract him.

"Death cannot be the end of consciousness," I said with absolute finality.

He absorbed my words, yet his alarm didn't lessen. He visibly shuddered, still stunned by his first glimpse of my fangs. I had to continue.

"Mountains once were barriers to human passage, but we learned to scale them," I said. "Oceans once limited our travel, yet now we sail them. The upper airs were once unreachable, yet balloons fly above the clouds. As science advances, barriers fall. Is not time such a barrier? We all exist trapped in time, but will not science someday master that which flows us from our cradles to our graves? What then will become of those long dead? When we can return to any time at which they were alive, will anyone truly be dead ... or will they just be ... unvisited?"

The look of shock upon Jonathan's face lessened, and he shook himself, ashamed to have again lost control in my presence.

"I ... I've never thought about it, but it must be true," he said, rather clumsily. "That's an amazing thought!"

"You must think deeply to fully understand this concept, for there are aspects of this which I still ponder," I said.

"Tell me more, I beg you!" Jonathan pleaded.

"Have you not seen a fly dash away from the hand that swats at it?" I asked. "Does not the deer flee the wolf? Clearly, all creatures fear death. What does that tell us?"

"What?" he asked. "Pray, tell ...!"

For a moment I doubted my plan; *could he not see the obvious?*

"We see the world around us, but unless everything that exists is visible, then we don't see everything," I explained slowly, as if to a child. "To know everything, we must become reservoirs of all knowledge; we must be aware of what all men think, and then determine which thoughts are invalid, inconsequential, or irrelevant to our goal. However, since animals also fear death, then it is equally obvious that animals think, and to know all, we must consider the thoughts of animals."

"But animals ... think poorly ... if at all!" Jonathan argued.

"It is not for facts we consume the thoughts of animals, but for clarity," I said. "Humans lie, to ourselves and to others, until truth is but a single grain of sand upon a beach of falsehoods. The study of animals reveals far more about the base nature of men than the thoughts of men."

"Ahh, I understand," Jonathan said. "By recognizing the concepts of those who know only truth we can divine the lies of those who believe falsehoods."

I grinned, for I couldn't help being impressed.

"You have a gift for insight and eloquence. I'm glad to host you in my home."

I'd much to do, and it was far past midnight; my guest must be tired, despite his carefully-arranged appearance. I decided to end our first evening together, as far as he was concerned. With my mind, I reached out to my distant brothers, and called to them, and commanded them to respond to their master. A moment later, languid, mournful howls filled the nearby forest, echoing through my hallways. Jonathan startled again, and looked about, visibly shaken.

"Listen to them: the children of the night. What music they make!" I said, and I rose from my chair. "Ah, sir, you dwellers in the city can't enter into the delights of the hunter. But you must be tired. Your bedroom is ready, and tomorrow you'll sleep as late as you will. I've many demands upon my time, and have to be away until late afternoon, so sleep and dream well!"

"I thank you, generous host, and I hope we may continue this discussion tomorrow," Jonathan said.

"It would be ... my greatest pleasure," I replied.

I closed the door to his room and waited outside it, breathing deep breaths to control my lusts. As he prepared himself for bed, I listened carefully, for his movements were swift and certain, without the agony of one whose body has succumbed to the ravages of time. Even through the thick door I could smell his delicious scent, which lingered in the air and was nearly-overpowering. Yet I was determined; quenching my thirst upon him would spoil my carefully-orchestrated plan. I had to resist; *the lives of my people depended upon me.*

Yet his heart beat loudly, and I could feel each pulse in his arteries, even through the thick door. Memories of the taste I longed for and despised haunted me, yet I forced back my hungers. Finally I walked away, more silently than a shadow in moon-glow, after he fell helplessly asleep.

I'd much to do; he'd awaken during the dreadful day, and no one would be there to greet him. I wrote him a note and placed it where he'd find it:

"I have to be absent for a while. Do not wait for me. --D."

Then I cleared his dishes, but I didn't wash them, for that would never be done. Normally I commanded my brides to do such chores, although they worked poorly and were lazy, driven only by their immortal thirst, but I'd banished them from this part of the castle, for their strength to resist our cursed appetite was pitiful. However, once cleared, I arranged new breads and cheeses, and a clean place setting for Jonathan to find tomorrow, and then I descended into the dungeon of my castle where I'd imprisoned my loves.

"He's here!" Loritá snarled as I unlocked their door and entered. "We can smell him. We must taste him!"

"He shall not be touched," I said darkly, my tone implying a beyond-the-grave threat.

All three of my maids hissed angrily, but none dared to refute my commands. However, my orders would be forgotten if they spied my guest, so I stayed firmly between them and the unlocked door. They glared at me, their eyes red, their snarls showing gleaming fangs. I watched them closely, for they'd fulfill their lusts ... even against my commands.

Dark and olive-skinned, Loritá was my eldest, my first deathless lover, a peasant whose beauty was astounding even before arising into the perfection of immortality. Now she was a temptress without compare, a seductress who knew every trick to inflame the desires of men, taught by centuries of expertise in hunting would-be lovers ... and convincing them to accompany her to some dark and discreet hideaway, where amid their writhing satisfactions they'd never realize they were dying.

Miëta, my princess, the daughter of an emperor, was wise, cunning, and dangerous, the only maiden on Earth who posed a threat to me. Of all those who inhabit the worlds of the living or the dead, Miëta was closest to being my mental equal, and she understood the depth of my purposes, and even my feelings nearing compassion, which she didn't share. Her delight of cruelty intensified in the two centuries she'd walked the night. Killing was no delight to Miëta, for death ends the suffering of her victims. She was my torturess, to whom I send those who anger me.

Hēlgrēth, my last true love, was born of the young races in Europe's farthest northwest. Her bright, sun-radiant hair and azure eyes shone like the stars of sapphires, and enhanced the innocence of her appearance, her gentle, deferential manner which was her trademark. Her mild demeanor dispelled all reservations her victims might have, as with submissive bearing she set aside worries and doubts, and with hands as soft as a newborn canary she lays men down to a deep sleep from which they'd never awaken. Even her fangs were small and delicate, and the sharpest, for she could bleed a sleeping victim to death without ever awakening them.

Loritá, Miëta, and Hēlgrēth stared at me, three different glares, all the same hate. I alone stood between them and their closest source of gratification. Once they'd had many sisters, but those maids dared to seek their own nourishments among my people, who knew and understood what they were ... and how to destroy them ... or worse: *they defied my will.*

In the end, after I've departed Castle Drăculea, long after my current guest is drained of every drop of life, hunger will force my nocturnal trio to seek frequent sustenance, and the neighboring villages will eventually rise up and destroy them. On that day I'll be sad, for at one time I loved each of them, but they've become anchors that tie me to this life, to my ancestral bonds, which I'm determined to escape.

"Where's the meal I commanded?" I ask them.

Hēlgrēth moved aside a cloth and lifted a tray, prepared as I'd ordered, and she approached with slow deliberation, flowing across the broken flagstones.

"Master, will you not explain ...?" Hēlgrēth asked sweetly.

Her pleasantness affected me, yet I couldn't succumb. Miëta watched and listened, and my only fear was that she might perceive my intention, for she alone could thwart my purpose.

"I said I'd explain, but not yet," I said. "I'll give you his name, Jonathan Harker, but I warn you again; he's forbidden ... until my business with him is completed."

"What business is that?" Loritá asked, gliding to the other side, as if to distract me, yet I kept my focus on Hēlgrēth, for only she was close enough to attack without warning. I didn't fear them; I excelled all enemies, for I was the ultimate warrior, trained from birth to conquer and command, a Prince of Transylvania, and now the King of Eternal Darkness.

"You know the penalty of defiance," I warned them. "Curb your hungers or you'll never feed again. Trust me: when I'm finished you may drink your fill."

"We smell him on you," Miëta said, her very tone an accusation. "He's young and strong. Will a single drop remain after you've finished him?"

"We're dry as dust," Hēlgrēth said. "Can we have nothing now?"

"The night's almost spent," I said, and I reached out and took my guest's meal from Hēlgrēth's graceful hands. I glanced at the tray; it was food fit only for the living. "I'll bring you something as soon as I may."

As I stepped back toward the door, all three women hissed at me like vipers, eager to bury their fangs in living flesh. Yet I heeded them not; I firmly closed and locked their door behind me. Through the stout wood I heard Hēlgrēth scowl, and then Loritá screamed in anger. As always, Miëta made no sound, offering me no evidence I could use against her. I'd have to feed them something soon, but I had to be certain they were starving first; I couldn't allow them to increase their numbers, creating others in the hopes of killing me, as several of my past maiden-lovers had tried ... *right before I killed them permanently.*

Hurrying back, I set Jonathan's next meal beside the bread, cheese, and my note, where Jonathan would find all. Then I began my other chores, including feeding and watering my horses for the day, as my maidens couldn't perform their usual duties. I made sure all the doors out of the section of the castle where Jonathan slept were locked; it'd ruin my plans if he strayed upon secrets he didn't need to learn. Then I felt the customary weakness saturate my limbs; *the cocks would soon crow.*

With no small amount of trepidation, I returned to my maidens and locked myself inside with them.

"It is time," I said, and jeweled daggers seem to spike from their eyes. Yet they'd no choice; our weakness was evident. I gestured for them to precede me and followed at a safe distance.

Our resting-chamber lay in my vast dungeon, topped with a high ceiling, under which our coffins lay. On the bottom step I waited, watching as my three lovelies, my immortal damsels of death, opened their lids and reposed themselves in their customary positions. I stared at each of them in turn and held them long in my gaze. Admiration and appreciation of beauty is a trait that enhances with age, and long centuries have imbued me with a love of beauty far greater than I possessed when last my heart beat. Only when I heard the first cock's cry did I ascend my stairs to my topmost earthen platform, where my own splendid coffin lay. My weakness was almost complete, yet I couldn't risk being attacked while I lay helpless; I had to wait until they were as sedate as I. With my last ounce of strength, I pulled my lid down over me, and it slammed shut like a cannon's boom, as I was too weak to restrain it. Then exhaustion took hold; I'd accomplished many trying tasks for one as aged as I, who'd not fed in almost fifty years.

But soon I'd feed again.

On May the 6th, Hēlgrēth screamed at me as I moved to unlock the door ... and to seal them in for another night. I'd commanded them to be silent, for fear their shrieks would alarm my guest, but they were hungry, and I, too, felt their desires.

"One more shriek and you'll have not a sip of my guest; I'll let your sisters suck him dry," I warned her.

Hēlgrēth bit back a retort as Loritá grinned, but Mïeta glared.

"Creatures of the night shouldn't be caged," Mïeta snarled. "Our curse shall turn us."

I met Mïeta's eyes with a stare as baleful as hers. She was pushing me, hoping for a reaction that would reveal my secret.

"I'll bring you relief soon; you'll not starve," I said, locked on her gaze. "Restrain yourselves for but a few more nights ... or I'll restrain you ... forever."

"What does this mortal give you that's more important than us?" Loritá demanded.

Believable lies filled my mind; a few choice words would settle them, but I'd taught them to detect falsehoods, and I preferred to never utter lies; lies were monsters fools unleashed upon themselves. I was a Count of Hungary, a Prince of Transylvania; I wouldn't be consumed by my own deceptions. Yet I dared not tell them the truth; *combined against me, I wasn't certain I'd prevail.*

"All I've ever had I've shared," I said firmly. "All you have has come from me. How dare you question me?"

My question was answered by doubt, and in Miëta's expression, sheer disbelief, but they spoke not another word. I unlocked the door, closed it, and caged them behind me.

From a special crypt where the chill never ends I fetched the full pot I'd placed there 'ere my guest arrived, and I carried it up the long stair to the kitchens, where all was waiting. Quickly I threw dry firewood into the hearth, lit it, hung my pot upon an iron hook, and swung it into the rising flames. Assured that the fire wouldn't extinguish, I proceeded up the great stairs and unlocked the door to the wing in which my guest resided, careful to relock it behind me. His bedroom was empty, yet a brief search found him in my library. My low table in the center was littered with my atlas, English magazines, and newspapers, which I'd had shipped here, though none were of a recent date. Here I'd placed books of various subjects: history, geography, politics, economics, botany, geology, and law, all relating to England and English life, British customs, and formal manners. One of my favorites, a picture book describing in detail the various types of popular horse-drawn carriages, had been moved aside. Jonathan was reading my copy of Whitaker's Almanac, and my London Directory lay beside him. He looked relieved to see me, and hungry, although his hunger paled before mine. To alleviate his worry, I saluted him with a friendly gesture.

"Forgive me, my dear friend, but the business that called upon me lasted far longer than I'd expected," I said. "I hope you are well rested."

"Thank you, I am," he said. "I thought I heard your servants shout from outside, but none came near enough for me to see."

"The needs of a royal personage such as myself demand their presence as well," I said. "My servants are below, and your dinner is being prepared."

"You're too kind," Jonathan said, and his face showed a relief I could only envy.

"My dear friend, I'm glad you found your way here, for I'm sure there is much here that will interest you. These companions ..." I laid an icy hand upon one of my books, "... have been good friends to me, and for some years past, ever since I developed the idea of going to London, these books have given me many hours of pleasure. Through them I've come to know your great England ... and to love her. I long to walk through the crowded streets of your mighty London, to stand amid your whirl and rush of humanity, to share its life, its changes, and its deaths. But alas! As yet, I only know your tongue through books. It is through you, my friend, that I must learn how to speak properly."

"But, Count," Jonathan said, "you speak English well!"

"I thank you, my friend, for your too-flattering estimate, yet I fear I'm but a brief journeyman upon the road I'd travel. I know the grammar and the vocabulary of your English, but I know not how to express myself."

"I beg to disagree," Jonathan said. "You speak excellently."

"Ah, but were I to speak in London, all would know me for a stranger," I said. "That's insufficient. Here, I am a noble; a *boyar*, which was originally a Russian title ranking below prince. Here I'm the master of all. But as a stranger in your land, I'm no one; men know me not, and to know not is to care not. I'll be content only when I can speak like the rest of Londoners, so no man who hears me stops and says *'Ha! A stranger!'*.

"So long I've been master of all that I'd be a master still ... or at least speak that no other should master me. You, Jonathan Harker, come to me as agent of my friend, Peter Hawkins of Exeter, to tell me all about my new estate in London, yet I must have more. You shall, I trust, rest here with me awhile, that by our talking I may learn the proper English intonations, and I ask that you tell me when I err, even in the smallest way. I'm sorry I was away so long today; forgive one who has many important affairs."

"Of course," Jonathan said. "But ... other than your heavy accent ..."

"Yes ...?" I asked. "Please speak."

"Only because you ask, and meaning no offense," Jonathan said. "You do seem to speak in ... very long sentences, and that would be noticeable by most Englishmen."

"I thank you," I said. "I shall endeavor to make my speeches shorter, yet I beg your pardon, for one as aged as I, the thoughts we're accustomed to dwell upon are often complex, with many details, connecting myriad facets of human experience, of which I am greatly endowed, and thus are unable to be conveyed in a few ..."

I stopped, realizing from the slowly-rising eyebrows on Jonathan's face, that I was speaking exactly as he'd commented. Spontaneously we both began laughing, and humor, so rare an experience for me, warmed my cold heart.

"I hope I didn't intrude by reading your books without permission," Jonathan said, obviously trying to quickly change the subject.

"No man should ask permission to gain knowledge," I said, still smiling. "Read any book you fancy, and go anywhere you wish in the castle, except where doors are locked, where of course you would not wish to go. There are reasons for all things here, and could you but see with my eyes then you'd understand better."

"I welcome any knowledge to aid my understanding," Jonathan said.

"Understandings take time, and must be digested slowly," I warned. "Beware you don't understand too quickly, or you'll consume dry facts without comprehending their fullness. Transylvania isn't England. Our ways aren't yours. Doubtless, here much will be strange to you. From what you've told me of your experiences, you've already witnessed some strangeness. I pray you: explore slowly. Each course must be devoured fully ... if you'd truly experience your feast."

"Indeed, I have been mystified," Jonathan said. "No doubt the fault is mine for not understanding your local customs, but many here seem ... afraid of you. Also, the coachman who brought me to meet with your driver stopped several times; seeing a dim blue flame spout up suddenly in the woods, he halted his horses and ran into the forest. Yet the blue flame, whatever it was, always vanished as mysteriously as it came, and each time he slowly came back, grousing and discouraged. He said that on a certain night of the year, last night, all evil spirits hold unchecked sway, and a blue flame appears over any place where treasure has been concealed."

"Those treasures have lain hidden for hundreds of years," I explained. "The region through which you journeyed last night was fought over for centuries by the Wallachians, the Saxons, and the Turks. Why, there's hardly a foot of soil in this region that hasn't been enriched by the blood of invaders and patriots. In old days, when Austrians and Hungarians came in hordes, our warriors rode out to meet them: men and women, the aged, and even our children. All awaited our enemies in the rocks above the passes, to sweep destruction upon the invaders with artificial avalanches. Also, there are secret paths throughout these mountains, where my people have hidden treasures and fled without detection, and thus my people are fancied to have unholy powers to evade men's eyes. When the invader was triumphant, he found but little, for whatever existed hid sheltered under friendly soil."

"But how can treasure remain undiscovered when there's so specific a pointer to it, if men would but take the trouble to follow it?" Jonathan asked.

Reluctantly I smiled, again displaying my teeth.

"Because your peasant driver is at heart a coward ... and a fool. Those flames only appear on one night; and on that night no man of this land will, if he can help it, stir outside of his doors. And, dear sir, even if he did, he wouldn't know what to do. Why, this peasant you tell me of, who sought the blue flames, wouldn't know where to look for that same spot in daylight. Even you, I dare be sworn, wouldn't be able to find those places again, ... would you?"

"You're right," Jonathan said. "I know no more than the dead where to look for them."

I smiled at his reference.

"For searchers, there are many dangers in this land, perils of bird, beast, and spirit, yet we shouldn't discuss those now, for you must digest what you've learned 'ere you sup another meal," I said. "Come, tell me of London, and of the house you've procured for me."

"Forgive my remissness!" Jonathan exclaimed. "I have maps, photographs, and drawings in my satchel; if you'll pardon me, I'll fetch them."

With a gesture from me, he returned to his room. I used the moment to light more candles, for I wished to see clearly what I'd purchased. When he returned, he showed me all of the documents he'd brought, and I memorized each at a glance – they matched what I'd already learned from my correspondences with other businessmen from his country, of whom Jonathan was ignorant. We spoke long about the residence and area, and I fear I spoke too freely.

"How could you know that?" Jonathan asked. "You sound ... as if you've already been there."

"My friend, is it not needful I should know? When I go there I shall be alone, and my friend Harker Jonathan -- nay, pardon me, I fall into my country's habit of putting your patronymic first -- my friend Jonathan Harker won't be by my side. You'll be in Exeter, many miles away, working on papers of law with my friend Peter Hawkins. So, tell me specifically about my estate, and why you chose it."

"It lies near Purfleet, on a by-road, where I came across just such a place as seemed to be required by your letters," Jonathan said. "The estate is surrounded by a high wall, of ancient structure, built of heavy stones, and hasn't been repaired for decades. The main gates are tall, of old oak and iron, all eaten with rust.

"The estate is called Carfax, no doubt a corruption of the old *Quatre Face*, as the house is four-sided, agreeing with the cardinal points of the compass. The estate contains in all some twenty acres, and many trees grow upon it, which makes it in places gloomy, and there's a deep, dark-looking pond or small lake, evidently fed by hidden springs, as the water is clear and flows away in a fair-sized stream.

"The house dates of all periods, I should say, back to mediæval times, for one part is of immensely-thick stone, with only a few windows high up and heavily barred. It looks like part of a keep, and it's adjacent to an old chapel or church. I couldn't enter all of it, as I had no key, but I've taken kodak stills of it from various points. The house has been added to, but in a very straggling way, such that I can only guess at the amount of ground it covers. Only a few houses are nearby, one being a very large home recently formed into a private lunatic asylum. It isn't, however, visible from your grounds."

"I'm glad it is ... I mean ... it's ...old and big," I said with all honesty, trying to mimic his style of speech. "I myself am of an old family, and to live in a new house would kill me. A house can't be made habitable in a day; and, after all, how few days go to make up a century? I rejoice also that there's a chapel of old times. We Transylvanian nobles love not to think our bones might lie amongst the common dead. I seek neither gaiety nor mirth, nor the bright voluptuousness of sunshine and sparkling waters. My heart, through years of weary mourning, attunes not to jollity. But the walls of my castle are broken, its shadows many, and cold winds breathe through my broken battlements. I must have a home of a newer build, which bows to my comforts: I love the shade and shadow, and would be alone with my thoughts."

Something in my tone made Jonathan look up questioningly, and I fell silent. In the rare pleasure of conversation, I'd forgotten myself; *despite that he'd soon die, I couldn't allow this stranger to glimpse my soul, if my curse had left me even that.*

Angry that I'd revealed myself too much, I rose and walked out of the room. Jonathan called after my abrupt departure, his voice full of surprise, yet I left his cry unanswered.

My plans were set. *Jonathan had already seen too much.* Knowledge is power, and I can't allow others power over me. When I enter his England, my chosen feeding ground, I must arrive unknown, unrecognized, hiding in the shadows I choose. My plans were set, and I couldn't allow myself the weakness of liking Jonathan; *his last delights would be the kisses of my brides.*

Locking his door behind me, I hastened to the kitchen to check on Jonathan's meal. It was nearly done,

and so I took a few precious moments to rest; I'd not pushed my stiff, dry body to this much movement in years, and the pains I normally felt doubled under my current exertions. The smell of Jonathan's blood, so warm, so close, was drawing me faster toward madness. I had to resist, yet always, one word dominated my thoughts:
    Soon!

Jay Palmer

Chapter 2

Bubbling and steaming, I served his dinner on a wide tray, weighted down with a roast of pig and many vegetables in a hearty broth, smelling so good I was tempted to taste it, although I knew the ill effects human food had upon me. Heavy it was, for it was several meals worth of food, yet I carried it up to his small dining room, and found him again in my library.

"Aha!" I said, "Still at your books? Good! But you mustn't work always. Come; I'm informed your supper is ready."

As he seated himself at my table, Jonathan pointed up to a painting hanging by the door.

"Forgive me, but this painting is masterful," Jonathan said. "When did you pose for it?"

I couldn't help but smile.

"This was my father; a great man," I explained.

"Your family resemblance is strong," Jonathan said. "The same jaw, and the same forehead; you must have looked much like him in your youth."

The sweet compliment warmed my heart, for I cast no reflection and had previously held only hope that I resembled my father. Yet I frowned; *I couldn't afford to like Jonathan as much as he deserved.*

Despite my reservations, we talked many hours on countless subjects, and I reveled in the delight of sharing my knowledge and insights, which no other man on Earth comprehended. Meanwhile, I studied his mannerisms, dialect, and intonations, which I'd have to mimic perfectly to pass for an Englishman. Jonathan was often amazed, and drank eagerly at the spring of my wisdom. Again, I should've restrained myself but I couldn't help it; this mortal would soon be leaving this world forever. *The least I could do was reward him with knowledge he wouldn't live to pass on.*

Jonathan did offer a few more comments on my patterns of speech and pronunciation, and each time I thanked him and adjusted accordingly.

Eventually the cry of a distant rooster warned me it was nearly time.

"Morning again? How remiss I am to let you stay up so long. You must make your conversation less interesting, that I may not forget how time flies."

With that, and a few benefic farewells, I left ... and waited until he fell asleep to set his morning meal.

Mïeta stared at me as I unlocked and entered our chamber. I glanced about; Hēlgrēth and Loritá's coffins were already closed, their lids tightly shut. I smiled; *they think I'm deceived.*

"Dawn has come," Mïeta said, a scowl of derision in her voice. "You tempt the weakness we share with the nearness of your guest. You must have reasons; share with me your mind. Do you test us ... test me?"

I said nothing, but I firmly closed and locked our door, sealing us inside. Then I stared at Mïeta; *she must think me a fool, I, who have never been fooled.*

"You are recreant with your thoughts," Mïeta said. "Come, share with me, as you used to. Let us join in purpose as we have joined in mind and body so many times. I yearn to be one with you again."

Mïeta stepped forward. She was wearing her favorite cloak, black silk, and it clung to her shapely form. From its concealment, a pale hand reached to her throat, released the clasp, and the black fabric flowed from her bare shoulders to collapse around her slender ankles, revealing my goddess of Asian beauty in her naked voluptuousness, the temptation of luscious desire so great that, once I'd seen it, I couldn't let it succumb and be ravaged by time. Even after centuries, so beautiful was she, raven-haired, white-skinned, youthful and pert, a silky softness ever tempting me to meld us into one, flesh into flesh. She was vampiric perfection; she inflamed even the cold lusts within my withered shell, such that I longed to succumb to her once more. No man could resist her naked wondrousness, and I yearned to yield to her persuasions.

But she was the trap ...!

"Hēlgrēth," I said softly. "Loritá. I am not deceived."

Mïeta's look of passive desire suddenly burned with hate.

"Let us out!" Mïeta cried.

"Soon," I promised. "I give you my word; Jonathan will be yours."

Silently Hēlgrēth and Loritá stepped into view, from shadowed alcoves on opposite sides of me. My anger grew; *they should've known better!* Mïeta knew the depth of my military training, the thought I put into tactical planning; no doubt her hunger made her think I'd surrender my reasoning to share her coffin again. We hadn't mated in forty years; she refused to lie with me when my skin was so decrepit; she preferred me soft and young.

However, I dared not disrupt my timetable. *Their punishments would come ...!*

"Your trap has failed," I said to Hēlgrēth and Loritá. "Mïeta's charms have miscarried; I wasn't distracted, as was clearly your purpose ..."

"We hunger ...!" Loritá said angrily.

"You shall drink before I; I swear it!" I said.

"Master," Hēlgrēth said. "Do you not still love us?

How can you deny we who've loved you forever?"

Hēlgrēth was my greatest seductress; her passive appearance, reticent and demure, disguised her deadly nature far more than Miëta, my queenly tower of voluptuous elegance, or Loritá, my dark, aggressive temptress. Even over I, Hēlgrēth's powers of seduction held sway, but my supremacy of will was greater than theirs. I stood like a mountain, unmoved by their beauty, apparent longings, and invitations to pleasure.

Miëta bent her knees deeply, without bending her spine or slumping her shoulders, displaying the grace I'd always admired, and reached down and plucked her silk cloak from the ground, then rose to face me undaunted. She made no attempt to cover herself; at this point, a display of false modesty would appear comical, demeaning to her meticulously-guarded dignity. Yet her eyes burned with fires I knew too well; *madness was overcoming them*. Soon I'd have no choice but to surrender Jonathan, or someone else ... or our shared bloodlust would drive us to violence.

I stood and waited as dawn's weakness grew stronger in me, and finally my brides succumbed. One-by-one they entered their coffins; Miëta paused to fling her black silk cloak back about her shoulders and fasten it at her throat, concealing her unparalleled charms, 'ere she lifted the lid of her coffin and slid into it as water pours from a pitcher. Seeing I was watching, she closed the gap in her cloak before she lowered her lid. I waited, feeling the rays of the unfortunate sun shine over the distant peaks to touch the crumbling walls and towers of my castle; *oh, how lucky they are, even the cold stones, to be touched and warmed by the rising sun which gives life to all not cursed and damned.* My aged body endured the weakness only because I willed it to, and my will is iron; I can't be thwarted ... not even by me.

Assured they'd rise no more that night, I slowly descended to and crossed my wide floor of broken, uneven stones, every step mortal agony. Rigidly I proceeded, slowly, so as not to succumb to dawn's exhaustion. In my cavernous dungeon, step-by-step I arose toward my salvation: large, black, and marked with the name and crest of my family. I needed both hands to lift its lid; herein lay my sanctuary, my morbid throne of eternity, where even the power of daylight fails. Here alone lies comfort while the daystar circles across the Heavens, banishing lesser lights. I struggled not to fall in, but to arrange myself so my body didn't awaken sorer than now, and finally I relaxed as any corpse should, safe in my tomb. I'd no strength to gently lower my protection; I pulled with the last of my strength, and my lid came crashing down, deafening my ears, and then wondrous oblivion washed away my pains, and the brief taste of true-death caressed me.

Consciousness slowly returned on May the 7th. As my weakness was ebbing, a sound so soft only I could detect it alerted me. The sun was near setting, but already I felt my night-strength returning, and with it came enhanced senses. I've been the wolf, *the hunter,* the bear, *the lumberer,* and the snake, *the slitherer.* I felt more than heard the soft steps of bare feet upon stone; *my brides were approaching.* With the first movement of evening, I reached out and set my palms against the inside walls of my coffin; in the stillness of a crypt, even the slightest movement stirs the stale air, and I felt my brides creeping towards me with stealthful treads, barefoot to muffle their approach, but I'm the deadliest hunter and the wisest warrior.

I heard no chink of chain nor soft scrapes of coiled rope; their intention wasn't to bind me within my coffin, as others have tried. Miëta, Hēlgrēth, and Loritá have seen what I do to those who betray me or seek my doom; I feared no physical attack, as they knew my fighting skills exceeded theirs.

This would be a mental attack.

I steeled my thoughts; *I couldn't let them in.* The

human mind is susceptible to the slightest intonation. Some sights can make a grown man weep, or frighten a woman into fainting. Even an expression could mesmerize, and evoke longing, sorrow, or sympathy so intense it can shackle the observer more firmly than manacles, despite any determination to resist. Ageless, all children of the night can master these expressions, so commanding that comprehensive discourse can occur using only our eyes; most mortals are quickly overcome by our power. Miëta is especially good at forcing her will over others, yet subtle enough to persuade while distracting, a mistress of temptation to influence the unwary.

    I waited patiently; I could sense them just outside my coffin. They must've fought their weakness to arise early; their night-strengths would come upon them slowly. I relaxed like the dead, allowing the sunlight above my lands to slip over the horizon and dim the sky. The night-strength came upon me slowly but fully, unforced, and I waited to embrace it.

    I closed my eyes ... and then I lifted my lid.

    Suddenly, before my lid was fully opened, it was hurled upwards by a force not of my own. Bodies leaned over me, suddenly, intending to startle, to catch me by surprise, doubtless with practiced expressions so strong mortal men would cry out in fright.

    I smiled, my eyes still closed; *without seeing them, their expressions couldn't affect me;* I'd surprised them ... and they know I'm too powerful for psychic attacks.

    Prepared, I opened my eyes at last; Hēlgrēth and Loritá stared back at me, their planned expressions faltered, bewildered by my failure to respond, silently voicing alarm at their own impotency. Miëta alone maintained her composure of command, and so stern were her eyes mine were instantly fixated upon hers, unable to turn away. Yet I never feared; these tricks I'd mastered 'ere they were sired. I'd taught them their use ... and their sway. Hēlgrēth and Loritá attempted to resume their practiced looks, their attacks of appearance, but they'd been made feeble by my simple, unexpected counter to their combined attacks. With a force of mastery I alone can claim, I wrenched my basilisk gaze from Miëta and stared at both of them. The stark fury of my expression frightened them, dilating their eyes ever so slightly – *I almost smiled at their weakness.* Unaffected, my brows remained steely, allowing no doubt of my determination. My pupils stared directly and undaunted, my eyes unblinking, unwavering, staunch and relentless. My pallor was calm, untightened, denoting my resolute confidence in my just and rightful persistence. My expression was murderous, but not twisted with maddened rage; my chin was lifted, my poise stiff, as signifies my noble parentage, which only Miëta could equal.

Hēlgrēth and Loritá faltered and fell back, unable to bear my gaze. Both were too strong and clever to be overwhelmed, as any of us could do to a mortal, yet they couldn't bear the fury of my righteous displeasure. I was their master and sire into eternal deathlessness; *this attack was a betrayal!* Fear filled their eyes, their heads withdrew, and they turned away, crumbled and ashamed.

Miëta faced me solo; *no fear marred her eyes.* Her hunger radiated, her longing for substance, the warm, sequent need we shared. So strong was her visage my bloodlust awoke unbidden, and my dust-dry mouth slaked, desiring the rich diet that sustained us, and my mind reeled, needing refreshment as much as she. I was strong enough to tackle Miëta alone, to absorb any emotions her masterfully-executed expressions might engender, but over the endless appetite we shared even I held little power. I wavered, glad I'd focused first on Hēlgrēth and Loritá, her weaker sisters, as Miëta's intense focus would've left me unprotected from their lesser assaults. However, this wasn't a contest between equals; I was the font of the curse they bore, and my curse came straight from the one divine God. I was Drăcula; I flee before no assault and quaver before no challenge. Neither Miëta nor I accepted defeat, but in an instant, we both knew it was over.

If she'd won, then my hungers would've overpowered me, and I would've led them upstairs to the young, foreign feast we would've shared. Not until my thirst was slaked would I have given thought to my complex plan. Yet neither of us would succumb. She wouldn't relent before me, and hungers hadn't dimmed my mind and detracted; no victory would be won here today, *and without victory, Miëta wouldn't feed until I allowed it.*

Miëta fell back as I climbed from my coffin, and I seized all three in my gaze.

"This betrayal is unworthy," I said. "Your master exceeds all concerns, even your hungers. Now back, all of you! My plans include your feedings, but in the sequence I choose. Obey me!"

My voluptuous temptresses withdrew, shielding themselves by retreating behind my coffin, stepping as far back as my tall earthen mound would allow without crawling down its steep ledge. With a final glare at them, I strode down my steps, ever listening behind me, wary of pursuit. Luckily none came, for Miëta had indeed awoken my hunger. I walked straight to the door of our burial chamber, unlocked it, exited, and locked them inside for another night of starvation.

I could allow this effrontery, but soon they wouldn't be able to control their urges any longer; *I had to feed them someone.*

Not tonight; I had important duties.

Again I went through the process of preparing a meal. I slipped quietly into the locked dining room to set it, and then I went in search of my guest. I found him shaving in his bedroom, with no sign of suspicion or dread, and I eased my concerns; *Jonathan was growing accustomed to my daylight-absences, and probably accepted it as just another strange custom of this land.* I was grateful for his complacency, for this simple young man was helping me achieve my ultimate plan. I greeted him by placing a friendly hand upon his shoulder, and I spoke cheerily in the style of England.

"Good morning."

Jonathan jumped, startled, as if my presence were the last thing he expected. I was taken aback, for I was so accustomed to my usual habit of walking silently, mastered over centuries, I'd forgotten to give him warning of my presence. Then I spied a revulsion to awaken even my horror: *Jonathan had propped a looking-glass, a mirror, upon the shelf, and was using it while he shaved.*

I hadn't seen a mirror for decades, for I never allowed them inside my castle; mirrors reflect light, and creatures of darkness cast no image upon them. In the mirror, with his face turned from the door, Jonathan commanded a wide view of the room behind him, such that he would've seen me enter, were I a mortal such as he. With this mirror, Jonathan could discover my greatest secret ... and undo much of my plans.

Yet, even worse than the mirror, the sweet scent assailed me, the tantalizing odor I desired most. In being startled, with a razor against his soft, mortal flesh, Jonathan had slightly cut himself, and as he turned around, my eyes fixated upon the precious, most wondrous crimson refreshment trickling from his wound. Hunger exploded upon me worse than I'd ever felt before, enraged by the exposure of Miëta's so-recent psychic pressures upon my demonic nature. My sanity inflamed, my desires roared, and I succumbed to my madness.

Blood! So beautiful! So delicious! Youth! Strength! I must have it ...!

I lunged forward, determined to drain this foolish child, this intruder upon my darkness, and suck him to his last drop. Yet, in the first instant of my attack, my eyes fell beneath his bleeding chin, and there I spied the dreadfulness that hung innocently, formerly hidden by his shirt and tie: *a crucifix! The symbol of the God that had cursed me!*

Not in four hundred years had I foundered, limp and indecisive. My maddening hunger ached ... *but the cursed crucifix!* That holy symbol was as daylight to true believers, and so Jonathan must be one of the faithful, for the weakness of day splashed over my entire being. I staggered, and almost fell, overwhelmed as if the sun itself was unexpectedly bathing me with its burning rays. I was stronger than those I sired, yet I hadn't drunk blood for so long I was powerless against its holiness.

Jonathan startled again, but seeing my weakness, his strong hands reached out and caught me as I staggered. *My prey was helping me, steadying me: saving me!* With his support, I slowly reclaimed my balance and struggled to maintain my composure.

"Th-thank you," I said, those unfamiliar words choking against my throat.

What was I to do now? I was indebted to a man I'd decreed must die. Where was my honor, the integrity of my long-dead family ...?

Jonathan's young face and naïve expressions were easy to read: I'd scared him, the look in my eyes as I first saw his blood could daunt any mortal, but his gentle nature overcame his fear; *this wasn't a peasant to be killed without regret. This man had noble blood in his veins, even if he didn't know it.* I couldn't change or delay my plans, but I'd no longer enjoy their execution.

"Take ... care," I said, recovering myself. "Take care how you ... cut yourself. In this country, it's more dangerous than you think."

Then, as my strength partially returned, and I became my own master again, I stepped forward and seized his shaving glass, *the mirror that could ruin all.*

"And this is the wretched thing that has done the mischief!" I cried. "It's a foul bauble of man's vanity. Away with it!"

I stepped to his window, flung it open, and hurled the wicked talisman of narcissism to the winds, to shatter in the deep forest far below. However, my weakness was profound, and my full strength wouldn't return while I basked in the glow of that awful talisman; I couldn't abide the presence of a crucifix so prominently displayed, especially with the sight and scent of blood driving me mad. Snarling, I pushed away from the window, strode to the door, and departed, leaving Jonathan stunned and speechless behind me.

Locking Jonathan in his section of the castle, I descended to my foyer, and there I hesitated, and slowly sank to sit upon my stone steps; *who was really the prisoner here?* Below was the cage containing my beauties, and above, the cage holding my guest. I was the prisoner, trapped between my feeders and their feast.

Slowly my strength returned, yet I dared not face Jonathan again tonight. Midnight came and went, and finally I roused myself; I was succumbing to the greatest threat of all, the sapping of my will by circumstances beyond my control.

With a growl, I rose. *I wasn't a common man; I walked wherever I willed, and slayed whatever displeased me! I didn't bow before the will of others, and I didn't let chance decide my fate! I commanded all ... including myself!*

I hurried to my stables. With a speediness I didn't think my aged, dried husk of a body possessed, I saddled a horse, mounted him, and rode out under the stars. The winds of the night blew past me, and I forced my horse faster, for I'd far to go.

I galloped past the camp of the Szgany gypsies, but I didn't slow my faithful steed. The Szgany are descendants of ancient Transylvanian, Moldavian, and Bukovinan bloodlines, minor nobility, and distant cousins of mine, although so far removed they knew nothing of our relation. They and their families serve me, when I call, and for loyal services I don't prey upon them. Yet they are fearful, superstitious men who cower before me; *I can't respect them.*

To a distant village I rode, and there I reined in and tied my horse to a tree far outside their town. These people knew me, and my hunger, and how to destroy me. However, even in my aged body, I had no equal among them. I feared them not, and when I slid amid the shadows of their dwellings, they heeded me not. Even their animals were mostly unaware of my presence, and I was careful to give no warning.

It was too late to expect wanderers upon their streets, and their houses were fortified against me with holy symbols, but I snuck into a barn, and there found a young man and woman asleep, entwined in each other's arms, under blankets, in a tumble of hay. She was a dark-haired youth, pretty, but he was laden with muscles, such as my brides could turn into one of us ... and use against me. Without hesitation, I raised my fist and smashed into his skull with all my might; the pain was unbearable, and my weakness manifested, for he wasn't killed, but rendered sufficiently unconscious to be no threat to me.

With the reflexes of a Transylvanian noble, I seized the shocked girl before she could scream, and held her while she struggled, my hand covering her mouth and nose until she suffocated and passed out. She was still alive, but as unconscious as her lover.

Chuckling, I tore her dress from her, and searching the barn, I quickly found a knife and a small pig. I carried the struggling piglet to the unconscious couple, slit its throat, and let its blood paint the girl's dress, the man, and the knife, which I then placed in his hand. Then, carrying the piglet and the naked girl, I returned to my horse, hurled her over its back, and threw the piglet's carcass into the bushes. When found the next day, beside the bloody dress of the girl, and with the knife in his hand, he'd be accused of murder, and my part in this deed would remain unknown.

Of the girl, she'd alleviate the hunger of my brides; *my plan could then continue.*

I rode back as the night waned, eager to return, to present my brides with this feast. I yearned to taste her myself, but once I started, then I wouldn't stop, and Jonathan was sure to notice the physical change in me which feeding would engender, which no science known to him could explain. I needed Jonathan; through our conversations I was learning to adapt to the new life I must soon begin ... which would end my fast ... and my entrance into a realm with unlimited prey. I could feast like a mortal ... *every night!*

When I presented my brides with their dinner, Hēlgrēth and Loritá squealed with delight, but Miëta approached with a frown.

"I prefer my victims awake," Miëta sneered.

"How would you explain her screams to my guest?" I asked casually, ignoring her barbed tone. "Would you defy me again ... I ... who bring you such treats?"

Miëta said nothing, but approached the naked, unconscious young girl. Hēlgrēth and Loritá had knelt beside her, and each had lifted a long arm. I smiled; when drinking alone, a major artery is best, but when sharing, secondary veins were preferred, lest the body be emptied too quickly. Miëta knelt and lifted a leg; a thin artery on the inside of the calf would provide her ample sustenance. As one, they bared their fangs, bit, and let the first, strong streams of refreshment spew into their eager mouths.

Fighting to resist my hunger despite the overpowering sight and rising scent of blood, I watched until they drained her dry. Keeping the girl unconscious was done for more than one reason; more than once, some of my hungry brides had raised a victim without my knowledge, and trained her to assassinate me; those brides now adorn the dirt of my earthen mound ... *as dust.*

Once their feast was truly dead, I hurried back upstairs. Slipping quietly into Jonathan Harker's bedroom to tidy it up, I set out a clean bowl of shaving water and made his bed. It was important to keep up the pretense that I had servants; when finished, I slipped back out unseen. I'd wanted to talk to him again, but the night's efforts had exhausted me, and dawn was coming.

I needed sleep.

On the evening of May the 12th, after laying his next day's breakfast of *mamaliga*, a plain porridge of maize flour, and *impletata*, an eggplant stuffed with spicy forcemeat, I presented myself to Jonathan Harker, and delighted in a most enjoyable conversation, wherein I recited my family history.

"My dear Count Drăcula, please forgive me," Jonathan began, "but I'm quite perplexed. I wish to be respectful to all of your local customs and traditions, but in one case they so conflict with the social expectations of my England that I can't help but remark ..."

"Please, if anything troubles you, do speak your mind," I said. "You're my guest, and it would a great insult to my house if you were displeased."

"I'm not displeased," Jonathan said. "It is simply I'm ... confused. I came here from England to assist you understanding the purchase of your new estate, yet I'm left alone ... without seeing a soul, every day. I don't understand ..."

He broke off, and I shook my head, contriving an excuse that wouldn't be a lie.

"You ... cut yourself, ... remember?" I said slowly, my voice heavy with regret. "Perhaps in England you don't have such a custom, but here ... in Transylvania, a guest is not only honored, but protected. For you to have come to any injury under my roof is a great dishonor. I am ... saddened you suffered such a mishap ..."

"Oh, it was nothing, just a scratch," Jonathan said.

"Blood is sacred in these lands," I continued. "Some bloodlines, such as mine, transcend a thousand years into documented history, to the fall of the Empire of Rome, in which my family first gained prominence. We Szekelys have a right to be proud, for in our veins flows the blood of many brave races who fought, as the lion fights, for our lordship.

Here, in this whirlpool of European races, the Ugric tribe bore down from Iceland the fighting spirit which Thor and Wodin gave them, which their berserkers displayed to such fell intent upon the seaboards of Europe, aye, and of Asia and Africa, too, until the peasants thought werewolves had come.

"Here, too, when my ancestors came to build this castle, my people met the Turks, whose warlike fury had swept the earth like a living flame, killing all, until the dying peoples held that in Turk veins ran the blood of those old witches, who, expelled from Scythia, had mated with devils in the desert. Fools, fools! What devil or witch was ever so great as Attila, whose blood flows in my veins?"

I held up my arms, signifying the summit of the mighty bloodline within me, and then gestured at all of Castle Drăculea.

"Is it a wonder we're a conquering race; that we were proud; that when the Magyar, the Lombard, the Avar, the Bulgar, or the Turk poured their thousands across our frontiers, we drove them back? Is it strange that when Arpad and his legions swept through the Hungarian fatherland, he found us here; that we confronted the Honfoglalas here? When the Hungarian flood swept eastward, the Szekelys were claimed as kindred by the victorious Magyars, and for centuries, to us was trusted the guarding of this frontier of Turkey. Aye, and more, we manned the endless duty of the frontier guard, for, as the Turks say, *'water sleeps, but the enemy is sleepless.'* Who more gladly than we throughout the Four Nations received the *'bloody sword'*, or at its warlike call, quicker flocked to the standard of our king? When was redeemed that great shame of my nation, the shame of Cassova, when the flags of the Wallach and the Magyar were hurled down beneath the evil Crescent? Who was it, but one of my own race, who as Voivode, crossed the Danube and beat the Turk on his own ground?

"It was a Drăculeşti! Woe be it our own unworthy cousin, when he'd fallen, sold his people to the Turks, and brought the shame of slavery on them! Was it not a

Drăculeşti, indeed, who inspired others of our race, who in a later age again and again brought his forces over the great river into Turkey; who, when beaten back, came again, though he walked alone from the bloody field where his troops were being slaughtered, since he alone could ultimately triumph?

"They said he thought only of himself. *Bah!* What good are peasants without a leader? Where triumphs the arm of war without a brain and heart?

"After the battle of Mohács, we threw off the Hungarian yoke, and those of Drăculeşti blood stood beside their fallen leaders, for our spirit had never brooked that we weren't free. Ah, young sir, the Szekelys, with the Drăculeşti line in their heart's blood, their brains, and their swords, can boast a record unrivaled by mushroom growths like the Hapsburgs and Romanoffs.

"Those warlike days are over. Blood is too precious a thing in these days of honorable peace. The glories of the great races are a tale fully told."

Jonathan Harker sat amazed, his eyes huge, but finally he recovered.

"My most ancient and noble lord, I didn't understand the fullness of your ... incredible history!" Jonathan said. "Never did I mean to impinge upon your hospitality, and not one word of reproach shall ever be uttered by me; I swear it!

"However," Jonathan continued, "... to be clear, my small insight was upon the act of leaving a guest alone ... every day ... from sunup to sunset. I don't criticize, but I seek to understand."

"In England, such a thing would be unforgivable?" I asked.

"Yes, of course," Jonathan answered. "Why ... I haven't even seen one of your servants ... in all the days I've been here."

"Again I must beg your forgiveness," I said. "I have servants, three of them, but it's best you never see them. Servants here aren't like those in England; there, servants are paid, and can be trusted to do guests no harm. Here, servants are slaves, and only by my will are they restrained. Unfettered, they show no loyalty. Fear them, Jonathan Harker. I've forbidden them from your presence for your safety ... while you have drops of blood to spill, my servants are a deadly threat."

His eyes widened with alarm and surprise, and a moment of disbelief passed where he fought to find words to reply.

"I ... I don't reproach, but I'm unused to being alone for so long," Jonathan said. "I understand royal duties consume your daylight hours, but ... could I not join you? I'd be no trouble, and I'd be delighted for the chance to learn more about your culture."

I shook my head.

"It's not for your sake I haven't included you in my daylight requirements," I told him. "Those with whom I must deal suspect I'm withholding secrets from them, and would take great offence at the idea that I'll soon be departing these lands forever. It'd be a great difficulty to have them know of the business negotiation we're concluding. Even to make them aware I'm guesting a businessman of England would enflame suspicions."

"I'm sorry I'm such a vulnerability to you," Jonathan said. "Are all your dealings so mysterious?"

"Knowledge is the greatest power, and those with whom I deal wield power beyond your reckoning," I said. "Often I must divide people by what knowledge they possess, and separate them as to keep them from sharing. My hope is that I may continue this practice in England, for I don't appreciate anyone knowing my affairs too deeply. Tell me, my friend; can a man in England have two solicitors ... or more?"

"You might have a dozen, if you wished," Jonathan said. "...but it wouldn't be wise to have more than one solicitor engaged in any single transaction, as only one could act at a time, and to change in the midst of a business enterprise would be certain to militate against your interests. You might have one man to attend, say, to banking, and another to look after shipping, and more, in case local help were needed in a place far from the home of another solicitor."

"I'm delighted, but could you not explain more fully?" I asked. "There are subtleties I don't fully comprehend."

"I'll be glad to illustrate anything I can," Jonathan said.

"Excellent," I said. "Your friend and mine, Mr. Peter Hawkins, lives under the shadow of your beautiful cathedral at Exeter, which is far from London. He buys for me, through your good self, my estate outside London. Now, here let me say frankly, lest you should think it strange I've sought the services of one far from London: *my motive is that no interests might be served save mine.* A solicitor with a local residence might, perhaps, have some secret purpose of his own, or a friend's, to serve. Thus I went afield to seek my agent, to Exeter, in order to purchase my estate in London. Now, suppose I, who have many affairs, and wish to ship goods from London, say, to Newcastle, and Durham, and Harwich, and Dover. Might my affairs not be done by consigning each shipment to a different solicitor ... one in each of those ports?"

"Certainly, and it would be most easy, but we solicitors have a system of agency, one for the other, so work can be done locally on instruction from any solicitor, so any client, simply by placing himself in the hands of one man, could have his wishes carried out by many, without troubling the client with unimportant details."

"Yet," I said, "I'd be at liberty to direct these dealings personally. Is it not so?"

"Of course," Jonathan replied, "and such is often done by men of business who don't like their affairs to be known."

"Good!" I said, and then I went on to ask about the

means of making consignments, and the forms required, and discussing of all sorts of difficulties which might arise, yet by forethought could be guarded against. Jonathan explained all these things to me, and left me under the impression that he was a wonderful solicitor. I admired the youth, who could've served me well, but I had to stick to my plan, even where distasteful. He'd have been a helpful contact in England ... if he'd never come to Castle Drăculea.

"Have you written since your first letter to our friend Mr. Peter Hawkins ... or to any other?" I asked.

"I haven't, for I saw no opportunity of sending letters," Jonathan said.

"Then write now, my young friend," I said. "Write to our friend and to any other; and say, if it please you, that you shall stay with me for another month."

The look of surprise on his face revealed displeasure.

"*A month ...?*" Jonathan asked.

"I desire it much; nay, I'll take no refusal," I said. "When your master, or employer, whatever you will, engaged that someone should come to me on his behalf, it was understood that only my needs were to be consulted. Is this not so?"

Jonathan swallowed hard before agreeing I was correct.

"I pray, my good young friend, you'll not discourse of things other than business in your letters. It'll doubtless please your friends to know you're well, and that you look forward to getting home."

I slid open a drawer in his desk and took three sheets of notepaper, envelope paper, and sealing wax, and gave them to him. He accepted them with a perplexed, forced smile.

"I trust you'll forgive me, but I've much work to do in private this evening. You will, I hope, find all things as you wish," I began to exit, then paused at the door. "Let me advise you - nay, let me warn you, should you leave these rooms, you'll not by any chance go to sleep in any other part of this castle. My home is old, and haunted by many memories, and bad dreams await those who sleep unwisely. Be warned! If sleep overcomes you, hasten to these rooms, for only here will your rest be safe. If you be not careful in this respect, then ... *my servants may find you.*"

After locking Jonathan inside, I hesitated, unsure for the first time in decades. I didn't like uncertainty; this was my reason for wanting an Englishman to stay so long with me, to leech from him everything I might face in his country. England was the most technologically-advanced civilization on Earth, and I'd dwelt too long in a country where inventions centuries old were still considered new and controversial. What I'd not expected was that Englishmen, if my guest was their representative, would be as open-minded, as freely-spoken, and as thoughtful as any youth of Jonathan's age could hope to be; *never had I encountered his like!*

Chapter 3

On May the 15th I needed certainty to restore my resolve: *I needed my diaries.*

I headed to my central keep, down the wide stairs, up to my private study, and through it to my foremost tower. My diaries were my most precious possession, and the only cargo I was leaving behind that I couldn't do without; here alone they'd be safe. I'd never transport my diaries by ship, for the possibility of them being lost at sea was unthinkable. No one was allowed to know they existed; I slew and drank the masons that had sealed their entrance, and even my beloved brides knew nothing about them.

I arrived at my window to the world, which plummets straight down over the cliff, a path no man but I could traverse. My affinity for even the lowest animals had taught me skills no others knew, and only those skills allowed entrance to my vault. I took several moments to steel my strength, as my aged body would be pressed to its limit; finally I opened my window and eased out. Yet I didn't turn around, to descend as a man; booby-traps I'd long ago installed protected my diaries. To descend as a man, deadly spear-tips stabbing out from hidden crevices would impale you or drive you off the wall, to plummet down my cliff. To open my vault, you had to descend face-first, as the lizard climbs.

The stone blocks in this part of my castle are smooth, the mortar tight, the places where fingers and toes could secure themselves few and hard to see. I kicked off my shoes before I exited the safety of my study. I reached out, fastened my hold in the exact spots, as I did every time, and I crawled out onto the wall, to cling like a spider, defiant against the whistling mountain winds, and inched downward. Had I blood in my veins it would've all rushed to my head, but not a drop oozed through me, so I crawled down the wall without hesitation. No fear stayed me; I was a Count of Hungary, a Prince of Transylvania, and the greatest warrior ever born. I descend the exterior wall of my castle heedless of danger ... twenty feet, thirty feet, until I reached the stone with the gap underneath which hides my release-lever. When pressed, ten large bricks slid inwards, opening a passageway, and I seized the smooth iron bar, placed there a'purpose, released my toe-holds on the cracks between bricks, and let gravity fling me inside.

I lowered my feet to the floor of my vault, and then I leaned out of its entrance and gazed down at the smooth bricks below me; one touch, one moment of weight upon their cracks, and spears would've impaled me; even one such as I would've died. This was my plan, for this vault had to be safe from violation ... even by other undead.

Releasing the counterbalance, the wall returned to its place, sealing me inside. The air was dry, all moisture sucked away by an intricate series of baffles installed long ago, leading to pipes descending far below. No priority equaled the safety of my diaries, my journals of death, recorded thoughts and insights spanning the centuries of my life. Someday, when the foolish mortals have succeeded in killing off every race over pointless religious and political arguments, when no more blood sustains me, then these books shall stand as the sole record of the paths of my mind in the days of mankind, and alone sustain me when all else is still.

These caves are deep and intricate, only one who knows them well wouldn't get lost, or could detect the secret door which leads to my forbidden chamber: *my vault.*

I opened the intricate lock, knowing someday I must install a newer, less fallible lock than this one, which is more than a century old. Although I can somewhat see in the dark, I light a candle and hold it high, for the sight of my illuminated vault always delights me.

My vault shined before me, deep granite walls lined with fine veins of gold, flowing from a high, limestone ceiling where blue and pink quartz erupt as if frozen in a white waterfall that splashes down to the floor, stationary in time, as I am trapped in eternity. Tiny gleams of my single candle reflect back at me from every surface like stars in the heavens, and amid their gleaming, twinkling radiance, I see my ornate writing desk, topped with four rows of strong iron shelves, only the lowest shelf half-empty. Upon these shelves lay my books, my diaries, each an account of my thoughts and experiences since God's curse claimed me. Reading my books, I can see my numerous threads of thought run and grow throughout the ages, remember my mistakes and discoveries, and recall my early explorations of every continent on Earth, my discussions with the wisest men and mightiest kings; *my hunger for knowledge has ever driven me.* These books contain reasonings and understandings no mortal could conceive in a single lifetime, and ponderings upon the endless mysteries which only I can imagine, although I've yet to fully grasp. All the wisdom of mankind is summed up in these books, my history, my diaries of death ... and the deathlessness I endure.

It started an eternity ago. The Carpathian Mountains were filled with people, primitive villages, yet happy and contented, safe in their mountain loft. But death was coming: the Sultan Mehmed II had vowed to conquer all of the lands to the West, to extend their Empire to the Atlantic Ocean, and someday eastwards to the Pacific Ocean. The armies of the Turks were vast, and we thought no power on Earth, not even all the armies of the West, could stop them. Even if we could gather all of our disparate forces into one great army, the Turks, led by the boyars of Targoviste, would destroy us.

I gathered my small army and rode to Walachia to meet their vanguard, a small troop of 2,000 sent to survey the roads and keep the bridges open. We fought a costly battle, and I was wounded, as were most of my men, but my wound wasn't fatal, and in the end we captured 400 of their men, although we'd lost many times that number.

Here I was faced with the greatest decision of my existence, living or dead: what could I do to save the West from utter destruction against overwhelming military forces, reputedly as formidable as the dreaded Mongols ... or before them, the Huns?

My troops had only won our minor skirmish because of our weapons and tactics; a Carpathian war-spear was a 10-foot long pike, too heavy to throw, but stout enough to impale a charging stallion, and thus we'd defeated their advance troop of horsemen. Yet fighting couldn't win this war; I had to rely upon something else.

The idea was nightmarish, but all soldiers have superstitions, and that was my only hope. For eighty miles up the only road an army could travel through the Carpathians, I had my men dig holes, and bury the bottom halves of our war-spears, points up, solidly in the ground.

Upon these deadly stakes, with much struggle, sometimes fifteen of my men against one Turk captive, we sat them upon the points of our spears, and pulled them down until they were pinioned, trapped, and stabbed from their buttocks upwards through their ribcages, with the steel points of our spears emerging through a shoulder, a head, or a mouth. The lucky ones died instantly, while the unlucky cursed me amid screams of agony.

To my knowledge, that was the source of my curse, which has kept me undead unto this day; *God heard and heeded the terrible screams of those men.*

It was a monstrous victory. To this day, the screams of those Turks and their tormented curses ring in my ears. Those screams haunt my worst dreams, the nightmares of Count Drăcula.

We spaced them out, so the Turks marching toward us would pass by one impaled Turk every few minutes, for days, every day, as they marched into our lands.

At first, the Turks were enraged. Those unfortunates who still lived couldn't be saved, and they died in the arms of their kinsmen. The rest were already dead, and many had been dead a week before they were found. Yet the Turks approached us slower; *their superstitions tortured them.*

Then came disease; sickness exudes from the dead, and those who travel beside them often fall victim to its grasping clutches. One day before the Turks reached my castle, they were stopped, unable to continue; *fear and disease had beaten them to a standstill.*

In the end, it was these enemies, fear and disease, foes no army can fight, that defeated their horde. The Turks turned back, dragging their sick, abandoning their dying. They marched home. Never again did the Turks seek to conquer my homelands; *I'd saved the young civilizations of the West.*

But the curses of the impaled had been heard by God, and His fury was vented upon me.

Count Drăcula, a name many in the West had never known, the Hero of Hungary, the Destroyer of the Turks, soon became known by other names; the killer, the blood-drinker: *vampire.*

Impaling became the greatest punishment in my lands. Soon I could leave a gold cup beside a well ... and no man would steal it, fearful of the punishment I dealt. Peace and lawfulness came to my lands, but then my curse crept in, and I suffered worse than any who'd defied me.

Why had I been cursed? What else was I to do? Had God desired the enslavement and slow-murder of my people, of His faithful worshippers, whom I sought to save?

In this hallowed place, my vault; here alone was I at home, free to think as I will, to be what I am, curse and all.

I am Drăcula!

My castle above was crumbling to ruin; soon rotted timbers would give way, ceilings collapse, ancient stones break free of their mortar, and walls fall. This vault, its entrance walled with iron and sealed in the hidden heart of the caverns that once laid open in the cliff-face, held the greatest treasure on Earth; my books, my memories ... transcribed by my own hand. When all else of this world is gone, these books and I alone shall remain.

Even if my castle falls, this vault will remain.

Yet my body rots, and I must feed. Soon the pain will grow too great for my mind, and I will take from the living the feast to end my famine.

I must leave my beloved Transylvania, the home of my clan, the land of my ancestors, before I feed again!

I saved these people. I'm their rightful liege. I'm the master of these lands and the lord of all who dwell within them. I can't forsake my heritage, but neither can I feed upon my children; *they've suffered enough.* I must go elsewhere to seek sustenance, a new home, while I rebuild my strength and fortune, which has slowly trickled away as the centuries passed.

Then, young and wealthy again, I shall return in a hundred years, or maybe two hundred, when my people have forgotten me and fear the name Drăcula no longer. Then I shall rebuild, a new castle, stacked upon the foundations of the old, an modern palace worthy of my ancestors, with their lineage clearly depicted in every hall, a place of wonder and learning; *a new center of the living world.*

It was for this reason I chose England: the most contemporary of cities, with a population so vast few will notice those who vanish to sustain my appetite. There I'll find a new bride, not a beautiful harridan of fear and loathing, but a woman of wisdom and intellect to share with me the endless eternity of night ... as all else falls to dust.

This is my plan. This was why I summoned help from the island-nation I'd soon invade, to siphon off its strength and secrets: England; *the reason Jonathan Harker was in my castle above me.*

My plan was sound. I must carry it through. I liked Jonathan Harker, yet he was a small sacrifice, one of many that must be paid to insure my success.

I sat at my desk, opened my latest diary, uncorked my ink bottle, took my quill in hand, and began to write. I must document this quandary I feel; I must pour my feelings into my diary, that I'll have it centuries from now, when specific memories fade.

Hours later I corked my ink bottle, sprinkled resin upon my freshly-written words, and rose to leave. I felt better; my mind was clear. Dawn would come soon, and I dared not leave my brides alone all day, to awaken without me ... hungry again.

Chapter 4

The next evening a remarkable change occurred. After serving his meals in the dining hall, I came upon Jonathan Harker, not reading, but praying, his head fervently bowed. As he rose, I could feel the crucifix hanging around his neck, although his shirt concealed it.

"Forgive me, my friend, if I have interrupted your private moment," I said.

His eyes blazed at me, fear and desperation evident; *as one who has seen every expression, I can't be deceived.* Yet he smiled, a wan, accusatory smile.

"Forgive me, Count Drăcula, for in all of our conversations, I've never asked about the most important thing of all," Jonathan said.

"Important ...?" I asked. "What's so important ...?"

"God!" Jonathan said forcefully, more a challenge than a question.

Were Jonathan not an innocent and my guest, I'd be infuriated, but I preferred to obey the rules of hospitality.

"God ...?" I repeated. "Please, ask your question."

"Do you believe in God?" Jonathan asked.

"Believe ...?" I asked, amused. "Certainly not: I know that God exists, so I have no need to believe."

My answer startled Jonathan, so much he seemed to shrink before me, his inflated sense of alarm punctured. He stared disbelieving, and then sat down upon a chair as if he would've fallen.

"*Know ...?*" Jonathan asked. "How can any living man know ...?"

I laughed; it was a forced laugh, yet it put Jonathan totally out of reckoning. His bright, youthful eyes stared at me incredulously.

"I'm older than you, older than you expect," I said. "I've visited every continent on Earth and learned every language. I've spoken with kings and wizards in words your young language can't translate, for your tongue has yet no words equal to their concepts. I've seen and experienced things beyond your grasp ... and all I've learned convinces me there is a God."

"In-indeed ...," Jonathan stammered. "I ... I'm glad to ... hear it."

"Be not, and be not deceived," I said warningly. "I take all matters of God most seriously, and have devoted more time to understanding His purposes than you've spent breathing."

"You ... you understand God ...?" Jonathan asked.

"Of course not," I scowled. "No man can understand God, any more than a dog, which you pet before leaving the house, comprehends what you do while you're at work. Yet it is in the attempt to understand God that mankind raises its thoughts to the highest level we may achieve. Do you not agree?"

"Yes ..., I think," Jonathan said. "Forgive my ignorance again, Count Drăcula, for this is a new concept to me."

Upon the table was an opened bottle of wine and an empty goblet; I poured a generous amount and handed it to Jonathan.

"Think upon this new concept, my dear friend, and answer me this: what does it tell you?"

"Tell ...?" Jonathan asked.

"Human thought excels most while thinking about God; what does that tell you?" I asked softly, offering him the chance to discover a trace of my wisdom. "What does that ... imply?"

Jonathan turned his head slowly, his eyes unseeing anything in the room.

"God ... thinks ... higher than us," Jonathan said.

"Exactly," I said.

"But that's obvious ...!" Jonathan argued.

"Then don't stop," I urged. "Keep thinking ..."

The expression on his face was wondrous. Here was the novelty I sought, the sole pleasure left to an immortal life.

"God ... wants us ... to think ... about Him," Jonathan said.

"Keep going," I said, excitement in my voice. "Think farther than you've ever thought before ..."

Jonathan wracked his brains, puzzlement obviously straining him.

"God wants us to think ... like Him ...?" Jonathan asked.

"And how do we know that?" I asked.

"Count, I fear for my soul to continue ...," Jonathan said. "What if I say wrong ...?"

"What if you say right?" I asked. "Don't stop when you're so close: how do we know that God wants us to think about Him ... and like Him?"

"Because ... God rewards us ... with higher thinking ... when we think about Him," Jonathan said.

"Why...?" I asked.

"Why ... so we ... think higher," Jonathan said.

I grinned, widely; even I couldn't hold back this smile.

"Thinking ...!" Jonathan practically shouted. *"God wants us to think ... higher!"*

"Exactly so," I said. "Of that conclusion, I am certain."

Jonathan's face was aglow with delight.

"My dear Count, ... what you've given me ... *words can't express ...!*"

"I didn't give this to you," I said, smiling. "I guided; you comprehended. This is the difference between polymathy and perspicacity; the former does not teach half of what the latter imparts."

"I can't wait to share this with my pastor back home," Jonathan said. "What an insight ... and it was there, obvious, all along!"

"The obvious is the most elusive of secrets, my friend, for few ponder its depths," I said, and to my surprise, Jonathan rose and fervently shook my hand.

"You're a marvel, my dear Count Drăcula," Jonathan said. "When you come to England, I hope you'll allow me to call upon you."

I steeled my nerves, which stiffened at this comment, although my young guest didn't notice.

"I'll never deny you entrance to my house," I said, which was sadly true.

However, Jonathan was too lost in his new thought to consider the change in my voice, the sudden seriousness which filled me.

"Tell me more," Jonathan said. "I mean, ... guide me."

"Comprehension takes time," I assured him. "Each concept is like a brick in a castle; you must take time to mortar each firmly in place before you set another concept atop them."

"But I want more," Jonathan said. "Please, share with me ... something ... anything!"

I gestured to his chair, and he sat back down.

"My friend, if we are to discuss such subjects, then I must be brutally honest with you," I said.

"Please do," Jonathan said.

"I told you that I believe in God," I said, choosing each word I uttered carefully. "I do, for I've seen and known His power, as there are things on this Earth that could exist through no mortal effort, which can only be attributed to God."

"Like what?" Jonathan asked. "What proofs ...?"

"Curses," I said. "I've seen, and known, what God does to those who displease Him."

Jonathan stopped, as if he'd been slapped.

"Belief in God means you acknowledge His existence," I explained. "It doesn't imply subservience to His will."

"*What ...?!?*" Jonathan asked, for clearly this thought had never occurred to him.

"I know God exists, but I do not worship Him," I explained.

The incredulity on Jonathan's face matched the horror I'd seen there when I first met him.

"But ... *He's God...!*" Jonathan argued.

"Indeed," I said. "But I could never worship a ... a Machiavellian God."

Jonathan pressed back in his chair ... and then made the sign of the cross. I flinched, but tried not to recoil. Though his face visibly paled, I continued.

"God is Machiavellian," I said with absolute certainty. "God has a plan, according to His followers, and all the pain and suffering of every person who ever lived on Earth will be justified by His plan. Is that not the story?

"But how much suffering has truly happened? How many human lives have ended in excruciating misery on this planet since man first walked upon it; ten billion? A hundred billion? Half-a-billion people inhabit the Earth right now, even to the bottom-most corner of what you call the New World, the Americas. Even to distant islands trapped in the middle of oceans, wherever man can travel, life thrives. Most generations reproduce every twenty years; five times the population of the Earth cycling through every century, back through all the ages of Rome, the empires of Egypt, and an eon before that, into civilizations remembered only by drawings left on cave walls. A trillion people ... and most died in utmost agony, sick, starving, or aged beyond their body's ability to endure.

"This is God's plan? The bulk of humanity dies in anguish? What plan could justify endless suffering? What reward is so great that a trillion people should be tormented beyond comprehension, brutalized by their very nature, cursed ....?"

My words failed me; I was getting too personal, revealing more than Jonathan needed to hear.

"What kind of merciful God makes a plan to hurt and murder, ... yes, murder, for He has the power to stop it ..., those whom He claims to love?"

As I expected, Jonathan had no answer. *How could he?* I've read and reread the many versions of the Bible for centuries, searching for clues, but it's all been mistranslated and edited too many times, from too many questionable sources, to have any universal meaning left. I've sought out the wisest priests and cardinals, and been quoted the weak answers God gave to Job, who was easily placated ... or crushed under God's fury, when His imperfections were pointed out, until Job relented. God was clearly angered by Job's questions, and He became defensive, as even the lowliest human does when their flaws are revealed.

"Machiavellian ... I know the word, but I confess ... I don't know its source ... or implications, and I fear to speak wrongly of matters so grave ...," Jonathan began, and I waved off the rest of his sentence.

"Machiavellian comes from Niccolò di Bernardo dei Machiavelli, an Italian historian and politician, who died in 1527."

"I know of him!" Jonathan exclaimed. "He wrote 'The Prince'."

"He's best known for that work," I said. "Did you like it?"

Jonathan looked abashed.

"We briefly discussed it in college, but I never read it," Jonathan said.

Without hesitation I rose, plucked it from a high shelf filled with books, and presented it to my guest.

"Consider it a gift," I said. "Machiavelli is the founder of modern political science, but his true gift was ethics. Like Plato, Machiavelli expounded a philosophy of realism, as opposed to the perfectionism of Socrates."

"Those philosophers I've studied," Jonathan said. "Plato insisted men should focus on the real world, and accept the harshness of life, while Socrates, Plato's teacher, insisted men should focus on the ideal ... and always strive toward it."

"Jonathan Harker, you delight me," I smiled. "Few men of these lands study sciences so ancient. Yes, Socrates was an idealist, while his student Plato was a realist, and see how differently those philosophies were treated in different centuries. In his day, Plato was hailed as a great thinker, and richly rewarded, while the wealthy forced Socrates to drink poison. Yet Machiavelli, despite his personal loyalty and generous nature, was reviled for his realist philosophy, which the commoners of Florence claimed *'endorsed behavior that was evil, selfish, and immoral'*. Machiavelli died a very sad, humbled man, denying the reputation his writings had branded upon him."

"You speak as if you knew him," Jonathan grinned. "Even you can't be that old."

I grinned back; *what would he say if I told him the truth?*

"I'd have to be four hundred of years old to have known him," I said astutely. "But the change of political impressions, and their resultant reactions, between the centuries, is of serious importance, worthy of deep study. What does this change in preferred philosophies tell you?"

"I'd say that ... simply, between ancient Greece and the Renaissance, morals changed," Jonathan said.

"Which morals?" I asked.

"Why ... the moral definitions of good and evil," Jonathan said.

"And ... what does that tell you about the nature of good and evil?" I asked.

"That the definitions of good and evil are social perspectives," I said.

"Precisely," I said. "A hero of one age can be the villain of the next."

"Yes, but I'd take it a step farther," Jonathan said. "In ancient Greece, power came from the few and dominated over the many, and the will of the few was considered 'the good'. In the Renaissance, after the ravages of the Black Death, true power came from the many, and the few, the wealthy and powerful, had to be more careful of the laws they made and the justice they dispensed, for they feared both revolution and excommunication; thus what was best for the many, rather than the few, became the definition of 'good'."

How many generations had been born and died since I was last surprised ...? My eyes widened and my jaw grew slack as I drank in his words. After all these years, a new concept was a treasure beyond my imagining! *I couldn't wait to get to England, where I was sure to learn more!*

"Jonathan, today I'm your humble servant," I said. "Today you're my teacher, and I your grateful pupil. If there's any reward I may bestow upon you, anything in my lands, it's yours ... from now until the end of your days."

I hesitated; again, *I was speaking to a doomed man.* I felt dishonest, but my needs were greater than his. He was my guest, but only until I departed this castle forever. After I was gone, Jonathan would be the guest of my brides ... and I wasn't responsible for what they'd do to him. I suspected that they'd consume him, but would they also raise him to join our kind? A wonderful friend he'd be, a boon companion beside which to wander the world, but his knowledge of me was already too great. In friendly conversation, I was showing him my mind, and that posed a great danger to me, if he should live to come to England. But no; my brides would finish him; *their appetites knew no bounds.*

"Forgive me, my friend, but little remains of the night, and I've many duties tomorrow," I said.

"I understand," Jonathan said. "If you would, I've written the letters you requested ..."

Jonathan lifted two sealed envelopes from a small table.

"I'll see them mailed as soon as possible," I said, and I took the two envelopes from his hand. "Good night, my friend."

"Dear teacher; your words have troubled me, but I'll do what I can," Jonathan said. "Tonight ... I'll pray for you."

Hiding my contempt at his supposed generosity, I feigned a smile.

"Pray, if you wish, but I beg you, don't pray upon your knees," I said. "Today Christians display their faith by making themselves small, as if the lowest groveler were the most devout. Before the Renaissance, true believers proved their faith by seeking to be like God, by excelling at mental, physical, and moral triumphs to enhance their glory, and to make of themselves a greater reflection of the One Divinity. We Szekelys prefer the former: God heeds best prayers uttered by deeds."

Such a waste to kill him, I thought as I carefully unsealed and opened his letters. I read each carefully; one was a letter to his employer, explaining his ongoing task as pleasant, but taking longer than expected. His second letter was more personal, a missive of passion to his fiancée, Miss Mina Murray, in which he described little of his business, but spoke as if referencing a former letter I'd not seen, in which he chided her for her modesty, claiming she was as beautiful as her friend, a girl named Lucy Westenra, whom I could only assume they both considered a prized beauty. He referred to Mina as an assistant schoolmistress, and professed his love and devotion to her in each paragraph, and swore that he'd never know joy again until he was home and reunited with her. My only puzzle was the word *'shorthand'*, which I didn't recognize, but it didn't bother me. Both letters were interesting insights into my guest, and I folded and resealed them, determined to post them soon. However, such a journey needed to be early in the night, and I had need to lay Jonathan's next meal before I left, yet not appear before him until later in the night.

As I unlocked our dungeon chamber, Miëta, Loritá, and Hēlgrēth stared at me.

"How long will this go on?" Loritá asked. "We weary of this prison."

"You'll remain here until I let you out," I said firmly. "My guest must know nothing of you."

"Can you bring us no plaything?" Hēlgrēth asked. "We hunger, and these walls are so confining."

"I brought you that girl and you sucked her dry," I said. "Your indulgences have made you weak; you can't resist hunger's slightest touch. I should make you fast for a year ..."

Long we glared at each other, yet I said nothing more; all that needed to be was said. Finally I started to walk down toward them.

"What are you planning?" Miëta demanded.

Loritá and Hēlgrēth stood silent; apparently neither had expected Miëta's outburst.

"Count Drăcula doesn't speak on command," I said defiantly. "My mind is deeper than even you know, Empress Miëta, and my lineage greater than yours. Tire not my ears with pointless entreaties! My patience is as thin as elder-blood."

I strode down the steps proudly, causing no small pain in my aged body, but I felt as if I were alive again, a prince in the fullness of his strength. I didn't fear any physical attacks tonight, for my time in my vault and my charming conversation with Jonathan had strengthened me. Loritá and Hēlgrēth stepped back as I neared them, but Miëta stood defiantly in my path.

With a strength she hadn't suspected, I seized her throat and lifted her into the air. Miëta startled, but she was too poised to thrash about helplessly; she bared her fangs and glared down at me. Finally, after my mastery over her was evidenced, I set her down behind me, and she clutched at her throat as if pained.

"Master, have you ... dined?" Hēlgrēth asked.

"I haven't tasted blood since last we feasted together," I said, staring so hard Loritá and Hēlgrēth blanched. "But soon ... we'll all feast ... when I command it."

I turned my back upon Miëta, a little disappointed when she didn't attack. With a cruel grin, I ascended to my coffin.

"I warn you again: no one who attempts to thwart me shall see another moonrise," I said. "Now enter your coffins; day approaches."

I lifted my lid and settled myself comfortably, more relaxed than I could remember. The scent of fear I'd engendered among my brides wafted over me like perfume. I needed them to be afraid, for their fear was also keeping them from finding an exit from this prison; my maidens could be quite clever, when need arose, and I was too cautious to trust any prison could encase them forever. I needed no fear today; dawn saps their strength worse than mine. When I heard my brides close their lids, I lifted mine down slowly, and drifted into oblivion.

With the early sunset, I arose to find my maids still in their coffins. I climbed carefully out of my coffin; the exertions of the last few days, as painful as they were, had loosened my joints some, and I was moving more freely. I hurried upstairs, cooked and laid out a sumptuous meal for my guest, and then slipped back down to my stable. Feeding them all, but saddling only one horse, I rode out in my disguise, cloak, hat, and false beard, braving the last rays of the sun as it sank over the world. I'd far to go, and business to conduct.

Riding fast, I soon reached my first destination: the camp of the Szgany gypsies. I rode right into their midst, and women screamed as I was recognized. Those sitting around their huge fire, holding plates of cooked meat, jumped to their feet. From one of their traditional, many-wheeled Hungarian coaches, a small house built on a wagon's frame, came a shout for everyone to withdraw and raise no weapon. I sat upon my powerful steed, my thighs feeling the flexes of his ribs as he breathed, as a tall, elderly man with thinning white hair swept off his hat and bowed low to me. He seemed both humble and simpering, as if he expected this to please me, and he wore clothes of both France and Germany: a short jacket, a round hat, and home-made trousers, a too-large white shirt with billowing sleeves, and a wide belt with bright cloth strips fluttering from it. He doubtlessly distinguished himself with this flamboyant, foreign outfit, as most of the men wore baggy, dirty-white trousers, linen shirts, and leather belts nearly a foot wide, all studded with brass nails, and wide-brimmed hats. Unlike this fool, the others wore high boots with trousers tucked into them, and had long black hair and heavy moustaches. Many, including the women, had short blankets wrapped around them to protect them from the wintery night wind, even in summertime. This fool threw off his blanket before he approached me.

"How may we serve you, Master?" he asked.

My teeth grated; all these walking feasts, these vessels of refreshment, ate at my insides; *how I longed to leap down and devour all of them!* But no; they were my loyal subjects, and it was to save them that I must depart. I reached into my pocket, drew forth the envelopes containing Jonathan's letters to his employer and fiancée, and held them out.

"Yes, Master; your will be done!" he said, and he hurried forth and took the envelopes. "We will take these downriver and post them, just like the others."

"I shall require your services soon," I said. "Twenty men with wagons, axes, saws, hammers, nails, and shovels, to perform a task I desire. Be at my castle, at this hour, six days from now. You will build me fifty large, strong boxes, fill them with dirt, and transport them to the sea."

"We are yours to command, Master," the old man said.

I reached into my pocket, withdrew six of my precious silver coins, and let them fall, tinkling against my steed's heaving sides, to clatter upon the ground. Then I surveyed them all, for it might be centuries before I saw them again. They stood terrified of me. For thirty years I hadn't come to their camp, and when I began my correspondences with England, it was they who dispatched my letters and brought me replies.

"Guard yourselves!" I commanded, speaking up so that all could hear. "In ten days, after your men return from the duties I require, you must quickly leave this land, travel far away, and not return for at least a year. Obey me ... or all of you will die!"

They were good, strong people, but ignorant; not one of them could read or write. After my mission was accomplished, even if it took three hundred years, I'd return to find them exactly as I left them, only then our bonds would grow closer. Through them, new masons, laborers, and artists would be contracted, and my castle rebuilt, a center around which my empire would rise. I'd teach them, not only the petty sciences known in England, but understandings few mortals comprehend. At my command, they'd breed and grow plentiful, and import the sacrifices I needed to sustain my vigor. Their gratitude then will be as strong as their current fear, and my distant cousins would eventually arise to be the greatest peoples of the world.

These fools wouldn't understand; their faces showed fears never witnessed on my countenance. With a haughty snarl of disgust, I turned my horse and raced from their sight.

My plans were coming to fruition. At least my people, the Szgany gypsies, would be safe; my brides would seek feasts closest to them so they could return to my castle before dawn ... *until the villagers realized I was gone.*

I turned down a road seldom traveled, and within two hours riding across the Mittel, I reined in at the outskirts of a village I'd not visited in half a century. Noises were coming from a large house, but I dismounted and crept along the sides of the outlying dwellings, until I saw signs of my prey; a stick-pony ... and a rag doll ... laying outside a house surrounded by small footprints. I reached out with senses only ten lifetimes of experience exposed. I heard dim heartbeats ... old hearts and young hearts. I smelled fresh blood, and circled their house until I knew the positions of every heartbeat in the dwelling, and then I settled in a shadow; *I'd need all of my strength for this.*

Some thoughts all people share, even I. We need not voice these thoughts; they resonate and radiate around us. They're hard to grasp and difficult to maintain, but I focused all of my formidable determination into them, and filled my mind with those thoughts alone ... until I wasn't alone. I concentrated, radiating my thoughts, and heeded only the subject I desired, the faintest heartbeat closest to the window whose shutters I pressed against.

Gradually, without breaking my mental radiance, *I called.*
I yearned.
I invited.
Time passed slowly; my prey was asleep, but I heard his heartbeat quicken and, finally, approach. I heard a wooden latch slide back. The shutters swung wide; a young boy stood before me, his eyes closed, still asleep, but obeying my summons. I needed to be quick; I must seize the boy, which would certainly wake him, and then flee to my horse, and ride back to my castle.

Yet, as I rose before his helpless, innocent form, a gurgling noise distracted me; an infant, with a heartbeat so faint even I didn't hear it, lay in a crib; *an infant will suit me better.* Even a boy could be used by my brides, but an infant holds only one purpose; I stared at the sleep-walking boy, focused my will upon him, and changed my orders. Without hesitation, the boy walked to the crib, lifted the infant, and brought him to me. I took the newborn into my hands, lifted it out through the window, and as I closed the shutters, I commanded the latch be slid back into place, and grinned as I heard it softly grate, wood against wood. My last command was to the boy, to return to his bed, and there sleep peacefully.

I hurried back to my horse, carrying my living prize, when suddenly it wailed, screeching; a piercing cry. I covered its tiny mouth too late; a deep voice cried from the village.

"Oy! Who goes there?"

Two men stepped out from behind a house; *I'd been seen!* I climbed onto my horse's saddle, but they were running toward me fast. I couldn't afford to be delayed; with one hand, I grabbed my false beard, lifted it to capture the brim of my hat, and swept both off my head.

My visage in the moonlight halted my pursuers, and my angry hiss bit like snake-fangs; they recoiled in horror at the bloody gleams of my eyes. As they stood frozen, I spurred and rode off. This wasn't part of my plan, curse those fools, to remind this sleepy village of whom they once feared. Yet it was a minor flaw; I rode hard, trailing only dust, leaving them far behind. When next I returned to these lands, the children of these men will have died of old age, and their offspring will laugh to recall the silly tales of their aged grandfathers.

Thus are all generations deceived.

Hours later, well past midnight, I returned to my castle. My horse was weary, for I'd allowed him few rests, and he returned to his stall willingly, and I rewarded him with extra water and grain.

Taking the infant, whose cries annoyed me so greatly I'd wanted to fling it into my path and trample it under my horse's hooves, I headed to my dungeon.

As I reached the iron door to my chambers, I, the Prince of Darkness, stood horrified: *my locked door stood ajar!*

Desperately I hurried upstairs. *Was Jonathan alive ... dead ... or undead?* My brides would've had to penetrate three locks to enter Jonathan's rooms. The first door I came to was still locked; I unlocked it, hurried up the stairs, and found his rooms empty.

Had they betrayed me?

Quickly I set about, searching the small section I'd allowed him, when I discovered another alarming sight: a wooden door, partly broken ... *from the inside!* Jonathan had also escaped! *But did he flee from my brides ... or succumb to their voluptuousness?*

Not in four hundred years had so many unexpected events occurred with such rapidity! *What if I was too late? Had my plan already failed?*

I forced myself to remain calm. I had to forget my urgency, restrain my trepidations, and overlook my fear. Jonathan, if he still lived, had a heartbeat, and I could sense it faster than I could search a hundred ancient rooms and hallways. I drew myself into my mind, and then I reached out. I felt nothing, which meant that my brides may already have cornered him, but I forced myself to continue; this was a large and labyrinthine castle, 457 years old, and much had fallen to ruins.

Sensing nothing, I began walking down a central hall. My brides could hide from my senses, but I kept my eyes open, hoping to glimpse them, or at least a footprint in the dust. Long I searched, and then, a cry; *Jonathan was screaming!*

With a speed I didn't think my aged body possessed, I ran toward the outburst, and ascended a narrow stair whose dust had been disturbed by four sets of footprints. I dashed into a moonlit study, and there, before my eyes, knelt my three beautiful brides, their mouths affixed to my guest.

"*How dare you touch him?*" I shouted. "*How dare you cast eyes on him when I've forbidden it? Back, all! This man belongs to me!*"

Shocked, all three lifted their faces to me, terror of my vengeance widening their eyes ... the blood of my guest smeared across their faces.

Suddenly Hēlgrēth laughed, a ribald coquetry.

"*You never loved aught but yourself!*" Hēlgrēth chuckled.

Miëta and Loritá joined Hēlgrēth in her laughter.

"We're young again ... and united strong!" Miëta warned.

"Queens of the Night feast where we please!" Loritá shouted merrily.

Drunk on blood, all three of them; *I was too late!* I ran to them, and even Miëta's attempt to rake my face failed; she was no warrior. My blows battered them, and then I seized and hurled them across the room as violently as I'd ever impaled an enemy. I stepped toward them, determined to kill them all, and then ... Jonathan's dazed eyes opened and looked upon me. *He was in a stupor, but he was alive!* How much he would remember of this night, if he lived, I didn't know, but my plan hadn't failed yet.

Laughter erupted from my brides, mocking, sadistic laughter.

"Give him to us," Miëta commanded. "We're not done, and he hasn't suffered. We won't kill him, or turn him, but the music of his screams shall chorus through these halls and fill our still hearts!"

"We're filled with life!" Loritá said. "Master, fill yourself! Feast with us! Feed, and be young again!"

Only Hēlgrēth kept smiling, as if some secret goaded her.

"Once you loved me," Hēlgrēth said. "So I thought, but I was wrong; if you'd ever loved any of us, you wouldn't deny us this man."

Love ...? Did any of my brides truly love anymore ...?

Did they ever love me, or was that a simple delusion of my youth? Was that why I was leaving them behind ... to seek a new land ... or to seek a new love?

"I love," I said. "When I'm done with him, you shall kiss him at your will. Now go! *Go!* I must awaken him, for there's work to be done."

"We aren't satisfied," Miëta said. "We crave his agony."

"You're intoxicated; you've had enough," I said.

"What of our fun?" asked Miëta. "Have we nothing to play with tonight?"

With a low laugh, she pointed to the bag which I'd thrown upon the floor, and which moved slightly, and issued the soft cries of a waking infant.

As the baby cried, Jonathan lifted his head to stare at them. Loritá jumped forward, snatched up the bag, and all three women peered hungrily inside it. Their laughter rose, and as one, all three ran off, fading into the shadows, taking with them their precious new toy.

Jonathan swooned.

After depositing Jonathan in his room, and repairing the door so he couldn't escape again, I burst into my dungeon, a sword in my hand.

Cries of the infant filled my dungeon. Loritá, Miëta, and Hēlgrēth were circled around a table; Miëta held a lit candle, Loritá a small blade, and Hēlgrēth a bloody scissors. I stooped to examine the lock; tiny scratches around it told me they'd picked it.

I closed, relocked, and tested the door before I was convinced that its lock wasn't broken beyond repair. Then I descended and approached them; they didn't look up to see me until I was only five feet away. Miëta turned, exuberant, her widest grin stretching her blood-smeared lips thin, as the deafening cries of the agonized infant drowned out all other noises.

With a motion worthy of a champion duelist, I stabbed my sword forward with all of my might; the point of my sword penetrated deep between her breasts, spilling her newly-drunk blood. My sword stabbed through her heart, out of her back, and its point hovered over the table upon which the tortured baby lay.

Miëta screamed to deafen God Himself, and clutched at my hilt, her clawing fingernails digging into my hand. Loritá and Hēlgrēth screamed and turned to run, but in one sudden motion I flung Miëta to the ground, yanked my blade from her chest, and sank it into Loritá, through her back. Loritá's scream was different from Miëta's screech of surprise and pain; Loritá had seen most of my punishments, and Loritá's scream effused pure terror. I didn't chase Hēlgrēth as she ran off, but left my sword long inside Loritá, enjoying her screams as they mixed with the wails of the infant.

Finally I flung Loritá down to lay by Miëta, who was still gasping in pain on the cracked flagstones. I glanced at the infant; *my brides' tortures had left nothing worth saving.* With a sudden slice, I brought my sword down and ended the infant's suffering by dividing the babe into halves.

The sudden silence was broken only by the soft patter of Hēlgrēth's pointless flight, and of agonized moans from Miëta and Loritá. I looked at the severed infant; dead blood was poison to us, so in killing it, I'd wasted its nourishment. *That would hurt them worst of all.*

"Don't make me chase you," I shouted to Hēlgrēth. "Accept what you master gives ... or worse will come."

Hēlgrēth peeked out from behind a pillar.

"There's no escape," I warned. "I'll be merciful. Come; *disobey me now ... and I'll behead you.*"

Long moments passed as Miëta and Loritá lifted their heads, terrified by my words. They'd need to feed several times 'ere they'd be free of the pain and damage I'd done to their undead bodies, but to be beheaded; *only damnation awaited us beyond this world.*

"Master, have pity ...!" Hēlgrēth's high voice whined, but she knew better.

"Come!" I commanded, determined that I wouldn't repeat my command again.

Half of Hēlgrēth's face became visible as she peeked around a pillar, and then it vanished. I waited, for any first move on my part would be seen as a sign of impatience, but eventually I wearied of hearing Miëta and Loritá writhe, and started forward.

Hēlgrēth stepped out, into full view, her expression forlorn. Downcast, she seemed diminished, a smaller woman, and slowly walked to her doom with reluctant, shuffling footsteps. I stood imperious, awaiting; they'd defied me, and if I didn't punish them harshly, then they'd only become bolder. Also, I no longer worried about them turning Jonathan Harker, for they'd need every drop of him to begin their healing. However, they'd revealed to him the nature we shared, and now my plan was injured. Jonathan would remember, for I hadn't been there to cloud his mind; controlling him would no longer be a pleasure.

For this betrayal, my brides must pay with their most prized attribute: *their vanity.*

Never had any bride crossed my dungeon so slowly, especially not at my command. Hēlgrēth seemed so sorrowful I'd have expected to see tears on her cheeks, were she mortal. The distance between us lessened until she stood just outside of my sword-range.

"Master, forgive me," Hēlgrēth said gently, her voice barely heard. "Our hungers ... we are dominated. You are the first, the elder, the sire of all our kind; we're weaker than you ... not by choice. We fight against our nature, but ... your curse ... we're powerless against it. Please, Master; spare me now, and I'll be your slave forever."

"You are my slave," I said. "All that walk the night are mine. Now you must pay ... with your heart ... or your head. Choose!"

Hēlgrēth whimpered softly, and she bowed her head.

"This is my favorite dress," she said, looking down at her flowing raiment. "At least ... spare it."

When I said nothing, Hēlgrēth lifted her hands, undid the bow before her cleavage, and reached behind for her laces. Slowly her dress was undone, and she pulled her arms from its bodice, and then slid it down over her gentle hips, pushing it toward her ankles. Hēlgrēth wore nothing underneath; she stepped out of her dress, lifted it, smoothed its wrinkles, and laid it aside over the foot of her coffin. She stood unclothed, bright and radiant, sunlight blonde everywhere, with skin like kissed cream, perfect in shape and hue. Her sad blue eyes drilled into mine, which struggled to deny her angelic perfection which never failed to arouse, her soft curves of sensuous ecstasy which drew the eyes of men and women alike. Beauty is a power unto itself, a magic that weaves its spell and numbs the mind. Over a century had passed since I'd first marveled at her ultimate allure, and still she was mesmerizing. Many times I'd explored every inch of her body and I desired only to explore her again.

Could I spare her? Wasn't there some other punishment? To mar perfection was a crime, *and was she not perfect ...?*

This was her power, I reminded myself, *her tool for enslaving fools who saw only the angelic, not the demonic.*

I rammed my sword between her shapely breasts all the way to the hilt.

As she fell, I let go of the sword, leaving it stabbed through her, heedless of her agonized cries; *the extra pain would teach her not to test her powers against me.*

I walked up the stairs to my coffin, and there I turned and stood, looking down upon my slaves.

Miëta and Loritá still hadn't arisen; if they couldn't crawl into their coffins before dawn then they'd be further weakened, and easy prey, should I wish to worsen their torments. Even if they did make it inside their coffins, they'd waste months trying to regain their full strength and beauty. Miëta alone glanced at me; her hateful glare would've killed a normal man. I stood unmoved, determined to watch; dawn was yet an hour away, and I'd add degradation to their suffering; *none defies a Drăculeşti with impunity.*

Jay Palmer

Chapter 5

At dusk, I arose early. Hēlgrēth, Miëta, and Loritá lay where I'd left them, on the floor, unconscious and weak, my sword beside them, caked with their dried blood. I strode past delighted; *they'd cause no more trouble.* I locked the door behind me and hurried to the kitchens; quickly I started a fire and gathered enough cold food for Jonathan to eat, and then I ascended to his dining room. As I entered, Jonathan stepped out from behind the curtains and faced me as I stood, still holding his meal in my hands.

"*What Godless manner of thing are you?*" Jonathan demanded.

I hesitated, and then I set down his meal upon the table with far less care than I'd ever given it.

"You weren't meant to see them," I said to Jonathan. "They were ordered not to touch you. They've paid dearly for their effrontery ... both to your person and my commands. You won't see them again whilst I command this castle."

"*What are they?*" Jonathan demanded. "They were so ... stunning, lovelier than any woman I've ever seen, even my Mina ... even Lucy Westenra ...!"

"They are curses," I said. "Curses upon this land, which is far older than your England. Transylvania is not just mountains and forests and rivers; the Carpathian Mountains were once a place God favored, but now a place God shuns."

"How dare you speak of God ...?" Jonathan asked. "You live with demons ...!"

"You speak of demons, who've only briefly glimpsed them," I retorted. "I, who know every pit of nethermost Hell, have seen Lake of Fire and Pearly Gates, more than any living man ..."

"Are you not a living man ...?" Jonathan asked. "Are you ... *one of them ...?*"

"I'm your host ... and your benefactor," I said. "Without me, my maidens would've emptied your veins, and you dare accuse ...?"

"I wish to depart ... *now!*" Jonathan said.

"You'll not remain here much longer," I assured him. "I've learned all I can from you, friend Jonathan. I speak as you do; I can enter your cities and pass by unremarked, invisible amid your millions."

"That's why you brought me here: to help you invade ...!" Jonathan began.

"Beware, Jonathan Harker!" I warned. "My powers are greater than you can imagine. You'll do as I command, but I'll grant you one favor: obey me, and I won't take your life. Defy me ... *and you'll never return to your Mina."*

Jonathan stared at me as an angry child might stare at an adult, ignorant of its impotence. I saw him glance at the table; upon it lay a sharp knife. I reached out to the table, took the knife, and held it out before him. Trepidation colored his features; *did he think that I'd use it on him?* No, I took the knife, bared my left arm, and slowly, never taking my eyes off Jonathan, I cut a shallow slice across my forearm. When I finished, I held out the wound for Jonathan to inspect; *not one drop of blood leaked from my cut.*

Jonathan reeled, almost fainted, and fell back against the window.

With both hands, I grasped the sturdy metal knife by each end ... and easily bent it.

"You will write three letters," I commanded Jonathan. "The first should be dated June 12th, the second June 19th, and the third June 29th. The first letter must say that your work here is nearly done, and the next that you will start for home within a few days. The third letter will report that you've left my castle and arrived at Bistritz. I'll return for your letters by midnight; if they're not written, then I'll personally introduce you ... *to my brides.*"

Utter horror met this declaration.

My next days numbered among my worst: *my novelty was gone.* Fear had replaced innocence; my friendly conversations with Jonathan had ended. Jonathan regarded me as his kidnapper, an enemy, and when I attempted conversation, even offering him knowledge no other man knew, all I received was suspicion and mistrust.

My days fell into horrible mindlessness, recalling my centuries back to the origin of my curse. Worse, because of my recent novelty, these days seemed even drearier. Jonathan knew he was my prisoner, and every evening I expected to find his room empty, that he'd escaped during the day. To thwart him, I'd summoned my friends, several local wolf packs, to haunt the forests surrounding my castle. The days and nights echoed with their howls; *they sang unto me.*

On May the 28th, twenty Szgany gypsies arrived at sunset, and I put them to work. First, I ordered them to construct fifty large wooden crates, and I told them that, once they were finished, they'd dig up dirt from the courtyards of my castle, fill the crates, and drive them to Bistritz. There they'd seek a barrister with whom I'd already exchanged correspondences, and he'd have the crates loaded aboard a ship. To their surprise, I paid them in advance, and then I warned them in the old language:

"Inferorum quia pretium."

They understood: '*Hell hath its price!*'

The next evening, one of the gypsies rang a bell upon my doorstep until I appeared. With a bow, speaking no words, he handed me two envelopes. Both were addressed with the handwriting of Jonathan Harker, although his name wasn't on them; I'd never seen these letters before.

I entered Jonathan's chambers and found him reading my books. I held up the two sealed envelopes.

"The Szgany have given me these, of which, though I know not whence they came, I must, of course, take care to see what they contain. Alas! One is to my friend Peter Hawkins; the other ..."

I tore them open and read their contents. The first was a call for help, a plea for rescue with desperate urgency. As I looked at the second, I saw not writing, but a series of strange ciphers new to my eyes. I knew every language on Earth, and to be stymied by this implied an unworthy secretiveness.

"This is a vile thing, an outrage upon friendship and hospitality!" I waved the ciphers at him. *"I see they aren't signed ... so they can't matter to us."*

With iron self-control, I calmly held both letters and envelopes over the flame of a lamp until they caught fire, and then I dropped them onto a plate only as their last bits were completely consumed.

"You've no concept how much I miss your ignorance," I said to Jonathan. "Our former conversations were as ... moonshine ... to me."

Jonathan only glared, and so I left, locking him inside.

I went to inspect the work of the Szgany, and found several crates already built exactly as I'd commanded. My brides had arisen, but they were pained and weary; *they needed blood,* yet I ignored them; they'd taste nothing until I left, and then all the hounds of Hell wouldn't stay their thirst.

Having no other concern, I went to the kitchens, as I'd not yet prepared Jonathan's meal. This took longer, for the stores I'd purchased for him were running low, and I was down to cooking smoked meats and baking bread, which I was unaccustomed to doing. However, I still had a great store of wine, and so I took him a full bottle.

After setting his meal in the dining room, I found him drowsing on the sofa with my favorite book on modern carriages on his chest.

"So, my friend, you're tired? Get to bed. I may not have the pleasure to talk tonight, even were you willing, since there are many labors awaiting me; but you will sleep, I pray."

"Prayers from you are blasphemies," Jonathan sneered.

At midnight, I climbed to my secret vault and wrote many new pages in my diary, trying to quiet the unease in my soul ... if I still had a soul. I hated myself, regretted that Jonathan must die, and consoled myself that soon I'd be among thousands like him. I felt better after hours of writing, and returned to my castle refreshed and calmed.

Before dawn, I entered Jonathan's rooms and found him asleep. While he snored softly, I removed all blank papers, inks, and quills; he'd be sending no more letters. Fearing he might try to escape, despite my wolves, I also took his warm coat and shoes; he'd never survive the wintry heights of my mountain barefoot, even in the midst of our summer.

When I entered the dungeon, my brides were standing together.

"Master, we crave your forgiveness," Hēlgrēth said, gesturing to her sisters. "We were wrong. We're yours to command. Please, the pain overwhelms, and we're weak ... give us relief!"

"You'll have relief soon, my sweets," I said, and I kissed each one of them upon the lips; *our last kisses.* "Trust me, as you used to; your time is coming. Now come, dawn approaches. Let me help you to your rest."

"We hear hammers," Loritá said. "What are they building?"

"That you shall also know soon," I replied.

Supporting them, I led each of them to their coffins and helped them to lie down, and I closed their lids carefully before I went to my own. Something bothered me, but I couldn't guess what; their weakness seemed greater than I'd expected ... *or were they pretending?*

At dusk on June the 24th, I arose and departed before my brides lifted their lids. As the hammers of the gypsies pounded and the saws grated through the last logs, I made Jonathan his breakfast and carried it to him, but he'd noticed his missing coat, shoes, and paper, and he accused me of being a thief. I ignored him. However, after locking his door behind me, the hammers of the Szgany suddenly ceased, and a terrible scream, a woman's scream, came from outside. Curious, I hurried to a balcony, where I looked down to find a moonlit peasant woman pounding upon my doors with her fists. She looked up and saw Jonathan leaning out of his window, around the curve of his tower, and she screamed at him.

"*Monster, give me my child ...!*"

She threw herself onto her knees, and raising up her hands, repeated her cry in tones which obviously wrung the heart of my unwilling guest. She tore at her hair and beat her breast, and abandoned herself to all the violences of extravagant emotion. Finally, she threw herself forward, and, though I could no longer see her, I heard the beating of her naked hands drubbing against my doors.

This was the mother of the child my brides had delighted to torture ... that I'd chopped in two.

With Jonathan and the Szgany watching, I didn't wish to show my powers. I stepped backwards, inside, out of the moonlight, and called to the night in a harsh, metallic whisper. My brothers heard my call, and as I repeated it, many howls answered; *they were coming.*

As my brothers poured into the courtyard, the Szgany fell back, yet the wolves heeded them not. Of the woman, she gave no final cry, and the feral growls of my brothers fell hungrily upon her.

Two evenings later, I awoke with a strange dream in my head. I'd dreamed Jonathan had opened my coffin in the daytime, while I slept, but I had no time to dwell on dreams; *my time had come! A new world awaited me!*

Then I felt the strange pain; I reached up and felt a gash in my forehead that had no explanation. *Had Jonathan discovered me during the daytime?* If so, how had he gotten through the iron door? *Was there another entrance, so ancient neither I nor my brides knew of it?*

It didn't matter; this wound would soon vanish. I was lucky indeed that Jonathan knew nothing of my kind, and wise I'd revealed no truths to him, or I might never have awakened. I couldn't blame Jonathan; although no man attacks a Drăculești with impunity, I was his jailor, and I'd sentenced him to death; *what wouldn't I do to someone who'd imprisoned me?* His fate would be punishment enough.

On the evening of June the 29th, although it wasn't part of my plan, I felt the need for a last visit with my friend. Arising before my brides, I made a special hot meal for Jonathan, and I carried it up to him.

"My dear Jonathan, my plans are complete," I said. "Tomorrow, my friend, we must part. Your letters home have been dispatched; tomorrow I shan't be here, but all will be ready for your journey. In the morning come the Szgany, who have some labors of their own, and also come some Slovaks with wagons. When they've gone, my carriage shall come for you, and bear you to the Borgo Pass to meet the wagon from Bukovina to Bistritz. When you've had time to reflect and understand the needs that drive me, you may regret that you didn't appreciate my hospitality. You'll always be welcomed here, should you choose to return."

"Why can't I go tonight?" Jonathan asked, yet his eyes were affixed to the newly-opened gash he'd placed on my forehead. I reached up and ran a finger along it, letting him know I knew its source, but I kept my voice calm; *it amused me to see him shudder.*

"Because, dear sir, my coachman and horses are elsewhere," I said.

"I'll walk," Jonathan said. "I want to leave now."

"And your baggage?" I asked.

"Leave it for your servants," Jonathan said. "Consider it *my gift ...!*"

I shook my head; *I'd mourn his death.*

"You English have a saying which is close to my heart, for its spirit is that which rules our boyars," I said. *"'Welcome the coming; speed the parting guest.'* Come with me, my dear young friend. Not an hour more shall you wait in my house against your will. Come!"

I led him to the door beyond his dining room, unlocked it, and allowed him to exit his prison. I lit a lamp, and gestured for him to proceed down my hallway. Together, we descended the long stairs, and across the grand hall, and finally came to my front doors. I opened one, but as I did, I sent out a silent call to my brothers; howls filled the night air.

"Hark!" I said. "Hear them, the children of the night! Walk, you say? Indeed, if you think it wise ..."

I stood aside and held the door open for him. For a moment, I thought he'd actually go. Then, as we stared at each other, wolves began to pour into the courtyard through the open gate. Seeing Jonathan, they raced forward hungrily.

"I'll ... wait till morning," Jonathan said, and he buried his face in his hands.

I pushed the door shut moments before my wolves reached it, and I heard their snarls of complaint as I slid the heavy brace into place, its iron chains clinking.

I held out my ring of keys to Jonathan and, to his amazement, I surrendered them to him.

"I set you free," I said. "By mid-morning, I'll be gone. Farewell, Jonathan Harker. You're a good man, wise for your age. I've been honored to call you my friend. When you reach your next destination, know that you arrive with the respects of Count Drăcula."

To his amazement, with a smile, I walked away, leaving my keys in his hands.

As I began to descend the stairs toward my dungeon, I heard footsteps behind me; Jonathan was following me. *The fool! What other secrets did he hope to learn?*

I came at last to my iron door, and lifted up the only key I had left. I unlocked the door and stepped inside.

Hēlgrēth, Mieta, and Loritá stood there, waiting for me, surprised by my early return.

"Master, please, we are your slaves, but we need ...," Loritá said, and then she startled, seeing the gash in my forehead. *"Master, what happened ...?"*

"My young guest is more violent than I thought," I said, a wry smile dancing on my lips. "Heed it not; it will vanish when I feed."

"We must feed, too," Mieta said, and she took a step forward.

"Your time is not yet come," I said. "Have patience! Tonight is mine. Tomorrow night is yours, when you may feast."

Suddenly, in a rage, Jonathan Harker threw open the door behind me. I turned to look at him, and we all stood frozen. His expression wasn't fearful, but defiant, ready for a confrontation.

A moment of silence passed, and then Mieta laughed, slowly and deliberately, bubbling with wicked mirth. Loritá and Hēlgrēth joined her, laughing at Jonathan.

"Tomorrow, you're ours!" Mieta shouted to Jonathan. "Then you shall pay for harming our Master!"

Amid echoing peals of malevolent laughter, Jonathan fled.

I watched Jonathan dash up the stairs with great sorrow; *I missed our conversations, and this wasn't how I'd wished to be parted with him.* Alas, he was only a young mortal. I wasn't to blame for his mortality.

"And now, I require only one thing," I said to my brides. "You will obey me, will you not?"

"We're your slaves," Hēlgrēth said.

"Tonight is the night of fruition, and if you don't obey me tonight, then your heads will separate from your shoulders," I said, and even Mïeta flinched at my commanding tone. "Obey me now, and don't ask why. Go into the farthest back rooms, and remain there, and don't come out, don't even peek out the door, until dawn commands you to seek your sanctuaries. Go now, or you'll not live to know why."

My brides exchanged confused glances, then stared at me hesitantly.

"When ... when will you break your long fast?" Mïeta asked.

"Tomorrow night," I said. "Our fasts shall end together."

This seemed to placate them and, together, with lingering, wary stares, they walked back, beyond the pillars, into the shadows. There were many back rooms in my dungeons; most were built as cells for prisoners, but I had no desire to lock them in. My brides had served me well over the long, dreary centuries. I didn't wish to end their faithfulness, however forced it might be, with their soon-to-come deaths on my hands.

At one time, I'd loved each of them ...

I waited until I heard a distant door close; and then my deeds in Castle Drăculea were done. I dropped the key to the dungeon atop Mïeta's coffin and passed through the iron door for the last time, not bothering to lock it.

With decisive steps I climbed to my stable; as I'd commanded, the Szgany had my horses ready, fed, watered, and strapped into their harnesses, this time pulling one of their large wagons. Atop the wagon were two of the large crates the Szgany had made for me, eight feet long and four feet wide, filled with fresh dirt, again as I'd commanded.

I spent almost an hour working with a shovel; after I'd wrenched a lid off, digging into the earth in one of the boxes, which I half-emptied. Then I cast aside my shovel, and went to a stall filled with hay. Pushing aside the hay, I pulled out a gleaming black coffin, much smaller than my luxurious regal throne in which I normally reposed, but more suited for traveling. The lid of this coffin was removable, and this would allow me exodus at any time. I drug this coffin to the wagon, and, using all my strength, I lifted the coffin and placed it atop the dirt, then took the shovel and filled dirt in all around my snug coffin, until only the lid showed. I removed the lid, braced the lid of the box, and sat down inside my travelling coffin. At last, I pulled the top of the crate over me, firmly secured it in place, and set the lid of my coffin overtop me to keep off the dirt as we journeyed, and then I laid back, eager to begin my adventure.

With a single spoken command to my trained horses, they began moving forward, pulling my heavy wagon out into the courtyard where my servants awaited them. Minutes later, I heard the voices of my ignorant cousins, and someone stopped my horses and climbed aboard my wagon, making my wagon shake, and sat upon the gotza, from where they'd steer the horses. The other drivers, each with wagons loaded and horses ready, had been awaiting my steeds to join them; with the cracks of several whips, they carried my crates of dirt, and, unbeknownst to them, myself, out of Castle Drăculea.

A major stage of my plan was complete, and a new stage beginning. All was going as planned. A smile curled my lips: *tomorrow night ... I'd feed again!*

Rattle! Shake! Thump!
The rugged ruts of the road, unseen from the inside of my coffin, tossed me sideways, and several times almost bounced me against the lid of my coffin, which I had to fasten to keep from flying open and letting loose dirt rain upon me. This travesty of a comfortable ride lasted four hours, for it was many miles from the heights of Castle Drăculea across the Mittel to the Sereth River, called the Siret in olden times, which runs up and around the Borgo Pass. It's a wild, fast river, with many twists and cutbacks, which feeds into the Fluviul Dunarea, which flows all the way to Bistritz, where it joins the great waters known since before the Romans as the Black Sea.

The Black Sea connects to the Mediterranean Sea, which leads to the Atlantic Ocean ... and then to England.

I sighed, relieved when the jarring motion finally stopped, and then strong men, my Szgany, could be heard grunting, lifting my great boxes, and carrying them to their rafts. Finally they jostled my crate, and I was lifted and carried, only to be put down on what I assumed was their raft, for splashing, rushing waters surrounded me.

Two hours after we'd stopped, my journey began again. The raft bobbed against the heaving of the wild waters. I heard the shouts of the poles-men struggling to keep us in the center of the current, and calling to other men on their rafts. Were these not all skilled oarsmen, I wouldn't have trusted them, but these men frequented this river and knew its turns.

Hour after hour, while the sun rose, we floated down river out of the Carpathians. Not in a hundred years had I journeyed this far from Castle Drăculea, and it bothered me to think I'd never see my beloved ancestral home again.

Its crumbling ruin no longer looked pleasing; I remembered the celebration I attended as a child, when the last of the masonry had been completed, and when my father, Lord Drăculeşti the Tenth, had feasted the architects and masons that had built us so wondrous a palace. Then, Castle Drăculea had been sturdy and strong, clean, with bright flags and banners everywhere, its halls filled with light and the laughter of children. My aged grandfather had proclaimed to all that Castle Drăculea would last a thousand years.

If not for my curse he'd have been correct. My family would still be alive. Repairs to our castle would've been timely and appropriate, and my ancestral home wouldn't have fallen to tottering ruins, threatening to topple over the cliff during every storm.

Material destruction is transitory; soon a new Castle Drăculea would rise in its place, and I'd reclaim these lands as my own, not as a feared demon or monster, but as its wise, powerful, and rightful king.

Dusk came slowly, and then night fell, yet we were still on the river. I remained inside my coffin. I already missed my beautiful brides. Their treachery and secretive ways, over the centuries, seemed of small account now; indeed, staying wary of their plots and intrigues gave my mind fertile ground to dwell upon, rather than become as sleepy as trees. Their pleasures, before I began my fast, would fulfill the lascivious dreams of even the most licentious deviant, but even those delights paled as years uncounted passed by, leaving the four of us untouched.

Strangely, now that I'd left, and was traveling farther away each minute, I didn't miss Jonathan Harker. I'd liked him; he would've made a good heir for my teachings, but he was a common man. Doubtless I'd find many his equal in the cities of England. *Would my brides suck him dry at once to alleviate their pain?* I suspected so, but it was also possible they'd torture him for his knowledge of my plans, or even feed him of their own blood, and raise him to take my place. *A merry meeting that would be when I returned!* But no, Miëta had always longed to rule, and this would be her chance; *she wouldn't let a refreshing meal stand between her and the throne of Castle Drăculea.*

I had no fear that my brides would try to follow me; *why would they desire to become subservient again?* They stayed with me for protection, for many of my other brides, driven by bloodlust, had snuck off to seek sustenance in the local villages; all had ended up as dust, staked, beheaded, exposed to sunlight, or consumed by fire. Some had thought to make themselves queens, to rule over the peasants, and raise a vampiric army to challenge me; they would've been wiser to flee into distant lands and never be heard from again. I am the father, the parent, the Grand Sire of all my kind; their strengths are but shadows of mine. No, my brides wouldn't follow me; Miëta would attempt to replace me and rule as queen, and either the local peasants would besiege Castle Drăculea, once they realized I was no longer there, or Loritá and Hēlgrēth would rebel against her. Within a year, they'd all be dead ... truly dead.

My thoughts grew hazy; dawn was approaching. I sighed, and listened to the oarsmen shouting to each other, commands and warnings of rocks and dips, and the splashes of the river that rushed us along. My thoughts vanished into the dreary day-sleep.

BLOOD!

Sunset awakened my hunger, heightened by the smell of edibles so close at hand. *I could feast again!* I no longer had to worry about killing my own people. *Never had I needed sustenance so badly!* My stomach ached, so much I almost cried out. My mind reeled, lost in a fog, but I had to resist ... *fifty years I'd waited ... just a few hours more!*

I was still on the water and I couldn't emerge on a raft. My whole point in leaving Transylvania was to keep from killing my countrymen, and a poor exit mine would be were I to again feed upon those who'd served me faithfully. My hunger was great; soon I'd succumb to its madness. With unparalleled effort, I remained myself.

Minutes past endlessly and hours crept by. If I could've doubled up in pain, I would have, but the confinement of my traveling coffin was tight, unlike my royal residence in Castle Drăculea. I also had to be silent; sloshes of water were still audible, but they were calmer; *we were far downriver.*

Eventually I heard shouts to dock at a specific place, beside a tall ship. We came to a stop, and the raft tilted strangely as a grinding-scrape told me we'd run aground on a sandy beach. Shouts came to tie an anchor rope to a post. Then I heard the name of my barrister, to whom my shipments would be consigned, and then a long silence followed. I suspected some of the men had gone to seek my barrister, and when they came back, long after midnight, we pushed off the beach, as I assumed it must be, and poled farther downstream.

At length I heard voices I didn't recognize, but ropes flopped onto my raft, and we were quickly bound to a dock. The rest didn't take more than an hour; my coffin tilted, first one way, then the other, and suddenly I was lifted, swinging, and raised above the voices; *I was being loaded onto a ship!*

Apparently I was neither the first nor the last crate, but at least another hour had passed; only a few hours remained until dawn. I waited for a pause in the distant voices, and when I heard no one nearby, I opened and lifted off my coffin lid, which I gently set aside. But when I tried to lift my crate's lid, it wouldn't move.

Fool! I cursed. *They'd stacked my crates, and mine wasn't on top!*

Each of my crates were at least a thousand pounds, and took many men or a strong winch to lift. I pressed against my lid, from the inside, but even my great strength failed to budge it. *Would I be trapped inside here, going mad with hunger, this entire trip?*

No! I had to get out!

I listened closely, and heard the sounds of waters splashing against the hull of the ship. I could be motionless when I chose, and slowly I detected that the sounds were strongest on my left side, and there I reached, stretching out my arm, and touched the boards on the inside of my crate; there was over a foot of space between the top of my coffin and the lid of my crate, wherein I could maneuver my removable lid and escape. These crates were built out of fresh, new boards, still dripping sap; I pushed as hard as I could, but the sticky board didn't break. Frustrated, I gritted my teeth, and called upon my full vampiric powers; my fingernails were long and sharp, hard as iron, and older than the trees from which these boards came. I dug my nails into the wood and tried to claw a hole through them, but I couldn't; *I was trapped.*

Frantic, I felt all around, but found no hope until I reached up, as high as I could, and found where the boards met its sturdy frame, three inches wide and two deep, to which the side and end-boards were nailed. I could feel the points of the long nails sticking through the wood; here the boards were affixed together, and here they'd be weakest. I couldn't break these new boards, but if I could pry them out, nails and all ...

Desperation took me. My madness was coming on. I dug my nails into the gap between the boards, pried, pushed, and hungered so much I almost screamed in fury. My relentless and growing appetite fed me a strength I'd never known; the top board moved, and with a loud *creak!*, the nails gave an inch. I was close; I pressed harder, pushing with all of my might, and ...

Success! The board pushed free!

A sprinkle of dirt and rocks poured from my crate.

"Avast!" cried a voice. "Did you hear something?"

I froze, silent as the grave. A still moment passed.

"Just settling; those boxes are new, still wet," said another voice.

I hesitated, but the sounds of footsteps faded, and then I could wait no more. *My plan!* I kept reminding myself, but it sounded like a voice from a stranger. The gap where I could move was small, but I'd climbed mountains believed to be unscalable, descended into narrow caves deep in the Earth, and waded through swamps that would kill any living man; I forced my way out of my coffin, through the gap, and out through the hole where I'd pried the side-board loose, and I pulled my legs behind me until I fell upon the inner hull of the ship.

I was free ... and hungry!

Fifty years ... fifty years of fasting ... *and my time had come again!*

I forced myself to stand still, to resist a minute longer. I could smell the blood of the sailors ... *so close* ... but I'd need these men later. *I had to resist.*

Once, when I was a little boy, my father had shaken his head at me. I'd come home from a romp in the forests outside our new castle, as I'd been ordered to stay out of the way of the masons building it, and I'd returned with a wolf-cub I wished to keep.

"You must give him back to the forest," Father had said. "But, before you do, heed all the lessons you can learn from him. A wolf can't be tamed, no matter how hard you try; he'll chew our doors, our walls, and our furniture, because that's a wolf's nature. Heed this lesson, my son: you can't fight nature. Let him go. This small animal is to be respected, even honored: don't look down upon that which can't be tamed, for you are Drăcula, my son, and you must never be tamed, not by pain, desire, or women. Always be what you are, not what others would make you."

With cautious, furtive steps, I crept through the bowels of the ship. The open cargo doors above shined more than enough moonlight for me to see, even if mortals would be stumbling in shadow. I slipped up the creaky steps and noted the voices of sailors still bringing in cargo, with a boson shouting orders. Many men, Cszeks and Slovaks, were carrying small barrels up the one gangplank; I waited for a gap in their line, and when no one was watching, in the pale starlight, I slipped off the ship, down onto the dock, and wound my way through stacks of goods waiting to be loaded. This was a large port city; thousands lived here; *my hunt would be easy.*

Not far off, I found an illsome tavern, lively with song and laughter, and near to it would be those who begged; *no one would miss them.* With my head bowed to shadow my features, I walked past the beggars in a hurry, heedless of their outstretched palms, and turned into a dark alley behind the tavern. Waste and rubbish filled that horrible place, but there I halted, hungering.

"Good evening, sir," said a slurred voice behind me. "They don't let no one come into their kitchen, and there's no other place to go back here."

I smiled; *it was their nature to come to me.*

"I say, for a few shillings, or a doubloon, if you have one, and if you're knackered, I'll take you inside, and we'll both have a drink."

His footsteps came closer; *he thought I was his prey.*

"Thar's no one back here but us, and I pref'r to be a gentle soul," he said as he stepped up right behind me. "How's about you be a sport and share me a coin or two ... so your clothes don't get ruffled?"

I unbound my hunger. In an instant, I turned, seized his head, and slammed him back against an empty crate. My left hand closed on his neck, my thumb driven into his throat, cutting off his air with a grip that could snap his neck, had I wished, but dead blood wouldn't sustain me. With wolfish angst, I bared my fangs and bit into him.

Blood! Sweet, warm, pungent life ... flowed into me! The taste ...! My delight ...!

The artery under his left ear spewed, and I sucked with ravenous abandon. He struggled, hit and punched, and we bounced off the crate, but I needed his liquid essence; I pushed him backwards until his head impacted the outside wall of the tavern. He staggered, but my thumb rested upon his windpipe, and he couldn't catch his breath. I couldn't risk detection, so I drew back just long enough to let him see my face; wild eyes, my blood-filled mouth lusting for more, the gash of the shovel creasing my forehead, my ghastly pale skin; he startled, as if realizing I was Death Incarnate come to end his wicked ways.

At last, my fast was ended ...!

Some men fight Death, while others quail; *groveling worms beneath Death's boot.* This man seemed torn, as if afraid to die, but too frightened to resist. Slowly his lack of breath weakened him past the point of consciousness. He collapsed in my grip, and I held him pinned against the wall and feasted deeply. His taste was Czech, lowborn and common, but I didn't care. *Blood filled my mouth again!* In my veins, his blood felt overpowering, its essence of life refreshing; the demands of my curse were finally fulfilled. Like air to a drowning man, I sucked every mouthful, every drop, releasing fifty years of denial in one wondrous and succulent moment.

I was alive again! Fresh blood flowed inside me!

Long, magnificent minutes passed, and I sucked until I'd drained him dry. When the blood pulsing through his veins grew too little, his heart stopped, and no more came to his neck. I let his corpse fall, almost staggering backwards, my body scintillating, my brain awash with a dazzle to blind the thoughts of any mortal man. *Food ...!* Only those who've died of hunger and thirst could comprehend the relief I felt; *vigor, strength, and fluidity surged within me, an unholy baptism of delicious, savory blood!* I, who'd lived centuries and endured destitution of my most-essential need longer than any mortal man, stood in disaffirmance of the curse God placed upon me, now quenched by a single depredation.

I wanted more ...!

I glanced down at the ruin of the vessel of a man before me, swathed in ragged, dirty garments, a corpse with nothing to justify its existence. *I am the blessing God sent to you! I ended your suffering, lucky fool! Be sure to mention your gratitude for God's plan when you grovel before St. Peter at the Pearly Gates!*

I turned away, hungry still. I felt light, almost giddy, yet I couldn't allow myself to become intoxicated. I was far from my castle, and from the small coffin which was my temporary sanctuary; should my ship sail 'ere I boarded her, that would leave me stranded to face the approaching dawn.

Soon I'd feel my old self returning, my full strength, and the pain of this withered shell would depart. Then I'd be young and strong forever ... *as long as humans existed to feed me.*

Slipping back onto the boat proved even simpler than getting off it. I heaved a small barrel onto my shoulder, used it to hide my face, and walked aboard like a common sailor, without anyone looking at me. Veering away from the others, I set my burden down so it blocked the narrow passage behind me, and then I slipped down a flight of narrow stairs into the hold. There I crouched in the deep shadows; sailors were transferring boxes lighter than mine to the fore, and when they'd departed, I returned to my crate, where the board I'd pried free was still hanging loose. Dawn was more than an hour away, yet I'd feel better if I rested and let the delicious warm juices inside me deliver their benevolence. I slid as ungently into my crate as I'd slid out of it, and entombed myself with delight, eager for the healing to begin. As soon as my coffin lid was secured, I drifted off ... and slept like the dead.

I awoke the next night to find my pains still abundant; one feeding would cure me only a little. I was hungry again. Yet I was rocking strongly; *my ship was far out to sea.* It would be many days before I reached my destination; I'd have to feed sparingly from now on, *but I would feed!*

I stayed in my coffin for another three hours, resting and recovering my strength. I'd no business wandering about; the risk that I'd be discovered was too great. If these fools knew what they sailed with, they might abandon ship, giving themselves to the sea to avoid surrendering their lives to me; that would leave me alone, and I was never a great sailor. Worse, they might ignite their ship during the day, leaving me to burn in it, to die in flames as they died in the sea.

Once I'd been aboard a ship as it sank; my dead body floated, and I'd have died with the dawn. Yet I swam to the bottom, and clung to a rock, and there awaited the night. The weight of the water crushed me, yet as few pains are fatal, I'd no choice but to endure. The daylight weakened me, but the water in my lungs couldn't choke breath I didn't have. At night, I fetched a heavy chain from the wreck, and wrapped it about me to hold me down, and climbed over the strange cliffs and around the mysterious pits of the ocean's depths. It took me months to travel underwater, but what else was I to do? It was my first fast, which proved to me that I could survive without fresh blood, even though it pained my body greatly. When at last I sloshed up onto a shore, far from civilization, I'd had to bury myself in sand, day after day, until I found a tiny village whose primitive dwellers had the sweetest blood I've ever tasted.

As I waited, I tried to listen, to estimate how many men sailed this ship, but it was too noisy. The ship was smaller than I'd expected, a Russian schooner named 'The Demeter', and I was worried; the larger the ship, the more food I'd have. It was too late to change; *I'd manage with what I had.*

Late that night I crawled from my confinement and searched the hold, determined to know all about the ship I was aboard, but I found nothing of interest. I went fore, located a small set of steps leading upwards, and in searching them I found the cramped sleeping quarters for the men; fourteen bunks, most of them empty. This troubled me, so I crept to the top of another short stairs, and there heard the men, still on deck ... and throwing dice ... from the sounds of their laughter.

Returning to the hold, I searched aft, and found many thick rolls of carpet stacked; carpets pleased me; Castle Drăculea had few, for most had rotted so badly they could be swept into piles of dust. I'd like carpets such as these for my new residence, and of course, the new Castle Drăculea ... when I had built it.

For now, carpets and boxes of consignments were worthless to me. I found another stairs to a closed door, and after listening, I slowly opened it. To my delight, it didn't creak at all, but the room was vacated, so it didn't matter. The silent door opened upon a galley, which held two long tables for the men, with a wooden counter upholding wide, fat pots sitting on an even wider stove, which was still giving off heat, and the only light streamed from an open vent in the front of the stove, and illuminated dishes soaking in a half-barrel, the foaming, soapy water sloshing back and forth. Doubtless the cook was waiting until morning to clean, after the rocking of the ship had made his chore easier.

I quickly examined the galley and found a cupboard of food fit for the living, not nearly as rich as the repasts I'd purchased and cooked for Jonathan Harker. Six kegs were stacked against the wall, some marked 'water' and others marked 'grog', but I required neither. However, I found a two-pronged cooking fork; *I stole and pocketed it.*

Carefully I threaded my way up another short stair to the deck, staying behind other crates; I was glad my crates were below; boxes on deck had to be tied down, and the brightness of day shone on them. Yet I was able to peer at the sailors; they looked like countless other men, rugged, rustic, and slovenly, with beards as full as they could grow them, and each held a wooden mug in one hand. To my surprise there were only nine of them. One was clearly the captain, for he puffed a large bone pipe and was a head taller than the others. Another was a cook, round and flabby, and wore an apron smeared with soot and stains. Two wore uniforms; these would be mates, subject only to the captain's commands, and five sat in ragged garments, strong and sturdy lads; these were the working sailors.

Having no wish to reveal myself, I took the occasion to slip into the one chamber I'd not explored; the captain's quarters. A lamp hung from chains affixed to the ceiling, and its glow was dim, but more than enough for me. I found a long sea-chest, and opened it to discover a cache of rifles, pistols, gunpowder, and shot; this captain was prepared to arm his entire crew in case of attack ... or to fight all of them, if a mutiny broke out. I also found several thick coats, one of sealskin, and three pairs of tall boots. A smaller chest held five bottles of rum, and a purse under his mattress held a wealth of coins, mostly silver, which was quite a lot for any man of the sea.

However, the only item that interested me was his book, the ship's journal, which was set out, and upon opening it, I found carefully written entries for almost every day, going back three years. I read the last entry:

On 6 July, we finished taking in cargo, silver sand, and boxes of earth. At noon we set sail. East wind, fresh. Crew, five hands ... two mates, cook, and myself (captain). Should be at Bosphorus by 11 July.

I grinned; I liked men that kept journals, for it was always interesting to see how others thought. Of course, mortal writings were naught compared to my diaries, where the musings of four hundred years lay detailed.

Nothing else existed on the ship. This was undesired; I wished my presence to remain unknown, and yet to have a ready supply of food. My hunger, having been slaked once, longed for more.

I snuck back down into the bowels of the ship and sat upon a small crate. I felt disgraced: *I, a Prince of Transylvania, was hiding like a mouse in a haystack, unable to reveal my presence for fear of what peasant sailors might do.* Finding me, I could be slain in my daylight weakness, or, in my deep slumber, they could throw me overboard, or sacrifice their lives by burning the ship itself. Drowning couldn't slay me, but it might be months or years before I washed ashore, and I'd no desire to suffer, helplessly adrift, wandering the depths with no idea when or where I might find land.

My dilapidated condition was a shame upon my house, and the fault was mine. When I'd first realized what I'd become, the enormity of my curse, I should've embraced it fully, explained it to my family, and assumed the coronet as was my birthright. Had I done so, I'd have become the famous immortal Ruler of the Carpathians, and doubtlessly King of Hungary by now. I could've ordered my kinsmen to repair my crumbling castle, and they would've done so gladly. I'd be on my own royal barge now, guarded by trusted retainers, headed to Windsor Castle, my visit expected by my royal cousins in England. But, in my ignorance and shame, I'd begun my immortality badly; I'd been ashamed of my curse, terrified of its unknown effects, and fled into shadow and isolation.

That was my mistake. *If God had chosen me to be his devil on Earth, why should I not rule here, as the Evil One ruled in Hell?* If God hadn't intervened, if only the curses of those whom I'd impaled had brought His doom upon me, *then was I not free to use my curse as I willed, for the eternal glory of the Drăcula clan?* Either way, I didn't need to choose isolation; there were more than enough unimportant fools, like that blackguard who'd accosted me behind the tavern, upon whom I could feed. Had I assumed command of my armies, and led them to glory and conquest, then I'd have had an endless supply of enemy captives to satisfy my needs. They'd be brought to me every night by my loyal soldiers, instead of me having to prey upon peasants who feared and hated me.

This was the cost of my mistake, the price I pay for my folly; hiding in the depths of a smelly ship while my inferiors lounged on deck. Soon I'd undo my error, and unravel the steps that led me to cower here. My mistake could be undone; I'd no longer walk in shadow, but claim the pinnacles of power which I could take at will. I'd wear my crown at last, and the mortals who'd prefer me beheaded, burned by sun or fire, or staked to the Earth, will then cower before me. I'll arise greater than ever, a King of the Night, and any army powerful enough to threaten me shall find an army of undead assaulting them, and laying to waste any city that defies me. With the powers I possessed, the world was mine to take ... *I only had to seize it.*

Patience, I told myself. *One step at a time.*

Long after midnight, all went to sleep save the youngest, who was set to watch. The great wheel, mounted on the aft castle atop the galley and the captain's quarters, was tied off; the captain and other sailors didn't trust this boy to steer. I waited until all else was quiet, save the sea and snores, and crept out of hiding. His back was turned to me; he was pacing back and forth, probably to stay awake.

I reached out with my mind; his thoughts would be simple, as was he. Filled with many dreams, on a lonely watch, during a hot summer night, a boy at sea was concerned only with his place among his companions. I knew sleep better than any mortal; I willed comfort, rest, and drowsiness into his mind. It was no small effort, for such mental controls, without being seen, are difficult, impossible for vampires with less than two centuries of practice.

He staggered, then resumed walking, and finally sat down. His yawns told me my mental-focus was accurately targeted, my efforts successful. Yet I didn't want him unconscious; I needed to insure he didn't cry out and awaken the others. I waited, feeling his mind slowly blur and dim, and then I slipped across the deck.

His eyes widened in sheer dismay as I revealed myself to him. His face, seeing mine, paled, and his slack jaw fell open, disbelieving the horrid apparition that was my countenance. I towered over him, an evil spirit of the sea, borne upon an ill-wind, a harbinger of doom. Any cry he might've uttered was swallowed in the shock of seeing a total stranger appear in the midst of a wide ocean, upon a small ship with no known passengers. Surprise and my connection to his mind left him mute.

I seized upon his hesitation, and performed such tricks as could dazzle most mortals, mastering changes in my expression to access and confound the thoughts of the weak-minded. He stared mesmerized; I delved into his soul, and finally I left him stunned beyond any response. I kept his mind dazed and drew out the fork that I'd stolen; I stabbed it into his throat, but into a lesser vein; I didn't want him to die tonight.

Blood ...!

My hunger was less ravenous tonight, but I thirsted for recovery from this aged, withered shell that had entombed my spirit for the last fifty years. I supped slowly, savoring the rich, warm flavor, the dense, life-filled red syrup, the sap of humans which only mortals can generate. This youth was also common, but tastier than the foul, base scoundrel upon whom I'd broken my fast; when I'd cared only for a container I could empty into myself. Now I remembered the subtle differences that quality and breeding infused into my diet, the myriad and exquisite flavors to be enjoyed by selective feeding. Yet I forced myself not to dwell upon taste, lest I drain him dry. I drank until warmth tingled inside me, against the endless cold of the grave which haunted my frame, and then I drew back, hesitantly, but with firm resolution.

At my command, the boy fell into a deep slumber, and I placed the two-pronged fork into his hand; when discovered, it'd give the sailors an excuse for the punctures upon his throat, to preclude their searching the ship for a different cause.

I walked like an emperor should back to my crate and entered my coffin. Securing my lid, I laid back and let the warmth of his blood course through me. My plans had been diminished by the unexpectedly small crew, but not denied; I'd arrive in England young and strong.

Young blood ...!

Jay Palmer

Chapter 6

  I awoke at sunset to a strange sensation. I felt ... fluid, less dry than I could remember. I'd expected an easing, but there was something more, something which tingled in my mind more than my body. I felt ... exhilarated, almost excited, not only ready but eager to begin my new life in England. By now my brides must've realized I wasn't coming back and become frantic; the blood of Jonathan Harker wouldn't sustain them for long. They were smart, devious, and powerful, but they weren't warriors; *I'd never have to worry about their betrayals again.* That thought alone bathed me with relief, for they alone knew my mind and weaknesses. Once they were gone, nothing could stop me: *England would be my ultimate feast.*

  I needn't dwell upon the dreariness of the remainder of my voyage, save for my slow healing. On July the 11th, we arrived at the port of Bosphorus just as the sun was rising. Before I fell into my daily sleep, I heard Turkish Customs Officers board and inspect our vessel, and on July the 12th, at dusk, the same happened at Dardanelles. Every night I arose and fed, and my body grew younger and stronger. Soon my crustiness was gone and I felt robust as a man in his fifties. On July the 16th, one of crew, Petrofsky by name, had taken over the nightly watches, but my attempt to mesmerize him failed; instead, I drank every drop of his blood and cast him overboard. I soon heard the crew grumbling more, with frightened voices, but my strength was increasing; soon I needn't even fear the sun.

On the morning of July the 17th, one of the men, Olgaren, glimpsed me, but I vanished into the hold so quickly he told the captain I might've been a ghost. The crew was openly angry, and searched the ship, even opening several of my boxes, although not the one I slept in, nor did they crawl around the back to discover my point of egress.

The next night, before I began my nightly exploration of the ship, I snuck back into the captain's quarters and found a new entry.

> *Mate reported in the morning one of crew, Petrofsky, was missing. Couldn't account for it. Took larboard watch eight bells last night; was relieved by Abramoff, but didn't go to bunk. Men more downcast than ever. All said they expected something of the kind, but wouldn't say more than there was 'something' aboard. Mate getting very impatient with them; fear trouble ahead.*

The next night, after the sailors took to their bunks, I was disturbed by the captain's latest journal entry:

> *On 17 July, one of the men, Olgaren, came to my cabin, and confided to me that he saw a strange man aboard the ship. In his watch, he'd been sheltering behind the deck-house, as there was a rain-storm, when he saw a tall, thin man, who wasn't like any of the crew, come up the companion-way, go along the deck forward, and disappear. He followed cautiously, but when he got to bows, he found no one, and the hatchways were all closed. He was in a panic of superstitious fear, and I'm afraid his panic may spread. To allay it, I shall today search the ship from stem to stern.*

Four days of rough seas, followed by a brief respite, gave the sailors something else to discuss, but several still considered the ship haunted. In the storm, I drank another sailor dry, this time a mate, and delivered him to the frothy brine, hoping the storm might be blamed. His blood made me feel even younger, and I watched delighted as wrinkles faded from my aged hands. Days later, when a real storm tossed us about, I drained another, and the heat and power within me felt as if I'd consumed a raging bonfire.
I felt alive!
Fog set in as we neared England, making my movements aboard ship easier. I slew at will; my flexibility had returned; *I no longer felt dry or aged, and my strength of old was recovering.* I drank another sailor and the cook, following my plan. Only three remained. *None who sailed with me could be left alive when I reached England.*

Only one sailor died well. Digging into my boxes, and finding the trail of dirt my feet had left, he spied me emerging one evening. Before I could stop him, he fled up the stairs and onto the deck, which was laden with fog.

"Save me! Save me!" he shouted to the captain. *"You'd better come too, captain, before it's too late! He's there! I know his secret now! The sea will save me; it's all I have left!"*

Without hesitation, he dove overboard, preferring to be consumed by the sea rather than me. The remaining captain and first mate shouted to the waves he'd dived into, but he never resurfaced.

That night, I took the first mate, leaving only the captain alive. We were close to our destination; *I'd no fear now.*

On August 7th, I emerged to find that the captain had lashed himself to the great ship's wheel, steering The Demeter directly toward land. In his hands he held a crucifix, and his eyes fell upon me with a horror that shriveled his soul. The crucifix weakened me greatly, yet I was strong again, and his self-made bonds prevented resistance. I drank him dry, but his crucifix left me too weak to untie the ropes around his wrists. Standing behind him, my hands upon his arms, I steered The Demeter our last few nautical miles. Before dawn, I heard the crashing surf, and spied land.

England, at last ...!

I steered away from the docks, toward a sandy beach; the safety of the ship no longer mattered. I left the corpse and fled from the weakness of his crucifix.

In the bow of the ship, I watched the foreign shore approach, and smiled. *My time had come!*

Once, as a little boy, I'd awoken to the howls of wolves, and fled to the safety of my father.

"Son, never be afraid," my father had said. "Those night-howlers aren't enemies, but trusted friends. Watch them, as often as you can, for wolves are great teachers, if you have the wisdom to learn. When outmatched, wolves gather and attack as one; then nothing resists them. They howl to instill fear, which is a powerful advantage over those who cower. God didn't make all men sheep; some men God made wolves, and their blood is ours: *clan Drăculeşti, the Wolves of God*. Fear no wolf, my son. Be the wolf."

Many eyes watch the sea, even at night. I couldn't let them see a man leave the ship, lest a search begin.

I descended to all-fours.
I perked my ears and bristled.
I licked my chops.
Be the wolf!

The last son of Drăculeşti entered his new land of conquest on August the 8th. As The Demeter ran aground on a sandy spit, I jumped over the rail, onto English soil, and ran off. The ship no longer mattered; *here I could feast at will.*

It's no small effort to transform into a wolf, or any other shape, or to transform back. Amid the hazy thoughts of the primal hunter I ran for miles, away from the coast, and there I found a shadowed garden in which

I resumed my human appearance. Then I sought out a victim, a wandering constable, and killed him, leaving his empty carcass sitting upright upon a bench, leaning against a tree as if sleeping. He had a respectable supply of coinage, which I took, for I'd need it, and I added it to the coins I'd stolen from the captain after he was dead.

Following the lessons I'd learned from books, and from my conversations with Jonathan Harker, I hailed a one-horse cabriolet, or hansom cab, as it was called, which I'd read about but never seen. I loved modern carriages, and had toyed with ideas to construct one myself. The wonderful design of a hansom cab allowed for enhanced speed, with the safety of a low center of gravity, which made for smooth cornering. I gave the driver directions to a town nearby my purchased residence, and rode looking at the strange houses and trees, with the English wind in my face, delighted by my choice of new feeding grounds.

From there I took a second cab; a phaéton, a sporty open carriage with rigging for two horses, although this phaeton had only one horse, and the driver sat so near its tail they looked to be one. It had a light, minimal frame atop four extravagantly large wheels, with a cloth canopy to shade its passengers. My plan had been to use three different drivers to get to my house, to maintain secrecy, but as the dawn lightened the sky, I needed to get to safety.

My first view of my house was only its roof over a tall, overgrown stone wall. It looked both impressive and foreboding, exactly as the drawings and photographs of Jonathan Harker had shown it. It seemed a castle compared to most English homes, although it was pitiful compared to my mountaintop fortress. Yet I had no time to admire it; I paid my driver and sent him off just as dawn lit the horizon. Then I fled indoors.

All night before August the 10th I suffered without a coffin, sleeping atop dirt foreign to me, which would weaken me, in the high-ceilinged basement beneath my chapel. The day passed outside, yet I found it hard to sleep.

Before sunset I heard movement above me; the letters I'd sent from Transylvania, and the note I'd placed in view of the front door, had been found. Shortly into the night, I removed my clothes and shook them free of dirt while my crates were delivered into the gallery beside my chapel. From a doorway I watched as each box of earth from my homeland was set in place by burly workmen, and then they departed.

I examined my crates, and found the one containing my coffin, the boards of which had been nailed back together. Strengthened by the blood of the sea captain and constable, I pulled three of the crates, including the one containing my coffin, down the steep steps, dumping out a small mound of Transylvanian soil for me to sleep upon. I had no time to move the rest; *I'd much to do.*

Only a mile from my new residence was the Purfleet Marketplace, with many charming shops, and merry customers walked about under lanterns that banished the darkness. I stayed in shadow as much as I could until I spied what I needed: a vestments mercantile office, which the inhabitants of England called a *'clothing store'*. I entered, and was greeted by the first real smile I'd seen in ages, from a man who questioned the source of my Carpathian garments and suggested I select something more modern. His cheeriness and deferential manner endeared him to me, and within an hour I found myself in fashions the like of which I'd only seen in photos. I selected several garments, and this man carefully fitted them to me, marking all but one of them with chalk, and promising to have them tailored to fit me even better.

However, while I stood in the strange new clothes, he took hold of my arm, which stunned me, and then he tried to pull me in front of a full length mirror, at which I almost pulled him off his feet. Greatly confused, he again tried to get me to view myself in his mirror, to which I adamantly refused; astounded, he gaped, but finally he acquiesced.

In one pocket I had several gold coins I'd brought with me from Castle Drăculea; I offered him one, and was amazed to be informed he couldn't exchange such a valuable coin, and thus I was given credit, to take with me one suit, the one that fit best, and to pay for it upon receipt of the others, after his seamstress had adjusted them to my build. I was taken aback by such innocence; I'd intended to kill this man, but I bowed to him and thanked him instead. Dressed in style, I carried my old clothes with me as I left, and shoved them into a tall bush only a block away.

Then I was astounded by an action I'd never encountered. As I walked back to my home, I stepped into the light of a streetlamp, and found my path blocked by three men, strangers I'd never seen. These men stopped at once, and with a demeanor I could only call *'friendly'*, they bowed to me and begged forgiveness for interrupting my stroll. I was taken aback by the intimacy of being spoken to so casually by strangers, who didn't seem to fear me at all. They seemed happy, and stepped aside to clear my route to pass them by, and as I did, they wished me a *'good evening'*.

Confused, I continued on my way, only to find their courtesies weren't uncommon in this land; not a block away I saw two gentlemen stop and actually bow before a lady, who accepted their actions as quite normal, before she proceeded to walk past them.

I dare say that, before I left the lamplit area, I felt positively lighthearted. *England would be a wonderful new adventure for me, a great place to rebuild my wealth and prepare for my triumphant return to Transylvania.*

I didn't feast that night, for I'd decided to commit no murders near my new house. Instead, I returned to my purchased abode and began to explore it, learning its every room and passage. Jonathan Harker had described it accurately; it was huge and complex, with many renovations over the last century, with thick stone foundations of the fortress it'd once been. Its disrepair showed, but only a of few years, which could be easily mended. Two large halls, worthy of royal audiences, were adjacent to galleries with many empty bookshelves, which I longed to see filled, and a dozen bedrooms, some of which still held furniture. I found kitchens and pantries worthy of Castle Drăculea's prime, with a dining hall worthy of a royal feast. In the moonlight, from the high windows, I spied the small lake that lay within the confines of the stone wall surrounding my new estate. I felt exhilarated, eager to explore the heavily-wooded grounds around my lake. Yet my outdoor adventures would wait for another night, for there was much indoors yet to be discovered.

My greatest surprise: I discovered a narrow catacomb under my chapel, where many coffins lay, filled with the remains of this dwelling's former inhabitants. The narrow, winding passageways converged upon my central chamber, almost a cave, directly under the chapel. This chamber, I decided, would be my makeshift dungeon, where I'd sleep every day.

Seeking out the dark corners of my domicile took the rest of the night. I was certain I hadn't seen everything before I heard a distant rooster warn of the coming of dawn. Holding aloft a candelabra I'd found in a furnished bedroom, secure in my residence, and wearing a suit of the latest fashions of my newly-adopted land, I set my travelling coffin atop my layer of dirt from my homeland, and laid down to comfort myself, content that my plan was working out better than I'd imagined.

The next evening, as soon as the sun set, I walked to the Purfleet Marketplace and hailed a cab, another cabriolet, which I directed to a distant district, wherein I could feed. However, I purposefully avoided the shadows and walked in clear sight of the local inhabitants. I wondered what I looked like, for I no longer seemed to shock those whose gaze crossed my features. Clearly I was a foreigner, but my new clothes seemed to instill a familiarity, as if by accepting their styles I became acceptable. Seeing their faces smile at me engendered the strangest feeling, like the warmth of a fire inside me. Once I'd traveled the world, seeking the cause of my curse, and discovered civilizations as different as the living from the dead. Never had any welcomed my presence like this strange, young land.

Their gaiety was intoxicating. Before midnight I was smiling back at strangers smiling at me, bowing to gentlemen who returned my bows cheerily, and stepping back before ladies, who accepted my gestures as cultured and respectable. This was the environment I longed for in my isolation of the Carpathians; when I returned, I'd fill elegant halls with folk of this ilk, and invite my distant cousins so they may learn these modern mannerisms.

After midnight, the streets seemed to bleed away its crowd, as if by some unspoken command. Constables, men wearing drab matching uniforms with strangely-domed hats, wandered about with many a *"good-night, gents!"* on their lips, as if informing people it was time to seek rest. I was taken unaware when a constable asked my business, and if it was nearly concluded. I politely assured him I was seeking a cab, hoping to distract him ... and perhaps carry him into some shadow where I could feast upon him. To my surprise, he blew on a small, rather loud, simple musical instrument he wore on a loop around his neck, and within moments I was boarding a large coach with no idea where I was going.

"West," I told the driver, and he turned his horses toward London.

Twenty minutes later, after I'd ascended to sit beside the driver, I pushed his blood-drained carcass forward, so the wheels of his own coach crushed him. When his body was discovered, his death wouldn't be blamed upon the small pricks of my teeth, but upon the more-obvious cause. His blood had a trace of nobility to it, although he was so base I doubted if he knew of it, but

I felt greatly refreshed. I drove his coach to the outskirts of another district, from where I hailed a different cab to drive me home. To my delight, this cab was a plush and extravagantly brass-trimmed Victoria, an elegant French carriage first made for George IV. I examined it closely, delighted by its construction. It was essentially a phaeton with a coachman's box-seat, which my beloved book back in Transylvania claimed was popular amongst wealthy families. On its low body was a plush seat for two passengers, and its raised driver's seat was supported by an iron frame, topped by a calèche canopy, and drawn by two elegant horses; *I was truly riding in style.*

Dawn was four hours away when I arrived. I didn't have my driver drop me at my gate, but at the large, Doric house beside mine. I paid his fee, and tipped him generously, as I'd learned was customary from observing others. According to Jonathan Harker, this classic abode housed a large lunatic asylum, which made it the perfect neighbor for me. I needed a servant, and where better to shop for one weakly-minded?

Standing outside my neighbor's mansion, it took a while for me to regain my self-control. Walking among the happy peoples of England, I'd adopted a casual nature compensatory with my newfound environment, a complete contrast to my lonely ruins with murderesses for company. Yet I soon mastered my accustomed level of concentration, regaining the depth of my immortal mind. I began to reach out, into the asylum, feeling with my instincts, with the peripheral faculties of my senses, to find what I needed. I disregarded women and the elderly, and those too thoughtless to be aware of themselves; I'd no need for a mindless puppet, whose every move I must command. Finally I located a suitable subject, a man whose mind was filled with fears. He reminded me of the Szgany gypsies, whose presence always disgusted me, for they lived their whole lives in fear, never seeking to amount to be more than they were born.

I finally located him, at a basement window low against the ground, on the very backside of the asylum. He was gripping the bars desperately, his eyes ablaze. I stooped and looked at him closely, examining the terrors on his face with an expert's eye, while keeping a tight grip on his mind.

"You ... are ... *Renfield*," I said, grasping at a name amid his mental chaos.

"Yes!" he said, although he looked even more frightened. "Please ... get me out of here! I don't belong in here!"

"How did you arrive here?" I asked. "For what crime were you imprisoned?"

"No crime, good sir, if it please you!" Renfield insisted. "That is, I'd had a bit of the drink, and didn't know what I was doing, and the horrors came upon me ...!"

"*Horrors ...?*" I asked.

"The horrors, yes, they prey upon me, sir," Renfield said. "Witches, devils ... I don't know who they are, sir, but they attack me at my weakest. That's why I like to stay drunk, sir, so I can't hear them when they come ...!"

"What do they look like, these ... horrors?" I asked.

"Please, governor, don't play parlance with me," Renfield said. "I never see them, except in nightmares, but I hear them, as clearly as I hear you."

"I need a servant ...," I said.

"I'll serve you ... if you get me out of here," Renfield said.

"What I require most is loyalty," I said, my tone unflinching. "My secrets are mine, and to a servant who blabs even one word of my doings ... only the grave rewards him."

"I'm your man, sir!" Renfield said. "I'm here; just bring me a sharp saw to cut these bars ...!"

"I need no saw," I said. "Will you swear to me your life and soul, that you'll do all I ask, and never speak of me to another living mortal ...?"

"I'm your slave, if you free me!" Renfield said.

I had my doubts, for this man was lowly and destitute, barely more intelligent than a dog. Yet I was unlikely to find better in this neighborhood, and I'd little patience shoveling dirt. I knelt down, gripped one of the iron bars blocking his window, around which was littered many yellow feathers, and pulled with my vampiric strength. My recent feedings empowered me; the thick iron bar wouldn't give, for not even I could bend such, but the half-rotted wood in which it rested slowly crumbled and broke apart. I pulled carefully, to be as quiet, and do as little damage, as possible. Mr. Renfield gasped, and his jaw fell open as the hard wood finally gave way and the bar pulled free.

"You ... you're the master ...!" Renfield exclaimed.

Twice more I performed my feat of strength, and soon two more iron bars lay beside the first. Renfield pulled himself up and squeezed between the remaining bars, and wriggled like a hooked worm until he'd pulled himself free. Then he stood up and started to run, but I seized and held him firmly.

"Replace the bars in the window," I commanded Renfield. "Make it look as if they're still part of your prison, in case someone should come looking for you in the night."

"No one will ...," Renfield began, but my hand seized his throat and squeezed with no less force than it had taken to pull his iron bars free.

"My servants don't argue ... *they obey!*" I hissed softly, as if I were a deadly serpent about to strike, and I flung him to the ground.

Renfield lay sprawled upon the grass, and stared at me with a horror worthy of my curse. He was a sturdy, muscular man, but my strength was greater than human.

"Yes ... Master," Renfield said, and before we slipped away, he replaced the bars and packed moist dirt around their bases to hold them in place.

We crossed the grounds to my house. I set Renfield to the task of digging dirt out of my boxes. While I hid my coffin, he filled a large bucket from the stable, and then he carried it down to the central cavern below my chapel, dumped the bucket upon my pile, and returned for more. This was slow work, and Renfield kept casting me frightened looks as he labored.

My mound of dirt grew scarcely two feet taller before the roosters began crowing.

"Enough ... for now," I said. "Leave your bucket, return to your cell in the asylum, and after you enter, reset your bars so no one will know you've been gone. Remain there all day, and return to me only after night has fully fallen, when no one can see you cross the grounds. Obey me, and I'll reward you with liquor. Disobey me ... and you'll not live to see another dawn."

"Yes, Master," Renfield said, his pallor whiter than I'd ever worn, and then he fled.

After he'd left, I looked down at the pathetic mound of dirt he'd piled. Soon this would be a small rise, not as grand as my former mound under Castle Drăculea, but sufficient to insure my full strength each sunset. As to Mr. Renfield, I'd keep him as long as I'd use for him; his life wouldn't last a second longer than his usefulness.

Mr. Renfield reappeared an hour after sunset the next day, August the 12th, after I'd again hidden my coffin in my catacomb. I set him to the task I needed most. To my astonishment, he obeyed without question. As he dug the precious dirt of my homeland, I informed him he must be careful not to mix this dirt with any other, and that I needed to be elsewhere, but would return before dawn with his reward ... or his punishment. Renfield started to reply in his subservient, timid manner, but I walked away from him, unwilling to be drearied by groveling.

At the marketplace I hailed a hansom cab, and again directed the driver to a distant popular location, or so I'd surmised from the map I'd studied in Transylvania, but we arrived at a quiet, empty crossroad where no one was about. Bothered, I informed my driver that I was seeking an area not far from this where there were shops and taverns, and he knew exactly where to go. Ten minutes later we entered a lively section of town brightly festooned with streetlamps and people. I thanked my driver greatly and tipped him well.

I was determined to challenge myself tonight, and so I entered a pub and bought a flagon of brandy. The barkeep filled a small cup to the brim and left the flagon beside my glass, grinning like every merchant in England seemed to do. I sat upon the chair beside another man, who eyed my flagon but said nothing. I could drink, and eat, but mortal actions weren't conducive to one nourished solely by blood. Still, the brandy left a delicious taste upon my lips, and it combined well with the spicy environs. I pretended to drink while I glanced all about. I kept my ears open, eager to hear what was being said.

Novelty! In Castle Drăculea, every night was the same, until I cringed to feel the sunset. Here, nothing was familiar, not even my distrust of strangers, a facet of human nature I'd thought eternal, but no one in England seemed to share. I swam in delight at my new surroundings.

Two serious men discussed a business transaction where a third and absent partner was suspected of double-dealing, and considered possibilities of how they could prove it. A group of young men debated their chances with the local daughter of a very wealthy gentleman, and their assurances of wealth and position if they could but impress this lovely innocent toward marriage. Two ladies with enormous hats compared the qualities of their maid-servants and the dubious influences young, low-born women might have upon their husbands.

That evening, as the crowds were starting to thin, I found myself walking with my flagon of brandy toward an unknown section of town, when I was accosted by a woman of surpassing girth, most of which seemed to be formed of her breasts, which were squeezed into a gown of such tightness and revealing nature that much of her breasts rose from her bodice like the curved tops of baked loaves.

"Governor, now you wouldn't be so unkind as to pass a lady by and not give her a sip of your libation, would ye?" she asked.

I was so perplexed by her question, directed at me, that I fumbled my reply.

"Madame, I'm a stranger here, and know not all your ways ...," I said.

"Oh, dearie me!" she exclaimed. "Well, let me do the honors!" She reached for my flagon as if to take it from me.

"Madame, if I may," I said, drawing the flagon out of her reach, "I think we might reach an acceptable arrangement ... if we could find somewhere ... less visible."

"Oh!" she laughed, smiling all the time. "Follow me! I know just the place!"

How strange was this land where dinner invited the diner!

She led the way along an outer brick wall devoid of windows. We emerged in a dark garden, where above us, long marble steps led to a magnificent house whose every window showed lights.

"Here, governor," she smiled, "Is this secretive enough for the gentleman?"

"Indeed," I said.

Too dark to use mesmerism, I reached into her mind, which was as open as a lidless box, and upon my first touch, our first and only connection, she tried to scream and run away. I grabbed and pressed my hand over her mouth, and with ease toppled her so her head smashed against a rock wall, and she lost consciousness.

I had to go carefully, for I didn't wish to soil my new clothes with her blood, or ruin my trousers by kneeling on the soft dirt; I began with her flabby arm, and bit into her inner-wrist with a hunger becoming accustomed to frequent feeding. *How had I denied myself the taste of blood for so long?* I leaned over her, careful not to drip onto my trousers or let her essence spew upon my jacket. She didn't taste good; she had a sour, heady flavor, but I drank deeply. I didn't empty her; I drank more than enough to satisfy me, and then I left the flagon with her; she'd appear to have fallen down drunk, and thus I'd avoid another report of a murder in a district not far from my home.

Afterwards, I hurried back to the marketplace, found the bar about to close, and again asked if I might purchase another flagon for the long ride home. The confused tavernmaster agreed to this, and soon I was in a cab being driven home, my reward to Renfield clutched in my hand.

Arriving several hours before dawn, I was delighted to find Renfield still hard at work, and my mound much larger, which would secure the strength of the woman I'd half-emptied. I instructed him to find an elegant wardrobe from one of the bedrooms upstairs and carry it down here for my use, and he promised to obey. Renfield was elated with the flagon, and drank the brandy as greedily as I consumed my elixir.

"This is only the beginning," I said to my new servant. "I can bestow gifts like no other ... even immortality ... if I'm served well."

To my eternal wonderment, Renfield didn't seem perplexed or excited by my offer. He frowned and fidgeted, as if uncomfortable.

"Begging your pardon, Master," Renfield muttered. "They say fools and children can see things hidden from the wise ..."

He broke off and looked down, as if afraid to meet my eyes, and took a long swig of brandy to strengthen his resolve, which seemed to be crumbling before my eyes.

"What do you know ...?" I demanded.

"Can people who live in asylums know anything?" Renfield said softly. "Even if we knew anything, no one would believe us, and the wilder our stories, the heavier our chains."

"Tell me," I commanded, making my voice irresistible.

Renfield shuddered, but he seemed too frightened to refuse.

"Your eyes ... Master," he said. "Your eyes ... they're like ... windows. I see you, but ... it's like looking through a plate of thick glass. You're there ... but you're not ..."

This wasn't the first time I'd heard these words ... if never from a voice so timid. Their implication was that my curse had rendered me soulless, which I didn't believe ... although I was far from certain. Centuries of consideration had led me to contemplate this question, and I'd concluded that I probably had a soul, although no man could claim ownership of such a commodity; it was a gift, but from whom? *This was more proof of the existence of God.*

"Your perceptiveness pleases me," I said to Renfield. "Someday I may rely upon your awareness, but you must tell no one; this I command."

"I obey," Renfield said, "but I ... don't understand."

"You will," I said. "Someday you'll know all, and stand beside me, if you earn my trust. I have the power to free you from death ... and make you one of the great!"

"Great ...?" Renfield's voice cracked, and he looked more frightened than ever. "Oh, no, Master, please ... don't make me great!"

Novelty, my greatest joy, has a dark side; I stood astounded, bewildered by his reaction.

"Not great ...?" I asked. "Explain this to me."

"Greatness is a curse!" Renfield said.

"Curse ...?" I asked, incredulous. "No man who walks under Heaven knows more than I about curses. How is greatness a curse?"

"A monstrous curse," Renfield said. "I'm a plain, honest man, Master, a laborer. I'm happy to move your dirt, if it pleases you. It's a simple task ... requires no thinking at all. I'm not expected to do anything more, especially not more than I can handle. I don't want to die; I want to live, but to be great ...!" He visibly shook, like a wet dog, as if he could shake off his fears. "If I were great, people would ... expect things of me, amazing things, and then wonderful things, until they wanted things beyond my ability ... and then ... I'd be a disappointment. I don't want to disappoint anyone; I'd be ashamed."

"Ashamed ...?" I asked, my voice deepening with anger despite my effort to restrain it. *"Ashamed of greatness ...?"*

Renfield assumed the terrified expression of many of my victims, seeing their death approach. I was furious; *how dare he insult the ultimate desire of my life ...? Of my family ...?*

With tremendous force of will, I relaxed my shoulders and the glare of my eyes. Renfield still quavered before me, but I squeezed a smile out of my features and adopted a tone of fatherly interest.

"Count Drăcula doesn't harm those loyal to him," I said, although the memory of Jonathan Harker, who'd taught me so much, flitted through my mind. "Perhaps this is a cultural misunderstanding, or an error of translation, as I'm new to your England. Please, fear not your generous master, who will reward you again for your continued service. Pray, open your mind and your heart ... and explain this *'curse of greatness'*."

Renfield looked as tremulous as a child, quivering, cowering before me, but I remained still, tall and proud, and eventually he spoke.

"Please, no offense to you ... or any other, but ... greatness ain't for the likes of me," Renfield said. "A hard day upon my back ... and a bottle to ease my nights ... are all I deserve ... and all I ask for."

"But why ...?" I asked, honestly curious. "Why would you not desire to rise in power, wisdom, and prestige?"

"Them things are traps, begging your pardon," Renfield said. "Forgive me, Master, but I'm not ... you. My opinions mean dirt, and I prefer that. Knowledge is dangerous, and people don't like folk they fear. People like you ... Forgive me! ... people born to greatness, it's no effort for you ..."

"Have you no desire for greatness, to rise above your fellows ...?"

"No, Master, no. If I found that I was ... unequal to the challenge ... t'would be shameful."

"But are you not ... ashamed ... to be common?" I asked. "Just like any other ...?"

"I'm hidden among the many," Renfield tried to force a grin, but he was hiding a frown. "No one expects anything of me, and so I'll never be tested ... but if I tried to be great, and failed ..."

"But what if you succeeded?" I asked. "What if you could become great ...?"

"There's the rub," Renfield said, lowering his head and smearing the sweat on his forehead with his dirty sleeve, as if hiding before my stare. "As one of the many, I know my place, and I'll never know what might have been. If I tried to be great, and failed, then I'd know for sure that I wasn't good enough: better ignorance of success than certainty of failure."

I gritted my teeth, but held my expression calm. With a dismissive gesture, I signaled that this conversation was over, yet I couldn't hide my disgust.

"Return to your cell, and come back tomorrow night," I ordered him. "Speak to no one. Tomorrow, when you arrive, continue with your task. I want thirty of those boxes emptied down here."

"Yes, Master," Renfield said, and he left quietly ... drinking brandy from his flagon as he walked, shoulders slumped, head bowed, and his tail between his legs: *a mouse of a man.*

Considerable restraint prevented me from going after him and killing him. I didn't want Renfield dead, for I needed a lackey to perform my menial tasks, but his attitude infuriated me. *How dare he?* Yet I checked my revenge with the knowledge that Renfield, even now, didn't understand how he'd insulted me. *He did live in an asylum ...*

Greatness was my family tradition. For generations, all of my fathers were great men, each driven to further prove our importance. I'd been raised to be superior, by lesson and example. *Greatness was a goal for all men!* Even when my father stood beside men who were taller, no man ever held his head so high and proudly, and even the tallest bowed before him. As a commander of armies, before the Turks brought my curse upon me, I'd commanded some of the strongest and fiercest warriors ever born, but all reverenced my authority, dissuading their own greatness before mine.

Renfield ... *he was a small man, if a man he could be called.* He bowed before me like the Szgany gypsies, but in my absence, at least they became men. I'd seen them, from the shadows, boasting of their courage while hunting, against other men, and while fighting rival clans. Their fear of me, whom they considered supernatural, a spirit of evil, was pardonable, as no man can fight a spirit. Yet Renfield ... abhorring greatness ... *this was an insult!* How can those who seek greatness arise to the heights of glory if those whose shoulders they stand upon would ... debase themselves, and lay prostrate for fear of recognition? *His very existence eschewed the philosophy I stood for!*

Only once had I failed in my greatness, and for that mistake I'd atoned for decades. Solitude I'd sought, ashamed that I'd murdered my own family. No blood had ever tasted so foul upon my lips as the blood of my father; *I should've made him like me, to live forever!* Yet my young self was ignorant of my power to infect, and so my family had died. Those I didn't kill fled and vanished into the countryside and became lost to all knowledge, even mine. Only my cousins, the Szgany, remained alive of what was once a family destined to rule.

As I brooded, a rooster crowed, and I fetched my small coffin and laid it atop the dirt Renfield had piled higher. My greatness was coming: *I needed to be patient.*

Night after night my familiarity with the countryside grew. Renfield knew much about the local areas, and we explored my grounds together. Walking through the thin, young woods, I found charred remnants of a much older wood beneath it; over a hundred years ago there must've been a fire which surrounded my house, consuming this forest, but these new woods grew atop the old; a sad loss, but life always continues.

On one of my distant outings, I met a wealthy man who was a banker by trade, by the name of Lord Manfred, a solid man in all physical measures, but whom age had whitened and withered. He was a good man of business, to all apparent clues, but upon deep mesmerism, which was hard to invoke over one so strong of will, I learned he'd acquired much of his wealth by payments which the English called *'blackmail'*. He'd spent his days discovering secrets important to other men, and collected annual fees for not revealing them. He was a clever man, such that most of his unhappy benefactors didn't know his identity. When I awoke him, I convinced him he'd fallen prey to over-consumption of alcohol, and I'd cared for him during his unconsciousness.

In the nights after that, it was a simple matter to let him intoxicate himself, and then subject him to my powers of persuasion. Under my influence, he revised his conditions of payment, whereby my solicitor in Sheffield, Samuel F. Billington & Son, would receive all the future funds he collected, and deposits would be made to an account which I set up with my real estate solicitor in Colchester, Carter, Paterson & Co., whose deposits would be verified by a reputable house of accountants in London, who'd send monthly statements of my investments to me. These multiple dealings cost me considerably in fees, such that I banked only three-fifths of what I was paid. Yet the blood of the banker, Lord Manfred, was old blood, refined, with a known ancestry tracing back almost to my birth; his blood carried a delightful piquancy, a flavor of aged sweetness I'd almost forgotten. It amused me to no end that his secrets died with Lord Manfred, but those being blackmailed would never know ... and thus keep paying.

These payments, however, would never be sufficient to buy me a new Castle Drăculea; I had to be watchful for more opportunities. It would be easy enough to rob those I killed, but murders for profit irked me, for it besmirched my family reputation with the brand *'thief'*. No, such a peasantry occupation wasn't how I wished to enrich my new status, my birth of the Drăcula reign. My empire would arise proud and noble, and my powers would easily provide me with all the secrets I needed to invest my blackmail-profits properly.

However, my new-found interest in financial matters brought to me a new novelty, which made every evening a pleasure: I purchased my first English newspaper on the day it came out, and upon learning such documents could be delivered to my residence with little cost, I purchased no less than eight subscriptions, and had Renfield build a tar-roofed box beside my iron gate just for the purpose of receiving my local and London newspapers, and protecting them from the rain.

The rain, I discovered, came far too frequently for my taste. England was often soggy and boggy. I almost killed a shopkeeper for laughing at me as I purchased a brolly ... and had to ask how to use it. The rain made hunting for potential victims more difficult, such that I fasted some nights rather than explore England in a torrential downpour. Yet I soon found districts, especially those near the river, where the poor and lonely dwelt in abject desolation, and where the chief industries seemed to be begging and prostitution. Here I found unlimited prey, and while drunks and whores left a sour taste in my mouth, as long as I left them partially alive, not drained dry, the local murder rate didn't rise perceptively.

One morning, just before dawn, I arrived home with a prize: upon wandering the streets, I'd come upon a likely victim offering to do detailed sketches of people for half a crown ... or a simple drawing for a sixpence. I'd no reflection to view, but this young woman, who proved to be a talented artist, sketched a picture of me so resembling my memories of my father that I thanked her profusely, doubled her payment, and left her alive and unconsumed.

The sketch of me was amazing. I did indeed resemble the painting of my father Jonathan Harker had recognized; I appeared young, perhaps less than thirty, and very muscular. My face was handsome; had the artist seen me as Jonathan Harker knew me, white, skeletal, bald, and aged to monstrousness, doubtless she would've screamed, fled, and never drawn again. I had some white hairs mixed with black, and the same deep-set eyes I remembered from my youth, from my last sight of myself in a mirror, before I was cursed. Despite a prominent hawkish nose, my face looked bright and intelligent, as eager to succeed as I'd been in my father's presence. My skin, I knew, was a shade darker than that of the men of England, and I had a thin, pointed beard which was mainly gray, which made me look older, and perhaps wiser, even if it wasn't currently fashionable in this land. I was pleased, and I placed the drawing in the central room of my manor, and admired it often. Days later, I had Renfield install my portrait in a large, ornate frame which had once housed an oil painting of two men, and we hung it over my mantle, near my new desk, upon which I'd begun to write a new journal; *my diary of my English adventure.* This diary, I knew, would someday sit in my vault beneath my new castle, alongside my other recollections.

Renfield was kept busy rearranging the furniture in my house, which I'd selected from the few rooms containing any, to fully-furnish my main rooms. He was no longer allowed beneath the chapel. In the chamber in which I'd had him build my mound, of which his last act was to scour the grounds within my walls for sturdy rocks, such that he'd built a short stone staircase in my central chamber, of seven steps, very even and well-made, that I could ascend to the top of my mound. To my knowledge, he'd never seen my travelling coffin, for I'd always hidden it in the catacombs before he arrived, and fetched it after he left.

After forbidding him to ever enter my sub-chapel chamber again, I purchased and had delivered to my house a modern English coffin of exceptional size, comfort, and beauty, lined with white silk, and cushioned as if one would spend eternity laying upon a pillow. I placed my new coffin atop my mound, stashing my traveling box in the catacombs.

My new coffin was wondrously wide, clean, and comfortable, and made me happy. My plan was working perfectly. I was starting to think of England, my adopted country, as less of a feeding-ground and more of a second home.

I was considering buying a piano, having heard the marvelous music they made, and wondering if my nightly powers extended to artistry, when an event of amazement startled me; I read a name in the newspaper that I recognized. It was the name of a woman whom Jonathan Harker had discussed with his fiancée in their correspondences, and a photo of her was printed in the newspaper. She was indeed an angel born upon Earth. Her name was Lucy Westenra, and she lived only thirty miles from my residence; *I determined to meet her.*

Renfield's nightly absences had been discovered at last, and he was moved to different quarters, and his loosened bars repaired with such craftsmanship even I'd have difficulty penetrating that window again. I didn't mind, for I no longer needed him for nightly chores. Apparently he'd made several attempts to escape, and was caught and punished, yet his taste for fine brandy had grown since the first flagon I'd given him, but he never spoke of me or my chores. Of that I was grateful, for he was a resourceful man, useful when needed.

One delight of England surpassed all others, and my first discovery of it, after reading an advertisement in every one of my newspapers, was the theater. I had to arise early, and brave the sun before it set, but I was stronger now that I was feeding again, wore a tall hat, and stayed in the shadows as much as possible. I was weak in the daylight, but I'd become familiar with the customs of English society, such that I could sit in a bar and converse with any man, and none could discern I'd not been born a native. Therefore the risk was slight, and it felt good, sitting in the theater, watching a play, an opera, or a ballet.

Upon those stages, tales of adventure, romance, and tragedy earned loud applause from the attendees. Although it was expensive, I secured an entire box upon the left wall, for I disdained the company of others as I watched. My solitude in my box earned me a notoriety I'd not expected; apparently it was unheard of for English gentlemen to sit alone in a box meant for ten patrons of the arts. Yet I was a Prince of Transylvania and disdained to sit among the commoners upon crowded benches.

It was there, at the theater, that I first glimpsed the radiant beauty mentioned in Jonathan Harker's correspondence: Lucy Westenra. She practically glowed, as a light in a room of shadows, wearing a white and pink dress revealing a shape divinely wrought, with hair like a flaming torch upon her head, and skin as smooth as a polished pearl.

I'd found my new bride!

I admit that I stared, but I wasn't the only one, for she was surrounded by suitors and admirers. Her hair was apple-red, and shiny, such that the bright lights of the theater foyer made her glow. She wore a wide, white collar, with sparkling gems upon thin swirls of polished silver about her throat, and her beaming smile never faded from her precious lips. Her eyes were green like the delicious-smelling artemisia annua, or 'Sweet

Annie', beloved by my Asian flower, Miëta, who'd once had it brought and planted around Castle Drăculea just for the pleasure of its scent. Lucy was young, like Hēlgrēth, my blonde beauty, but Hēlgrēth had been shy and demure before I drew her into eternal night; Lucy Westenra held the attention of every patron in the theater with a casual delight that bubbled like champagne. Her laughter excelled all forms of music, and as her voice reached my ears, I felt the playfulness of youth for the first time in centuries. Lucy exuded joy and merriment, walking in a cloud of contentment and frivolity, and I, who'd mesmerized countless victims, stood rendered helpless by the power I'd so often used.

Yet I didn't approach her, for I stood alone, and it seemed undignified to become of those fool suitors vying for her attention. I'd bide my time, and learn all about her, and then approach her at a setting more suitable for my purposes.

I was in a carriage, on my way home, when reason returned to me; *many times I'd been infatuated by beauty, and what was the result?* Loritá, Miëta, and Hēlgrēth, my vicious, hungry brides, greedy, starving with an eternal bloodlust countless murders couldn't satisfy. Before I'd abandoned them, I'd sworn I'd seek brides of greater usefulness, queens worthy to sit beside me upon the throne of the world, whence I took my rightful place. Loritá could never have sat there, for she was ravenous, direct, willing to snarl and crawl among the wolves for a single drop of human blood. Miëta was wise and strong-willed, but she'd place herself even before me, her sire, if I stood between her and a beating heart. Hēlgrēth had been my last hope, but Hēlgrēth held no thought longer than absolutely necessary, and flowed with whatever circumstance would bring fresh blood to her lips.

What did I know about Lucy ... save that she was beautiful?

What made me think she could be a queen?

Nights passed in endless frustrations ... and none of my frustrations were caused by their source. I searched the popular gathering-places of England within many miles of my house, but I returned unsatisfied. I feasted on blood of all types: wealthy women, muscular men, and even a university professor, but all tasted bland and unsatisfying; none inflamed me as I longed to be sated. Newspapers became exasperating, and my few attempts at conversation caused only arguments. Disaffection followed me everywhere, made worse because I knew what was affecting me.

No one, living or undead, not even a Drăculeşti, is perfect. We're all victims of unspoken desires, cravings we dare not voice even to our closest confidants, and needs which burble unwelcomed out of our secret minds, which the newspapers say was recently renamed our *'subconscious'*. Our greatest frustrations are when desperate needs haunt us, but a path to their fruition we've yet to ascertain.

From each unknown need emerges an even worse threat: *thought-blindness.* Minds are quick to justify actions, especially when those actions are unjustifiable. Our minds generate rationalizations without considering what we truly believe. Then our thoughts align with pre-conceived justifications to support our desires ... rather than acknowledge facts.

Our desire to be right blinds us to the falseness of logical supports which we never investigate for fear that we might be wrong.

Age is my biggest advantage; children see only actions, teenagers notice reactions, adults divine intentions, and the wise recognize the motivations of others. Only the wisest, the most-mature of any age, can see these external forces manipulating them.

Few mortals look at themselves impartially, and for those who can, their reflections are often unpleasant. None of us exist as we truly wish, and many avoid their reflection for fear of reality, compounded with the dread of death all mortals share. Even immortals share this, for I've watched vampires terminate their existence, often by their own hands.

Can I, the fountainhead of my curse, die?
If so, what would happen to all I sired?

I desired that answer greatly, but not enough to test it. I'm four and a half centuries old, wise beyond the comprehension of one lifetime, and I view my own actions, reactions, intentions, and motivations more intensely than any living soul.

On August the 18th I admitted I was unhappy ... *because I wasn't sharing my time with Lucy Westenra.*

I'd only one choice; I had to meet her, to study her, and learn if she was worthy of becoming my immortal queen ... or only of satisfying my appetite. I resolved, once I knew her, I'd consume her if she didn't match my requirements.

Self-deception is the key to all folly. I'd be tempted, as I'd been with Loritá, Miëta, and Hēlgrēth, but this time I'd be strong. This time I'd prevail. This time I'd be ... *a Drăculesti.*

Facts about the legendary Lucy Westenra weren't hard to find; her recently-deceased father was one of the wealthiest and most noble men in England, with numerous titles and coats of arms, and the history of their family was well-documented. Her address was well-known and easy to find on a map. For her beauty, as much as her wealth, Lucy's life was a common theme of the busybodies who authored local newspaper articles, and photos of her were often published, as they drew the eyes of every reader. Gossip of her was equally available, if one dared to drop her name or ask a question about her in a pub; never had I heard of a more-celebrated woman.

I had to meet her!

Chapter 7

Only a few nights later, on August the 20th, I knew as much about Lucy Westenra as could be derived from local newspapers and tavern gossip, yet those nights passed quickly amid excitement, as if my tedious broodings belonged to another age. I walked byways with a light step, bowed deeply to strange women, and greeted men with a smile, although I still disliked shaking hands. My resolution to meet Lucy had relinquished my dismay and filled my still heart with novelty. I had only one problem; there were no direct roads to Hillingham, her district, for rough hills and small rivers, which could only be crossed at distant bridges, separated us. The ride to her house from mine would take almost two hours.

The next night I arose early, and then waited for the strength of the sun's absence. As I waited, childhood memories returned.

As a child, playing in the woods, I liked to bring home pets, few of which I'd get to keep. This time I'd captured a small bat. It was a feeble creature, weak and helpless, and I questioned father about the symbol of our house, which was a bat. To my surprise, he took the winged rodent from my hands, and led me to a small, empty room far in the back of Castle Drăculea, which had only one high, open window. Taking out a scrap of cloth, he had me hold the bat while he tied the cloth over its eyes, rendering it blind.

"Look, my son," father had said to me. "Blindfolded, the bat can't see; now watch what happens."

Father tossed the bat into the air. Sightless, it flapped three times around our room, never once hitting a wall, the ceiling, or the floor, and then it flew straight out the high window.

"Bats needs no eyes; bats always know where they're going," father said. "Drăculestis are like bats: whatever hardships lie before us, we never lose our way. We know our destiny, and nothing denies us. A mighty future awaits you, my son; know your vision, and become whatever you must to succeed. Choose your future ... and drive toward it. Be the bat."

Be the bat!

As I resumed my human form, I staggered, weakened from my winged efforts; *it was a long flight.* Transformation was overwhelming, and its pains faded slowly. Reason returned ... as if I were awakening from a dim-witted nightmare; *the mind of a bat is too small to contain the fullness of human thought.* I leaned against a tree for support and gathered my strength and faculties for ten minutes. I stood in a sparse woods outside a huge mansion, a monolith far newer than my home. Lights beamed from its many windows and loud music drifted under the pale moonlight.

I glanced first to the moon and judged the time; I had to return before dawn lightened the sky.

I walked toward her house leisurely, stopping to admire the sleeping blossoms of her garden. If I were seen, I might be taken for a resident of her house, and so I strode with casual ease. A party seemed to be occurring, for applause and laughter coincided with the breaks in the music, and then the melody and tempo changed and began afresh. Others passed by me in the garden, walking in pairs, and I bowed politely to them, and spoke when needed to avoid suspicion.

I needed to gain entrance ...!

Easily I found a door to a busy kitchen, which was open and venting heat from stoves and ovens. I stepped up and spoke to a cook working by the door.

"Forgive me, sir," I said. "I'm avoiding ... a woman. May I enter here?"

"I understand," the cook smiled. "Please ... come in, good sir."

Access provided, I entered Lucy's home, hurried domestics acknowledging me with subservient avoidances of their eyes. I passed through the kitchen, and followed the line of waiters carrying wide platters of food towards the source of the loud music.

Never in all of my centuries had I entered a room such as I found before me. Chinese emperors and French kings couldn't claim such abandon in colors and textures, or so much light and sound, nor a gathering so overflowing with gaiety. A bizarre mixture of new and old styles met my eyes, fresh paintings of men and women posed as if from centuries before, marble statues of cherubs and mythological deities, all laden with newly-bloomed flowers, and ribbons hung everywhere. Yet foremost were the people, a crowd of dazzlingly-festooned figures, men and women in garments that I recognized as the latest fashions, colors sparkling of rich fabrics and gems uncountable, and the motions of dance circling endlessly in the center of a magnificent ballroom lost in a miasma of swirling joy. The deafening mixture of music and laughter vied with a roar of conversations almost shouting to be heard, yet obscured in a cacophony illegible by any ear, living or undead.

I stood amazed and inspired; *this was what I wanted, the goal I sought.* This gala boasted the best in the world, a grand aspiration to which all mortals could achieve, the pinnacle of humanity celebrating its climactic height, the culmination of eons, arisen from the darkness of mankind's humble beginnings. A festival of the living danced before me, which was exactly what I wanted for my next bastion of the undead. Whence a new Castle Drăculea arose upon the ruins of the old, this was the throne room I wanted, a palace of life and learning, filled with passion and aristocracy, all loyal to me. This room, this revel, would fill my halls, my lands, and all the lands I'd send my armies to conquer. This was the floorplan for my new throne of Earth, my heart of civilization, which would last until the mountains fell.

But where was Lucy Westenra?

My chance of finding her in this crowd was unlikely, but I held off asking; I needed to observe more of this unrepentant revelry. I accepted a glass of red wine from a servant, only for show, and strode through the midst of celebrants into the heart of joviality. I walked as if strolling through a dream. *Too long I'd lived in shadows and darkness, too long brooding upon the mysteries of death.* Novelty assaulted every sense I possessed; *the novelties of life!*

A laughing woman suddenly bumped into me, turned and looked up into my face, and her startlement seemed to fill her with delight. She smiled at me coyly, and for a moment I caught her scent under the heady perfume of unbloomed roses she wore; she reeked of youthful blood, a veritable feast of energy and vitality, such that my desire to taste her swelled. Yet she seemed to take my affront for trickery, for she laughed and said:

"No frowns! This is a party!"

I stood filled with wonder. *This girl, in fact, these youthful people ... had no fear!* They ran about like children, playing games with a mindlessness they should've long outgrown. By their age, women in Transylvania carried daggers to protect themselves against thieves ... and crosses to safeguard against me. Men their age worked or hunted ... in lands where prey often hunted the hunters. These young folk seemed completely unaware of peril or threat ... *even when it walks among them.* Was their innocence a token of backwardness, as any dweller of the Carpathians would consider it, or a token of superiority of an advanced civilization, to have removed all dangers from their midst?

Would these people be slaughtered if faced with a real threat? If so, did all civilizations grow strong only to weaken themselves? Or were they strong in ways I couldn't perceive?

The young lady before me was joined by two laughing young men, and with scarcely a glance at me, they pushed into the crowd, as if heading for a worthy destination. Quickly they became lost from view, but I slid between other guests, following their direction. I felt alarmed at how often I was touched by strangers, bumping elbows and dodging to keep from running into me. Never in my life had I walked so casually, unnoticed, through a throng oblivious to a heart not beating.

    I chanced to stop at the edge of the dancers, joining a line of older people watching the flow of grace and refinement twirling in rhythm to the musicians' spritely tune. I'd never once danced, but I recalled a few dances I witnessed as a child in my father's house, but those were strict and rigid compared to the frivolity of these dancing pairs. They moved in ... not perfect coordination, displaying widely differing levels of skill, but in glad cooperation, the better dancer compensating for the few stumblings I witnessed. Also, no chastisements were inflicted for failures, such as would've happened in the old days ... as if mistakes were irrelevant. While not perfect, each pair danced in unison, and I was impressed by both the dances and the dancers.

    I wondered ... should I learn to dance ...?

    "Aren't they marvelous?" a woman's voice asked.

    Despite my increasing familiarity with local customs, I was still taken aback by the boldness of English ladies. This woman was mature, perhaps fifty years old, wearing a voluminous gown of purple silk beaded with pearls. Her graying hair was bound up so none of it fell upon her neck but hovered inside a fan of some iridescent material that seemed pinned to the back of her head. She was looking wistfully at me ... and at the dancers.

    "Indeed," I said, for I knew such was an acceptable reply.

"I am the Countess Mariella du Haugh," she said, and she extended her hand to me.

"Count Drăcula, at your service," I replied, and I grasped her hand and kissed it.

Of all the customs of Englishmen, the kissing of hands was my favorite. Upon pressing my lips to the back of a woman's hand, I could inhale her deeper than in any other way, and almost taste the warm blood flowing so closely beneath her skin. It was like sampling a meal before it's served, a tantalizing tease of what could be had if I chose to avail myself. This woman was of mixed blood, noble and common, with a unique essence I could savor slowly, but I desired not to soil this evening with murder.

"I'd love to dance, if you would," she smiled.

"Alas, most lovely lady, I'm not trained in the art of dancing," I said, and a look of doubt filled her eyes. "I was born and raised in the east, where sons are trained to be warriors, not dancers."

A visible sigh displayed her disappointment.

Begging her pardon, I wandered back into the crowd, away from the dancers, and found another servant carrying a large tray of dishes. I held up a hand to stay him, deposited my undrunk glass of wine upon his tray, and asked if he knew where I might find Miss Lucy Westenra. He pointed me to the far side of the musicians, and I thanked him and redirected my steps.

Finally I saw her, my beautiful Lucy, standing among a group of people her own age. Amid their laughter, they were shouting at each other to be heard over the music so close by, instruments being played with such intensity even I could barely hear her voice. Lucy looked flushed, as if she'd been drinking and recently dancing, her eyes alight upon her companions.

Yet I couldn't simply walk up and intrude upon their conversation, however naïve it might be. I had to speak to Lucy alone, but upon observation, I doubted if that would happen tonight.

However, I was determined to meet her, and my eagerness brooked no delays.

"Oceans of love ... and millions of kisses!" Lucy cried as she waved to a couple escaping arm-in-arm into the crowd, and I noticed she spoke as if singing, with a voice pleasant to my ear.

I strode forward like a Drăculesti, boldly. The minds of these young fools were putty in my hands; as they turned to see me, surprised by my sudden appearance in their circle, I projected a command, a promise of novelty to be had, behind them. At once, each of Lucy's friends turned and faced away from us ... and began talking to each other as if of their own choosing.

Lucy seemed stunned, and confused, at being suddenly left alone with me, despite the many figures surrounding us.

"Have no fear," I said to her, speaking plainly over the volume of the musicians. "I can restore their attentions, if you wish."

Up close, Lucy was indeed beyond comparison in beauty and grace, and in this light her hair shined like bright rose petals. The harlequin green of her eyes glittered, mesmerizing, and I smiled, seeing bewilderment upon her dazzling face.

"Behold," I said, and I snapped my fingers, again reaching out with my mind.

As one, all of Lucy's friends turned back to face her, their conversations flowing as if no break had occurred. One young man asked Lucy to dance, and a girl asked if she liked this song, while the others engaged in topics equally banal. Yet Lucy's eyes locked on me with a fixed stare, more-powerful than I'd expected.

"I am Drăcula," I said to her. "Count of Hungary, Prince of Transylvania, Vlad Drăcula, at your service."

I smiled, yet kept my fangs carefully hidden. I knew my purpose, and it stood before me. *I'd arrived ... and I'd conquered.*

Lucy looked unafraid, yet unable to speak, as if any confirmation of what she'd just witnessed would condemn her senses. Yet concern never showed on her face. If anything, she looked stern, as if she'd intimidate me.

"It's but a simple trick," I said, glancing askance at her friends.

I held out my hand to take hers, although she hadn't offered it.

Slowly her hand rose, almost against her volition, and I lightly kissed it, relishing in a scent so pure and wholesome I hungered for its taste.

"Miss Lucy Westenra, daughter of Eorl Glenford Westenra, betrothed of Lord Godalming," she introduced herself.

"Charmed to make your acquaintance," I said, and I released her hand, lest she become alarmed.

I drank the vision of her as I'd imbibed so many: greedily. Yet I remained passive of expression, lest she feel threatened. Her friends followed her line of sight to my face, but as the portrait artist had revealed, I was strong and handsome, appearing only slightly older than they.

"I'm delighted to feel so welcomed at your gala," I said, half bowing to her. "I thank you for allowing me to attend."

Her hand had never fully lowered; I reached out, took it, and kissed it again. Then I stepped backwards, performed a half bow, and walked away.

I could feel Lucy's eyes following me.

The party became a veil to me, sheer and transparent, a loud, moving lace woven so finely I could walk right through it. I felt as if I were floating upon a cloud flowing swiftly up a mountainside. The exuberance of the dancers and drinkers and celebrants played a descant harmony which arose far above the intonations of the musical instruments braying, tinkling, and piping their notes.

I'd met my prey ... my Lucy ... and she would be mine.

I availed myself to witness many displays that night. Not amazements of jugglers or acrobats, but of people, their means and their ways. Almost everyone here was vying for attention, indulging in outrageousness for the sole purpose of arresting the eyes of everyone nearby. Some seemed to be drunk, their antics boisterous, imprecise, and amateurish. Others were overly-loud, as if volume could attract what their content lacked. Yet all were imbecilic; chaff in the wind, easily blown, clinging only to that which they accidentally brushed against, only to be blown away by the next wind. *Did none of these people have goals and ambitions that lasted beyond a single moment?* I bided my time, watching and learning, as a predator, although part of my mind was enrapt with the joy of having finally met my dear Lucy ... and anticipations of future meetings.

After nearly an hour of wandering amid the drunken revelers, I discovered a distant, quieter room filled with bookshelves and a large, roaring fireplace where only men stood amid thick clouds of cigar smoke. I selected a snifter of brandy, and walked among them, listening. One group of men was talking politics, debating the value of their wars in South Africa. Another man insisted that only hired mercenaries should actually fight in their wars, and all Englishmen should be their ranking officers. A third group was cursing the taxation of goods shipped across the English Channel to France, while a fourth conversed on the conditions in the *'Rebelled Colonies'*.

"President Grover Cleveland and William McKinley are both going to wish they were like Mark Twain: reported to be dead," one man said, and all laughed except one.

"They found gold again ... in the Klondike," the frowning one groused. "That should be our gold!"

"America isn't our colony anymore," his friend answered in a tone heavy with impatience.

I glanced at them, amused, and one of them seemed to catch my eye; a short fellow with a waxed moustache.

"Who's this?" he asked, looking at me. "A new face, one which I don't think I've had the honor of meeting ...?"

"Count Drăcula, at your service," I nodded politely to him, and he took my hand and shook it vigorously.

"Count ...?" one of the other men asked. "May I ask your lineage ...?"

"Of Hungary, from where I've recently journeyed to explore your England," I said.

"Ah, Hungary!" the short fellow exclaimed, pulling at one long, pointed end of his moustache. "Now there's an area I've always hoped to visit."

"I know only of its location upon maps," said another man. "A rugged country, isn't it?"

"It's a country where ones strength is always challenged," I said, proudly describing my homeland. "Only the mighty survive. We don't have the education and pleasantries of England, but we're an old line, descending back to the Romans."

"Indeed?" said the man who'd asked my lineage. "Perhaps England should look more closely into the lands of Hungary."

"That's why I've come ... to investigate the lands of England ... *before we're investigated,*" I said.

This sparked jovial laughter among all of my listeners, and I obliged them with a pretense of understanding. Not one of them, I was sure, would last a single night in the Carpathians, with nothing but their etiquettes to protect them from cold, hungry wolves.

"Forgive me if I've interrupted," I said. "I believe you were discussing America ..."

"America, yes," said the short man. "Have you visited there?"

"I know of America, but my knowledge is dated," I said. "Shortly after it was discovered, I ... that is, my family sent a representative there to discern all he could, to learn the languages and converse with strangers so distant no blood tied them with Europe."

"Ah, that would be when those shores belonged to us," said the tallest man of their group, who was very bald and observed me through a monocle.

"I fear those shores were all that England ever owned," I said. "The breadth of America, its vast width, and its length to its bottommost tip, were populated by many proud warrior races. Back then, the people of the north spoke of a great empire destroyed by plague less than a century before Columbus, and an even greater civilization, boasting much wealth, existed in the southern continent below America."

"Your spy must've spent many years there," one man said.

"Nearly forty years," I replied. "My family was always ... thorough."

"Do you intend to stay long in England?" asked the man who'd asked my lineage.

"I'll remain ... until my curiosity is satisfied," I said.

I conversed with these gentlemen for almost an hour on trivial matters, mostly related to business dealings, before I grew bored. I was looking for an opportunity to depart politely when the greatest gift I could've asked for suddenly entered the library.

Lucy Westenra appeared as a flame in a dark cave, making all else a reflection of her light. She smiled, and every old man vanished to my eyes.

Several greeted her, and she paused to show respect to each, but she blithely excused herself and, to my delight, approached me.

"Count Drăcula," she said, seeming demurely polite for an act so bold.

"Miss Westenra," I half-bowed to her.

"If I may intrude, gentlemen," she turned her attention to face the self-acknowledged aristocrats with whom I'd been conversing. "My betrothed and his friends have asked to meet Count Drăcula."

"I'd be delighted," I said, and I inclined to her, that she might lead me to better company.

With pride undisguised, I walked arm-in-arm with Lucy through and out of the company of elder men. All followed me with their eyes, some with curiosity ... others with jealousy. Hateful stares targeted, yet their sources loitered impotent and unimportant. My curiosity was piqued only by Lucy; I swirled my brandy as I walked beside her, confident and delighted.

"Miss Westenra, if I may ...?" I asked as we left sight of the stogy room and its patrons, but before we got too close to the music to hear.

Lucy turned to look at me, and it was as if my curse had been lifted. Her piercing green eyes, her soft, painted lips, and her dazzling beauty dimmed the brilliance of the central room and everything in it.

"Yes, Count Drăcula ...?" Lucy asked.

"Please, call me Vlad," I said.

"Only if you'll call me Lucy," she smiled. "I'm glad I found you; I wanted to know how you managed ... what you did."

"I hide no secrets from you, Lucy," I said, "but to understand the ways of the Carpathians requires more than explanation; words can't express what can only be experienced. I'd be delighted to show you ... but not here ... tonight. This ... ostentatiousness ... is unfamiliar to me, and such displays are best done quietly ... and privately."

Lucy's penetrating eyes drilled into me, but I was too old not to recognize the look of deep thoughts passing behind her eyes. Introducing me to her fiancé and his friends was a ploy; *she wished to speak to me alone, but no privacy would be allowed to us here.*

"I do wish to know ...," she said.

"If I may call upon you at a less-festive time, then I believe you'll understand all," I said.

Lucy eyed me carefully, as if she had the power to discern truth from appearances, but even I wasn't so wise.

"Do you promise ...?" Lucy asked.

"The word of a Drăculesti is truer than the vows of lesser men," I said.

"I'll hold you to that," Lucy said. "Will you come and meet my betrothed?"

"If you wish it, I'd be delighted," I said.

I forced myself not to smile; her betrothed was doomed, but such trivialities were beneath my consideration, for after untold thousands, the death of a single mortal was like the weather, inevitable and ordained by God. I couldn't consider any man to be my rival, for my strength, knowledge, and wisdom excelled other men's as theirs exceeded their pets. To the betrothed of Lucy Westenra I'd be congenial and friendly, as I'd recently been to Jonathan Harker.

Lucy took my arm in her hand, a very bold and forward gesture for a woman of any homeland, and drew me through the crowd to a small stairs leading up to a private level, a wide balcony overlooking the dancers. There I was presented to three men, one exceedingly sturdy, of a rugged, muscular build, and the other two tall and thin, but growing into worthy shapes of manhood. Lucy introduced me to the rugged man first, speaking loud to be heard above the musicians.

"Count Drăcula of Hungary, may I introduce you to Mr. Quincey P. Morris, of America, a brave and honest soul, if ever one was born outside of England," Lucy said, and we shook hands roughly.

"A shore'nuff pleasure to meet you, to be sure," Mr. Morris said with a heavy, drawling accent I'd never before heard.

"Count, this is Dr. John Seward, the noted physician and psychiatrist, who manages an immense insane asylum," Lucy said.

This introduction alarmed me, for there was only one such asylum in this area; *this man could be my neighbor!*

"A pleasure, my good count," Dr. John Seward said, and his handshake was less forceful.

"My pleasure," I replied. "If I may ask, in what district do you practice?"

"In Carfax, near the river," Dr. John Seward answered.

"That's good," I said, "for I didn't wish you to practice upon me."

As I wished, this generated a jovial laugh.

"The unexpected always happens," Dr. John Seward retorted with a smile.

"And this," Lucy said, beaming with unrepressed delight, "this is my betrothed, Arthur Holmwood, the son of Lord Godalming."

"The honor is mine," I said, offering my hand.

Arthur Holmwood had a firm, calm assurance in his handshake; here stood a man of culture and breeding. It pleased me that Lucy would find such qualities attractive, as I was deeply endowed with aristocracy, as well as uniqueness of mind.

As I shook his hand, I couldn't help but feel that my curse, as I so often called it, was in this instance a blessing. I was suddenly glad to be a vampire. This thought evoked memories of debates I'd argued with myself for centuries, so many times I knew them by heart, although I could never end them with any logical conclusion. *Had God intended me to live this long? Or had He intended for me to kill myself, when I realized the horror He'd made me?* Most men of power created their own worst enemies, who eventually supplanted them. *Was I cursed to become a threat to God?* In all humility, I had powers no mortal could claim, but to create a single speck of dust out of nothingness was beyond any skill I possessed. Great I was, *but how could anything born of woman be equal to God?*

"Count Drăcula, welcome to England," Arthur said, and merriment suffused his voice. "Lucy says you're newly arrived, and you performed a trick earlier ....?"

"A simple distraction, but not one I'm prepared to repeat," I said. "I'm new to England, traveling from my distant homelands to witness your great cities."

"If there's any service we may offer you, it's yours," Arthur said. "Thank you for coming to our engagement party."

Novelty isn't always a good thing; I'd no idea that I was invading the celebration of the upcoming marriage of my soon-to-be bride to another man. Yet no hint of disturbance showed upon my face: I smiled.

"It's a carnival of wonder to me," I said, glancing at the dancers circling entwined. "In my country, customs are very strict, and the young don't cavort freely."

"I pray you aren't offended," Arthur said.

"Not at all," I said. "It's always interesting ... to see something new."

"You must tell us of your homeland, Vlad," Lucy said to me. "My Arthur is very traveled ..."

"Alas, this I can't do," I said with a half bow to Lucy. "Forgive me, but my lands are obscure and treacherous, and such topics are ill-suited to a celebratory setting."

"Dang, but I twig you jest like a nobleman," Mr. Morris said, raising his drink in salute to me. "I avoid the fancy gibber, when I can."

"I beg your pardon, sir; I'm newly acquainted with your language ...," I said.

"Don't mind Quincey," Dr. Seward said. "He's all bluff and bluster, but he's a lot smarter than he pretends."

"Nonsense," Quincey insisted with a jovial falseness apparent to everyone. "Now, you stop them mind-documentings, John! You know I don't trust 'em!"

Everyone laughed, and so light was their mood even I chuckled.

"I'm grateful that you've all made me feel so welcome," I said. "Miss Lucy found me talking to those who dragged me here, for I feared to intrude upon the happiness of those I'd not met."

"You're always welcome in our house," Lucy insisted. "Now, tell me, Count ... I mean, Vlad: is there a Countess Drăcula?"

"Alas, I've never been carried to an altar," I said.

"Beware, Count: Lucy has many unmarried friends and an eye for matchmaking," Arthur said. "Consort with her and you'll soon find yourself betrothed."

"It would be impolite to contradict one's host at the celebration of his engagement," I said to Arthur, and Quincey laughed loudly at this, but I saw no reason for his outburst.

"We have to have Vlad for dinner," Lucy said to Arthur.

"Yes, please," Arthur said. "Lucy loves throwing dinner parties. Leave us an address where you may be reached ..."

"... And beware of every she-cat Lucy exhibits you to," Quincey laughed.

Again, much joviality.

"I'm honored," I said to Arthur, and I shook hands with him again. "Of course, I trust you'll do me the same honor ... *and allow me to have you for dinner?*"

"Of course," Arthur replied, and I smiled widely; *for the first time in four hundred years a dinner had accepted my invitation!*

Tired of shouting over the noise, we watched the dancers, and Lucy began to sway with the music, obviously to suggest to Arthur that she wished to dance. His invitation came a moment later, and I noticed she acted surprised, as if his offer were spontaneous. This, too, delighted me; *Lucy was a woman of superior intelligence and cunning.*

After they departed to become dizzy upon the dancefloor, I excused myself with handshakes to Quincey and Dr. Seward, insisting that my 'friends' would be wondering where I was. I'd accomplished all I'd intended, and required a strenuous transformation and flight to return to my home. I left my brandy snifter upon a table and strode through the lively merrymaking, relishing every sight and sound, but I'd had enough. This novel festivity would give me much to reflect upon, and required time and concentration to fully comprehend.

Yet each memory would be a delight.

Alone, I strode into the gardens, past pairs of wandering lovers, and found a place where no one would witness my shape-shifting. Then all complex thoughts left me.

Be the bat!

Consciousness returned as the pain slowly diminished; I was outside my house, inside my grounds, near the side-door to my chapel. I glanced up; the stars were dimming; in less than an hour dawn would tire me. After my exertions of the night, I'd be very weak tomorrow night; *I'd need to feed.*

A soft noise, barely audible, made me turn around. Shock widened my eyes: Renfield lay there, fallen upon the grass, sprawled, as if he'd fainted.

Had he seen me transform?

I couldn't forgive this. I couldn't let my secret be revealed. I reached into his subconscious mind, seized him, and took control of all that he was. Like a marionette, he rose upon the strings of my commands, and finally stood before me. His eyes were now wide and filled with horror; although controlled, he was awake.

"What have you seen?" I demanded.

"I ... I've ... seen your ... greatness," Renfield stammered.

His words calmed me.

"What will you do with this knowledge?" I asked.

"Nothing," Renfield said. "I'm ... already considered mad; I've no desire to prove their diagnosis."

I considered these words, contemplating if I should feed upon my servant, but hesitating; now I knew the man who ran his asylum, and I'd no wish to be questioned by Dr. John Seward for an inmate whose body might be found on my property. Renfield was apparently smart enough to realize what I was thinking.

"Master, I'm your slave ... your silent slave," Renfield said. "Please, allow me to keep serving you. *Don't ... kill ... me ...!*"

I surveyed him closely.

"If one word of what you've seen escapes your lips ...," I deepened my voice to a command that would resonate between his ears forever.

"Never, Master ... *I swear!*" he pleaded.

I nodded my acceptance, for I felt weak and exhausted.

"Open my door for me ... and follow," I said.

Obediently Renfield held my door as I entered the chapel, passed through it, and entered my main rooms. There I rested myself upon a tall-backed chair, and Renfield stood in silence by the door.

"Come to me," I commanded. "Sit before me."

Renfield hurried and lowered himself to sit upon the floor, for I'd no desire to look up at his face.

"Tell me what you saw."

Renfield swallowed hard, then bowed his head.

"I escaped from my cell shortly after midnight, after the bed-check," Renfield said. "I came here and searched for you, but realized you were out. I didn't know how long you'd be gone, so I ... begging your pardon, Master ... took a little refreshment ... to steady my nerves ... and waited for you. But it was starting to get light, and I didn't want them to know I was gone, so I was heading back, when ... when a huge bat dropped from the sky and hovered right before me. I'd never seen such a thing ... bats usually fly so fast ... and then ... then the bat became ..."

Fear effused every word he spoke, so I doubted if he'd tell a soul, but I was curious about what he thought of the spectacle.

"This is but a fraction of my true strength," I said.

"Master, *you're a god ...!*" Renfield said.

"Godhood comes in many levels," I said. "I've no use for worship. I require obedience."

"I'm whatever you make of me," Renfield said.

"So, have you reconsidered my offer?" I asked.

"Oh, no," Renfield said. "I'm unfit for glory."

"You fear me ...?" I asked.

"Yes, Master ...," Renfield said.

"What do you fear more than me?" I asked.

"Nothing ...!" Renfield insisted, but I could hear the lie in his voice.

"I command truth ...!"

Renfield looked even more base and ashamed than I'd ever seen.

"I fear what all my kind fear," Renfield said softly, barely a whisper, as if only his terror of me dragged the words from him. "Death, but also the time we spend awaiting it. Death comes to us, to all men ... who aren't gods like you ... and women, of course. Sometimes we wish time would stop, to delay our deaths. Sometimes we want time to speed up, as death will eventually take us anyway, and the waiting becomes unbearable. That's why I like the drink, sir, as much brandy and whiskey as I can hold; drink takes away time ... and it's time we suffer from the most."

"Do you know what happens to mortals ... when they die?" I asked.

"Not a clue, Master," Renfield said. "I know what the priests say, but my life's unfit for Heaven, so my choices are an eternity of Hell ... or some unknown fate ... perhaps even worse."

"To fear most what you don't know is the height of folly," I said. "I've seen thousands die, more horribly than any Hell, and I've spent centuries pondering death; *death isn't to be feared.* Death is the culmination of all you've achieved in life, the pathway to a new level of being. I've never seen a ghost, but I've felt them, as tangible as a hammer, lurking, haunting the shadows of my mind. Even animals sense the dead, when they're close by. Your fear is a lack of faith, a disbelief of your own senses. Weakness of mind fills an ocean of doubt, and doubting men drown for fear of swimming."

"Please, Master ...!" Renfield begged, cowering before me. "Such thoughts require drink to banish ...!"

How I wished Jonathan Harker were here to discuss such topics; he would've found this conversation fascinating. But again, I must allow for weakness in others if I'd claim strength for myself. This poor wretch was a mental pygmy before Jonathan, and even less before me; *he'd never comprehend elevated thoughts.*

"Go back to your cell," I commanded. "Don't return until I call you."

Vampires seldom dream, but I awoke on August the 21st smiling, the eyesome memory of Lucy Westenra haunted my thoughts. Dreams of her felt pleasant, so sweet I lingered in the silent darkness, letting her lovely visage fill my mind, before I raised my lid and rose from my new, comfortable coffin. *Lingering solely upon*

feelings, especially those delicious and desirous, was an intoxicant little different from brandy or whiskey. Letting feelings overwhelm you was one of the great joys of existence, and an agreeable way of passing time, although it did little to advance one's ambitions. Still, we're all made of past experiences, and controlling our feelings molds us, either into the person we want to be ... or in the wrong direction. Lucy was still only an option, as I'd not yet determined to make her immortal, but her beauty was mesmerizing, her voice enchanting, and her intellect tantalizing. She made me feel young again.

Even a king of darkness needs light.

I changed into commonplace-attire, rather than the formals I'd worn to meet Lucy. Then I went outside only to find the sky spitting rain. I returned to fetch my brolly, and felt foolish as I walked under its protection, but I contentedly arrived in the nearby populated district, and climbed inside a carriage, mostly dry. Despite my disgust of the many strange customs of this land, where men cowered before a little rain, I had to admit that dryness made my ride more comfortable.

I returned to the waterfront, where I found a strange gathering under a sign: *'Salvation Army meeting'*. They asked for a donation, claiming to be an important charity for over thirty years, yet they were many and sober, of no interest to me. Food walked about elsewhere, poor and plentiful, those who wouldn't be missed. I avoided the crowded, lamplit streets, as I needed no witnesses.

Unrepaired buildings soon surrounded me, crossed by thick boards, nailed to their outsides, to support their crumbling structures. Nothing looked clean. Rags, parts of broken devices, and scraps of severed ropes lay discarded all about, plugging the clogged gutters, alongside empty crates, and atop termite-eaten barrels. The dirt road beneath my feet was pocked with ruts between piles of horsewaste. Yet with my night-sight I navigated with ease while remaining in shadows.

Noises of lively music and conversation wafted from behind closed shutters and doors of taverns, while the utter silence of the rest of the docks drank in their sounds, washed away by cascading rushes and river-splashings against pylons, and the endless pit-patter of falling drops. I flitted with ease from devastation to decrepit shanty, and from dark alley to crumbling warehouse, a strolling shadow of death.

A splash of boots disturbed a puddle behind me; *I was being followed.* I grinned and didn't look back; this innocent land always provided a hunted chasing the hunter. I looked for a suitable spot and spied a wide alcove covered by a ragged awning; in its shadows no one would witness my feast. I headed directly for the inky darkness, amused at the delight my stalker must be feeling, seeing his prey seek the precise location they'd choose.

As I reached the solid wall, buried in shadow, I spun and faced my attacker. He was a monstrous brute, tall and twice my width, but I was a prince trained to fight since birth ... with centuries of practice.

As our eyes met, he hesitated not a second, but marched forward with confident stomps, a sneer that might've been a smile twisting his cruel, unshaven face, and sinister determination. His monstrous bulk swayed with a swagger, certain of his purpose. His arms spread wide, as if to cut off any hope of my escape.

I reached out with my mind and stopped him only a pace away. His mind was weak beyond measurement; *no doubt I could make him dance like a brutish puppet!* His eyes widened with confusion as he stopped suddenly, unaccountably ...

"You will become part of my greatness," I said, and I stepped within his range, grabbed his jaw, and turned his face to the side.

My brolly cast aside, I seized his rain-drenched shoulder with my other hand, bared my fangs, and bit into his jugular. Life spewed into my mouth, and I gorged my appetite, replenishing my strength from his abundance of physical muscle. His taste was vulgar but heady, with immense vitality. I had to drink quickly to spare my clothes, but such was my nature that I was accustomed ...

"Cromwick...?" called a voice behind him.

I startled; *my prey wasn't alone, and here was I, feasting...!*

'Cromwick' cried out, a bass bellow that resounded the intense fright of a man designed to frighten others. Surprised, I'd dropped my mental grip; my meal suddenly pushed away and stumbled backwards, clutching at his throat, eyes wide with horror.

He stumbled backwards, out from under the awning, and I realized he was far from alone. Five pairs of eyes loomed from shadows behind him, all staring around the behemoth I'd meant to drain, who was staring at me as if I'd ascended from Hell itself.

"Kill it!" Cromwick shouted. " *Whatever it is ... kill it!"*

Lesser men would've cowered, or drawn back, seeing themselves outnumbered by ruffians intent upon their demise, but fear was a despised state: *no Drăculeşti submitted to fear.*

Overwhelming odds delighted me, providing an opportunity to prove myself, and overcoming many defined superiority as no other act could. My six assailants spread out, cutting off any hope of escape, and slowly closed upon me. Vampiric tricks wouldn't avail me; *now was the time to unleash Vlad the Impaler ...!*

I snatched up my brolly and hurled it at Cromwick, and as he batted it away, I attacked the two on his left, driving them back, placing Cromwick's bulk between the three others and myself. One man held up bare fists, and the other grasped a broken bottle, ending with sharp glass shards. I managed to push away the bottle, which snagged and tore my damp coat. I seized his neck, and twisted it so hard I heard his bones snap. Then strange fists struck against my lower back and shoulder; *his companion was attacking that which he wasn't worthy to touch.* I spun to face him, seized and bit deeply into his neck, but I didn't drink; I ripped a hole in his flesh so wide his jugular spewed his essence upon my whole form.

Suddenly massive arms encircled me; *Cromwick had seized me from behind!* I thrashed and flailed, but even my vampiric strength failed, and I couldn't concentrate enough to transform while being simultaneously crushed and flung about.

Other men were shouting, and the intense agony of a sharp knife stabbed into my chest. The pain was overwhelming, but a good warrior turns pain to strength. My fists proved useless upon Cromwick, but I seized the hand holding the knife and yanked, pulled the blade from my chest, and drew it to my lips. I bit into the wrist holding it, and drank deeply, drawing the substance I'd need to heal this wound. Cromwick flung me from side to side, but I held tight, and the knife-wielder was tossed about with me. His blood washed over my pain, and I ripped the knife from his loosened grip. Then I was armed. Deep gashes I sliced in Cromwick's arms, and then I managed to bury the blade to the hilt in his leg. Almost instantly I tore free, but before I attacked Cromwick, I had to deal with his fellows, most of whom were attempting to flee. Here my vampiric strengths helped me run them down, and stab holes in each of their backs, before I returned to finish them. Then I faced Cromwick, who was clutching his badly bleeding leg and neck.

Paradise surrounded me; the air was thick with the intoxicating aroma of fresh blood, which pooled in the dirty, puddled street, and invigorated my senses. The fool whose neck I'd torn out was alive still, but he was crawling and weeping like a child begging to climb back into its crib. Only Cromwick shakily stood, and he backed away as I approached.

"*Stop!*" I commanded, but his mind was too horrified to dominate.

"*Wha-what are you?*" Cromwick demanded. "*Are you ... death?*"

"I'm life," I sneered. "You shall live forever ... in me."

Cromwick fell to his knees, and astoundingly, he began to pray. No doubt he had a Christian upbringing, for he recited The Lord's Prayer without missing a single word. I heeded him not; I didn't care where his soul went as long as his blood remained. He barely resisted as I put the blade to my twin punctures upon his neck ... and sliced deeply. He bled out amazingly fast, and I drank in his raw physical power, indulging in Hell's most luxurious feast. I stopped only when I felt his baleful life drain away. Released, he fell flat upon his face into the bloody mud with a sickening *'splosh!'*.

I staggered back. The knife wound in my chest hadn't fully healed, but I was bloated with life, with the passion of every feral beast, the wolf in me fully awake. I raised my head up to view the black sky, and to feel the rain splatter upon the skin of my face, as much a part of nature as the unnatural can be.

I was everything!
I was Drăcula!

The man with the torn neck gasped as I approached, fell onto his side, and I drank him until his heart stopped beating.

Slowly I began to feel the moisture suffusing my clothes; I was soaked, and not just with rainwater. *How was I to travel home like this?* My suit was ruined, slashed, and stained with blood no cleaning would remove. Yet I needn't transform; the night was mine, and I was wild and free, alive in my element, a son of the black mountains, born to forest and stream. I glanced around, determined to leave no trace I'd been involved in these murders. I snatched up my brolly. My home at Carfax was some twenty miles away, and it was still deep night. I checked each body to insure they were dead, and then I began to run, like a wolf, but in human form. When I came to a nearby park, I threw my brolly into bushes, unwilling to be burdened by modern devices of my adopted land. Just this one night, this moment, I was back in the Carpathians, living as I was born to live, intoxicated with the unleashing of my true self.

I ran all the way back home ... and I loved every step.

The next evening I awoke almost fully restored. The wound in my chest had healed over, although it could still be seen – another feeding would cure that. I needed a new suit, possibly two, in case this happened again, and a new brolly. I desperately wanted to see Lucy again, yet I feared formalwear might not be appropriate. I arose from my coffin in my formalwear, which I'd put on after washing, to avoid staining the silk lining of my pretty new coffin, only to hear a door above me open and close. I had to investigate, yet upon reaching the foot of the stairs, I saw the door at the top of my stairs open, and a figure stood silhouetted in moonlight streaming through the stained-glass window.

"*Master ...?*" Renfield called. "*Master, I'm here!*"

After an instant of surprise, I ascended the steps, pushed him backwards, and closed the door behind me.

"*Did I not order you never to enter that chamber again?*" I demanded.

"But ... I want to!" Renfield said, excitedly, his voice shrill. "Master, I've come ... to become great ... like you!"

Even in the dim light, I could see his eyes blazing. His lips were drawn back in a grin surpassing mirth, ecstatic, almost rapturous. I was taken aback at this change, for never had I seen him so.

"*Please, Master!*" Renfield begged. "*Make me like you, immortal, unfearing of death!*"

I glared him into submission.

"This is a change," I said. "Before, you didn't wish to be great ..."

"I do now, Master," Renfield said. "I'll give anything ... be your slave forever! Only give me life ... eternal life ... and I'll be anything you desire!"

At first I was confused, but then I recalled where I'd found him, and where he still lived. Renfield wasn't the first madman I'd met, but few madmen were constant in their afflictions. Most varied widely. So mild and meek he'd seemed, I'd assumed this was his normal state, but men aren't locked in asylums for timidity. His effusive joy, his desperation, and his boldness seemed to project the soul of an entirely different person.

"I can give you this gift, but its price doesn't change," I said. "I am neither living nor dead: I'm undead, and to arrive at my state, you must die."

"No, Master, please; I want to escape death!" Renfield said.

"No man escapes death," I said. "But I need not kill you tonight. Someday you'll succumb to the black shadow that haunts all the living. But my gift, my curse, can spare you from dissipation into the ethereal realms, and let you walk the night forever."

"Yes, Master!" Renfield was trembling with excitement. *"Give me that power!"*

"You're no longer young, and if you die tonight, with my curse in your veins, then you'll walk as you are for all eternity," I said. "But if you choose to wait until you're aged, then as an elderly man you'll face the endless years, unable to return to the youth you have today."

"No, don't kill me!" Renfield said. *"I don't care how I live ... as long as I live!"*

I considered his request. I liked having a human servant, as some chores like gardening and accepting deliveries must be done while the sun was up. Making him a vampire now would curtail his usefulness, and his mind was insufficiently strong to endure the passing of centuries, ignoring that I'd quickly tire of his ignoble company.

"Your mind has changed," I said. "Certainly it'll change again. Will you then hate me for cursing you?"

"No, Master, never!" Renfield swore, and he fell to his knees before me.

I surveyed him for another instant, groveling upon the stone tiles of my chapel, and then I shook my head.

"No," I said. "You're a good servant, but this gift requires years of service. I promise this: if your loyalty never fails ..."

I stopped as Renfield growled. Hatred radiated from his face, such that I was certain he was about to attack me. I had no fear of him; if I could slay Cromwick and his allies then Renfield was no threat. Yet I was about to lose my only servant, for by his demeanor, I'd surely have to kill him to subdue his maddened state.

"Wait," I said. "Perhaps ... I have erred. If you were to promise ... to swear upon your very existence ..."

"Master, I am your willing slave, loyal to you forever!" Renfield practically shouted, holding up his hands in supplication. *"I'll do your bidding forever! Anything! I swear!"*

I observed him another moment, disgusted, but also curious. Madmen hold a special fascination for me, as we're both extraordinarily different, although in dissimilar ways. I maintained staunch control over myself, greater than even the sanest man. Most madmen go in and out control, and the abhorrent machinations of their dementia offers clues to how lesser men think, although some levels of irrationality depart all conscious reason. The lunacy of Renfield shined obvious; no doubt he'd soon regret his pleas of this night. But then, my hold over him would be drastically increased, for once infected with my curse, no reversal exists. When reason returned to him, then I'd inform him there was a cure, and if he obeyed me, then someday I'd grant him that cure ... *which he'd only desire while rational!*

His cure would be the consummation of his newly-arisen corpse by fire, with a stake through his charred heart and garlic stuffed into every crevice, but he needn't know that.

"I'll make you immortal," I said.

With tangible excitement, Renfield watched as I removed my coat, unbuttoned my sleeve, and bared my forearm. Exposing my fangs, I held up my wrist and bit until blood flowed. Slowly I held out my leaking arm.

"I offer immortality, but you must take it," I said. "Drink of my blood, if you'd live until the stars fade. Drink, but be it upon your soul, for it's you who make this choice, not I."

Renfield seized my wrist and sucked with a passion even Miëta couldn't rival. I stood and watched; normally this was a sacred moment, but for Renfield, this was his decree of doom, the final, irrevocable verdict that his life would end twice at my hands, once when I needed him no more, and a second time when I banished him from this world forever; *madmen were unfit to carry my gift into eternal night.*

"Enough," I said. "You are now immortal."

Renfield's smile could've outshone the sun.

"*I am great ...!*" Renfield shouted. "*I'm great ...!*"

"Yes, but now you must tell no one, moreso than before," I said. "You stand upon the doorstep to eternity. Return to your dwelling ... to revel in what you've achieved ... and all you desire shall someday be yours!"

"Yes, Master! Thank you, Master! Thank ...!"
"You heard my command: *obey!*"

Trailing apologetic gratitudes, Renfield ran to the door, aglow with triumph, glanced back once at me, and then departed.

I shook my head. I'd assigned myself a new duty, to insure the world didn't suffer from his unrelenting appetites, if only to protect my secrecy. I hated burdening myself with menial chores, but Renfield could never be restrained if he awoke undead. Certain depredations were private, not to be trusted to the insane; I couldn't allow all of England to become aware of vampires.

The rest of my evening passed in calm pleasantness. After a coach-ride to a distant district, I purchased a new suit that fit without the need for tailoring, and a new brolly. Again, the tailor seemed determined to stand me before an accursed mirror. I promised to oblige, but I asked to be allowed to view myself in private. Confused, he allowed me time to stare blankly into his mirror. Yet, when I purchased both, I extolled upon my appearance in his suit.

I quickly found a local tavern, where a prostitute chose me as her wealthy mark, and I bought her more than enough drinks to render her speech inane, such that I had to practically carry her to her tiny room on the third floor of a nearby building. There, I gently pushed her onto her stained bedclothes, and she fell into a drunken stupor which only my power could awaken. Her neck was filthy, so I spread her legs, vigorously wiped a spot clean, and sipped gently from her exposed inner thigh, careful not to pierce the strong artery there. I didn't need to glut myself, stain my new suit, or ruin my formalwear, which I was carrying in a bag. Nor did I wish to kill her, for the six men I'd fought near the docks had undoubtedly been found with their throats torn apart. I didn't need another murder to happen the following night with the same wound.

    Blood thinned by alcohol has lively effects upon vampires. We don't get drunk, as the living do, but alcohol speeds the streaming of life's warm liquid through our cold veins. Yet fermented chemicals aren't the rich, intoxicating, satisfying flavor we relish. Drunkards generally taste sour, and while they're drunk, their blood is thinned to the point of being watery. Elder blood tends to be thin and bitter, while young blood has an undeniable vitality, with an unparalleled sweetness. Hard workers are tart, with an intense heady, almost caramel flavor. Sailors' blood tastes sharp and acrid, while farmers' blood is always rich, syrupy, and wholesome; it satisfies your appetite and lasts long in your veins. Smart people have a remarkably subtle zestiness and poets are especially succulent. Hard muscles produce a salty robustness of vigor and stamina, usually from men, while women tend to possess more subtle and enticing tastes, with a spicy zeal that lingers upon the tongue. Feisty women are the most pungent, almost peppery, and beauty is especially potent, so the taste of a gorgeous wildcat can be savored on the palate for days. Yet the most delicious blood flows in the veins of the oldest families, where breeding has been selective for generations, and where combinations of intellect, confidence, and strength of will produce a piquant tanginess that excels all others.

My tasty prostitute was young and hard-working, but in all other aspects completely forgettable. Perhaps, had she not been intoxicated, I'd have found her blood appealing.

Leaving her a few coins, weak but alive, I walked the streets refreshed, and hailed another carriage. I rode to my district of Carfax, yet I didn't hurry home. I took an hour to indulge in a local tavern, nursing a beer I'd never finish, and reading an evening newspaper. Finally I found the article I'd been seeking; a nasty fight had occurred near a prominent seaside warehouse not far from here. The reporter described a scene of unequaled violence he believed had been between thieves of rival gangs, each seeking sole claim upon the waterfront district. His speculations amused me, for there was no mention of witnesses or anyone escaping the *'tragic loss of life'*; none of those lives, not even the muscular Cromwick, could've ever amounted to anything but a tragedy. My concerns were eased; *again I'd not been connected to a series of murders.*

I returned home and found several letters addressed to me from my London accountants, and I quickly estimated my total financial worth and expectations, which were nowhere near where I needed them to be. I resolved to devote more time to my financial preparations, as those would take the longest to insure my plan came to fruition. Yet I wrote my replies with no thought more than I needed. Only one idea tantalized and held prominence in my mind: *tomorrow night I'd return to my dear Lucy, to judge her fit to rule the world at my side ... or drain her entirely.*

At dawn I descended to my resting chamber beneath the chapel, ascended the stone steps to my summit of Transylvanian dirt, and surveyed my sleek, shiny coffin. *Soon, perhaps only months from now, I'd need Renfield to make another mound, of local dirt, for my Lucy.*

Jay Palmer

Chapter 8

August the 3rd awakened me with childish nervousness. I paused to relish the alien sensation. Every night in Castle Drăculea I'd wandered my home with petty motivations and short-lived goals; I fed, watered, and exercised my horses. I called to my wolf-friends. I indulged in sensual trysts with my brides ... until my dried-up shell grew too withered to enjoy physical intimacy. Conversations were few, mostly arguments over our appetites. Even Miëta didn't share my passion for knowledge. My lust for intellectual stimulation macerated ... until Jonathan Harker. Since him, I'd become a new person, not only younger, but almost alive, enticed by novelties I'd never imagined existed. *Why had I wasted so many years?* Now I'd live forever in the center of the world. When at last I returned to my familiar mountains, then I'd bring the world with me. Never again would shadows haunt me; my name would be synonymous with supremacy, intellect, and fashion.

And I'd have a queen worthy to sit beside me!
I restrained my enthusiasm to keep my perceptions untainted. Not once in every century did beauty and grace combine to produce someone as stunning as Lucy. I had to be stalwart and discerning,

keeping my final goal in mind. I couldn't be swayed by mere infatuation.

I dressed in my new suit, combed my hair, and donned a top hat suitable for the occasion. After posting my business correspondences at the nearest station, I hailed a cab to a popular area, half the distance to Hillingham. The crowded streets delighted me, and I read a local newspaper that I'd never seen before. I considered seeking refreshment but I refused to stain my new suit on this important night, and it was too early in the evening to hope for trustworthy solitude.

As night deepened, I hailed another cab, this time a calèche, a light carriage with small wheels, with seats for four passengers, a separate driver's seat, and a folding canopy. It was the most comfortable carriage I'd ever known; its passenger section hung upon thick leather straps, which my book in Castle Drăculea called thorough-braces. It didn't rattle over cobblestones and swung very little. I gave the driver Lucy's address in Hillingham. My excitement escalated, yet I struggled to control it.

I paid the driver, watched him drive away, and then ascended the bars of a locked gateway with ease, and spent half an hour wandering around the dark gardens behind her house. Then I came across the perfect place, on a rise above a stream, surrounded by lilies and honeysuckle, sat a white gazebo, almost glowing in the moonlight, with a single wide, painted bench inside.

It was an hour past midnight, and most of the windows were dark. I headed toward her house and reached out to Lucy's sleeping mind:

'Come to me! Come to me!'

Minutes passed, and I concentrated harder. Not knowing where she slept in her father's mansion was frustrating, but finally I sensed a reaction, and I focused upon it until I was certain. She was in the southern wing, on the second floor, and I followed her sensation until I knew I was right. There, strengthened by closeness, I refocused my will upon her sleeping form:

'Come to me!'

Slowly I felt her yield. Moments later a door opened on a balcony above me; Lucy stepped out into the moonlight, still in her nightdress.

"Open your eyes ... and look down upon me," I commanded.

Her mind was still asleep, but her body responded without question. In the moonlight her exquisiteness was breathtaking, but I resisted; I couldn't release her now.

"Come, my beloved," I said. *"Come downstairs ... and outside ... to me."*

Minutes later a lock clicked and a door opened upon the patio to my left. Lucy emerged in glorious fullness, her unseeing eyes vacant, yet still beautiful. I held out my hand and she extended her arm; together we walked through the twilight across the footbridge.

In the gazebo we sat, side by side upon the bench. She was delectable, delicious to look upon, and my urge to touch her, to feel her womanly curves, was almost overpowering, yet I hadn't come for a momentary debauchery.

"Lucy, you walk in a dream ... but also there's reality," I whispered. "Nothing exists for you to fear, for never in your life have you been as protected as you are now. You're free to think ... and to speak ... anything that you like. I'm your protector ... and your friend.

Tell me everything. Speak, my dear Lucy; what reason would you have to fear me?"

Her mouth slowly opened.

"I ... don't ... know," Lucy whispered.

"Of course not, for there is no reason," I said. "Do you know who I am, Lucy?"

"No ...," she breathed.

"I am Count Drăcula of Hungary, Prince of Transylvania," I said. "We met at your party, and you called me Vlad. Do you remember me?"

"Yes ...," she said.

"You invited me to return, and I've done as you wished," I said. "That's why I'm here: to comply with your wish. Will you speak to me, Lucy?"

"Yes ...," she said.

I'd no idea how much of this night she'd remember, possibly none at all, but my goal was to discover her nature, to judge her worthiness. Still, I couldn't deny my heart, as if it were fluttering like batwings in a cloud of delight.

I'd denied myself the joys of the flesh too long. I yearned to be one with her, but I restrained myself; I had plans beyond what she could currently comprehend. To begin our immortal lives together, as I hoped, we couldn't start like debase animals.

"Tell me of yourself," I said to Lucy. "Tell me of your notable family ... and your childhood. Who is your oldest ancestor ... that your history describes?"

"Herman Maximus Westenra," Lucy said. "All of my family histories begin with him."

Herman Maximus Westenra, if any of her family history was true, was the son of a shipwright who'd taken to sea, and made his fortune trading in distant lands, and returned to England a wealthy man. He married a

French dowager, and inherited her family's titles and estates, and eventually became an earl, although how this was arranged was unknown. Lucy was descended from him through seven generations, and at this revelation, I hungered to taste her blood, for it must be scrumptious. She knew little of her other ancestors until she came to her grandparents, and most of her first childhood memories with them were of walks around these very gardens. They even rested in this gazebo, while young Lucy played with her toys, picked flowers, or splashed in the stream. In her mind, her grandparents were light, love, gifts, and frolicking free; Lucy knew nothing else about them.

Of her own parents, Lucy felt great love, especially for her father, whom she had lost two years ago. Yet her adoration was shadowed by their rigidity and frumpiness. Her father forced Lucy to learn to read, to care for her own things, and assume responsibilities for chores which servants would've gladly done. As she grew, her mother made her learn cooking and sewing, which was far more fun than cleaning and making beds. Eventually her father made her keep account books and track business transactions. As a break from these tedious tasks, Lucy was gifted with musical instruments, including a harp, for which she was assigned a series of teachers, who'd taught her well. Later, she learned that musical skills were intended to make her a suitable wife for a wealthy man, and Lucy thereafter refused to play, although she secretly practiced. *'Any husband worthy of me'*, Lucy told her mother, *'will love me without reservation'*.

Yet, despite her *'arduous upbringing'*, Lucy forgave her parents, for she was a creature of gentleness and honesty. She confessed to me, with her sleeping mind, that she was grateful to her parents, for she'd not grown up vacuous and dainty, as ethereal as her friends, whose heads seemed dazzled by the softest reflection. Lucy was neither naïve nor artless, and she'd been reprimanded many times for appearing too wise or inquisitive for a beautiful young girl approaching the age of marriage.

In her sleeping voice, Lucy boasted with pride of her insistence that she choose her betrothed, for she wasn't raised to have choices made for her. She had no lack of suitors; Lucy was a daughter of English aristocracy, and her reputation as an unrivaled beauty born to wealth preceded her. Only men of exceeding virtue and nobility were allowed in her company, and she put many suitors through subtle and excruciating tests, to determine the truth of their natures, before she considered their compliments sincere. Arthur Holmwood, the sole son of the fabulously wealthy and powerful Lord Godalming, was the only man to pass all of her tests. Of their eventual love Lucy was convinced.

Here I chose to intercede, for I had doubts to sow.

"My dear Lucy, as smart as you are, you know Arthur Holmwood is mortal," I said. "He may offer you all that he can, but when you're aged, fearing death, when you desire only to live longer, then Arthur will hold out empty hands."

For the first time since I'd met her, Lucy looked troubled.

"Don't fret, my dear," I said. "What no other can give, I can. Count Drăcula can protect you from all evils in this world ... even the specters of old age and death. Raise your eyes and look at me, dear Lucy." She obeyed, and I leaned closer, almost letting our noses touch, and letting her peer deep into my dark eyes. "See the truth inside me, Lucy. Where I appear to be young, I'm not. I won't deceive you, nor shall I ever lie to you: I'm 466 years old. Age doesn't touch me, nor shall it ever. I'll continue as long as the moon shines, and witness ages of men countless centuries from now. You need not fear death, either, for I've chosen you to become immortal. You'll never age or grow heavy, but always be light and lithesome as you are now. This I do swear, and the promise of Count Drăcula no mortal vow can equal."

I realized, only as I spoke these words, that I'd decided.

"It's almost time for you to return to your bed," I said. "You won't remember this night, save as a dream, and your dreams shall be glorious, wholesome, and fill your every desire. But I can't risk losing what I've found, and so, dear Lucy, now you must fall deeply asleep. Very deeply. *Sleep!*"

Lucy closed her eyes, and I felt my hunger rise with my desires, but I couldn't let them overwhelm me. I touched her precious, soft cheek with my fingers and slowly turned her head to one side. Her bare neck glowed in the moonlight like a promise of eternal gratification.

A soft sigh escaped Lucy's sleeping lips as I kissed her throat, first lightly, and then with increasing passion, until my fangs pierced her as gently as I could. She gave a startled cry but didn't awaken, and I indulged myself on a nectar so sweet only Heaven itself could've fashioned it. Her blood was like a rich, ripe tomato suffused and saturated with honey, vanilla, and cinnamon, the sweetest desert with the most sublime flavor I'd ever tasted. She streamed inside me like fresh cream overflowing with lustrous joy and sanguine vivaciousness. Lucy's heart and spirit were sprightly, a buoyant soul bursting with genial wisdom; hers was a taste of which even Count Drăcula couldn't tire.

With one bite, I knew Lucy would be my queen forever ... until the last night of this world.

Filled with her ecstasy, I drew back my cuff and sleeve as far as I could without tearing it, and exposed my wrist. Then, using my sharp fingernails upon my undead flesh, I cut a gash until my blood flowed freely. Cupping the back of her head, I raised her chin and pressed her sweet mouth against my bleeding wrist, letting my essence become hers.

The silent night seemed to thunder loudly, for my world had just changed. Lucy was joined to me forever, my immortal queen, to rule the night and all the lands. I alone knew this, but I knew so much I shared with no other that it was no surprise that earthquakes and lightning didn't herald the dawn of this new age, the age when a single throne would ascend above all of the empires of mankind. This night would become legend, when Lucy was instilled with deathlessness, and destined to be mine forever.

The second stage of my plan was fulfilled. No obstacle could stop me. Soon I'd rule this world ... with my eternally beautiful Lucy at my side.

The next morning I awoke troubled: *someone was outside my coffin.*

I was tired after my long flight home, yet I had to know who it was, so I lifted my lid and rose. At the foot of the stone steps he'd built, staring up at me, stood Renfield.

"Did I not command you never to enter here?" I demanded.

"What ... have you done to me?" Renfield asked slowly, a deadened despair filling his voice.

Apparently his personality had changed again; he was as I'd first met him, save that he was now infected with my curse. I climbed from my coffin and stood looking down at him.

"You asked me to," I said. "You begged me. You demanded it."

"What will become ... of my soul?" Renfield asked.

"Nothing can harm a soul," I said. "God made your soul and mine; do you really think I have the power to destroy that which God made?"

"You have the power to ... to damn what God made," Renfield said. *"Have you damned my soul?"*

I stared at Renfield angrily. He'd served my purpose, and done many tasks for me, but his usefulness was ended. His very presence here defied my commands. His disobedience meant my secrets were no longer safe with him. *But not now ...*

"There's a cure," I said.

Renfield's eyes widened.

"A ... cure ...?" he asked.

"Of course," I said. "A holy herb. I'll fetch it, if you like. Be here at dawn ... and I'll cure you."

Renfield swallowed hard, as if doubting me.

"I'll be here, Master," he said. "Thank you."

I hated to lie, but Renfield's mind was so ill-adapted to the truth that untruths were for his best. Yet for now, I needed him to perform a final task.

"I may need to host a dinner party," I said. "Clean the rooms upstairs as best you can. Stay at it all night. There's more brandy in the kitchen; help yourself, but don't imbibe so much your cleaning suffers. Start with the main rooms, and dust and sweep everything. Place wood in all of the fireplaces, and candles wherever light might be needed."

"As you command, Master," Renfield said, and with a last puzzling look at my coffin, he walked to the stairs and ascended.

I stood there, considering what I should do. I needed my house cleaned, if I was in fact to entertain guests, but mostly to give Renfield a task to occupy his mind while I pondered my options. Finding another servant would be easy, but finding one whom I could blackmail or intimidate into silence would be problematic.

Possibilities swarmed like bats. England had already altered me from the grave shadow that had haunted my ruined castle. In Transylvania, nothing was new, and my mood reflected its grim unchangingness. Now, my thoughts were like England, light and hopeful for success. I was enjoying the process I was undergoing, delighted to be living in a land of novelty. I'd seldom felt amusement since my return to Castle Drăculea, after my century-long investigation of all the lands of the Earth. Only when I was writing in my diaries did I enjoy my old life.

But now I had to be careful. Novelty leads to carefree abandon ... which leads to mistakes. I mustn't enjoy my new life so much that I forget my purpose, to *'be like the bat'*. My goals weren't only to remake my life, or to bring me out of eternal night, where I'd hidden since learning of my curse, but to remake my homeland, my people, and finally, the whole world. I'd not planned on remaking myself, but of course, we're all products of our environment. In my explorations, while traversing through horrific jungles, I became wild, a savage hunter. In this soft, young land of England, I must be careful not to intenerate my instincts, lest I spoil my ambition.

As King of the World, what affect would holding a supreme position have upon my mind? Would I become vain, intolerable, and grasping at every facet of existence, determined to bring all things under my control? If I did, I'd have to dominate not only whole empires, but the minds that ruled them ... and someday subjugate the minds they ruled. How far would this go? How much liberty could I afford to grant without my subjects becoming a threat to my rule? Would I become a generous, benevolent ruler ... or a greedy king without care for his subjects? What kind of emperor did I want to be ... and what type of environment would I have to create to insure that I didn't become something else?

Many men dream of elevating their lifestyles, but mortals seldom ask how their elevated status will affect them. Vast wealth enslaves the wealthy to eternal strife against those who'd steal their wealth. Endless love lasts only as long as both lovers do; few mortals can tolerate the faults of another for a single lifespan. Fame requires work to acquire, and must be constantly maintained.

To remake the world, my first task was to remake myself, for if not, then the world would certainly remake me.

The key to remaking a world was what you did after you conquered it. Simply to maintain control wasn't enough; someone had to have a vision of what the world should be. Yet my mind was still too dark for such ambitions; *Lucy would chart my new course for our world.*

I was hungry yet I didn't go out until late that evening. I wandered through the unlit rooms of my mansion, and silently passed by Renfield sweeping with a broom, a bottle of brandy nearby. I explored dark, empty passageways, illuminated only by starlight upon window sills. I brooded upon what environment would be best for an emperor. I'd seen emperors in Asia, and many kings in the west, and leaders of great nation-tribes in Africa and South America, both vast lands now being usurped by Europeans. I could come to no conclusion, and moreso, I was troubled. Walking through dark hallways with no direction in mind, lost in deep contemplation, brought me back to my days in Castle Drăculea before Jonathan Harker arrived. *Was I still that same man, distracted by purpose and novelty, my nature unchanged?* While any environment might affect me temporarily, would my long, immortal life not eventually restore me to my nature?

No, I concluded. Natures change. The more entrenched the nature, the harder change becomes, the more effort is required, and the longer it takes. I'd have to enforce my will over others for centuries to make my throne of humanity truly my own. My existence would become enforcing my will ... but that was only my path, not Lucy's goal.

I smiled. My immediate concern wasn't only the world I wanted to create, but also the company I allowed to inhabit my inner circle. This brought me to thoughts of Lucy, my beloved bride, who was already one of my kind, although she didn't know it. The world I shaped would affect her as well, and all who'd come into our inner-circle would affect us. Yet, as I dwelt upon Lucy, I lost my focus on distant plans ... and felt only current desires.

I had to see her again!

I found myself walking my grounds in the moonlight, and so I left. I hungered, so I hurried to the local waystation and hailed the first cab I found. The driver recognized me, for I'd used him before, so I rode for only a short ways before I let myself out, and minutes later I hailed another cab. This one I took eastward, ten miles closer to Lucy's house. Then I paid the driver with most of my few remaining coins and walked through the thinning crowd to a seedy section of town. There I planned to allow myself to be seduced, but a drunken man, stumbling from the door of a brothel, stole my attention. He called back to the women who'd just evicted him, and they offered to let him back inside ... when he found some more money. Although drunk, he was a big man, in the prime of his strength. I waited until the brothel door closed, and then I approached him.

"Excuse me, sir, I'm looking to hire a strong back," I said.

"Beg pardon, mister?" he asked. "*Money ...?*"

"Eight shillings, if that's enough ...," I said.

"What's th' job?"

"I've a crate to be carried to the stables and loaded upon my wagon," I said. 'It's nearby, but I can't lift it ..."

"Eight shilling' ...?" he asked, amazed.

"Forgive me, I'm new to your lands," I said. "Is eight shillings too much ...?"

"No, bless me, eight shilling' is jus' perfect," he said. "Show me tis box; I'll carry it, even t' Dover, if'n I must."

"Thank you, my good sir," I said. "You're most helpful."

I led the way, although I'd no clue where we were going. I simply chose the darkest route to somewhere where we wouldn't be seen, which appeared only a few alleys away, behind some houses.

"Hey, where dis box?" my prey complained.

"There it is ... just a little bit further ... on the ground."

I stopped beside a house with a stone wall, and he bent to peer into the shadows for a box that never existed. I grabbed his neck firmly and smashed his head against the stone wall, and when he tried to resist, I hammered him into the wall again. He finally fell, after a brief struggle, and I drank from his wrist, again careful not to soil my clothes. He was bland and sour, yet his strength poured into me, and I drank until he was so weak he wouldn't soon awaken, if ever.

Invigorated, I drew back my head, and only then did I let his unconscious body fall to the dirt beneath us.

Scream; an outcry burst above me, and I looked up. An old woman, poking her head over the rail of a widow's walk, stood looking down at me, screeching her lungs out ... and a bobby's whistle blew from the street. She couldn't have seen much, for we were hidden in shadow, but I couldn't attempt to flee lest I run headlong into the arms of a constable. I had only one choice:

Be the bat!

An hour later I was human again. I was in a strange woods, and it took several minutes of wandering lost through an overgrown thicket before I found a trail and spied Lucy's house in the distance. I wasn't surprised; I'd not concentrated on any destination, and my bat senses had returned me where I most wanted to be. It was again past midnight, and I was already here, so I decided to see my new bride again. I walked straight to her balcony and stood beneath it, and again I summoned her.

As my blood now flowed in Lucy's veins, my summons was instantly obeyed, and soon I was walking beside her, on the same path to the white gazebo past the stream surrounded by lilies and sweet-smelling honeysuckle. She was wearing nothing but her nightgown, flowing white layers of thin, blowing lace, and her true shape greatly pleased me. The moon was full, its bright light making her pale skin and vestments glow, and I felt refreshed just being in her presence, holding her hand as we walked.

I sat her inside the gazebo, just inside the shadows of its woven lattices, and then I stepped into the bushes outside of it, where she couldn't see me.

"Lucy," I called softly to her. "You're safe, and you must be calm. Lucy, wake up. Awaken now. Don't be alarmed. Open your eyes."

A soft gasp came from the gazebo, followed by a stifled, barely audible scream, quickly cut off.

"Lucy ...?" I asked.

"Ar ... Arthur ...?" Lucy asked, her voice alarmed.

"No, it is I, your new friend: Count Drăcula," I said.

Her face appeared at the open doorway of the gazebo, and she looked bewildered. I bowed low before her.

"Don't be alarmed," I said most genially. "You remember me; I played an unexplained trick upon your friends at your party, and you asked me how I did it. Do you remember?"

"What ... how ....?" she asked. *"What am I ... what do you ...?"*

"I promised to tell you how I performed my trick," I said. "I've now performed it twice: once upon your friends ... and now upon you. How do you think I brought you out here ... without awakening you?"

Lucy drew back into the shadows.

"Please don't scream," I said. "You're in no danger. You know this gazebo. You played here when you were a child ... and brought lilies to your grandparents."

Lucy's face appeared again, this time staring at me.

"How do you know ...?" she asked.

"I'll tell you everything," I said. "But see; there stands your house. You may run home, if you wish. I won't try to stop you. Rather, I'll stand here and watch until you're safely inside. Go now, if you must. But if you prefer to know the truth, how I can do things no other man can, then stay and listen. I'll answer every question ... and teach you my ... magic tricks, if you request it."

"You ... stay right there!" Lucy ordered, shielding her chest with her arms.

"My dear Miss Westenra, your safety is my utmost priority," I said. "Command me to go, if you doubt me, and I'll walk away in any direction you wish. Of course, the truth of my 'tricks' shall go with me ... and you'll never again get the chance to have your questions answered."

Lucy looked troubled, but she was hesitant.

"How did I get out here?" she asked. "Did you ... *carry me?"*

"You walked in your sleep," I said. "You came down from your bedroom, right outside your patio door, and walked beside me all the way here. I could show you your footprints, but I doubt if you could see them in this light. You weren't carried. I escorted you here, and then I awakened you."

"Why here?" Lucy asked.

"Conversation would awaken your household, if we were any closer," I said. "Nor did I wish to take you farther, for you might've been justly alarmed. I thought you'd feel safe here, close to your home, where we could talk freely."

Lucy shook her head, as if trying to fling the haze from her eyes.

"Take your time," I said. "I have all night."

A long moment passed, and then Lucy asked:

"Alright, how did you trick my friends?"

I smiled at her.

"The longer one lives, the stronger ones thoughts become," I said. "After only a few centuries, the thoughts of that person could grow so strong as to extend beyond the confines of their skull and permeate into the minds of others."

"That's ... impossible," Lucy said.

"And yet, here you stand, in this gazebo, talking to me," I said. "You were asleep, and so your mind was open and unprotected ... as your intoxicated friends were open to any new impulse or sensation, and I simply gave them one."

"Nonsense," Lucy said. "No one lives that long ..."

"I've lived twice that long, Lucy Westenra," I said. "Simple mind tricks like these are the least of my powers. I hold the secret to immortality and eternal youth ... both of which can be yours ... if you want them."

"You're mad," Lucy said. "Go away! Leave me alone!"

"Let me prove it," I said. "I'll prove it to you ... and then I'll go. Is that acceptable?"

"How can you prove it?" Lucy asked.

"I can do as I've already done ...," I said.

"No!" Lucy said. "Don't use your ... tricks on me!"

"Very well," I said. "What if I used them on birds? Do you like birds?"

"Birds ...?" Lucy asked.

"Birds nest about here, do they not?" I asked. "They're sleeping, and of very small intellect, easy to manipulate. I'll call them down to come and greet you, and land on your palms, if you wish."

"No," Lucy said. "You ... you're a bird-trainer ..."

"Well, then, what test would you have me perform?" I asked.

She stuck her head out of the gazebo, looking straight at me, finally awake, with both arms concealing my view of her chest.

"My late father had a dog, Rudolf, who still sleeps on his bed," Lucy said. "Call him out here, if you can."

"Gladly," I said, "but you must commit to me first what will happen if I succeed. If I fail, then your accusations are correct, and I'll leave a liar and a scoundrel. But, if I'm right, and I can bring your friend Rudolf out here, then you must accept that I have mental powers the like of which you've never seen. Are we agreed?"

"I ... agree," Lucy said hesitantly.

"Relax, if you can," I said. "I'll call Rudolf."

The effort was simple. Rudolf was sleeping, but he knew when he was being called, and I placed Lucy's image in his mind, the beautiful image I cherished, and called to him. Almost instantly I felt him respond, and a minute later his shaggy body came loping out of the patio door Lucy had left open, and he ran straight toward us.

"Here he comes," I said.

"Where ...?" Lucy asked.

"Look to the bridge; you'll see him soon."

Rudolf was a Bingley Terrier, about forty pounds, with pointed ears and wiry hair. As he ran closer, the moonlight revealed him to be mostly tan with a wide patch of black covering his back and most of his sides. He ran excitedly, as if glad to be called, and I understood why: for a human, mind-to-mind contact, however soft, can be disturbing, even annoying, and is often disregarded. To a dog, or a wolf, contact with a human mind accesses levels of thinking beyond them, as mortals would feel if they could sense the thoughts of God.

"Lord forgive me!" Lucy exclaimed as she heard and saw Rudolf approaching.

"I can send him back, or make him do tricks he's never been trained to perform," I said.

"How – how's this p-possible?" Lucy stammered.

"I'll tell you all, and I won't lie," I said. "Will you allow me to tell you?"

Lucy looked at me, her expression torn between astonishment and terror.

"You ... won't hurt me?" Lucy asked.

"I'll never hurt you, my dear," I said.

Slowly, for it was a long tale, I told her of my past, emphasizing my normal, happy childhood, my royal lineage, and my family honor. I told her how my father was almost slain, by an advance party of Turks, for refusing to bow before their leader, Sultan Murad II, and how I was left in command of our army when he arrived home at our castle, badly wounded, having barely escaped the Turks at the cost of most of his guards. I made sure Lucy understood my hopeless situation: my troops were outnumbered many times over by a rapidly-advancing enemy, and the threat of what would happen to all Europe if the Turks crossed the Carpathian Mountains, as Sultan Murad II intended.

Attentive to my every word, Lucy sat down on the bench, and slowly I approached her, othertimes pacing back and forth on the path before the door to the gazebo, or stepping one foot onto the boards of the gazebo to explain a relevant point. She was fully awake now, and listening intently. *Our future together was assured, for no power of my mind could erase a memory as strong as her focus would give this one.*

When I described my horrible decision, how I tortured the Turks, and left them for their fellows to find, alive or dead, I met her eyes only once ... and nothing but revulsion filled them.

I described the success of my gambit, if such it could be called. My impalings turned back the Turks; I had saved Western Europe. At this point, I came inside and sat beside her, but I kept my eyes lowered, upon the floorboards of the gazebo.

"I'd been so proud of myself," I confessed. "We held a great party, and while my father recuperated in his bed, my mother declared me the King of Castle

Drăculea, Lord of the Carpathians, and she placed a gold circlet upon my head, as the Turks had stolen my father's crown while he was their captive. I was heralded as the Hero of the West, and everyone praised me.

"But soon, as I rode out into the sun, which I did almost every day, an unexpected pain sizzled my flesh. My servants shielded me with their cloaks, which relieved me, and I fled into the shade of Castle Drăculea. The best physicians were summoned, but my condition grew slowly worse, and soon I couldn't abide even reflected sunlight coming from windows. The daytime sapped my strength, and I began sleeping during the waking hours, arising at night. I didn't know what was happening to me, and everyone was horrified by the mystery of my inexplicable illness.

"Food began to make me sick, and soon I could eat nothing solid," I said. "I was convinced I was dying.

"My father got better as I got worse. He prayed for me, and commanded everyone in Transylvania to pray for me, and everyone willingly did.

"Lucinda was the daughter of a nearby Earl, whom my father had hoped I'd marry," I said, and I dropped my voice to a whisper. "She heard of my illness, and brought her father's chief physician to Castle Drăculea. He was as perplexed as any of my family's doctors, and he prescribed strange herbal baths, designed to protect my skin from the sun, and servants were sent to gather rare ingredients. But I never took those baths. That night ... my life changed.

"In the dark of the moon, Lucinda came to me, and she sat beside my bed and held my hand. I was in agony, for I could neither eat nor drink, and yet my hunger was ravenous. I'd consumed nothing for weeks, and I raved and raged in my daylight sleep ... and writhed in agony every night. I had no conscious thought but one: *I had to eat or die."*

I kept staring at the floorboards, struggling to avoid meeting Lucy's eyes. I hadn't repeated this story for a century, and still the words resisted me.

"What happened?" Lucy asked.

"I don't recall it clearly," I said. "A madness took me, and when I came to my senses, I felt fully restored. Moreso, I'd grown stronger. I surged, powerful, with muscles like iron, and my mind clearer than ... than it'd ever been. I was ... evolved. I was more than human."

"And then I saw ... what I'd done," I hissed, my words barely audible. "Lucinda ... was dead. In my madness, I'd fed ... upon her. Her body lay still upon the floor beside my bed. I'd drunk her blood, consumed her life's fluids, and drained all she had. I'd not meant to. I didn't choose to do this, or recall doing it. But her blood filled my mouth and stained my nightshirt; *there was no denying I'd killed her.*

"My father tried to cover it up, but my screams, at the horror of my own action, drew servants to witness the scene. Rumors spread across the Carpathians like wildfire. I was declared insane and imprisoned by my own guards in the dungeon of my family's castle.

"Lucinda's father came with a regiment of cavalry and demanded vengeance. My father had to choose between my life and a war that would kill hundreds of our people. He agreed to a trial, and commanded me to be silent, but my family honor wouldn't let me lie. I confessed my crime before all. I blubbered the words, for the health Lucinda's blood had given me had quickly faded. My description of my madness swayed no one.

With no other recourse, my father sentenced me to be hanged.

"But that night, before I was to be hanged, father came to me. My hunger was overwhelming. I begged him not to enter my cell, but he wouldn't listen. He sent the guard away, then unlocked my door, intending to steal me from the noose I'd earned ... and which I deserved.

"My next awareness: I was inhumanly powerful, and my father lay dead at my feet. I'd murdered again, and this was too much; using my newfound strength, I fought my way past our guards, overpowering men I could've never out-muscled before, ran to our stable, and stole a horse. The next thing I remembered was riding frantically down steep mountain paths, desperate to get away. I didn't know where I was going or why; the person I needed to escape from ... was myself.

"When the sun rose, I freed my horse and tried to hide from the solar glare. I crawled under thick fir trees, but they were no help; I ran to find ease, blinded by the light, my skin smoking, and finally I threw myself in a narrow ravine and pulled a pile of brambles over me. Leaves didn't help, but I'd used my enhanced strength to yank the strong vines, and a shower of dirt and rocks fell over me. This helped, so I buried myself as best I could, in a shallow grave of my own making, and hid from the day.

"My horse was caught, and the woods around me searched, but they didn't dig, so I wasn't found. Yet I could hear them as they walked above me. They called me a monster, a fiend of Hell. And I was convinced ... they were right.

"My life was over," I said. "I'd been struck by a curse so powerful only God could've decreed it. To this day, I don't know why I was cursed; it was the greatest injustice in history. And my curse was made infinitely worse by the fact that I had, in my madness, discovered my own cure: *human blood.* To spare myself, others had to bleed.

"I couldn't live with this infirmity," I said. "I couldn't allow my life to continue at the cost of other lives, especially not my family. I'd found a cave to hide in, and spent several days and nights praying inside it. I tried to drink the blood of animals but their juices made me as sick as any other food. The only drink I could stomach was human blood, yet I was determined to never murder again. When next I felt the madness approaching, I drew a sword I'd stolen from one of my guards, held its point at my chest, and I fell upon it.

"Pain: I can't describe the agony. The sword pierced my chest, right through my heart ... *yet I didn't die.* I laid there for almost an hour, praying for death, before I pulled the steel blade out of my chest. I was alive, although no mortal man could endure such a wound. I discovered, to my regret, that I'd become immortal. It was the worst miracle ever; *God wanted me to live ... to suffer.*

"I laid writhing, in agony, but after a few madness-induced feedings upon peasants, over the course of weeks, I recovered, and soon I was restored, as I'd felt when I stood over Lucinda's pale and shrunken body. I became whole ... and stronger than ever, even my scars faded.

What was I to do? I couldn't die, and my existence was causing the murders of others.

"They hunted for me, and several times they caught me, for twice I came stumbling out to fall upon my knees before them, begging them to kill me. But their swords proved no more adept at justice than mine did, and they fled, crossing themselves and calling me a demon usurper."

Finally I looked up at Lucy, ashamed at the shock in her eyes.

"I don't blame you," I said. "And I didn't bring you here to be a victim; I've no intention of harming you. I want you to understand ... fully ... what God did to me. I never asked for this. I was a good, pious man, even as a child. But that was 430 years ago. Since then, I've lived four hundred years as a helpless victim of God's curse, but those days are over. With experience comes wisdom, and I've had ten lifetimes to consider and contemplate why I was made immortal. I understand now God's purpose for me, and why I can't die: *I must live until God's purpose is fulfilled."*

Lucy stared at me, amazed.

"You know ... God's purpose ...?" Lucy asked.

A faint smile passed over my lips.

"God has yet to reveal His full purpose to me," I said. "Yet I'm convinced that such a purpose exists, and that I alone am meant to achieve it. I was the savior of His church in Europe, and perhaps that's why I was chosen. Until then, I'll do what I must, and minimize my feedings as much as I can, sparing the insanity I've learned to resist far longer than I could when my curse was new and unknown.

"Yet, there's one other problem, which I discovered while fighting, and which I must tell you," I said. "I've developed many powers of shape and mind, which only immortals can develop, but this I discovered by accident: my blood, the blood of others I've consumed and flows through my veins, carries my curse.

Humans who drink of my blood ... become like me: *powerful ... and immortal."*

I lifted my eyes and looked full upon the beautiful face of my Lucy. She was as near to me as English customs allowed a young lady to be, and wearing less than any young lady would dare wear before any man who wasn't her husband. Her loveliness was breathtaking; *she'd make a wondrous queen!*

Yet she looked at me with myriad emotions flashing across her expression: hatred, curiosity, disbelief, wonder, sympathy, and ... *most of all ... fear.*

"You ... can make others ... immortal," Lucy said finally, "but they must drink ...?"

"Those who drink of me share all aspects of my curse, my strengths ... and my weaknesses," I said.

"And ... why have you ... chosen to tell me ...?" Lucy asked.

"That's for you to decide," I said, and I stood and bowed to her. "Lucy Westenra, I confess that I find your beauty mesmerizing, and it bodes ill for any relationship, even a bond between close friends, to begin with a lie. Thus I decided to tell you all, my every secret, and let you decide ... if you wish to be ... my friend."

Lucy sat contemplating me, Rudolf sitting at her feet. I considered seeking into her mind to learn what she was thinking, yet I decided to honor her with privacy; *Lucy wouldn't take kindly to invasions right now.*

"It'll be morning soon," I said. "You must return to your bedroom, so no one knows you spent the night elsewhere. I'll take my leave. You may tell others of me, if you wish, but they'll claim you dreamed this meeting, and if you argue with them, then they'll say you're mad. I advise you to remain silent, and keep my story, and our meeting, secret.

"With your permission, I'll come again tomorrow night, and we'll meet here again ... to continue our conversation. You'll have time to dwell upon all you've learned tonight, and I'll answer the questions you can't ask yet.

"But I'll leave you with one final proof of my power. You must steel yourself; what I'm about to show you shall amaze your mind, possibly beyond your power to remain conscious, but I wish to be fully honest with you, and so I'll show you that which no other is allowed to witness. Are you prepared, my dear Lucy? Are you resolved to again witness power beyond your wildest imaginings?"

Lucy stared uncomprehendingly, and then slowly, silently nodded.

"Then I take my leave now, for I'll be gone before you comprehend what you've seen. Farewell, my dear, beloved Lucy! Think carefully upon what you've learned and witnessed. I'll come again tomorrow night to converse with you further."

Out of habit more than anything else, Lucy extended her hand when I reached for it, and I kissed her hand in a most-proper and chaste manner. Then I stepped back, fully into the moonlight; *it was time to show her everything.* I smiled at her, for our first private conversation *(that she'd recall)* had gone splendidly. I stood in the bright moonlight and spread my arms wide.

Be the bat!

Jay Palmer

Chapter 9

With the usual pains I assumed my human body next to my once-untended gardens. Renfield had been weeding, I was delighted to see, and a few early-blooming flowers were now visible. I liked flowers, for their beauty reminded me that not everything needed to exist forever. These flowers were the reverse of my curse; their blossoms closed at night and opened to thrive in the light of the sun, yet even in the light of the moon sliding toward the horizon, now casting shadows, I admired their closed buds.

I entered my house to await the quickly-approaching dawn, my mind filled with every sensation of Lucy. Being near her had been a delight, and her sharp mind perceived unique considerations, from which most people would've recoiled. I'd not told her everything, but eventually I would. *I wondered how she'd feel about becoming queen of the world?*

The sun was rising, yet my immediate purpose couldn't be performed this early. I wandered about my rooms, found Renfield had done a lot of cleaning, and in the main room, Renfield lay snoring in front of a dying fire, his head upon the arm of a large padded chair, an empty bottle of brandy at his feet. *I'd need more brandy, if he was to continue in my service.* I'd also need plates and silverware and tablecloths, if I was to host a dinner party. I'd need more clothes soon, which I could buy at night, but to acquire more money, a sufficient amount to keep in reserve, I'd have to visit my bank, and that I could only do during the day.

I awoke Renfield and sent him home, and then I paused, looking at my framed portrait over my fireplace. I did resemble the portrait of my father, which I wished I'd stored in my vault. I lit a candle and held it up to illuminate my sketched face, for I was fascinated. *This was how Lucy saw me.* Lucy saw only a strong young man, approaching his thirties, not his five hundredth birthday. I was a handsome gentleman with dashing features in a new European suit, not a skeletal wraith haunting a crumbling castle inhabited by three unrepentant murderesses.

Lucy saw what she wanted to see. Yet what would happen when Lucy learned the fullness of my nature, as all women in relationships eventually do. *What would Lucy see when she knew me well?*

After several hours of pointless speculation, it became time to brave the daytime.

Donning my tall hat, my gloves, a scarf, and my overcoat, I headed out into the deadly sun. I'd look strangely dressed, girded for winter in the late summertime, yet I had no choice; I'd make this venture as quick as possible. Daylight does more than drain my powers; the sun prevents me from transforming, healing, feasting, and all mental feats, even communicating with strange animals. Walking a single mile would seem exhausting, and lifting the lightest object would be a chore. I'd resist better if I'd recently fed, and the richer the blood, the stronger my resistance. But I hadn't fed tonight ... and my recent transformations had cost me much.

With a deep breath, I pulled my scarf tight about me and opened my door, fighting my instinct to recoil. The agony of bright sunlight touched me. My skin instantly dried, as I'd become while fasting, and even my clothes weighed me down. Yet I wasn't a man to cower before a challenge, so I forced myself out into the deadly, poisonous world. I headed to the waystation, staying in the shade of tall walls, houses, and trees as much as I could. I hailed the first covered coach I saw, a heavy clarence, which most Englishmen called a 'growler' from the sound it made on London's cobblestone streets. Growlers were enclosed, four-wheeled, two-horse conveyances with a projecting glass front and seats for four passengers inside its sturdy, enclosed cabin. The driver sat outside the carriage, on the front, above the window. I climbed inside and closed the curtains before I gave directions. My bank was an hour's ride from my residence, and already I felt tired. I hid inside the growler as the light outside grew brighter, listening to the clip-clops of the horses' hooves, dragging me farther from the safety of my coffin, and hearing the monotonous grinding of its wheels.

When we arrived, I ordered the driver to wait, again emerged into the sun, and quickly hurried into the shade of the bank's covered entrance and through its wide doors. Fortunately there was a doorman, as I was uncertain if I could've opened the massive doors.

As Jonathan Harker had instructed me, I asked to speak to a private clerk, and we entered a small office which, thankfully, had no windows. I presented him with my papers, proving my identity, and he took several minutes checking my signature against the documents I'd signed in Transylvania and mailed to his bank more than six months before leaving.

Satisfied, his attitude toward me became warmer, and my request for a withdrawal quickly managed. Fifty crowns and fifty shillings were delivered to me. The clerk gladly provided me with a bag just big enough to hold all of them, but I divided them between three of my pockets and stuffed the bag holding the rest deep inside my coat. The clerk commented that this was wise, and I should be careful not to carry so many coins at once, especially not at night. I thanked him and returned to my waiting clarence.

I'd distributed the coins about my person because I was certain I couldn't lift the entire bag.

Despite my preference for anonymity, I instructed the driver to deposit me just outside the gate to the asylum, at the residence of Dr. John Seward. The good doctor wasn't evident from the street, and so I paid the driver and hurried as best I could, in my weakened state, toward my house, as the sun was high and shadows few. My walk seemed long and difficult, and I was having trouble staying upright, weighted down as I was. I passed by the mailbox Renfield had made for me, delighted to see it stuffed with newspapers, but I was too weak to carry them inside.

After closing my door, I collapsed upon my foyer floor. With trembling fingers, I unfastened the buttons of my coat, and then my jacket, and like a snake, I slithered out of both and left them to lie on the floor. I waited long minutes, hating my weakness but unable to deny it, before I remembered how weak I'd be tonight if I spent the day upstairs. I needed my coffin, but even more, I needed the dirt of my homeland. With unparalleled determination, and leaving my coin-weighted coat behind, I crawled to a sturdy table, pulled myself upright upon its stout leg, and stumbled to my chapel stairs, holding on to the walls as I climbed down each step.

Before I ascended my stone stairs, I knelt down against the base of my mound and pressed my hands against the cold dirt of Transylvania. The connection felt comforting, and a residue of strength came back to me, enough to climb my stairs, lift my lid, and collapse into my coffin. My lid fell with a *crash!*

I awoke from a dreamless sleep with one thought filling my mind: *I needed to feed.*

Long I lay unmoving, waiting for night to deepen, and then I pushed open my new coffin's lid, which seemed to weigh more than it ever had. I wondered if Renfield had managed to escape tonight, for I'd certainly ease my appetite upon him. Yet an hour slowly passed, and I heard not a single footstep above me. Finally I had to arise, and I climbed the steps to my chapel like the living nearing the extent of their mortality.

In my chapel, I glanced up at the huge wooden cross hanging by thick chains over my bare stone altar. *'Are You enjoying my embarrassment?'* I asked in my mind, but I turned away, never expecting God to answer, supporting myself by leaning against my spare boxes of dirt which were still stored there. Soon I'd be strong again.

Was my strength or weakness conducive to God's plan, or was He trying to teach me humility? If so, He'd chosen an unfathomable method.

Seeking to recover, I went outside and let the cool moonlight refresh me. I fetched my newspapers and returned to my main room, after collecting my coin-filled coat. I found reading newspapers both relaxing and exciting, for it gave me information about important local figures. In Transylvania, such insights required spies to access private confidences. Here, more details than any spy could gather were commonly known. As I read an article about the questionable morality of a member of the House of Lords, I amused myself by imagining an article based upon my life, and what such revelations would do to the populace of London.

Slowly my strength returned as night deepened. I needed to feed, yet I couldn't appear at Lucy's house before midnight, so I had time to waste in idle pursuits.

Strangely, I missed my wives; in Castle Drăculea, they'd led me on a merry chase, and I was constantly struggling to monitor their doings, to control their lusts, and keep them from going on rampages across my countryside. Miëta was especially troublesome, as she envisioned a world where armies of vampires obeyed her every command. What she failed to grasp was the same problem that she always gave me; vampires can create other vampires, but they've no means of control. Miëta could've created her vampiric army, but she'd need whole cities murdered to feed them, and within a century there'd be no cities left. Miëta assumed that, because of her status, intellect, and voluptuousness, her vampiric army would be eternally loyal to her. She couldn't comprehend how wrong this would prove, as Miëta had always been the least loyal of my brides.

England felt comfortable. In my long life, I'd suffered too much idle time ... and grown to hate it. Mortals assume immortality would provide a luxury of wanton idleness, but only because their lifespans are brief. With immortality, idleness metamorphoses from a momentary pleasure into a reviled annoyance. Few mortals could endure living to the end of time, if such ever comes, without taking a sun-walk. As my father had said: *'Be your future, and drive toward it.'* Without ambitions, and ever-increasing goals, immortality would be torture.

I must confess: the one concept I'd never grasped was un-ambitiousness. In many languages, ambitiousness had no antonym that fully contrasted its meaning, except for crude insults. I'd concluded long ago that such a concept was too contrary to my personal nature to coexist with my thoughts, yet I frequently spent nights striving to understand it.

So passed my evening. Had I not been tired from my daytime excursion, I'd have ridden a cab to Lucy's district, and transformed to return home. Instead, I rested for hours, and then left early to seek a distant meal. I avoided the Thames waterfront, as it'd been the scene of several recent murders, and would probably be subjected to increased scrutiny of the constables, or bobbies, although I didn't know if that was a second name for the same profession. Instead, I chose a peaceful district to the north I'd never visited before: Hornchurch.

However, after paying my driver and sending him away, I quickly realized Hornchurch was a poor choice. All of the shops in this district were closed, and its one tavern was small and, looking in through a window, I saw only three men drinking quietly; my appearance in their establishment was sure to be remembered. Also, there were no other cabs in view, and mine had driven off after I'd paid him; I'd no transportation to a better place.

I needed to feed.

I stood in the shadows, wondering if I should break into a residence and surprise its sleeping occupants, when a dog barked in the distance. Looking up, I spied figures darting among trees on a hilltop only a few minutes' walk away. Glancing to make sure no eyes were watching me, I aimed my course toward the hill.

My prey were boys, no more than fourteen, playing in the shadows. I grinned, for surely these boys had been put to bed by their parents long ago, and snuck out to test their adolescent limits. As I approached, their laughter reached me, and I varied my path into the shadows of the long, leafy branches. This proved troublesome, for leaves had begun to fall, and my footsteps would've been heard were the boys not making far more noise than I. I crept up close to them, not thirty feet away from the nearest, and peered at them from behind a tree trunk. Three boys, all about the same age; I didn't need all of them, just one, and if I took him quickly enough, then the others would assume he was hiding, and spend the remainder of the night searching for him.

These boys played with abandon considered deadly in the Carpathians, intent only on each other, with no lookout for forest predators. Each boy had a stick, two holding theirs like rifles, and shouting *'bang'* as they played. The third, the one closest to me, held his stick like a sword, and pretended to slash their roundshots out of the air.

It was child's play to place in his unsuspecting mind the idea that he should pretend to be shot. Instantly he threw up his sword and cried out, clutched his chest, and then fell over in a most-dramatic resolution. As I expected, both *'gunners'* turned their weapons on each other, having vanquished their inferior foe. While they focused on murdering each other, I dashed forward, snatched the slain *'sword-wielder'* from the ground, and made off with him, my hand pressed over his mouth.

His blood was delicious. Young and high-born, his vitality gushed through me with an almost euphoric zeal. Holding him quiet and still while I drained him proved difficult, for he writhed and struggled until the end. The aftertaste of his blood was like a fine port wine, lasting long on my tongue.

I found a nearby well, next to a quiet house, tied its rope around him, and lowered him into the water. When they found him, he'd appear to have drowned while playing, and few would notice the two small pricks on his pale, waterlogged skin.

Walking under the shadowy trees to make sure no one could see me, I transformed with one thought: *wing toward Lucy.*

Be the bat!

I didn't have to summon Lucy: she was standing beside the moonlit gazebo as I transformed. My first awareness of her startled me as much as she. She looked lovely, wearing the same flimsy nightgown, but now a long, white satin robe concealed her most-delicate curves. *She was still radiant.*

"How can this be?" Lucy asked, obviously shaken, but before I could reply, she shook her head and waved my answer away. "We can't stay here. I was

seen coming inside last night; I told them I was sleepwalking. Come, follow me."

Lucy led me along an uphill trail, which came out behind a church set on top of a hill. On the other side, near the abbey, a wooden bench was set where viewers could languidly gaze down from the hilltop at a beautiful valley filled with quiet residences and several small, dark, starlit lakes. Lucy directed me to sit upon the bench, yet she remained standing.

"Can your .... curse ... really grant immortality?" Lucy asked.

"All terms are open to debate," I said. "I've existed for centuries, as you see me now, but my heart doesn't beat; *is that immortality?*"

Lucy looked at me doubtfully, her cheerful face masked with seriousness. Hesitantly she approached me, and I held my arms wide, offering her free access. Slowly she lowered her head and pressed an ear against my chest, and I pretended to be unaffected, but the scent of her hair reminded me of violets and jasmine, and the touch of her, so close, filled me like a breath of pure, sweet air after a rainstorm.

Eventually, she drew back equally slowly, her eyes wide with amazement. She grabbed my wrist and felt for a pulse; I surrendered my limb to her investigation with a smile.

"Satisfied?" I asked. "To your knowledge, no one can live without a beating heart. I offer you ... new knowledge."

"Why me ...?" Lucy asked.

I smiled, and for a moment, I let my true feelings show upon my face.

"You're pure light," I said. "Lucy, you're too young to see yourself as I do, not only as the beautiful person you are, but as the brilliant goddess you could be ... for centuries untold, passing untouched through long years into worlds yet to be. Your personality effervesces joy and innocence and spritely delight; no darkness could extinguish you. I need your light, Lucy. I need you to illuminate a soul sundered by centuries of darkness and more pain than any mortal can experience. I intend to reclaim my crown and birthright, but I've no desire to create a land of darkness, mirroring my former existence. I came to England because here shines the light of mankind, the highest learning and sharing, the richest culture, and the pinnacle of all man has yet achieved. The world I'd reshape must reflect your light, and no source glows brighter than you. I need you beside me, to be my queen, and banish the blackness in my heart ... and all the world."

Lucy stared at me with the icy glare of Miëta.

"I'm engaged to Arthur Holmwood ...," Lucy said.

"You are," I said. "I only offer, I don't insist. Yet you're a smart woman; would Arthur willingly share this curse with you? Would Arthur surrender every sunlit day for the rest of his life to explore the night for all eternity? He's a worthy man, I agree, but he's ill-equipped for immortality. You must choose for yourself, Lucy, for your memory of this decision will haunt you unto your last conscious thought."

Lucy's glare intensified, and then she diverted her eyes, turning to face the moonlit valley.

"I've given Arthur my pledge," Lucy said.

"I'll not stop you, if you should choose to share this gift with him," I said. "But beware, sweet Lucy; you wouldn't appreciate this gift being forced upon you, nor would Arthur. You must decide your own future, and give him the same choice, if you wouldn't risk his displeasure."

"*Arthur would never ...!*" Lucy started, and then she bit her lip and fell silent.

I said nothing, letting her dwell upon her own thoughts, which I could feel racing through her mind. She stood long in the moonlight, looking away from me, and I spent every moment admiring her. Lucy was perfect: smart, thoughtful, beautiful, and yet bubbly, as if the youth of all children danced in her heart.

How wonderful it would be to have her rule the world beside me!

"You must tell me everything," Lucy said. "Everything about your curse ..."

"Sit beside me," I urged her. "Hold my hand ... and I'll tell you everything."

Hours passed in luxurious splendor. Lucy took my hand reluctantly at first, but as our talk ranged widely and through countless experiences of my past, her grip became more relaxed, and at times possessive. When she asked a probing question, she'd squeeze my fingers as if to milk the answer from me. As much as I could, I spoke honestly. I told of my lost brides, and why each had failed me, and exuded praises upon the very qualities which she possessed, that would succeed where my former brides failed. The only information I withheld was of our secret meeting, our first rendezvous, which she'd never remember, and how I'd already infected her as a creature of the night. If she agreed to accept me, then there'd be no harm in repeating the operation. *If not, then she'd still be mine someday.*

"Must you feed so frequently?" Lucy asked.

"No, but weakness comes with fasting, just as if a mortal stopped eating," I said. "Without feeding, our strength, resistance, mental powers, and transformative abilities quickly fail."

Lucy considered this, and suddenly yawned.

"It's late, and you're tired," I said. "I must return home ..."

"Must you sleep in a coffin?" Lucy asked.

"It has advantages," I said. "Night-strength returns quicker, and it protects during your daytime-weakness. We don't sleep as mortals rest, able to awaken at the slightest noise; perhaps that's why we awaken so strong, as we rest deeper while we sleep."

"Will you come again?" Lucy asked, almost desperately.

"Tomorrow night, but we must take care not to be seen," I said. "I wouldn't see your honor disgraced any more than you would."

"I'll be discreet," Lucy promised.

"Does this mean ... that you've made your decision?" I asked.

Lucy clenched her teeth and looked down.

"I'm ... considering it," Lucy said.

"Perhaps you need ... a more intimate experience," I said.

"A bite ... won't ... turn me, will it?" Lucy asked.

"Only the taste of my blood can do that," I said.

Lucy swallowed hard, as if steeling herself.

"Taste me," she said.

How can one express the realization of their dreams? I raised the edge of my cape against the wide view of the valley, for this was a personal moment, and I'd no desire to share it. Lucy never closed her eyes, but watched as I drew closer, my face almost against hers, and then I hesitated expectantly. With some trepidation, but displaying her strong will, Lucy leaned her head back and willingly exposed her bare throat. My hunger flamed, but I controlled my lusts; *this was only a taste of what would soon come.* I exposed my fangs and lowered my lips to her skin with slow deliberateness, basking in the ecstasy of the moment.

    I kissed her flawless neck, breathing in her scent, intoxicated by her perfection. I could feel her blood pulse just under her skin, coursing through the wide artery just two tiny pricks away. *I had to be gentle:* I set my fangs to her skin and softly pressed.

    Ambrosia spewed into my mouth, a taste like Heaven afire that warmed my soul like godly gratification. I felt transformed by a flavor sweet and exotic. The glory of life filled me, a zesty tang that nearly overwhelmed my reason. For this taste I'd slay thousands, or fast a whole century. Never in 400 years had any sensation fulfilled my mind as the innocent delectability of Lucy's blood.

    I stayed my lusts; *now wasn't the time to make her my queen.* Lucy would choose that moment, and well-rewarded I'd be for giving her that choice. As before, I'd only lightly bitten her, leaving the smallest punctures, and the delight of Lucy's essence would linger on my tongue, to be savored for days. Slowly I ceased to drink ... and kissed her blessed soft, tight, pale skin. I yearned to kiss her more, to lick her throat clean, but I dared not press my affections, lest she resist. Finally I drew back, licked her blood from my lips, and gazed into her eyes.

    "I'll give you all you desire," I promised. "You'll never grow old, and you'll have everything wealth and nobility can buy. The Queen of England will envy you. I don't ask you accept what I offer, I merely place myself before you, your servant, if you'll have me. Eternity ... and all it holds ... is yours to take."

Lucy lifted her hand to her throat, which was bleeding only a trickle, dripping down onto the shoulder of her white satin robe. She drew back her hand and looked at the red drops on her fingers, lost in awe.

"*I ... don't know,*" Lucy said. "*I ... need time.*"

"Take as long as you want," I said. "But each day alive, the sands of time pass, and even my powers can't reclaim them. Your eternal youth begins the day you join me."

"I ... must go home," Lucy said. "Please ... can I see you ... transform again?"

"I can be other shapes, too, but they are more effort," I said. "Transformation is taxing, so I don't do it often, and only in one form can I reach home before dawn. When you've joined me, I promise, I'll show you everything."

I stood up, took her hand, and kissed it.

"Farewell, Lucy, my love," I said. "I leave you to the bale daylight, but I'll be yours again, at this same time, tomorrow night, right here."

Lucy's smile beamed; *she needed no words to accept my proposal.* My heart sang, and I released her and stepped back, pleased she wished to watch me. *She wouldn't be able to transform for at least a century, but what is a century to immortals?* I stared at her, sitting upon that bench in the moonlight, her fiery hair, her emerald eyes, the taste of her filling every corner of my being. I memorized her image; only it would support me until we were together again.

Be the bat!

I arose on August the 27th just before the sun set, and wandered impatiently about my house. Renfield had been cleaning, and had set up a dining room table with chairs, which he must've found in another room. *I'd have to purchase more brandy to reward him.* Donning my cloak and hat, I fetched my newspapers and read them until the light of the sun had fully left the sky.

Immediately I walked to the station, purchased eight bottles of brandy, and paid to have them delivered to my residence early tomorrow, during the day, with instructions to leave them on my doorstep if no one was at home. Then I hailed a hansom cab, rode west to another district, and then proceeded to Hillingham in comfort ... without transforming.

On my ride, I reflected upon the change of my mental acuity. I felt excited and alive, eager to be with Lucy again. My world wasn't filled with darkness, as I'd so often perceived: *I was in love!*

I smiled at the thought, at which I'd have once scowled. I was never in darkness. I'd allowed guilt over my father's death ... and Lucinda's murder ... to fill up my soul, and spilled my darkness onto everything around me. I'd hated myself for what I'd done. I'd locked myself in a crumbling prison and taken prisoners to insure my dreary and dour moods.

I'd been in love before. Loritá was my first, a beauty so mesmerizing I couldn't bear the idea of not making her immortal. But she hated me for converting her, and at first, she wished to kill herself, and then plotted revenge against me. As the centuries passed, her greatest triumph became inducing others to betray me without leaving a single clue pointing toward her involvement.

Miëta was to take me away from Loritá's untrustworthy nature, which I'd assumed came from her rebellious peasant-upbringing. Miëta was born of a Chinese emperor, raised in a palace, and as meek and mild a girl as I'd ever seen. She was beautiful, poised, cultured, educated, and well-bred; I was certain she'd be my immortal queen forever. But Miëta possessed her father's wrathful temper, and reacted accordingly ... once I'd taken her away from his control. Transformed, and as powerful physically as mentally, Miëta was free to be the woman she truly was: *demanding and intolerant.* She reveled in her freedom, and discovered the joys of subjecting others to torture, to further elevate herself.

Hēlgrēth was supposed to save me from Miëta, my greatest mistake, as she was soft and demure, as gentle as a flower. Hēlgrēth and I were exceedingly happy, but she was unwise, her mind unequal to the manipulations of Loritá and Miëta, who slowly twisted her into a creature of insatiable hungers. I'd thought a wife of lesser intelligence would placate me, but I was wrong, and I learned to my regret what men who prefer servants to wives often learn: *nothing separates two people as much as differences of mind.*

There were others, taken upon a whim, but most didn't last three months. Few mortals can endure the price of immortality, or overcome the fears of their religious beliefs, and they don't suffer long. Some kill themselves, running out into the daylight, and some attempted to slay me; *daylight would be a blessing compared to what I did to them.* Disloyalty was the one crime I couldn't tolerate, for such a sickness infects all those with whom it shares company. I collected all of their names in my diaries, which I greatly missed. I needed to keep making diary entries, but my preoccupation with Lucy drove all thoughts of documentation from my head ... *all a man in love cares about is his heart.*

Had I finally forgiven myself for my father and Lucinda's murders? Was that the change that had come over me? Was that why I'd finally left the crumbling ruin of my past to walk in the light of intellectuals?

Would I ever truly know?

I arrived at the gate to Lucy's manor and paid my driver, and then waited for him to depart. It was almost midnight, and I could sense Lucy was still in her house, so I took my time, strolling along lanes lined with flowers and young cherry trees, their pink blossoms long ago fallen, their branches now bare. The time and effort English people take to make their lands into gardens amazed me, yet I couldn't fault them for their attentiveness to detail and desire to bring all appearances under their control. Most of the customs of my homeland centered around functionality rather than appearance, and I understood that logic, but English ways seemed more elevated and sophisticated.

I arrived at the bench where Lucy had let me kiss her, but she wasn't there. I sat upon the bench and waited, and soon hurried footsteps approached.

"*Vlad ...!*" Lucy called, but there was an urgency to her voice.

"What is it, my dear?" I asked, delighted to see her.

"I can't stay," Lucy said, running up to me. "Arthur and his friends are drinking and smoking, and I must hurry back before I'm missed."

"How long are they likely to stay?" I asked.

"I don't know ... perhaps all night," Lucy said. "I have to hurry back ..."

"Do you want to stay?" I asked.

Lucy froze, and looked suddenly sad.

"Vlad, I'm confused," Lucy said. "This choice ... it's a terrible thing to ask of me. I want two lives, and I have but one ..."

"I could make this choice for you, but I told you what happened with Hēlgrēth, Loritá, and Miëta," I said. "You'd eventually blame me ..."

"I've thought about that, and I'm sure you're right," Lucy said. "No, I'll make this decision. Just please ... give me more time ..."

"My love, time is one thing we have in abundance," I said.

"Will you return tomorrow?" Lucy asked. "Please?"

"If you wish it," I said.

Lucy hesitated, and then suddenly she pushed herself forward into my arms and kissed my lips. It was a quick kiss, yet she pulled back with a smile, and then ran away, returning the way she came.

I didn't need to transform; I could've floated home.

It was a considerable walk to reach a district in Hillingham from where I could hail a cab. After several hours of riding, musing upon the kiss Lucy had given me, I arrived at a pub not far from my house. I didn't enter directly, but walked the length of the avenue and back, smiling at those whom I passed and doffing my hat to each lady, all of whom lightly curtsied to me, and some of whom giggled as I passed by. Most were young women who seemed attracted to my appearance. It was pleasant to be accorded the same courtesy and good humor as any other gentleman.

My love of England was growing.

I purchased a newspaper which I had delivered to at my estate, but which I'd only skimmed through in my haste to see Lucy. Inside the tavern, I was recognized by the bartender from my previous visits, and he poured me a foaming beer and greeted me as a friend. This was perhaps the most attractive aspect of life in England; my last *'friend'* had deserted Castle Drăculea with all of the others, within a year of my discovery of my curse, and I'd lived so long without friendship I'd forgotten the comforts it brings. I felt quite at home, sitting at a small table in the tavern, despite being surrounded by total strangers. I even caught a few friendly eyes glancing at me as I consumed every word in my newspaper. Occasionally I lifted my beer to my lips and pretended to drink, and no one seemed to notice the amount of beer in my glass never declined.

Beside the barman and myself, only five others remained in the tavern at this late hour, a couple of young men sitting together, and two elderly men toasting a woman of questionable morality, for whom they frequently bought another drink. Finally the trio departed, and when the two young men finally stood, I paid for my drink and departed. I considered following and consuming them both, but we were close to my house and I was simply in too good a mood; *no need to spoil it with murder.* I wasn't famished; Lucy's blood still energized me, and I was reluctant to spoil its taste with the sourness of strangers.

Renfield was sitting before a crackling fire in my house, staring at the flames. Beside him was another empty bottle. He moved to stand as I entered the room, but I waved him back down.

"You may wish to remain here, if you can, longer than before," I said. "A delivery of more brandy will be arriving today."

"Thank you, Master," Renfield said. "It's been nice, staying here, instead of locked in my cell."

"You seem to be able to escape at will," I said.

"The watchman on my new floor sleeps all night long," Renfield said. "In the basement, the watchman checked my cell each night."

"No problem with egress?" I asked.

"I stole a knife from the kitchens and carved out the wood around my bars," Renfield said. "There's a big oak tree just outside my window, and I can climb its branches easily enough. Master, may I ask you a question?"

"Of course," I said.

"Is my soul damned?"

I fell silent, and we stared at each other over a valley of social and intellectual dissimilarities.

"What makes you believe you have a soul?" I asked slowly.

"Why ... everyone has a soul!" Renfield insisted.

"Do they?" I asked. "Now think, Renfield; if everyone has a soul, then it's a common commodity; why would you care?"

"I ... *fear,*" Renfield said. *"Lakes of fire, pitchforks, ..."*

"What's a soul?" I asked. "Surely, if you value souls, then you must know what they are?"

"I ... well, no one really knows," Renfield says.

"Not true," I said. "What if every person on Earth has a different definition of what a soul is, and one person is right; how would that one person know that they alone possess the truth? To believe in something, no matter what it is, doesn't mean you know the truth. The question is: who would you trust to tell you if your definition of a soul is true?"

"God," Renfield said.

"Anyone ... closer to London ...?" I asked, amused. "A priest ...? A bishop ...? A pope ...?"

Renfield stared at me, his jaw slightly trembling, but making no sound.

"If you'd trust no one to answer your question correctly, then why ask me?"

Renfield considered this briefly.

"I'm sorry, Master," Renfield said. "I ..."

"I intend to answer your question, Renfield," I said. "However, before you hear my answer, let's be honest; you don't trust me to know the truth."

"Only God knows all truths," Renfield said.

"Ahh, that's another question entirely, which I don't think will serve us to dwell upon tonight," I said. "I've pondered upon these questions for centuries, and I'll share my conclusions with you, if you wish, but I don't expect you to accept them, nor will there be any punishment if you deny them. You're free to believe what you will."

Renfield held his breath expectantly, but I took my time and spoke slowly.

"A soul isn't something you have," I said. "A body is something you have. A soul is something you are. I believe a soul is human potential, which every child is born with, to arise and be more than what we are at the start of our lives. Some choose to be lazy and do nothing, and the worth of their soul reflects this. Some choose to be selfish and arrogant, and they're shunned by other souls. Some, such as you, my friend, seek similarity with others, and combine to make one great, unanimous whole. Others arise to the top, outshining all others. No demons jab pitchforks into the seared flesh of damned souls, but the consequences of some choices, like regret, can be a Hell unto itself. What a terrible thing it'd be to spend eternity trapped in regret!

"It's you, Renfield, who must answer to your own conscience as to whether or not you're content with the fulfillment you've given to the infinite potential with which you were born."

Renfield pondered this long, which seemed a great effort, and I kept silent and let him think. Thinking is a rare activity for some, and the deeper one thinks, the deeper one's able to think. I grinned, for I've always believed common men, such as Renfield, could think as deeply as a philosopher, if they tried, but most shun thinking for fear it'd ostracize them from their social order. A pity; *such people deny themselves the very answers they most-dearly desire.*

"Thank you, Master," Renfield said. "I've ... never thought of souls this way."

"I'm not finished," I said.

"There's more ...?" Renfield asked.

"Oh, yes," I said. "Whenever you ask a question such as this, whether you get an answer or not, you must ask yourself this: *why do you want to know?"*

Renfield looked hesitant, as if disturbed by this question.

"What are souls used for?" I asked. "Not 'what does God use souls for?' or 'what are souls?', but 'what do humans use souls for?'. Many inventions of man have been used for purposes unintended by their creators; why would men not use souls however they can?

"As souls have no definition which everyone agrees upon, it's easy to attribute to them qualities God didn't include," I explained. "Roman emperors believed souls were unequal, that their natures were naturally and undeniably superior. Wealthy families, the nobility, and religious zealots ascribe to this same assumption.

"In fact, by assuming a natural superiority that needs no proof, few of the nobility develop the motivation to attempt great deeds, and thus they often accomplish nothing.

"If your goal is to simply understand souls, then wait, and God will tell you. If you believe your soul makes you naturally superior, then you're condemning yourself to failure."

"How can you say that ...?" Renfield asked. *"More than any man I've ever met, you seek to be more than you were born to!"*

"I do indeed," I said. "But I seek my ambitions through my own accomplishments, not because I believe I began any differently than you. Mentally, physically, and financially, I was born your superior. Spiritually, we began the same ... as all men do."

I laid a comforting hand upon Renfield's shoulder, and tried to offer sympathy, but he pulled away.

"But ... Master, if you're cursed ... and I drank your ....?" Renfield began, and I smiled.

"Don't fear for your soul," I said. "God can reward ... or punish. Only your choices will affect His judgement."

Renfield stared at the carpet, then lifted his eyes to look at me. I didn't know what he was thinking, and I didn't care enough to penetrate his thoughts. Finally he drew himself away, turned to the fire, and stared at the flames.

I left him to ponder these mysteries. *I'd more important matters.*

Yet, as I descended the steps to the chamber below my chapel, Renfield's questions haunted me. If I alone never die, then I alone will never stand before God or be privy to His wisdom. Yet that thought assumed a benevolent God, not one who'd curse me as He'd done. This was a war, me against God; either I'd rise up and become master of all mankind, or God Himself must intervene. I'd spent centuries avoiding this war, certain I couldn't win, yet I'd hide from His challenge no more. My existence was a blessing or a curse; soon I'd know which.

My brief meeting with Lucy would've infuriated me ... *if not for her kiss.* That had surprised me, and I'm not easily startled. She was considering leaving Arthur, but she couldn't decide quickly; this meant she was giving my offer deep thought, which was promising. Had she forsaken Arthur without hesitation, would that've meant she had no loyalty or honor? But she hadn't, so I was free to assume the best of her.

Was I deceiving myself because of a brief infatuation?

Evening awoke me with a start: *someone was outside my coffin!*

Alarmed, I reached out with my senses and felt a male presence standing right beside my coffin, upon my mound of Transylvanian dirt. I prepared myself for violent action, but his familiarity calmed me: *Renfield.*

Bracing myself, in case he dared attack, I lifted my lid only to find him staring down at me with wild, flaring eyes and a maniacal smile, one hand holding high a glowing lantern.

"Master ...!" Renfield cried excitedly. *"Master, I'm ready!"*

"Stand back!" I commanded Renfield in a tone he couldn't disobey, and he instantly stepped out of my view. I arose, and found him retreated halfway down my stone stairs, but still facing me, almost panting: *Renfield was lost in his madness again.*

"Master, forgive me ...," he started.

"Did I not command you never to enter here?" I growled, barely containing my fury. *" Why have you disobeyed?"*

"Master, I've come to accept your bargain!" Renfield said, eager as a puppy and twice as energetic. "I want to be like you! Today! Now!"

"You defy my orders, and then beg a boon ...?" I asked.

"Make me a vampire!" Renfield demanded.

"Get down!" I shouted. "Down! You're unworthy to stand on this ground!"

A dozen emotions flashed across his face: anger, resentment, fear, delight, concern, determination, confusion, and pure joy. Yet he stepped backwards, down my steps, and I followed.

"Please ...!" Renfield begged.

"Silence!" I shouted, my voice driving into his brain so deeply he had no choice but to obey.

Renfield froze, his mind overcome.

"Do you no longer wish to serve me?" I asked.

"*No, Master!*" Renfield said. "*I mean, yes! I'll serve you forever!*"

"How can you serve me as a vampire?" I asked. "How can you tend my garden, my flowers that bloom only in the sun, or accept deliveries to my house in the daytime, as a creature of the night?"

"*I ...!*" Renfield began, but he had no answer.

"You begged for a taste of my blood," I said. "The very next day you cursed me for giving it to you. What will happen tomorrow if I sire you tonight?"

"*I beg you ...!*" Renfield said, his hands held out, palms up, grasping at air as if my will could be caught in his palms. "*Please ...!*"

"No," I said. "You'll continue ..."

The madness in his eyes gave me warning, and as he jumped at me, I dodged with the speed of a Transylvanian soldier, deftly caught his fist, and flung him to the ground. Renfield practically bounced to his feet and jumped at me again, but this time I had range and preparedness; with a fist hardened by centuries, backed by vampiric strength, I punched the left side of his head, just even with his eye. Renfield flew backwards and toppled to the ground, and for a moment I feared I'd granted his wish.

A groan uttered from his prostrate form, and his back rose and fell with heavy breaths, face-down upon the dirt floor of my chamber.

"*You will obey me!*" I said softly but forcibly, inferring unspoken threats. "*You live until I give you permission to die!*"

I reached down and picked up the fallen lantern by its woven-bark cord, which allowed it to be carried safely. The lamp's fire hadn't been extinguished, and shadows danced wildly as it swung.

"*Arise!*" I commanded, using all of my persuasion. He climbed shakily to his feet; he would've fallen were my mental powers not holding him upright.

"Learn the folly of defiance," I said, and I held up the glowing lantern. "Learn who's your master ... and why you must obey."

Through his daze, Renfield looked more frightened than I'd ever seen him. He tried to speak, yet I hadn't allowed him voice. I grasped his lantern by its bottom, and let its cord hang.

"*Reach out your hand,*" I commanded him. "*Place it atop the lantern.*"

Despite my dominance, Renfield hesitated; the metal top of the lantern was burning hot, sure to cook living flesh. The bark-cord existed to protect its carrier from burns.

"*Place your hand upon the lantern!*"

Forcing him with my mind, Renfield slowly lifted his arm. His trembling hand, with splayed fingers, rose over the lit, glowing lantern, and there it froze, unwilling to descend.

"*Obey me!*"

Renfield lowered his hand, and the hiss of searing flesh meshed with his cry of anguish. His face contorted into an expression familiar only to torturers. I held him totally, but the scorching of his flesh engendered writhings of his body even I couldn't dominate. The anguish of his burns resounded through his mind and reflected into mine, yet I gritted my teeth and endured as long as I could. Fifteen eternal seconds passed, and then I released him. He collapsed upon the ground, whimpering and clutching his branded hand.

"There's no madness greater than mine," I warned Renfield. "Never disobey me again! Now leave this chamber, and never enter it again! *Now! Or I'll char your other hand!*"

Blubbering, he crawled, one slow inch at a time, upon elbows and knees, clutching his wrist and sobbing. I severed our connection, which I needed no more. The scars of this branding would forever remind him of the penalty for striking his master. Not that I could allow this twice; *if he attacked me again then he'd greet the dawn headless.*

When we reached the top of the stairs, I seized and drug him to the front of my chapel, where I flung him to a heap before the altar, beneath the hanging stone cross.

"*Pray!*" I commanded him. "Pray to your God, if you think He'll save you. Let Him heal your hand, if He can, but don't expect it. God heeds not the prayers of men, nor rewards those who serve Him. Fear God! Or rather: *fear me, for I'm His instrument, and the torments you feel shall pale if you ever disobey me again!*"

Renfield cowered, cringing, trapped between God and me.

"Don't be here when I return, but be back in this chapel tomorrow night, ready to serve me ... *or else!*"

I walked away, convinced that Renfield's service couldn't last much longer. His madness was too dangerous to be allowed to carry my secrets. *Soon I'd have to kill him ... permanently.*

In my mailbox, beside my newspapers, I found letters from three different accountants, each detailing monies received and deposits made, and I quickly calculated my current assets. I needed to pay more attention to my finances, and devote more time to making business contacts, integrating myself with magnates who managed vast sums of wealth, that through them, and their manipulations, I could expand my worth into the fortune I needed.

Yet pursuing wealth would steal time from my associations with Lucy, which I could ill-afford. She was taking her time, making her momentous decision carefully, and upon that decision much of my future would be decided. If I didn't flame her desires and ambitions, I could lose her to her insignificant fiancé, Arthur, son of Lord Godalming. I had to stay near Lucy until she chose me.

An hour I attended to my required correspondences, and then I donned my hat, cloak, and brolly, for it was raining again. This boded ill for my meeting with Lucy, but I hurried to the station and hailed a covered phaéton, repeating my usual path.

Rain was falling even harder as I arrived, and I was delighted to find Lucy's mind already searching for mine, or at least, open for contact when I searched for hers. I informed her I'd wait for her inside the gazebo, and she agreed. Twenty minutes later, as I sat in the gazebo, Lucy appeared, in a modest green dress, wearing a thick shawl over her head and shoulders to protect her from the rain.

"Count Drăcula," Lucy inclined her head toward me.

I reached for her hand, but she offered it reluctantly.

"Count Drăcula, I ...," she began, as if reciting a prepared speech.

"Please, call me Vlad," I said, purposefully disrupting her flow.

Lucy sighed and began again.

"Vlad, I want you to know how honored I am by your offer," Lucy said. "As you're a foreigner, I'm sure you don't perceive how improper your proposal is."

"It's true I don't grasp all the social idioms of England," I said. "Is it proper for a woman to marry a man she doesn't love?"

Lucy seemed disturbed by my question.

"Please, Vlad, let me finish ...," Lucy said.

"I'll hear you out, but then you must promise to listen," I said.

Lucy nodded, then continued.

"As enticing as your offer may be, once a woman has given her word, then she can't impugn her honor, or the honor of her family, by redacting it. I've given Arthur my pledge to marry, and I can't undo that. I must ask you to be a gentleman and stop meeting with me in secret, for I can't be true to my word and continue with this charade. My pledge is given. You must now pledge to me that you'll stop coming here ... and never use any of your mind-tricks upon me again. You must promise to leave Arthur and I alone."

I stood, impassively waiting for her passion to expend itself, and to let her espouse every argument she had. However, she said nothing more, breathing rather deeply, as if she'd just endured a hardship.

"I see," I said at last. "You wish to end our ... clandestine meetings ... so you can be true to your word, and incarcerate yourself in a loveless marriage ..."

"I ... love Arthur," Lucy interrupted, but there was a hesitancy in her voice.

" ... and you wish to willingly grow old, wrinkled, and gray, instead of being young and beautiful forever. You'll gladly die, despite that I offer you immortality ..."

Lucy shuddered and looked down.

"Arthur's my fiancé," she said.

"Arthur's a good, sturdy man, if not a deep thinker," I continued. "I'm an immortal power, the strongest and wisest man on Earth, and the most travelled. I'm a prince by birth, while Arthur's father is only a member of the House of Lords, and there's no certainty his son will rise to attain his father's minor nobility. Arthur would make you his pretty housewife, to cook and sew and compliment him, while I offer you a throne, not only the monarchy of a nation, but of a new world order I shall install, and that shall last until God Himself chooses to end it."

"I've no choice," Lucy said.

"With Arthur, you've no choice," I said. "You're smarter than Arthur by far, and for a lesser mind to ignore your advice is a travesty of intellect. Married to Arthur, you may be disregarded for a brandy and a cigar, for the company of his favorite gallants, or for the adventure of a night free of you, whereas I seek to share your company not only every minute of every night, but I'd extend your existence to forever so I may never be deprived of you. You have a choice, Lucy: you could spend your evenings, to the end of eternity, regretting having impugned your honor while you sit upon the throne of the Earth, envied and admired, the culmination of your every dream ... or you can spend it alone, surrounded by maids and servants, fretting about where your husband is and why he stays out so late, and wondering, as old age creeps upon you, why you gave up eternal youth and beauty for the sake of a few words spoken in childish innocence."

Lucy looked abashed and said nothing, but I could also hold my tongue, and no mortal was as practiced at patience as I.

"You know ... so much, how can you not see right through me?" Lucy said. "I'm a ... prize to be won, an airy fairy, whom others have shielded from the world just to keep me innocent. I've never had a single real responsibility, or been punished for being disobedient. I flit about my social circle like a queen, although I know my family's money bought my crown ..."

"You deserve more than any mortal could give," I said.

"Who could remake me more than you ...?" Lucy demanded.

"Remake you ...?" I asked, unable to keep from laughing. *"It's I whom you must remake!"*

Lucy looked stunned, and I shook my head.

"I buried myself in shadows ... for centuries," I said. "When I left Transylvania, I carried my darkness. Not until I stood in your light were my shadows banished, and I stand before you remade, a happy man, willing to be remade again and again, as will doubtlessly happen in any immortal life.

"Lucy, we can't bind ourselves to the customs and traditions of any one time or place. Like Henry V said in Shakespeare's great play: *'We are the makers of manners'*. I seek not a trophy to sit idly beside me; my God-given powers can remake the world, but I need a wise and worthy queen ... to influence me, to keep me in the light ... to help me become the summit of all a man can. I need you, Lucy, to forever dispel my darkness, and help me shape every nation into the paradise it should be ..."

I paused, reached out a finger to lift her soft chin, and waited for her tear-dripping eyes to open.

"... or you can be a respectable housewife, doting on charities that'll never change anything, and wondering whose company your husband keeps when he isn't with you."

"Arthur would never do that," Lucy said.

"Other women's husbands do, and their wives wouldn't have married them if they'd thought they would," I said. "I do seek to persuade you Lucy, but the final choice is yours. Make the choice that's right for you."

"Lucy?" called Arthur's voice from the house. *"Lucy ...?"*

Lucy looked back.

"They'll come looking if I don't return," Lucy said.

"Must another evening be cut short?" I asked.

"After my *'sleepwalking'*, they're checking upon me," Lucy said. "I don't know when we'll get the chance to talk together ..."

"If you meet me at the gate, I'll bring a carriage, and we can ride around London all night," I said. "Tomorrow ...?"

"Tomorrow night I'll be at the opera," Lucy said. "And I must ask you, as a gentleman, not to call upon me again."

Not waiting for a reply, Lucy stepped out of the gazebo, into the rain, and hurried back to her house. I watched her go ... and smiled.

Opera ...?

Chapter 10

There were no unattended boxes at the opera, but three seats in a 2nd row of a box were available, so I purchased them all. The opera was Le nozze di Teti e di Peleo, written by Francesco Cavalli, and the poster inside the theater foyer said it was Cavalli's first opera, originally performed at the Venetian opera house Teatro San Cassiano on January 24, 1639 – *I was only 208 years old.*

The seven seats in my box I'd not bought were occupied by three elderly ladies, one of immense girth, and two young couples. The young men flipped a coin to determine which couple would sit up front with the ladies and which sat in my row. They were a friendly group, and introductions were formal and full of charming absurdities, both young men purposefully mistaking the age of the elderly ladies for women in their twenties, which made the elderly women giggle and titter. I was forced to shake hands with both of the men, who spoke deferentially to me, who was clearly their elder, and I kissed a hand of each lady, and then we sat down as the curtains were drawn apart.

A mythological theme graced this opera, which portrayed the wedding of Peleus and Thetis, and the infamous Judgment of Paris: Zeus held a banquet in celebration of their marriage, as Peleus and Thetis were to be the parents of Achilles. But Eris, the Goddess of Discord, was angered for not being invited, and so Eris arrived at the celebration with a golden apple from the Garden of Hesperides. Upon the prized apple was engraved the words *'For the Fairest'*, and she placed the apple in the center of a ring of goddesses.

Hera, Athena, and Aphrodite all claimed the sole right to the golden apple. Zeus was pressured to judge which of them was fairest, but fearful of insulting two powerful goddesses, Zeus declared that Paris, a Trojan mortal, would choose who was the fairest. Each goddess bribed Paris: Hera offered to make him king of Europe and Asia. Athena offered him wisdom and skill in war. Yet Aphrodite offered him the hand of the world's most beautiful woman, Helen of Sparta, wife of King Menelaus of Greece; Paris accepted Aphrodite's gift, and his choice sparked the Trojan War.

However, the opera was badly performed. The role of Thetis was sung by a terrible soprano, and Zeus by a bass so low his words were barely discernable. Eris, the Goddess of Discord, had a contralto voice that matched her character in its inability to hold a single note for more than a few seconds.

However, I wasn't there to enjoy the play. With ease I sensed for Lucy, and I quickly caught sight of her perfect pale face and scarlet locks. Instantly her head snapped to face me, and her eyes widened in fear; *she'd felt our connection.* I smiled at her, but she only glared, and then she took Arthur's arm and resolutely faced the stage. I noted which box they were in, determined to call upon them.

At the intermission, I proceeded quickly through the crowd and found them putting on coats and preparing to leave; doubtlessly Lucy wanted to avoid a confrontation, but I approached Arthur, held out my hand, and reintroduced myself. Fortunately, he remembered me from his engagement party.

"Count Drăcula, I was hoping we'd meet again," Arthur said, and he gestured to two men standing beside him. "You remember my American friend, Mr. Quincey Morris, and Dr. John Seward …"

"… The noted physician and psychiatrist," I said, and I shook each of their hands. "Gentleman, the honor of our first meeting is repeated … and an even greater pleasure."

Both men thanked me, but Lucy intervened.

"Darling Arthur, I may faint …," Lucy said.

"Forgive us, Count Drăcula, but Lucy's feeling ill, and we're departing," Arthur said.

"How unfortunate," I said to Lucy. "I enjoyed your celebration so much; I'd hoped for the opportunity to get to know you better, and share with you stories of my homeland."

"That sounds wonderful," Arthur said. "We're giving a dinner party on the 2nd of September, and we'd be delighted if you'd attend."

"I'm sure the count can't accept an invitation so soon …," Lucy started, but I laughed.

"I'd be honored, but I've business that'll keep me occupied until almost sunset," I said.

"If needed, we'll hold dinner for you," Arthur said. "Darkness is the proper setting for tales of the wild Carpathians."

"Indeed," I smiled, and Lucy glared at me. "Ahh, the curtain rises; I pray that your health returns, dear Lucy, and I will be your guest on September the 2nd."

Lucy seemed shocked and speechless, and Dr. Seward insisted they hurry to depart. I excused myself and returned to my box. The second act of the play was as dreary as the first, but I sat excited.

When I returned home, after feasting upon a drunkard in the alley behind the theater, I found Renfield missing, but after a brief search I found him deep in a back room, performing the cleaning I'd commanded. He bowed, circumspect; his burned hand heavily bandaged, doubtlessly still aching, but he was no longer in his rampant *'mindless exuberism'* state. He apologized for attacking me. I was pleased, for I now had a dining room fit for company, should the need arise, even if I had yet to hire cooks or purchase table settings. I informed him his presence wouldn't be needed for a while, and to return and stay in his cell until I called him. Without hesitation, Renfield promised to obey.

Three days I'd have to wait before the party, and I intended to use them well. I went out at sunset, as early as I could stand, and sought to enlist the locals in conversation about the wealthiest men in London, and how one could gain admittance to their circles. Several laughed, claiming the only way to get near wealth was to have so much money they invited you into their circle. Once there, they'd strip you of your wealth, and if they succeeded, then they'd kick you out. If they didn't succeed, then they'd resent being stuck with you; thus did the wealthiest men loathe each other yet share company... because no one else could abide them.

New topics of interest were discussed. The town of Ambiky had been captured by France, and this defeat was greeted by locals with angry frowns. However, in the Sudan, General Kitchener, the governor of the Egyptian Provinces of Eastern Sudan and Red Sea, had captured and occupied Berber, a city north of Khartoum, and this was greeted as proof of the *'British Right to Rule the World'*. Lastly, an inventor named Thomas Edison had applied for a patent for some device called a moving-pictures camera, and many arguments ensued over how pictures could be made to move.

Yet none of this, certainly not *'moving pictures'*, was likely to enhance my finances, so I excused myself. Apparently my best hope of garnering financial advice from the wealthy would have to wait until Lucy and Arthur's dinner party, where I'd be introduced to people whose company I couldn't yet afford to buy.

In the end, on the 1st of September, I bought myself a fresh new suit for the party, along with a black silk cape and top hat, of which I was assured were of the latest fashions, and I contented myself to be prepared; *I needed to be strengthened for my excursion to Hillingham.* I took a carriage ride to the London docks and found a pretty young prostitute willing to surrender to me *'anything I wanted'* for two crowns. On her corpse, I left two crowns.

My thoughts dwelt on Lucy, for she'd be dreading this dinner. I amused myself thinking of the many ways she might try to circumvent my arrival, yet she had no way of knowing where I lived. I smiled at her conundrum, but then I frowned; *I was taking a great risk.* What if Lucy did find a way to thwart me ... *or chose to reject me?* I wasn't considering every possibility. My thoughts were rapid, flitting quickly like flashes of lightning. Love, especially new love, whose passions set fire to your smallest arteries, was a thought-killer, sedating even the wisdom of sages. By accepting love, I was accepting a weakness I wouldn't have tolerated in Transylvania.

Love was a poison. Love seeped into the soul like a disease ... and couldn't be commanded to leave. *Could I leave England forever, even if I chose to, never to see my Lucy again?* Such thoughts I could contemplate, but my performance was doubtful. I was enjoying my new love, my new life, more than I'd ever enjoyed anything. I'd taught myself to shun humanity for shame of my infernal diet, but my need for humanity had remanifested with familiarity. Without fear or shame, I was suddenly human again.

Yet I couldn't deny myself from celebrating my upcoming triumph I'd hidden from for so long. My place in humanity was at the very top; *it was time I assumed the throne God had obviously empowered me to attain.*

Only then would I be avenged on God for the curse He'd inflicted upon me.

I smiled, feeling the sensations of imagined royal power wash over me. In dreams I was no different than any mortal. Imagined tantalizations swell the senses and feel more marvelous than their realizations. Reality would make a prison of my throne, where global responsibilities and formal duties would pile before me until I wearied of leaving my coffin. But, until I arise to that acknowledged supremacy, my anticipation of perfection would propel my actions.

"Count Drăcula, here by invitation," I said to the butler.

"It is my honor, sir," the butler said with a tone that meant he couldn't care less, yet he stepped back and invited me in with a formal bow and a gesture, and I dismissed his lie as unimportant. "The party is gathered, sir, and dinner will be ready soon."

I surrendered my cloak and hat to the butler, and he escorted me to a grand, ornate room where a lovely blonde lady was playing a piano with amazing skill. I stood in the doorway until she'd finished, and I entered as her applause began.

"Count Drăcula!" exclaimed Arthur Holmwood, seeing me cross the room. "Welcome! So glad you came!"

"My honor and my pleasure," I said, feigning a smile at Lucy's intended, and my eyes scanned the room until I found her, trembling, staring at me as deer stare at the wolf. I was invading her native environment, and inserting myself into the company of her fiancé, with the shared understanding I desired to prevent their marriage.

Even in her distress Lucy was beautiful.

Arthur rushed forward to shake my hand.

"Dinner is nearly ready," Arthur said. "The cook has been anxious for an hour, but he's an honest man and does his duty well. Come, let me introduce you around, and after dinner you must tell us of the mysteries of your homeland."

I felt like a prized trinket on display, yet I allowed Arthur to introduce me to his other guests, all of whom attempted to estimate my wealth solely by my appearance and titles, as if birth alone were the measure of a man. Their voices and mannerisms told far more about their greed, and their fears, than their words, but these were the very aristocrats I needed to help me invest wisely, the sources of information upon which I'd amass my fortune. I was formally courteous to all of them, introducing myself by shaking or kissing hands. Many were true bluebloods, and the scent of them was quite piquant and pungent, backed by generations of selective breeding, which the poor never manage. *I'd love to feed upon them.*

Dr. Seward welcomed me, and Quincey promised to counter my tales of Transylvania with stories of the 'wild west' of America, which I was interested to hear, as no white men had lived west of the Great River when I'd explored those lands.

At last we came to Lucy, and she greeted me with her usual gaiety, but I could hear the tremulations in her voice which she masked to all but me.

"It's always a pleasure to greet a lady of such excellent taste," I said, and I extended my arm to gesture at the furnishings, yet she knew that I meant more.

Lucy flinched, and raised a protective hand to touch the tiny scars which she'd hidden under a gold-laced choker around her lovely neck. *She'd invited me to drink from her, but she couldn't reveal that before her fiancé and guests.*

"There's no one I'd greet more warmly than a *true gentleman*," Lucy said to me, reminding me of her final words at our last clandestine meeting.

"Ah, the definition of a *'true gentleman'* differs in England from that of other lands," I replied. "I pray I may rise to the expectations of my hostess."

"I pray the same," Lucy said warningly.

As predicted, the summons for dinner came from the cook; Arthur listened to his whispers, which my enhanced hearing clearly heard, and then he made the announcement himself. As if tired of waiting, everyone rose at once, apparently having expected dinner sooner, but the sky had been free of clouds, and I couldn't fly here until night had fully fallen.

Dinner was a commensal delight, each platter colorful and steaming, as if prepared to please the eye as fully as the mouth. I do admire the taste of food, but it's a pale comparison to the warm richness of my traditional diet. I knew I'd be sick later, but I'd suffer that, and consider it worthwhile, in exchange for my intrigues of this night.

Lucy and I exchanged many furtive glances, and she appeared deeply concerned, such that several ladies commented on her quietness and inquired about her health. Lucy brushed off their concerns and pretended to assume her normalcy of effervescent joy, yet I heard her worried voice as if she were sobbing aloud.

I tried a bit of New Guinea fowl, which I'd never seen before, and vegetables that tasted as if they'd been cooked in a heavy gravy, but mostly I only picked at my food, for I'd no desire to make myself any sicker than I must. I engaged my time listening to the discussions around me, pretending interest in the gossip, at least about those absent from our dinner party. I was seated between a man who stank of tobacco, who seemed uninterested in any matter not involving business, and a married woman whose husband was travelling, who wanted to hear my opinion on everything, and who claimed propriety but seemed to take a personal pleasure in touching my arm with her fingers.

Finally I was rescued from her malapropos attentions by my host, who called upon me to speak.

"As you promised, tell us of your homelands, Count Drăcula," Arthur said.

"You would scarce recognize the pigeon-hearted peasants of my homeland as people," I said. "Transylvania is a pious, God-fearing country, far more than England, and inerudite, lacking sophistications common on your island. Seldom does any man or woman walk about without a protective crucifix, and never at night, when the infernals, absent from your modern island, stalk men's souls."

"*Infernals ...?*" Dr. Seward asked. "Are these local superstitions?"

"Young nations enjoy the blessings of God, but in days before your civilization existed, when terrors of the Old Testament visited mankind, demonstrations of God's anger were often wrought upon the unlucky," I said. "Those immortal curses of God still haunt remote milieus, avoided by those who fear them, but well-known by the inhabitants of primeval sanctums who, more than any young races, understand why God must be feared. The English boast universities of the highest intellects on Earth, and professors possessed of the summit of man's knowledge, but your scientists have yet to expose these horrors ... and live to report their existence. It's my hope to bring English enlightenment to my country, to illuminate shadows which evade detection. Only then may modern exploration and investigation reach into mysteries more ancient than your culture, and discover secrets buried by centuries of fear. Upon that day, I hope your intellectuals and my people may become equals, and join in the confrontations of these mysteries."

"*Gentlemen!*" Lucy raised her voice in earnest objection. "There are ladies present, and I fear this conversation may overwhelm them."

"Forgive me, Miss Westenra," I said. "I forget that the ladies of England are frail and delicate ... compared to women of my lands."

"Now that comparison I want in my ears!" Quincey Morris spoke up. "Exactly how do your women size up?"

This caused a titter of laughter around the table, and the young lady sitting beside Quincey playfully slapped his thickly-muscled arm.

"Not all of the terrors of the Carpathians are unknown by science," I said. "I've seen a young mother fling herself upon a wolf attacking her children, fighting barehanded to protect her offspring with no less savagery than the wildest beast. I once witnessed a woman dash into a burning house, heedless of injury, to rescue her elderly father. Yet I've also watched a devout woman willingly take her own life, rather than surrender her soul to one of those infernals whom you would call a 'superstition' ..."

"*Vlad ...!*" Lucy shouted.

I grinned, and many dinner guests glanced about, wondering to whom Lucy was speaking.

"You honor me, Miss Westenra, to recall my name from our first meeting," I said, unable to hide the mischievousness in my voice. "You're correct, and I apologize for upsetting you and your guests."

"I insist we change the subject," Lucy said with a stern finality that her sweet voice seldom carried. "Count, you attended the opera last week; what did you think of it?"

"I thought it wholly unjust," I said.

"Unjust ...?" asked Mrs. Effington, a blue-blooded elderly lady whom I'd been introduced to before dinner, another woman whose husband was travelling upon the continent. "How can an opera be unjust?"

"Injustice is the root of all evil," I said. "Besides forcing the audience to endure some truly terrible singing, the mythological theme of Peleus and Thetis is full of injustice. Eris felt she was unjustly not invited to the feast. Hera, Athena, and Aphrodite each felt it unjust that anyone could claim to be more beautiful than they. Zeus was the only god smart enough to avoid getting involved in the vanity of three overly-proud goddesses ... and the price of their dispute was the Trojan War, so thousands unjustly suffered because of a single unjust challenge."

"Very insightful," said Lord Godalming, Arthur's elderly father, whose illness I could smell. "But some injustices do exist naturally ..."

"Indeed," I said. "Some men are born weak, or poor, or sickly, and their lot is decided without consideration of the benefits of their intellect or empathy. The sickly live with injustice all their lives. Other forms of injustice are only perceived-injustice, yet those are often the cause of the greatest retributions."

"But justice does exist, does it not?" asked Mrs. Effington.

"There lies a mystery no mortal can answer," I said. "Injustice can be obvious ... but true justice is only surmised. God alone sees into the heart, and only by knowing a person's true motives can ultimate justice be declared. That doesn't make injustice a bad thing, but a worthy goal for all men ... and women."

"*Injustice is a goal ...?*" Dr. Seward asked. "That's something one of my patients might say."

"Perhaps you should confine me," I said to the doctor, and everyone laughed. "Surely, for inferiority to exist, there must be superiority, which some will always perceive as injustice. Yet blame not those who seek superiority, for only by their efforts has every invention been created, every opera written, and has mankind arisen above the base and ignoble to the heights England has achieved. It's beneficial to mankind for every man to seek to create the perception of injustice by attaining goals never before reached, and thus do we all arise."

"How elegantly said," Arthur said. "Thank you, Count Drăcula."

"Thank you, Lord Holmwood," I said. "But don't distract us with gratitude. Tell us, if you will, your opinion: given a chance to rise to greatness, is there any reason why any man ... *or any woman* ... should refuse?"

"I see no reason," Arthur said. "In fact, I'd say greatness is their duty, if they can attain it."

"We're in summative agreement, but we're men," I said. "Let's hear a woman's perspective; Miss Westenra, what do you think of your future husband's opinion? Should women always aspire to achieve superiority?"

Lucy's eyes flamed; she understood me well. To refuse, she'd have to give a reason why she wouldn't accept my offer, even if no other understood it, and to agree would bind her to me. Lucy hesitated, as if afraid to answer, and then a grin slowly spread across her face. She took a deep breath and met my eyes with unwavering conviction.

"Women don't need to aspire to a superiority we already possess," Lucy said.

Laughter exploded around the table, and many glasses were raised to Lucy, including mine. I'd not been mentally connecting to her during dinner, so I was unprepared for her witty and commanding rebuke, although it only enhanced my opinion of my future bride. She thought quickly, deeply, and yet was as bright and bubbly as a waterfall in summer; *a woman worthy of the throne beside mine.*

The rest of the dinner passed in a plethora of politeness and deference which sounded sweet to my ears, at first, but slowly took on the congealment of aged honey, and grew rigid and distasteful. The interests of these people annoyed me, for their conversations existed only to pass the time and for no constructive purpose, but I've learned in my examinations of social customs that English people prize most that which is superfluous, and so I feigned interest.

After dinner, as I expected, the sexes split; the women retired to a sitting room, while the men were ushered into a room where cigars were offered. I disdained cigars, for their odor was offensive to my heightened senses, and while the practice of smoking was pleasing, cigars were addictive, and the more one smoked, the stronger the addiction became. I hated the overwhelming need for tobacco, so much like my hunger for blood that I found it offensive, yet I needed to appear genial, not only for Lucy's sake, but for the sake of these men whose financial successes I hoped to replicate.

We men stood, as was the custom, while the women rose and departed, and then I followed as the men headed toward a different room.

"*Arthur ...?*" called Lucy's voice, and she came hurrying toward us, and to my surprise, she seized my arm. "Arthur, may I steal Count Drăcula for a moment? There's a lady here whom he must get to know better."

All of the men laughed, and Quincey overspoke all of their amusing comments.

"Ah, there falls Count Drăcula ... to bite the dust!" Quincey said. "Farewell, good Count, from the round-up of bachelors!"

I smiled at his remark, and then Lucy pulled upon my arm and led me away from the laughing menfolk. However, she didn't draw me to another woman, but into a narrow hallway, and then, glancing around to make sure we weren't seen, she pulled me through a door into a small, delicate sitting room filled with lace and baskets of knitting yarn.

"*You have to leave!*" Lucy said with an authority that amused me.

"Your husband-to-be shall wonder where I went," I said.

"I'll make a suitable excuse," Lucy said.

"But why ...?" I asked.

"*These are my friends!*" Lucy said.

"Am I not also a friend?" I asked.

"You ... you know ... *what you are,*" Lucy said.

"I am what you could become," I said.

"I'm engaged," Lucy said. "I can't accept."

"It's your choice," I said. "I won't force you. Your guests are safe from me; I won't feed here. But I'm enjoying your party; I've no desire to depart."

"I wish you to leave ...!" Lucy said.

"Go back to your women-friends and look at them closely," I said firmly, holding her eyes with mine. "Look at the dull weariness in their eyes, the deepening lines on their faces, and the colorless gray creeping into their hair. Look closely at the restrictions under which your sex lives. You'll suffer them all ... someday. You'll be what those elderly women are ... and then you'll die ... as they will, so late in life even I won't be able to save you."

"I ... I'll die ... a Christian soul," Lucy said, but the doubts in her voice rang like crashing cymbals.

"I'll return tomorrow night," I said. "I'll wait for you on the bench by the church. You may join me ... and become an immortal queen to rule this world ... or remain in your room and deny me ... and your dreams. I won't force you to come. I'll accept your absence as your final refusal ... or with your arrival, I'll give you everything you've ever desired ... and more. I'll give you the greatness ... that your fiancé spoke of as ... *duty.*"

I reached for Lucy's hand, and then I absently dropped her fingers, overcome with desire. I seized Lucy's torso in a desperate embrace and kissed her perfect lips, clinging to her as I'd embrace the glorious future that awaited us. We were the ultimate royalty, King and Queen of the Night, and I hungered for the position whose superhuman requirements God himself had given to me. My sudden amorous assault took Lucy by surprise, yet she didn't fight me, nor return my kiss with equal fervor, but meekly allowed my intimate touch, as if fighting against her own curiosity.

I could kiss her like that for all eternity!

When finally we separated, I bowed slightly to her, and said:

"Until midnight tomorrow, my love, when I'll await your decision."

I left her there, in the tiny room, and went to rejoin the men.

The stench of tobacco led me through the unfamiliar house to the large library which I'd briefly visited during my first invasion, during Lucy and Arthur's engagement party. As I entered, a titter of chuckles ensued, and a few men applauded as if I'd performed upon a stage.

"What's this?" Quincey laughed. "Still unmarried ...?"

I waited until their guffaws diminished.

"No Drăculeşti can be conquered by lipstick," I said, and every man cheered me.

Drowned in good humor, I pushed my way into the wall of smoke, selected a brandy offered by a servant, and approached Arthur, again surrounded by his closest friends.

"I can't say how greatly I'm enjoying your party," I said, raising my glass to my host, and I meant to offer a toast to him, but I never got the chance.

"Enjoying, indeed!" Dr. Seward interrupted my greeting. "Count, is that lipstick upon your lips?"

I hesitated; I was unused to kisses from women who wore lipstick. I wiped my lips and spied waxy pink smears upon the back of my hand. I made a mental note to myself: *Dr. John Seward was a smart and observing man.*

"No Drăculeşti can be conquered by lipstick ... but we do appreciate its source," I replied.

Again, laughter erupted. I let them enjoy their merriment; these men value their manhood based on the subservience of their women, but theirs is a pale shadow of dominance. My brides back in Castle Drăculea, if they still lived, would tear their hearts out and feast upon them, and they'd be helpless before their feminine wiles.

"Now, Count Drăcula, you can delay us no longer," Arthur said. "No women are here to pale before your descriptions of the Carpathian Mountains."

"Indeed, and I'd like to hear more of these *'infernals',*" Dr. Seward raised his eyebrows.

"Gentlemen, I will indulge you both, in recompense for your generous hospitality," I said. "My homelands of Transylvania are ancient, compared to your younger country, and yet are tamed far less. In winter snows, men seek firewood as a village, for those who enter our forests alone find themselves surrounded by savage wolf packs. Our pathways are rough and unpaved, for our mountains are rugged and high, with ravines a castle could crumble into ... and never be seen again. Education, so common in England, is scarce, for the principal occupation in hostile lands is simply to stay alive. We are graced with large, gentle animals, who seldom attack humans, such as moose and elk, but when hunted, these giants can slay with a fury no civilized man can equal."

Many heads bobbed, listening to my descriptions with rapt attention.

"As to infernals, these are not unknown to the men of England, only unseen," I said. "To that, I beg your pardon, all of your sciences must bow, for science recognizes nothing that can't be observed. Many are mentioned in your Bible, and disregarded as fancy by the doubtful, but the doubtful are historically proven wrong. The first white men to describe the mountain gorilla and orangutan were disbelieved, as were the first reports of the white rhinoceros, the giant python, and the ... vampire bat. Until these beasts were captured and brought to England, they were considered myths ... yet they were real enough to be feared by those who lived near them, even before Englanders knew of their existence.

"But what of creatures which can't be captured? Shall England continue to deny infernals because they can't be incarcerated in zoos?

"In Job, one of your Bible's oldest books, there's a Behemoth, described as a gigantic monster only God can tame, with a tail that sweeps the ground behind it like the trunk of a cedar tree. In the book of Revelations, there's a 'First Beast', with seven heads and ten horns, that rises from the ocean with the feet of a bear, the mouth of a lion, and the markings of a leopard. Abaddon, the Angel of the Bottomless Pit, whose name means 'Destroyer', leads a legion of locusts the size of war-horses, which have the faces of men, long stinging tails, flowing hair like women, and wear armored breastplates and crowns of gold. Their stings are reportedly so painful that 'men shall seek death and not find it'. The biblical Leviathan is a massive sea-monster, impervious to all weapons, which breathes fire and emits smoke from its nostrils. Lotan is a seven-headed giant serpent. And in many cultures, the Nephilim, the 'fallen ones', haunt the wilds and the wastes to prey upon lonely wanderers. My countrymen have many names for them: Ordog, Pokol, Stregoica, Vrolok, and Vlkoslak. They haunt the nightmares of all Carpathians."

I paused, and looked at the educated faces staring at me, rigid, determined to disbelieve.

"The family ancestry of Drăculeşti dates back to the fall of Rome," I said. "Distant explorations have been a hallmark of my ancestors, a tradition we cherish, and which I am continuing. Over two hundred years ago, a Drăculeşti circumvented the world, traveling to every continent, and witnessed great civilizations still unknown to England, in the bowels of Africa, in the continent below America, and in the high, frozen mountains of the distant East. Beasts they've seen, such as on the distant islands between China and Australia, where lizards larger than men, which could swallow dogs whole, crawl about upon primitive beaches. These creatures exist, gentlemen, whether or not science has documented them."

"I've heard rumor of giant lizards thereabouts," Dr. Seward said. "When the United East India Company was dissolved, Holland's royal family reported seeing such monsters, but no scientist has corroborated their claim."

"Perhaps we should journey there," Arthur said. "What a grand adventure that would be!"

"For this I came to England," I said with a nod of respect. "To bring the principals of your sciences to my lands, where terrors unknown must be respected and acknowledged."

"Respected ...?" asked Quincey. "I'd think you'd want them all hog-tied!"

For a moment, I held myself silent, forcing myself to not react in anger.

"It's a conceit of man to believe he can subjugate all things to his will ... or that he should try," I said. "That which God has made unstoppable shall never be tamed, any more than the wind or the tempest. That which God has imbued with powers far surpassing mortal man, that which never dies, naturally gains wisdom greater than any man could attain in a single lifetime. It's the right of that which is greater to rise above that which is lesser. No conceits change this. This, I fear, shall be an unforeseen menace to science as it spreads to surround the globe and learns all things knowable: not all of the infernals, as mentioned in your Bible, are mindless beasts, but immortal creatures whose intelligence far surpasses your own."

The expressions upon the faces of these Englishmen looked so horrified that they could've been mistaken for men of my homeland.

"Know you of such creatures, Count Drăcula?" Dr. Seward asked.

I lifted the glass in my hand to my lips, and wet them as if I'd taken a drink.

"I've no desire to be doubted, as have been all those who've first reported such sightings without proof," I said. "I believe as I choose, and invite others to seek the proofs they require."

"Ah, Count Drăcula, you delight me!" Arthur said. "When I asked for tales of your homeland, I expected peasant superstitions which any here could challenge, and here it's you that challenges us. Never have I enjoyed a story so much! But tell us one thing more, I beg you: do you truly believe that immortals exist today, on this planet, which are smarter than any living man?"

"That's not the question this educated company needs to answer," I said. "The question you should be asking is *'if you ever were to encounter an intelligence greater than your own, how would you recognize it?'*"

Every man fell silent and looked troubled, and glanced to their neighbors as if hoping for some plausible response.

"Well, I believe I've met an intelligence as great as my own, if not far greater," Arthur spoke up, and he held aloft his glass. "A toast, my dear guests: *to Count Drăcula!*"

As every man raised his glass, I couldn't help but smile.

After long good-byes and smiles to everyone, I departed with the crowd from Lucy's house. Lucy had vanished before I could thank her for her hospitality, but I entered my private carriage hopeful. Parties and new romances were truly much more pleasant than centuries of haunting grim Castle Drăculea, guilt-ridden, agonized, with bloodthirsty brides. I was beginning to consider revising my plans: rebuilding my fortune could require a century or more, and I'd no reason to hurry while England made life so joyful.

Outside, I was glad to select a full coach, black and solid-walled, such as the one I'd driven in Transylvania. However, inside my carriage, I rode east for only fifteen minutes before I frantically called for the driver to halt. Before the coach even came to a stop, I flung open the door and jumped out, and there on the street, I, Count Drăcula, Prince of Transylvania, vomited ... like a common peasant. The mortal food had tasted pleasant, and the few sips of brandy I'd actually swallowed warmed my insides like the blood of an infant, but the uneasiness of the carriage seemed to compound the queasiness I felt. Perhaps smoking an entire cigar had exacerbated my turmoil ...

"Governor, you all right?" came the voice of the driver as he climbed off his coach, and then a supporting hand gripped my arm.

"Yes," I said, and I spat, clearing my mouth.

"Don't let it bother you," the driver tried to reassure me. "We all drink a little too much sometimes. Better outside my coach than in it, I say. No hurry; we'll go when you're feeling better."

Several uncomfortable moments passed, and then the nausea passed. I felt embarrassed; in Castle Drăculea, I'd suffered old age and hunger for fifty years, and never had I succumbed to pain so quickly. Eating was poisonous to one cursed, but I'd needed to instill my presence in Lucy's environment, to show her that her previous life wasn't something she'd be losing, but something she could still possess after she was sired.

My success was in doubt. I feared what she might say in only 24 hours.

Quickly I assured the driver that I was recovered, and I reentered his coach just as another horse came into view behind us. I ordered my driver to hurry, as I'd no desire for others from Lucy's party to witness my weakness, and I pulled the plush curtains closed just to make sure.

Almost two hours we rode, for I'd given directions to Dagenham, a district near mine, and my strength had mostly returned, although I still felt relatively weak. I'd not fed, and transforming was taxing upon my nature.

I occasionally peeked through the curtains, and waited until we were in a shadowed, empty lane.

"Driver, halt! Halt!" I cried.

The horses stopped abruptly, and I jumped from the coach as I had before. As expected, the driver descended from the gotza and approached me.

I raised my eyes suddenly and stared into his. He startled, then hesitated, as if afraid. I focused entirely upon his eyes, drilling my thoughts deep into him; he'd probably never before seen such unwavering attention. My gaze arrested him, such that he stood flabbergasted, unable to respond, for nothing in his life had prepared him to gaze into eyes four centuries old, into pupils containing wisdom of a depth unimaginable by mortal men. Frozen by horrors of which common men know nothing, he never even whimpered, and I gorged myself. His blood was thick but bland, tasteless compared to the ambrosia of my precious Lucy, but I needed every drop of his essence. Once I started, I couldn't stop. Soon he started trying to fight back, but as his strength gushed inside me, his resistance became pitiful ... and finally he lost consciousness. I let him fall to the ground, empty, while I stood over him, renewed.

With ease, I tore some wide rags from his clothing, and stretched him out upon the road. He groaned: my driver was still alive, although he couldn't last much longer. Quickly I climbed to the top of his coach and mounted his gotza. As a master of horses, I urged these mounts backwards more than fifty yards.

Then I dismounted, used the torn rags of his clothing to cover the eyes of both horses, blindfolding them. Finally, resuming the driver's position, I cracked his whip, shook hard on their reins, and forced the horses to rush blindly forward. The driver's body lay prostrate on the road, and as I urged his horses to a gallop, I saw his head turn to look at me, and his mouth opened wide to scream. Yet he was too weak to move, and his feeble cry couldn't deter me; he'd be found in the morning, crushed by hooves and wheels, and no one would bother to look for two small punctures in his neck.

An hour later, I arrived home just as the distant horizon began to lighten with the dawn. I saw no sign of Renfield, so I went straight to my basement, seeking my coffin. Tonight had been a great triumph, but not until tomorrow would I know if I was victorious.

Sunset approached with the slowness of life. I awoke excited: *tonight Lucy would be mine ... one way or the other!*

No mortal could refrain from harboring feelings of resentment toward the person that killed them. Resentment had poisoned the love of my former brides. By allowing Lucy her own choice, I was blunting future emotional burdens, forcing her to accept the consequences of her choice, and perhaps evade an eternal life of blaming me for her death.

She'd be insane to reject me, trading decades of sunshine for eons of starlight. *Only a madwoman would choose to be dust!*

Yet my weakness, my vomiting upon the road after the feast, troubled me. My willpower seemed less now that I was young again. By regaining youth, had I given up my will of adamant that I'd developed in Transylvania? Where one plan, one carefully-thought-out goal, had sustained me, and kept me focused, now I was struggling to blend into a strange land, with customs I was only beginning to understand. I was trying to find a worthy bride, rebuild my family's fortune, and enjoy my new life; each effort was pulling me in different directions, diffusing my focus.

    I spent a long hour writing in my new diary, calming my mind, and then I fetched my mail and newspapers, read that one of my blackmail victims was late on their payment, and I assessed my total; the businessmen I'd met at Lucy's party would scoff at such tiny investments as mine. Perhaps I should reconsider acquiring funds more directly.

    I left for Hillingham, took my time, and switched coaches twice. Over-cautious, perhaps, but all of the drivers were talking about their colleague whom the constables claimed had been murdered. If he'd suffered a heart-attack and fallen off his rig, why was he trampled by his horses, whom he should've fallen behind?

    Drivers shouted this question every time coaches passed each other. These Englishmen, even the commoners, were observant and thoughtful; they weren't as easily fooled as peasants. Again, I should've anticipated this. That dead coach driver had been last seen in my presence, whereas I'd taken great pains to avoid connections to my other murders. Mistakes couldn't be tolerated. I couldn't afford sloppy thinking.

    Early revelation of my nature could undo everything.

    Love: *love was to blame.* Love consumed me, my thoughts riding clouds, dwelling upon fancies, not focused on reality. I was living in dreams of the future, ignoring details of the present. I had to focus and leave nothing to chance; *God was no fool, and I'd only learn too late if my goals thwarted His.*

Yet I reveled in my wondrous existence, too rapturous to decline. For the first time since I'd killed Lucinda, I was happy, unbound by the cruelties of God. Cold, clear thinking ... and love: these seemed incongruous, unable to exist simultaneously.

Love or clarity; if I could only choose one, which would I choose?

Pondering resolved nothing, but passed the duration of my ride until I paid my driver, urged him to be careful, and sent him off only a mile from Lucy's house. I set off across the winding cobblestone streets, admiring the houses of the wealthy, gleaming in the moonlight, until I reached the top of the hill and stood before the church.

There stood Lucy, arrived early, waiting for me.

Her alabaster skin shone radiant in the moonlight, her lips enticing, and her mesmerizing eyes reflected the gleaming stars. As I approached and bowed slightly to her, I couldn't but delight that, one way or the other, soon I'd be tasting her blood.

I held out my hand to take hers, eager, but she didn't offer her hand.

"I'm sorry, Vlad," Lucy said. "No man has ever offered any woman so great a prize as you've offered me, and I'm grateful, but I must decline."

I smiled; a lesser man might be taken aback by such false modesty, but Lucy was here, not avoiding this meeting. She wouldn't have come if she could've stayed away.

"May I ask, if it be permitted, why you prefer to grow old and die?"

A soft sniff reached my ears, as if Lucy were fighting to hold back tears, and a tremor arose in her voice, but no visible regret showed. *Was she trying to deceive me ... or herself?*

"I've given my pledge to marry," Lucy said resolutely, but the bitterness in her voice shrieked in my ears. "A woman ... especially one whom you'd make a queen, must be honorable ... worthy of her throne. How worthy could I be if I promise to marry a man and then withdraw my pledge?"

I softened my voice, trying to appear sympathetic, although my heart was leaping.

"Who asked you to cancel your promise?" I smiled at her.

Lucy startled, and looked up at me, confused.

"My sweet child, when's your wedding?" I asked. "Have you set a date?"

"I ... we ... wed in three weeks," Lucy said.

"Wed: to be bonded together ... until death separates you," I smiled.

Lucy's eyes flared; she instantly understood; *more proof that she was worthy!*

"I ... I ...," Lucy started.

"You'll be found alone, in your bed, with no pulse, and no heartbeat," I said. "To mortal eyes, you'll appear dead, but to one who sees all, you'll be a caterpillar in its cocoon, transforming into a new, eternal life."

"They ... they'll think ... I'm dead ...?" Lucy asked slowly, as if ruminating over her own words in her mind.

"And your promise to marry will be void," I said. "Mortals don't marry undead."

Lucy staggered back, her eyes staring blindly, her thoughts swallowing her concentration.

"Arthur will mourn you ... and be quite sad," I said. "His friends shall comfort and console him, and with their help, he'll slowly recover. Years will pass, and Arthur shall live long and honorably, never knowing that some lives extend beyond death. He'll age ... as you won't, and eventually succumb to his natural end ..."

"No," Lucy said. "I ...I mean, I want to live forever. I don't ever want to grow old. But ... *the price ...! Count ... Vlad, I could never take an innocent life! I couldn't do that!*"

I slowly shook my head.

"Lucy, I've been wholly honest with you," I said. "No mortal but you knows all about vampirism. But knowledge blossoms to understanding only with experience, and this knowledge is new, so you haven't thought it out. There's no requirement to end mortal lives. As I explained, before leaving Transylvania, I chose to fast for fifty years, and in that time I didn't taste a drop of blood, for the only substance available were my subjects and my distant relations. You allowed me to taste you ... and you didn't die."

"*I don't ... I don't have to kill ...?*" Lucy asked.

"No," I said. "Never."

Lucy staggered to the bench and rested her hand upon its back, leaning upon its wooden solidity for support. I approached her, remaining silent, giving her time to comprehend.

"*I don't have to break my vow to Arthur, I needn't kill, and I'll be young forever ...?*" Lucy whispered.

"Young ... and beautiful," I said. "And you'll be loved. But this is a monumental decision, and I don't wish to rush you. You have three weeks ..."

"No," Lucy interrupted me. "No, the longer I wait, the closer we come to the wedding, the more Arthur will suffer ..."

I hesitated, fighting the urge to rush into her embrace and make her mine. *I had to be patient!*

"Have you decided ...?" I asked.

"Wait," Lucy said. "I ... need time to think ..."

"I respect all who are thoughtful," I said.

Lucy turned away from me, staring up at the moon and stars, and then she exhaled deeply and strode a few paces away, and then stopped again, as if reflecting the struggle of her inner debate by frequently changing direction. Her silent turmoil lasted half an hour, in sudden, brief spurts of movement, in seemingly random patterns, followed by long moments of standing still. Finally she came and sat on the bench. All the while I stood watching, silent, ready to comfort.

"Does it hurt ... to die?" Lucy asked.

"Death is as painless as sleep, if you wish it," I said. "I can drain you to the point of unconsciousness, beyond your ability to recover. Days from now, I'll awaken you at sunset, and you won't even remember falling asleep."

"I've no wish to be hurt," Lucy said.

"You have the pledge of Count Drăcula," I said. "I'll never allow harm to come to you ... in this life ... or in the eternity we'll spend together. I'll be your devoted husband, forsaking all others, my endless existence bound to yours. Choose me, Lucy, and every dream you've ever had will come true. Soon you'll dream dreams no living woman has ever known. Be my eternal queen, Lucy. Will you have me?"

Lucy gritted her teeth, bowed her head, and shuddered slightly, as if forcing herself to perform an arduous task.

"Yes, I'll have you," Lucy said.

Suddenly we were kissing, Lucy no less ardently than I, and the paradise I'd dreamed of became reality. *I was in love! We were in love!* Effulgent ecstasies cascaded in showers of blithesome glee. I became the one transformed. After all these centuries ... seeking and failing ... *finally I'd found one woman I could love forever!*

Lucy clenched me tightly, fervently, and gave herself willingly. No words equaled the magnanimity of this moment, when the future king of the world had chosen his queen. I felt as one manumitted, unbound, free to arise even to the height of God.

I lifted my arm, pulled back my sleeve, and exposed my wrist. With a knowing glance at Lucy, I showed her my fangs ... and bit into my flesh. Blood flowed from my wrist: *vampire blood.*

Lucy stared at it, leaned forward to kiss my lips, and then took my hand, drew my wrist toward her, and lowered her lips to me. Willingly Lucy Westenra drank of my nectar, only wincing slightly as she swallowed.

Lucy willingly became a vampire!

Slowly she drew back and smiled, her eyes aware and alight, accepting immortality. I returned her display of teeth, and she nodded, then closed her eyes and tilted her head, offering her lovely throat.

My mouth opened, pressed against her throat, and gently I squeezed my fangs into her flesh ... *I mustn't hurt her!* Tantalizing, her delicious blood drenched my tongue, and she moaned, writhing, but she pulled me possessively tighter in her arms. A longing gasp escaped her lips, and the sweetness of her ambrosia filled my mouth with the blessed perfection of her essence, the balmy nirvana of her heart and soul. Her kindness became mine, and her gentility splashed throughout me, cleansing my mind and soul of every shadow; *let every part of her magnificence become part of me!*

"*Lucy ...?*" called a strange voice.

We both startled, stunned from our reverie. Lucy's eyes widened with fear.

"*Mina ...!*" Lucy gasped.

"What ...?" I asked, for I knew not this word.

"My best friend!" Lucy said, "She's looking for me ...!"

"We can't stop ...!" I said.

"She can't see us!" Lucy hissed wildly.

Seeing her alarm, I relented; *to refuse now would spoil her transformation, as would the murder of her best friend, and the voice that called was close.*

"Tomorrow," Lucy said. "I promise ... I'll be yours. Come back tomorrow."

"I will, my love," I promised, and although disappointed, with the faithfulness of a true fiancé, I rose and faced the moonlight. Footsteps approached us on the path; I'd no time to argue or seek another option.

Be the bat!

Chapter 11

Awareness melted out of primeval pains with one dim, primitive thought: *'home'*. I stood in my garden by the door to my moonlit chapel, a thin mist swirling around me. At first I staggered, and braced against the doorframe for support, until the pain departed. An amazing taste filled my mouth, and then I remembered: *Lucy was my self-proclaimed fiancée! She'd chosen me over Arthur Holmwood! Eternal night over brief days!*

I smiled, for in her choice she'd verified mine. Lucy would be an excellent queen, and our lives together wouldn't be dark and haunted, but filled with light, effusive parties, royal balls, and love to shame every relationship since the Garden of Eden, where God gave Adam and Eve dominion over all the Earth. Soon the name Drăcula would rise above Julius Caesar and Genghis Khan, and together we'd rule an empire as immortal as we.

Mina ...? Why did that name sound familiar...?

To no avail, I strained my memory, recalling every woman I'd met since my arrival in England, but I was certain I'd heard that name. I concluded that Mina was a lady whom I'd never met, who must've found Lucy missing from her bedroom and come looking for her, unaware of the delicate moment she was interrupting.

I was so close! So close ...!
Lucy had given me her pledge!
She'd chosen me! She'd chosen youth and global prominence over becoming the doting wife of a minor nobleman with little lineage. Her professed insistence that she must keep her word would now work in my favor, and tomorrow night would complete a major point in my plan for global domination. I'd partially drained Lucy; she'd be weak. Tomorrow, I'd drain her beyond her body's ability to retain consciousness, and Lucy would end her mortal life in sleep, painless, as I'd promised.

After an untroubled sleep, one thought overwhelmed as I rose from my coffin; *tonight Drăcula takes his bride!* No more interruptions or delays. If Lucy didn't come to me, then I'd enter her house and take what was mine, and even the protection of God would fail to save any fool keeping Lucy and I apart.

I arose quickly and changed into my best suit, as droplets of Lucy's blood had stained my lapels; soon I'd have to purchase another. The cost of new suits was a problem I'd not anticipated, but I could hardly draw attention to myself by frequenting a clothes cleaner to have bloodstains removed from shirts and jackets.

Rain fell heavily, and so I drew on my hat, cloak, and opened my brolly, holding it above me as I walked. Nothing could stop my errand, so I plunged through the wet branches and carefully threaded my way down the familiar route. As I passed Dr. Seward's asylum, a pair of eyes watched me, and I glanced up to see Renfield pressed against the wet bars of a second-floor window. I gave him a friendly wave, which he returned, and then I proceeded.

Again I traded coaches, noting that I was running low on coinage, and would have to soon brave the sunlight again to visit the bank. Perhaps, if it kept raining this hard, I could brave a day like today, so overcast the sun would prove little threat to me. I selected an elegant britzka, a long, spacious carriage with four wheels, with a wet, rear-facing front seat, but a folding top over the dry rear seat, which could be reclined at night for long journeys. It was pulled by two horses, with a raised front platform for the driver.

Inside the britzka, I relaxed; Lucy and I'd soon be joined in death, and her delightful company would make eternity a pleasure. She was smart enough to aid my plan, and working together, we'd conquer the world in style.

I wasn't alone anymore. My future bride had chosen me, and she was a strong-willed woman; she wanted to be mine.

I deserve this happiness. My duty had been to protect my people, and I'd defeated an army by the only means available. If God hadn't desired my victory, He could've killed me in battle. If God hadn't personally cursed me, then He'd allowed my victims to curse me. No man should have to watch himself murder his father and bride, and the misery of those actions had haunted me for four centuries. Now I'd turn the tables upon God. I'd claim a new bride, a willing bride, and together we'd build a future where I'd never know unhappiness. No longer would I have a curse; *from now on, Drăcula possessed the God-ordained sovereignty to rule the world!*

Due to the hard rain, I directed my driver to steer his britzka all the way to the church, where I paid and sent him away. There was a wooden eaves over the main entrance to the rectory, and there I took shelter from the rain. Lucy wasn't there, but I forced myself to be patient; it wasn't yet midnight, and why should she come early to wait in the rain?

An hour after midnight, I resigned to myself that Lucy wasn't coming. Gritting my fangs, but not letting anger consume me, I strode through the rain, under my brolly, down the long, wooded trail toward Lucy's house. Finally I arrived at the white gazebo by the stream. I considered strolling across the footbridge and breaching her doors to claim what was mine, but Lucy wouldn't appreciate me making such a show, and it was improper for a dutiful fiancé to conduct his actions without concern for the wishes of his intended. Instead, I reached out with my mind and found Lucy in an agitated mental state, arguing with someone. Both were in a temper.

I relaxed; *Lucy hadn't abandoned our meeting, but was being prevented from escaping.* Expanding my search, I focused on the person in closest proximity to Lucy; a young woman, demure and proper, but with a strong, unflinching will, so adamant it surprised me. Concentrating, I deepened my focus, only to discover her name: *Mina, the woman who'd thwarted my plans last night!* But I couldn't allow Mina to interfere again. If I delved into her emotions, so deeply I could control her, then I'd force her into an irresistible swoon, and free my Lucy to come to me.

I probed, my subtle thoughts heated by her domineering desire to master Lucy, for whom she feared. She believed Lucy was ill, suffering from sleepwalking, and possibly delusions, although I couldn't detect what evidences she claimed. *Had Lucy spoken out-of-turn ... and revealed too much?* Finally I pushed past Mina's rapid-flashing thoughts and forced my way into her emotions, into the raw depths of her heart ...

Jonathan Harker .....!?!?!

His happy image flooded my mind: the ingenious young man I'd welcomed into Castle Drăculea. Suddenly I remembered the name 'Mina': *Jonathan's letters!*

Mina was Jonathan Harker's fiancée!

The shock of this revelation broke my connection, and I grabbed tightly to the wet rail of the gazebo to keep from falling. *How could this be?!?* But slowly I recovered; Jonathan and Mina had discussed Lucy Westenra in their letters. From their correspondence I first learned that my Lucy existed, and that Lucy and Mina were friends; this unexpected intervention shouldn't have surprised me, and surprise is so rare a state for one as old as I that its perplexion seemed magnified. Yet this was again troubling; *why hadn't I anticipated this? Was I again succumbing to the foolishness of restored youth?*

I sat on the damp bench in the gazebo, too upset to care about a little rainwater, and began rethinking my entire plan. *If I'd missed this little detail, how many others had I missed?* I'd planned so carefully, over five decades. I'd abstained from drinking blood to remake myself before I remade the world.

Immortality is a crucible. Any being that lives long enough will eventually have tried and experienced everything, and cast off every idea that proves wrong. However, as falsehoods are cast away, confusion fills their void; *truth is not the absence of falsehoods.* To seek truth, I had to look deeper.

Truth is dependent upon the nature of he who seeks it. Mortals have time to explore only a few paths toward truth before their mortality proves itself, and are thus unlikely to chance upon their rightful path. For this reason, humans seldom comprehend truth, even when confronted by it, for they have no experience recognizing it. Immortals learn that you can't maintain a state where truths are perfect, for the nature of truth changes with the environment in which the seeker of truth dwells.

In my abstinence, I'd thought I'd found truth. *I was wrong.*

Movement distracted me; my beautiful Lucy emerged from her house in her nightgown, unprotected from the raindrops, and hurried toward me, yet she didn't get far. Mina burst out of the door behind her, called her name, and Lucy stopped; Lucy and I exchanged a frustrated glance, and then Lucy's shoulders slumped, and she shook her head, and simply stood there on the footbridge, in the rain. Mina caught up with her, forcibly seized her, and led her back.

My bride wouldn't join me tonight.

Mina was as young, and nearly as beautiful, as my Lucy, save that she had hair so dark brown it looked black in the glows emanating from the few lantern-lit windows beaming a wan brightness into the rainy darkness.

Did Mina know Jonathan was dead?

I watched as Mina hurried Lucy back home, waited until they were both inside, and then I lifted my brolly against the rain and began my long walk back to the nearest populated area, from where I'd get a carriage to carry me home.

I'd drink nothing tonight; I needed to think.

Early the next evening, I awoke determined. *No more interference! Lucy must be mine tonight!*

To insure this, I needed help, but not of any human-kind. *I needed a friend I could absolutely trust.*

While the sun was still high, I arose, dressed heavily in my wide-brimmed hat and cloak, and left right away. Avoiding the bright sunlight as much as I could, I took a carriage toward Lucy's district, but I didn't go to her house. Only a few miles away from Hillingham was a public zoo, where animals were locked in cages and put on display for visitors to gawk at; I directed my driver toward the zoo.

My long ride relaxed me. Despite the glaring sun, I was getting used to this long excursion, from my district to Lucy's, and I was certain I'd seen this driver, and possibly used this very hansom cab. On the way, I considered the similarities between my driver and I; yes, we were as different as night and day. He was alive while I was undead. He was a simple peasant who'd lived only a few decades, while I was an immortal prince possessing the wisdom of ages. Yet we were both facing much of the same existence. While my dreams were vastly more ambitious, we were both working toward our goal's achievement. We valued our existence and strove to continue it. We had personal likes and dislikes, and hated annoyances. We indulged in trivial delights whenever the opportunity arose. We were both struggling to understand the world around us, who God was and what He wanted, and our place in this universe.

The biggest difference between us was my centuries of pondering had given me an unparalleled depth of thought ... and the expectation of eventually proving which of the endless possibilities of God were true. We were both trapped on this planet, unable to leave it save by true death, moving along with the same passage of time, unable to slow the good times, so we can enjoy them more, or speed up the bad times, to make them pass sooner, and unknowing what experiences awaited us in times yet to be.

In the end, the biggest difference between great men and lesser men isn't opportunity, but ambition. What might this driver become, if transformed into a vampire, with centuries to learn and grow? I could give him that opportunity, but what of ambition? Would his goals expand with centuries of existence, or would he continue his mindless existence forever, plodding along only enough to survive, and seeking only momentary pleasures, and avoiding conscious thought and reflection at all costs?

Opportunity determines how far a man can rise above his station. Ambition determines how far he'll rise, given the opportunity. Other qualities have value; integrity, strength, courage, and even empathy, but these don't intrinsically raise the measure of the man ... or the woman. Only ambition elevates anyone above their birth-status and brings them closer to God.

'I'd say greatness is their duty, if they can attain it,' Arthur had said.

I smiled. *For a mortal, Lucy's would-be fiancé was a wise man.*

I wasn't the first vampire to seek a crown. Other vampires had tried to claim dominion over the world. In my first century, after I was cursed, I discovered, quite by accident, that an attacker whose mouth had been sprayed with my blood arose, after I'd killed him, to become another vampire. Astounded by this discovery, I'd tested my newfound power, and thought to raise a community of vampires to ease my loneliness. But they had no restraint, and seemed intent only upon glutting themselves with the blood of the living. Assaulted by bands of undead, whole villages were often slain in a single night, many of those villages holding the last remaining blood-ties to the Drăculeşti family. Soon these blood-craving murderers were making more vampires, without my consent, passing on my curse to their friends and family: creating an army of vampires to destroy all human life.

What if they'd succeeded? How would I feed after all humans had been slain?

Of all the mistakes I'd ever made that had been my worst. I assumed the obligation of correcting my foolishness, as no mortal could. I rallied my vampire army, claimed leadership of the murderers, and led small groups out *"to conquer other lands and spread our kind to the ends of the Earth"*... or so I claimed.

At dawn, I led each group into a trap I'd prepared, where only a wooden house could protect them from the deadly rays of the sun. There I abandoned them, and at noon, I ignited the building while they slept. Those weaker vampires burned in two fires: flames and sunlight.

When my deceptions were discovered, the remaining vampires rebelled against me, but I was a prince and a soldier, and I easily evaded their attacks. Over three decades I hunted and killed all of the remaining vampires. Some few escaped, and fled to distant parts of the world; my journey around the globe revealed that not all of my children had been slain. As I found them, I judged each: most I killed, as they were detestable. A few I allowed to live in isolation, as they were cultured and had sired no others of our kind. They welcomed me as their respected ancestor and paid me great homage. The rest learned of my presence before I could locate them, and fled for fear of me, and have remained hidden unto this day.

My driver's shout of *'Zoo'* interrupted my reverie. The scent of animals announced that we'd arrived.

Zoos are disgusting. Trapped behind bars, animals slowly rot; a sad way to observe them compared to how they exist in the wild. In my travels I'd seen all of these animals roaming free, and struggling for their daily sustenance, even as men do in their artificial environments. Yet the great sorrow of these beasts only I know, whose centuries-old mind can link with them, and sense the sadness they feel.

Yet, to release them without returning them to their native lands would be a death sentence. I came to satisfy my needs.

Following the unmistakable scent, soon I stood before a great gray-haired wolf, sleeping in an iron cage. Suddenly his hackles rose, and he jumped up, his eyes locked upon me, and he howled so loudly a zookeeper came running up and looked askance.

"Keeper, this wolf seems upset at something," I said.

"Maybe it's you," he said, looking me up and down and trying to peek inside my cloak. I smiled at him.

"Oh no, wolves like me," I said.

"Ow, yes, they would," the zookeeper said. "They always likes a bone or two to clean their teeth on about tea-time, which you 'as a bagful."

When the wolf saw me talking to the zookeeper, he stopped howling and quieted. He kept watching us both intently. The zookeeper spoke softly to him, and reached inside his cage to stroke his ears. The wolf ignored him, apparently accustomed to it, so I walked over and reached inside to ruffle his fur.

"Tyke care," said the zookeeper. "Bersicker is quick."

"Never mind," I said. "I'm used to wolves. My family raised them."

"Are you in the business yerself?" he asked.

"Not exactly in the business, but I've made pets of several," I said.

I looked hard at the wolf and he at me. At night, we'd be able to communicate fully, but in the daylight, there was nothing else I could do. With a nod to the surprised zookeeper, I strode away, left the zoo, and found a dark tavern in which to hide.

After night blessed England, and my strength returned, I strode back to the zoo. The gates were locked and lights extinguished, but such barriers were insignificant. Within minutes, I stood again before the great gray wolf, who was fully asleep. He didn't awaken at once, but I stared at him, preparing myself for the challenge to come.

Humans believe their minds are infinite in capability, and that no thoughts exist they can't conceive. *How wrong they are!* My thoughts, deepened over four centuries, amaze them, for the clarity and depth of my brain exceed theirs a hundredfold. If the mind of God ever touched them, if the thoughts that created the very universe were ever sensed, then humans would know at once that they exist only as a feeble spark before a raging forest fire, and gape speechless before a mind vastly superior to their own.

Thus is it for animals when a human mind contacts them. Abilities to reason and predict seem like magic and prophesy to those who can't grasp and compare simultaneous thoughts, and once contacted, those animals' personalities are forever changed. While they never gain our ability to extrapolate pure imaginings, they become aware of a consciousness that excels their own, and are humbled and tamed by it. So it has always been by those who spend their lives seeking insights into the mind of God, the philosopher and the scientist, each seeking to grasp a different aspect of divinity, which, after centuries of contemplation, I am only beginning to understand are the same.

I focused my eyes upon the sleeping wolf and reached out with my mind.

"Hear me, my chosen friend," I said.

Instantly the wolf jumped, as if awakened by a frightful dream, and he struggled to stand, to cower back into the corner of his confinement.

"Be calm, my friend, for I'm your rightful lord and master, and no harm shall I allow to come to you."

The wolf raised his eyes to me, and only I could read the horror in his face. Nothing in his brief life had ever prepared him for such a meeting, and he was foundering, lost in human thoughts.

"I am the essence of all you know, and I've been with your kind for years beyond counting," I said. "Only to a few of your kind do I open my thoughts, and then only in great need. I'll share my thoughts with you now, and if you listen, you'll be wiser, and happier, than ever before."

Hesitantly, braving thoughts never possessed before, the wolf opened its jaws and began to breathe easier. Slowly it inched forward. I could sense its fear, but also its amazement and curiosity. I reached my hand through his bars and exposed myself to its sharp teeth. He licked me, and I smiled, and he sensed my happiness.

"Like many of your brethren, we are now joined forever," I said. "I'm your kind master, and you're my loyal servant."

The wolf's joy overflowed, and we shared a deep bond. Yet wolf-thoughts are feeble, shallow, and primitive: the need to hunt, eternal wariness, fear of pain and death, anger at its imprisonment, a hunger to roam wild and free, a lust for companionship, and a tenderness for its own kind. Normally only these feelings filled his mind, but his thoughts paled before mine, as if I were a cleansing wave washing him into an illumination above his reckoning. From this day on he'd be tame ... and smarter.

"I need you," I said. "You must come with me, and be my eyes where I can't go."

His cage's lock was a simple mechanism. Half an hour later, I climbed the hill to the church by Lucy's house, my faithful companion at my side, wagging his tail and hanging his tongue, and pressing against my legs whenever he could.

As we reached the white gazebo, I sat and wrapped my arms around my companion; *how good it felt to be in the company of a wolf!* We shared long, undisturbed moments, lord and worshipper, and then I shared with him, silently, that I'd direct him without words, and he must proceed ahead alone.

With a flurry of licks from him and pats from me, my companion hurried off toward Lucy's house. Our connection was strong, and with my eyes closed I saw through his eyes, and felt his progress. I was low, ranging across the footbridge. Sharp pebbles stabbed my paws, yet I was eager, filled with delight. I slipped past pungent roses and gardenias, and their scents almost overpowered me; the noses of canines are far more acute than the senses of men. Even the grass smelled stronger than any scent in human nostrils. My nose became a new set of eyes, seeing a strange, hidden world.

The wolf was smart for its kind, and ran to jump up, my paws against the sills, and I pressed my cold, damp nose against every window. I saw the huge room where Lucy's engagement party had been, and the dining room not far from it, and soon spied a dozen other rooms I'd never seen. A woman was washing dishes in a kitchen. A maid was carrying folded towels toward a tall stairs. A long hallway stood dark and empty. Finally I peered into the library where I'd drunk brandy with Arthur and his friends. Servants sat with their feet on antique tables, drinking the brandy of their long-asleep masters.

Circling the house, I found a tiny stairs leading upwards; I directed the wolf to climb, and he found a long balcony on the second floor, and it had a walkway that passed by windows of many rooms, some of which had doors. My friend peered into each pane, and my eyes filled with every sight. Several rooms held sleeping people, but none were the goal I sought.

Then I spied her: *Lucy!*

Lucy was awake, sitting on a polished oak bed, writing something on a small wooden cabinet with short legs, designed to be used as a night-time writing desk. Thick comforters concealed her legs, and the walls behind her were painted with tiny, soft pink roses. I longed to reach out to her, but that would break my connection with the wolf, and I needed him still. I forced him to look about, and found that Lucy wasn't alone; beside her, sound asleep, lay an older woman with bound gray hair, whom I recognized as her mother. A snarl formed on my lips and on the face of the wolf; *I could brook no more delays!*

I turned the wolf's eyes back to focus on Lucy. In the light of a candelabra, she glowed as beautiful as ever, and I longed to take her. I pressed close, felt my wet nose squeeze against the glass, and drank in the sight of her.

Crash!

Tinkles of shattered glass rained down upon my fur. I shook my head; shards flew in every direction, and then I looked up. Lucy was staring at me, and her mother awoke, jolting up and knocking Lucy's tiny writing desk off the bed, where it fell with a hard, clunky crash. Lucy startled, but her mother drew in a deep breath to scream, and that I couldn't allow, for her scream would summon others, and my plan for this night would fail. I released my connection to the wolf and focused upon the mother, seizing her mind and silencing her voice.

My plan went awry. Holding Lucy's mother in my mind, I ran from the gazebo to Lucy's house, around the far corner and up the tiny, winding stairs my wolf-friend had found. A moment later, I stood beside the glass-paned door, from which the wolf had extracted its head from the broken pane. With determined steps, I flung open her door and entered her bedroom.

Seeing first the wolf, and then me brazenly stride in, proved too much for Lucy's mother. She gasped and clutched at her chest, staring agape at me, and then she swooned and fell limp beside her daughter. Lucy grabbed and shook her, yet she didn't respond.

Lucy turned to look at me, and I hesitated. *I'd come to claim my own, and Lucy had agreed to my coming.* Yet I must be gentle, as I promised, lest I create another Miëta, Hēlgrēth, or Loritá.

"Vlad ...," she began.

I silenced her with a gesture.

"Now isn't the time for fear," I said to Lucy. "I love you, and pledge to you a devotion that will outlast the stars."

Her reluctance left her face, and not a shadow of fear evidenced.

"I love you, Vlad," Lucy said, and she closed her eyes and leaned back her head, exposing her delicious neck.

Tiny wounds remained of my first tastes of her. I bent to the same spot, eager not only for her blood, but for the milestone this represented. *I'd chosen my new bride, and now she was giving herself to me; I was taking her into my world.*

Her velvety skin tasted like paradise, and slowly I set my fangs against her throat, feeling the pulse of her blood, so close, and with a brief nip, I penetrated to her flowing essence. Ambrosia like no other filled my mouth, and I wrapped Lucy in my strong embrace, held her tightly, and drank deeply. Her ecstasy filled me, and a warmth I've never felt before coursed through my veins. I was the one reborn, even as she was, with the purity and gaiety of a new and better age, a future I'd only dreamed was possible. Her taste blazed into my mind like revelations of divine comprehension, and I felt a peace I'd not known since I was a small child roving the carefree forests of the Carpathians.

I drank until Lucy slumped in my arms, and despite my desire to drink her dry, I released her. I'd taken more of her blood than any human could lose and survive, but I'd promised she wouldn't die awake, but pass over in her gentle sleep. Then I'd shadow her, and steal her corpse, and she'd awaken to a new life in my arms.

I glanced at her mother and sensed she was dead. Terrified beyond her ability to endure, and prevented from screaming, her heart had stopped. I shook my head; this wouldn't please Lucy, but she need never know I'd stopped her mother from screaming. I'd console Lucy, and mourn her mother beside her, and help her to do all that a dutiful daughter should, if only to please her, and ease her entry into eternal life.

Lucy lay unconscious, only hours from death. I kissed her soft lips, and then I rose, and with a lingering glance at her, a last look before her mortal attractiveness was transformed to immortal beauty, I turned and walked to her ruined glass door ... and closed it behind me.

My wolf-friend was still there, on the balcony, and we descended the stair together. I led him to the gazebo and beyond, into the woods close to the church, and there I knelt and petted him.

"My friend, you've pleased me greatly," I said to the wolf, and I needed no deep connection to sense its joy. "Now I must go, and you'll be on your own. You may return to your confinement, or ravage the countryside, if you wish, but men will hunt you while you're free, for the lands where you could run wild are far, far away from here. I can't say if we'll ever meet again, but I'll remember you, and you shall carry what I've shared with you all of your life. Go with contentment, my friend, and know that the bond we've shared can never be broken."

I held still and let him lick my face and rub against me for a full minute, and then I stood up, gave him one last pet, and turned my face to look at the moonlit sky.

Be the bat!

Long before dusk I awoke happy. I felt sanctified by the pure and wholesome young blood flowing through me. My beautiful Lucy would soon arise, perhaps tomorrow night, and then she'd be mine forever. I'd buy her the finest coffin and we'd sleep beside each other each day ... and rule the world by night.

Of all the states of man, happiness is the most fulfilling. Many times I've tried to qualify what happiness is, but the conditions and circumstances are so personal no equation exists. What makes one man jubilant can torture another; one man may thrill to the attainments of goals, while another celebrates only freedom from goals. Some cherish marriage and security, while others prize solitude and independence. Learning makes some happy, while others revel in blithesome ignorance, seeking solace only in drunken stupors.

The question isn't what causes happiness, but what makes you happy. For an unlucky few, no happiness exists unless those they care about are also happy. These poor souls suffer the sorrows of the world as their own, and so they endure countless miseries, but, long ago, I realized that those caring folk are the best people on Earth, the ones who often get pushed aside in good times, but are always there to cling to in bad times.

I was finally happy!

I arose, for I couldn't bear to lay still with so much energy filling me. Lucy's vitality and spirit coursed through me, and I was eager to do something, to be active in my new life. Fortunately, it was raining again, but not a hard rain. The sun was hidden, and so I washed, dressed, and checked my mail, and after writing a reply to my legal clerk in York, I took my brolly and braved the failing day.

Before I left, I noticed dust had begun to accumulate upon my tables, and I wanted my place to look nice for Lucy; I'd have to summon Renfield. I looked at the mansion of Dr. Seward as I walked past it, but I couldn't sense Renfield in the daylight; best I wait until dark.

From the position of the sunlight seeping through the gloomy clouds, I judged it to be late afternoon, and my first visit was to the bank. My daylight weakness seemed trivial, partly because of the absence of direct sunlight, but mostly because the blood of my beloved sustained me. I shielded myself under my brolly and stayed under trees and in the shades of buildings as much as I could. At the bank, I took out a large amount, leaving too little in my account for my tastes, and yet I had need of it. I considered using my powers to trick the banker into giving me funds from someone else's account, but no doubt that mistake would eventually be discovered, and then I'd face legal problems, which I wished to avoid. So I smiled, pocketed my funds, and left.

I went to the local tailor and purchased two new suits, as I did seem to go through them rather quickly. Delighted, the tailor called me his best customer, and fawned over my taste in clothes, although he still puzzled at my reluctance to look in his mirrors. At a nearby market, I purchased some more brandy for Renfield, whom I needed to clean my house. Then I took a fancy to enter a store that sold furniture, where I saw many admirable sets of finely-crafted beds, cabinets, and tables to fill the vacant rooms of my house, yet I let them be; Lucy may enjoy decorating, and I'd allow her to fill our house as best suited her tastes, which would be a small gift to ease her into her new life.

Yet we'd have to be careful; Lucy was celebrated throughout London and easily recognized by her beauty. The news of her death will fill local newspapers for days. To let her appear in public, and be recognized, would cause a great calamity. Worse, my next door neighbor was Dr. John Seward, a noticing man, who knew Lucy well; if he were to spy her from his lunatic asylum, it'd cause trouble indeed.

This was easily remedied with a disguise. Lucy would balk, but she'd slowly grasp that decades mean nothing to us, while humans age and die. In less than a century, no one would remain who knew Lucy as a living mortal.

I ended up in a tavern I'd visited before, and sat there until night had fallen, reading newspapers and eavesdropping on local gossip, which amused me. Yet nothing of consequence happened, and so I ended my last night of bachelorhood contentedly. After my glut of Lucy, I wasn't even hungry, and had no need to seek blood, even the best of which would taste bitter after my feast of perfection.

On my way home, I sensed Renfield with ease, and upon seeing him standing at an open window near a large tree, watching me from the 2nd floor, I stopped, and expanded my senses to reach his mind, which was dark and angry. He was in one of his moods again, cursing me for the gift which he'd once demanded of me. I ignored his ill-humor; he'd revert to acting like an excited lap-dog soon enough, and I gave him the command to come and clean my house.

'Lucy Westenra dies unexpectedly.'

When I opened my newspapers the next evening, I expected this headline to greet me on each front page, but it wasn't there. I scanned every page, looking for some reference; even the obituaries listed nothing about her.

Were they keeping her death silent? Had something gone wrong?

This was absurd! These newspapers printed every tidbit of nonsense and local gossip, and Lucy's death would be a countrywide tongue-wagger! How could they say nothing about it?

I had to know!

I arose, opened a window to the night's sky, and was about to transform when a sound distracted me. *Footsteps!* I tried to reach out with my mind, but I was racing over the countless impossibilities concerning Lucy, the absence of her obituary for which I couldn't account; I couldn't focus on yet another task. Instead, I marched through several rooms and found Renfield emptying a dustpan out a window.

"Master!" he recoiled with alarm, fear exploding upon his face.

I scanned the room with blazing eyes, and noted several cloths for dusting and a broom leaning against the wall, and slowly I restrained my anger.

"Thank you for attending to your duties," I said.

He stared at me as if in shock.

"Master, please don't kill me!" he said.

"You're not the cause of my anger," I told him, secretly amused he could read such intent upon my expression. "But someone is ... and they shall die ... *tonight!"*

Renfield's eyes widened even more, and he trembled.

"Command me, Master," Renfield said.

"You're performing the only task I require of you," I said. "I'm expecting a guest soon, and my house must be spotless. When you've finished, not before, help yourself to a bottle of brandy from the kitchen."

"I will, Master," Renfield said. "Thank you."

With a last glance, which I generously strove to keep from becoming a deadly glare, I turned to leave.

"Master ...?" Renfield asked.

I paused, and returned to face my servant.

"Master, when ... when I become ... like you ... will I be ... frightening?" he asked.

His question cut me to the quick; *I was failing at controlling my emotions.* Existence is a struggle between the rational mind and the emotions of the spirit. Where emotions maintain mastery, thoughts are overwhelmed and actions become spontaneous. Spontaneous actions are seldom rational, and often lead to consequences that only worsen their cause. I was too old and wise to get caught in that trap, but the fury in my dead heart was pounding.

I forced a deep breath to calm me down. I didn't need to breathe, but respiration was useful for its effects, even upon the undead. I had a plan, carefully laden and in the process of execution. *Was I going to ruin everything because of one more delay?*

No, I had to be rational. *Yes,* I needed to visit Lucy and discover the truth of her situation, but I didn't need to barge in unwelcomed and demand to know if Lucy was dead. The fact that I suspected her of dying, if bobbies were quietly investigating, might cause them to suspect, and investigate, me, and that I couldn't allow. My future business dealings required I maintain a low profile. To have detectives look into my arrival in England and my purchasing of this house could lead to revelations I'd no desire to have known.

"Renfield, what you'll become ... will be your choice," I said. "The gift of immortality requires the acceptance that change is eternal. Every century new experiences will fill you, you'll become wiser, more aware, and more free. You'll eventually understand concepts you couldn't guess at now. Who ... and what ... you'll be, you'll have the wisdom to decide – wisdom that you currently lack. Rest assured, my friend; whatever you choose, it'll be a wise choice."

Renfield smiled at me, and the relief on his face was easily read.

"Thank you, Master," he said.

Without another word, I swept from his presence.

In my main meeting room, before my favorite fireplace, I stared at the drawing of me I'd acquired from a local artist. From my framed portrait, my father's hard, strong eyes seemed to stare back at me from a face that only resembled his. *What would he say to me, if he could see me now?*

I'd lived too long without emotions of the spirit. In Transylvania, I'd spent a century denying all emotions, solely dedicated to pursuits of the mind. My every action was carefully thought out, and I moved with a stiffness caused mostly by my total emersion in rational thought. I was the embodiment of control, and therefore the ultimate in confidence, faultless, free of the errors of lesser men.

I'd also known no happiness.

Without the emotions of the spirit, success was assured. I'd purged myself of all liabilities, all spontaneity, and all frivolousness. I'd become the supreme being on Earth, incapable of mistake or blunder.

But that was my mistake!

I wasn't living. With emotions of the spirit comes passion and desire, and without lustful urges, what's the point of living? I'd become a miser of facts and analysis, hoarding them like a private treasure, and prizing what existed only in my mind. Now I was flourishing, awake, and walking among the living, sharing in their brief troubles; *I'd lived more since coming to England than I had in my last century in Castle Drăculea.*

Emotions of the spirit weren't to be denied, nor mastered, but partially controlled, as small punctures restrict the flow of blood. I was foolish to cut off emotions entirely. I needed to love again, to allow

Lucy's passions to respark the flame of my families' ambitions, which first lifted us above the peasant stock. I was bringing Lucy into my world, in a manner purposefully designed to avoid killing her light and happy spirit. I could allow nothing, not even my frustrations, to thwart my purpose.

As was written by Shakespeare in Henry V: '... *'tis the gentler hand which prevails.'*

Delays were to be expected. I must investigate before I act, to insure the correctness of my actions. I was in no hurry; *no power on Earth could prevent a mortal from dying.* If I was patient, and followed my passions thoughtfully, success was guaranteed.

I had to calm my temper!

Infuriations come from many sources, but the most insidious frustrations come not from external sources, but from exalted perceptions of self. All humans, mortal and undead, live inside our minds, and thus we are understandably fixated on ourselves. Some assume their exalted self-importance is shared by others ... each of whom have their own exalted perception. That's why mortals cheer when luck favors them, but feel slighted at the tiniest sting of the least perceived injustice. The wisest mortals, and the thoughtful undead, comprehend that luck that favors them usually makes someone else feel cursed, since that same luck didn't flow their way. Those smart enough to control their lives labor hard to align circumstances where luck can favor them, and take advantage when luck finally comes their way. Others are less likely to benefit from luck. Yet the idea that luck is deserved, or should fall in a certain way, is often the font of furious rages to blind even the rational mind ... and thus undo likelihoods that luck will ever profit us.

I'd labored hard to devise my plan. I'd willingly suffered deprivation to prepare myself for my ultimate challenge: to arise to the pinnacle my God-given vampiric abilities made possible. My centuries of experience and intellectual pursuits had gifted me the preparation I required; now I needed to step back and recall that I alone wanted the world to be ruled by me. My quiet entrance in England and low profile of dwelling was purposed to delay the challenges to my rule I knew would come, challenges dared by ambitious men seeking power ... and unwilling to surrender it.

If Lucy wasn't dead yet, then this was but a minor delay and easily rectified. She must've had medical help, perhaps from Dr. Seward, which troubled me; of all the threats to my plan, the greatest was my ignorance of England and its scientific advancements. In time, after I'd mingled in the affairs of Englishmen for a few years, then I'd be their equal in science and culture. Then would the supremacy of Drăcula be praised by all of England, and it'd be safe to make my presence generally known, although at least a century must pass before I'd feel safe to reveal my true nature. By then, my wealth and popularity would shield me from the stupid and narrow-minded, and the wealthiest and most ambitious men on Earth would surrender all they had in exchange for the ultimate gift of immortality. Then I'd become the richest and most-powerful individual in history, and together with the most-ambitious men as my loyal undead subordinates, we'd form a new ruling class to conquer and dominate every corner of the Earth.

Forcing myself to remain calm, I walked to the local shopping district, hailed a hack, and sat impatiently throughout the long drive to Hillingham. Unlike my previous visits, I directed the driver to steer past the front of her house, and then I shouted for him to stop, and wait there, right in the middle of the street. While stationary, I reached out to find Lucy, and easily connected with her mind, but she was deep in a dreamless slumber, and even my powers couldn't awaken her.

With a curt command, I ordered the driver to continue, and we rode past several houses before I commanded the driver to stop again, and this time I exited and paid him with a generous tip, which helped defer his curiosity as I walked away.

After the driver had driven away, I slipped into the shade of some trees, then wound my way back toward Lucy's house. Many windows were brightly lit, more than usual, and that alone was a sign something was amiss. On the main floor, I spied Dr. Seward talking quietly with an older gentleman I didn't know; they seemed to be discussing Lucy, but their voices were low.

No doubt Lucy was still alive due to some strange medicine unknown in Transylvania, administered by Dr. Seward. I gritted my teeth in frustration; eventually I intended to study all of the modern sciences, but such could be done in leisure time, after my plan was accomplished. Yet medicines couldn't stop me; next time I'd drain Lucy until no medicine could help.

I slipped outside the rose beds, circled the willow, and reached the outdoor stair my wolf-friend had found. Moments later I was peeking in at Lucy, asleep on her bed, with a servant cleaning up the room, folding blankets and wet-dusting the furniture. On the table beside her bed was a tray of small bottles; doubtless one of these was the vial whose contents had kept Lucy from the death we desired.

I waited patiently, standing in the shadows outside Lucy's door, as the maid finished cleaning, and then Dr. Seward and his elderly friend visited Lucy and examined her. Finally the lights were dimmed in Lucy's room, and still I waited. In the wee hours of the morning, after virtually everyone in the house was asleep, I entered. Lucy was still unconscious, and the latch on her door opened quietly. Like a whisper, I slipped inside.

Lucy was beautiful; as I knelt beside her, I couldn't resist the urge to kiss her lips before I kissed her throat. Yet when I bit into her neck, a shock struck me; the taste of her blood was completely different, strong and bitter, with only a little sweetness. For the first time, her taste repelled me, and I could only assume it was some horrible effect of the medicine that'd saved her life. But it was rich, healthy blood, and so I drank until her pulse was almost gone. When at last I lifted my head, licking the last drops from her sweet, white neck, I could almost feel her life failing, in her sleep, as I'd promised. She had almost no blood left; *no medicine could cure that.*

I arose with confidence, kissed her cheek softly, and stood, only to see a handwritten diary beside her bed. *Was Lucy writing about our meetings, or was she keeping up the pretense that she still hoped to marry Arthur?*

I picked up Lucy's diary and read the last entry:

9 September: I feel so happy tonight. I've been so miserably weak that to be able to think and move about is like feeling sunshine after a long spell of east wind out of a steel sky. Arthur stays very close. I feel his warm presence about me. Sickness and weakness are selfish things, and turn our inner eyes and sympathy on ourselves, whilst health and strength give Love reign. I know where my thoughts are. Arthur! My dear, my dear, your ears must tingle as you sleep, as mine do waking. Oh, the blissful rest of last night! How I slept, with that dear, good Dr. Seward watching me. And tonight I shall not fear to sleep, since he is close at hand and within call. Thank everybody for being so good to me! Thank God! Good night, Arthur.

With a satisfied grin, I set her diary back beside her bed and strode the walk of the victorious to her newly-repaired glass-paned door. *She was keeping my secrets ... leaving notes to spare the feelings of Arthur.* With one last look at Lucy in her final hour of life, I opened her door and stepped outside.
Be the bat!

Again, I awoke believing Lucy had died. Yet I couldn't trust luck any more. Once again, I'd have to travel to Hillingham to confirm the inevitable.

I arose with my old determination; *I was tired of patience.* If Lucy wasn't dead, then tonight I'd kill her by any means necessary.

Anyone who stood in my way would die.

No more traveling by coach. As painful and difficult as transformation was, I'd arrive at Lucy's door by my own power. *No more unexpected difficulties ...!*

A dim light still glowed in the western sky; *I needed to wait.*

I retrieved my mail, read a few letters and flipped through the ruffling pages of my newspapers with growing intemperance. Had I lost my mind in the joy of becoming young again? Youth had restored to me an exuberance I'd forgotten; my current spirit of delightful trivialities held no dominion in Castle Drăculea. I'd become too accepting of failure since I'd come to England. It was time I restored my intense mental discipline, which over the centuries had grown to surpass human control as an ancient god towers over a newborn in thought and memory.

When night fully encompassed my new world, I gritted my teeth, determined to fly to Lucy and return of my own power. I'd be hungry afterwards ... if I didn't feed tonight. Only one tower arose from my new home, a small room rising slightly above the roof with a view of the gardens. I ascended the narrow stairs to this cramped pinnacle of my domicile and opened its thick shutters, which creaked on rusty hinges. The moon was rising already. In an hour, I'd be with Lucy.

Be the bat!

The transformation agony died quickly, and I paid my weariness no more heed than a pinprick. I stood in the woods not far from her gazebo, and even from here I could see more lights than usual in Lucy's house. But all the demons of Hell wouldn't stay me tonight, nor prevent my success. *If I had to slay every living man and woman in Lucy's house to get to her, I would.*

I barely glanced at the white gazebo as I passed it, crossed the footbridge, and strode through the gardens to her house. The roses were blooming late in the season, and gave off a heady perfume which only one as aged as I could recognize as filled with the clotting scents of their failing life as winter approached. I hurried up the narrow steps and walked fearlessly across the balcony toward Lucy's door. I didn't care if someone inside the house saw me pass by their window. If they tried to stop me, then they'd suffer the wrath of a Drăculești.

At her door I reached out with my mind; *Lucy was there!* She was still alive, but asleep, her mind twisting with troubling dreams, and strangely hazy, difficult to connect to, as if her thoughts were barred from my entry. Through the glass panes of her door, I saw her angelic face, and I could wait no longer. She was alone in bed, her covers pushed down to her waist, writhing as if trying to awaken, some unknown darkness tormenting her dreams.

No one else was there. *I'd never get a better chance.*

I seized the handle to open the door ... and suddenly I recoiled, wincing, pained. My nose wrinkled and I almost choked. I released the door handle and fell back, gagging. *Something was wrong ...!*

... No! It couldn't be ...!

Garlic!

Well I knew that cursed flower, which the peasants of my lands grow in abundance, especially around their doors and in planters built into their windows. Transylvanian peasants know garlic offends me ... and protects them ...

... How could anyone in England know of my weakness ...?!?

The power of garlic over vampirism is understandable. Our senses are keen, our noses more acute than any human mortal, and the pungent scent of garlic, with its subtle healing properties, acts like a poison to the undead, an odor which seeps into our flesh and renders us useless, as lifeless as a real corpse. You can't heal vampirism, and all attempts only bring my kind closer to eternal death. True healing cuts like a slow scythe, decapitating us by inches.

I fell back, astounded, looking through the window at the sheer volume of my enemy. Lucy's room hosted a hundred garlic flowers, garlands strewn everywhere, encircling her bed. Each blossom was heavy with those hard, heady lumps which could suffocate my kind. *Why was it there?* Worse, I sensed those cursed plants not only adorned my Lucy's bedchamber, but had been rubbed all over the doorframe, such that it reeked. *How could anyone know this trick to defy me? Who could've done this?*

This was no accident! *Someone knew a vampire was visiting Lucy and had poisoned her room against me ... but who?* Englishmen didn't know about vampires ... or the charms used by Transylvanian peasants. But someone had sealed her room. In two steps, I stood outside her window, seeking another ingress, but it reeked almost as badly as her door. The inside of her window frame was smeared thickly, layered with oil of garlic, and flowers of it hung over the glass. *I was trapped outside!*

Only a fool stands outside a trap and waits for it to be sprung. I was revealed, and soon I'd be seen. I'd not come here prepared for combat, and I was still weak from my flight and the nearness of the poison. With a flash of hate, I considered transforming and fleeing back to my home, where I could ponder this mystery in safety. Yet such was the pungent power of the garlic that I couldn't transform, not while recoiling from the toxins of a hundred evil blooms, for that was the greatest effort my undead body could manage. I stepped back, and then strode silently away, along the route I'd come, this time careful not to be seen, and stomped with uncontrolled fury past garden, footbridge, and gazebo, following the trail uphill to the church and the bench where Lucy'd promised to be mine. There I stood and raged in silent turmoil.

There had to be an explanation! Perhaps one of my people, fled from my lands when young, had made his way to England, and seen the marks of my teeth upon Lucy's neck. They'd possess knowledge unknown to residents of this young country. Perhaps it wasn't a Transylvanian, but a stranger from another land, where another vampire ruled in secret, and their weaknesses were known. Perhaps it was another undead, one of those I sired when I was young and foolish, who lived in secret upon this island. The possibilities were endless, but I'd no way to know which was true. How could I know?

How could I not know?

My plan! My plan was being upset at every turn! Small deviances and setbacks I'd expected, and even anticipated, but knowledge of my nature was a major derivation from my plan ... *and could possibly derail it!*

I had to know how this had occurred. I reached out to my Lucy in her sleep, but the garlic fumes filling her nostrils smothered my attempts to waken her. *While she slept in there, surrounded by venomous vapors, I couldn't reach her!* Thoughts flashed through my mind like poisoned arrows. I could return and try to awaken her from her balcony by shouting or banging upon her doorframe, but such crude measures were sure to awaken everyone in her house, and as someone inside her house had purposefully barred her room against me. They might know my other weaknesses, and to alert them to my presence could expose me while I was weakened by garlic.

I mustn't be hasty and ruin my plans over this unforeseen misfortune. I must withdraw, recover my strength and wits, and return armed to deal with this threat.

I frowned deeply; I'd sworn to slay my Lucy tonight.

Someone would pay for this meddling!

Angry, I faced the sky, the moon now high amid the stars.

Be the bat!

The next evening I awoke ravenous, so hungry I considered summoning Renfield just to consume him, but that'd be a terrible waste of a servant already docile to my commands. *But his fellows ...!* Renfield wasn't confined alone, and I could choose my pick among the inmates of the asylum, so conveniently nearby, and one of the madmen would be blamed for the murder ...!

Yet that meant I'd have to enter the estate of Dr. John Seward, who'd recognize me in an instant. Even if he didn't, a murder so close could bring bobbies asking if I'd heard any disturbance in the night, and I'd no desire for official visitors. No, I'd carefully refrained from committing murder in my district, and I'd be a fool to change my mind.

I rose at once, dressed in top hat and cape, and trod a different path far around the nearby Purfleet marketplace, and by diverse avenues reached the end of the populated district, where shops gave way to inns and private residences. There I waited in the shadows, my stomach growling, until all of the carriages disappeared save one.

I stepped out into the glow of the streetlamp and whistled at the driver, who waved back, then turned his rig around and approached me. Having stepped back into the shadows, I re-emerged into the light, feigning difficulty, making my knees shake as I walked. When the driver stopped, and saw me tottering slowly toward his carriage, he lithely jumped down from the gotza, took my arm, and opened his door before assisting me to enter. Slowly, making my foot tremble as it rose, I lifted my foot to the small wooden step ... and seized his arm to support my weight. Then, I slipped inside his carriage, and I suddenly pulled with all of my might, desperation increasing my vampiric strength.

With a brief cry, the young driver was jerked forward, and I pulled him bodily in with me, clamping my hand over his mouth as quickly as I could. Burying his face in the thick cushions of his coach, I pulled aside his shoulder and sank my fangs like a cobra, deep into his neck, right into the huge pulsing artery. Blood spewed, faster than I could drink, but I lapped up all I could and sucked for more. He fought and thrashed and kicked until I'd no choice; with all the strength of a Prince of Transylvania and a warrior of four centuries, I released his mouth, raised my fist, and hammered down upon the back of his head like the pounding of a smith on steel.

The driver fell limp, unconscious, and I supped at his life's blood until nothing remained.

Many spots of blood covered my shirt and cape, but I didn't care. Someone in Lucy's house knew of vampirism, and possibly my identity. I'd no way to know this, but I dared not arrive unexpected if there was even a chance that someone in the house knew what I truly was. *Could Lucy have told ...? Had Arthur forced my secrets from her?* If so, then he'd die by my hand, but I had no proof; *Lucy was greatly weakened and could've talked in her sleep.* Or, as I'd already suspected, some person unknown to me, perhaps a fellow undead, could've intervened and plotted against me. *I'd never told Lucy about garlic, so how could she tell ...?*

Only at Lucy's house would I learn the truth.

I switched my hat and cloak for those of the driver, and with a mastery of horses surpassing any mortal, I assumed his seat on the gotza, cracked his whip, and drove his horses into a rapid walk. A pair of galloping horses in this district would draw attention and raise alarm, and another driver might recognize his rig and wonder why he wasn't driving, so I veered onto a side street and rode upon a dirt road rather than the cobblestones of the main street, and I stayed on the lesser streets until my passenger and I were far away. As I steered back to the main road, which I was forced to use to cross the bridges, I glanced inside the coach to find the bloodless body of the driver had slid to the floor, which would make it more difficult for others to see his corpse. I waited until I could see no other carriage upon the main road, and then I cracked my whip and drove my horses onward. The farther we got from my district unseen the less likely his rig would be recognized.

Despite my frequent journeys, I found identifying the landmarks difficult, but as hours passed, I focused on the shapes of the horizons, as a bat would, and managed to locate the general area. The large cross atop the church on the hill behind Lucy's house was rather unique, and once I'd spotted it with my undead night-vision, I was no longer lost. I drove my coach all the way up to the dark church, steered behind it, and edged down a narrow uncobbled lane hemmed with bushes and tree branches scraping the rig on both sides; possibly no one had ever driven a coach down this narrow dirt road. There I left the horses, who were doubtless thirsty, tied to a tree limb, and hurried along the narrow trail to Lucy's house.

At the white gazebo I halted, intending to spy before I approached, when I noticed an oddity: a black silk ribbon was tied around one of the gazebo's posts. In the darkness, surely no one but me could see it. I stared at this, wondering what it meant, and finally I untied it. As it fell free, a tiny scroll fell to the floor of the gazebo; I snatched up the paper, unrolled, and read it.

"Dr. Van Helsing is here.
I'm being watched.
Don't forget me.
-L"

A smile stretched my lips for the first time in days. *Lucy still wanted me!* Joy filled my heart, but as I reread the tiny scroll, the name *Dr. Van Helsing* took my smile away. *A doctor;* perhaps it was he who was keeping my precious Lucy alive, preventing her from joining me!

What kind of medicine could replace lost blood?

I stood there long, puzzling over what I must do. I couldn't endure another night without killing my beloved.

Past midnight, I slowly sensed that Lucy was weak and asleep, her lungs still filled with the poisonous fumes of that cursed garlic. Yet Lucy wasn't alone in the house; I ranged out, found a maid busy drinking her master's sherry in the familiar library, and I drove into her. She was drunk, her mind easy to penetrate and command, and I quickly captivated her. I gave her strict and clear orders, but softly, so she wouldn't suspect, and sensed her rise and ascend the stairs toward Lucy's room.

I stood tingling with excitement. The drunk maid entered the bedchamber of my sleeping Lucy, and busied herself removing all of the garlic flowers and garlands, stuffing them into a bag. As the fumes around her intensified, I commanded she let in some fresh air, and from my vantage point I saw Lucy's glass-paned door open wide, and then windows slid open from inside, and the foul fumes dissipated as her curtains blew about in the night air. Less than an hour after she'd entered the room, the maid left, taking with her the dreaded poisons, and leaving my path to Lucy open.

I hurried to the open door, taking every precaution. *Nothing must delay me now!*

Within minutes, I stood there, alone with my beloved, the lingering fumes noxious but bearable. I rushed to her bedside and sank my fangs into her pale throat without ceremony. I drank, gorging myself. As I emptied her, I sensed her consciousness slipping away. Again I ignored the strange, bitter taste of her blood, and I didn't stop until I felt her life precariously balanced on the edge of failing, her heartbeat stuttering within her breast. I left her just enough blood to die within minutes, in her sleep, as she'd requested, and thus she'd die exactly as she wanted. No medicine could cure her this time; before the next hour chimed, Lucy would be dead ... and then she'd be mine.

I drew back and looked at her neck, chalk white from loss of blood. The skin on my hands slowly darkened, as if I'd drunk a man's blood, while her pallor softened to a beautiful alabaster.

I sat beside her, staring at her, when I heard a cry from the outer room. With haste, I fled out the door, just reaching the shadows of the balcony before I heard the crash of Lucy's inner door flung open, followed by gasps of horror and a scream.

With the hunting skills of a Transylvanian prince, I slipped away like a silent shadow. Whoever was in that house didn't matter. Even if they knew everything about vampires, no mortal could stop Death when his victim was so primed.

I'd won. I'd succeeded. I'd proven myself a Drăculeşti.

Soon Lucy would be mine forever.
Be the bat!

Chapter 12

For the first time since I could recall, dusk awoke me a whole man. Lucy had to be dead, and my flight home had only slightly lessened the strange strength of the odd-tasting blood which filled me. I virtually leapt from my coffin, although never had I less need. Lucy's transformation couldn't occur during the daytime, and so tonight her evolution would begin. If it completed early, as some do, then tomorrow night we'd begin our eternal lives together, and if not, then the next night for certain.

I summoned Renfield, hoping to have him clean my house, but twenty minutes later strange, angry shouts arose from my garden. I froze, fearing I'd been discovered. Guards from the asylum were chasing after Renfield, who was running toward my door. I couldn't afford this attention, so I sent him a mental command to stop, and the voices grew louder.

They seemed to be fighting in my garden. I hurried to my chapel, and was amazed to hear angry shouts from just outside my door. Renfield was in one of his strange moods, a temper such as I'd never witnessed, and was fighting like a madman against multiple opponents. I realized his intent, ran to my door, seized the handle, and held it firm just as Renfield reached it from the other side. His insanity was blazing, and he raged against the asylum guards, and cursed them, but they heeded him not. With all of his might, Renfield pulled to open the door between us, but I stood on the inside, recently strengthened by the blood of my precious Lucy; I held the chapel door infrangible.

With great mental effort, I forced my way inside Renfield's troubled mind, which felt as if I'd shoved my face into a burning furnace, so wild and fiery was his insanity. Twisted thoughts burned as coals in a rolling forge, churning in endless circles of random impulses, fears so horrific only a Christian Hell could epitomize them. No sane thoughts permeated his ravings, and so I simply drove them all out with a blast of immortal anger so furious his lesser terrors quailed before it.

The shock of my intrusion stunned Renfield, such that he fell beneath the blows of the guards wrestling him. Their curses were no less vehement than his, and their punches and kicks rained until no movement showed resistance. Renfield collapsed under their assaults, and they dragged him from my door with no less anger than that with which they'd pursued him. Only then did I release my mental assault and my grip upon my chapel door.

Before they stepped out of hearing, one of the guards called out:

"We have him, Dr. Seward!"

I stood in silence, knowing what lay outside my door: Dr. John Seward, Arthur's friend, was standing in my garden, watching the recapture of his patient. If Renfield had raved my name, Dr. John Seward would've recognized it, and my location would be revealed. *Then what would I do?*

The voices of the guards trailed away; Renfield was being carried between them, back to his cell, too beaten to resist. I sighed; *I'd been lucky.* My presence hadn't been revealed, but it'd been a close call. *How did this happen?* My plan made no allowance for my residence to be known, and yet, my presence in Carfax had almost become common knowledge. *Again, I was taking too many chances, and where left to chance, most plans fail!*

I spent an hour wandering about my house, thinking. Someone in Lucy's house was protecting her against vampires; they must've recognized the tiny scars on her neck. Lucy was still betrothed to Arthur. Dr. John Seward was Arthur's friend. The knowledge that I was Dr. Seward's neighbor would connect me to the vampire bites on Lucy's neck.

I couldn't afford to be revealed!

Or, could I ...? My plan was made in a distant land governed by rules unknown in England, imagined by a stiff and rotting corpse, and now I was young, strong, and handsome. I had four centuries of cunning and canniness and the night-powers of God's curse. Why shouldn't I change my plan ... as long as my goal remained the same?

Or was I as mad as Renfield? Taking chances when there was no need made no sense, but making things more difficult, just to follow an unwritten plan, was equally foolish. Perhaps it was time I took a more active role in acquiring all I wanted. Why was I cowering in fear? I, before whom countless men have trembled? No; *it was time I took a more active role in my plan!*

I fetched my mail, of which there was only one letter: the weekly report of my accounts from my London banker, and determined I needed more wealth. Soon I'd want to spend all my time with Lucy, and trivialities such as making money would become an unwelcomed distraction. *I needed more money now.*

Of all the wealthy men I'd met in Arthur and Lucy's house, there wasn't one that stood apart from the others. All were bland, greedy, and insignificant, and any of them could provide me with all of the resources I needed. Yet there wasn't one of them whose company I'd enjoy, or who seemed especially interested in me. Their greed, contempt, and suspicions would be a hindrance to my plan; I needed someone who'd welcome my company, who'd invite me into their home and not spread word about ...

I had it! The one wealthy guest of Lucy and Arthur's dinner party who'd willingly offer me everything they had, and make my deception a joy: *Mrs. Effington!*

I frowned; to get in touch with her, I'd need to know where to look for her, and there was only one place I could gain such knowledge: *I had to go back to Hillingham.*

Slowly a new plan began to form in my mind. Whoever knew that Lucy had been bitten by a vampire doubtlessly suspected I'd be careful not to reveal myself, and especially not my address, to those protecting her. *Yet ... what if I reversed that?* I'd promised to invite Lucy and Arthur to a dinner party at my house ... what suspicions would be arisen if I just happened to drop off an invitation on the day she died, and hung around to offer my condolences to Lucy's grieving widower? That way I'd learn about Lucy and gain the address I wanted!

The irony of my new plan amused me. *Was I succumbing to the foolishness of youth?* Perhaps, but I could never go back to being a stiff corpse lumbering around a crumbling ruin. Like it or not, my old life was over. I hurried to my desk, took out ink, pen, and paper, and wrote a brief but very clear invitation to dine at my residence, and addressed it to Mr. Arthur

Holmwood and Miss Lucy Westenra ... and guests. With a laugh, I folded my letter, folded an envelope around it, sealed it with wax, seized my hat and cape, and strode out my front door.

Doubts nagged me during the ride to Hillingham but I shoved them aside. I was a prince, and if this was a mistake, then I'd deal with the consequences. As I expected, most of the windows at Lucy's house were dark, but some were blazing brightly. I paid my driver well and explained that I might be returning shortly, and if I didn't, I'd need his services no more this evening. He promised to wait fifteen minutes, no more, and then he'd drive away.

Invitation in hand, I walked up to the front door of the mansion and knocked loudly. Only a minute later, the butler I'd seen before opened the door.

"Good evening," I said to the butler. "I am Count Drăcula, a friend of Arthur and Miss Lucy Westenra. I'm not expected, but I was passing by and wished to have a word with them ..."

"Please come inside," the butler said. "Miss Westenra is ill, but I'll see if Mr. Holmwood is available."

I stepped into their foyer, and after closing the door behind me, the butler hurried off through a long hallway. I waited patiently, and noticed a telegram laid absently upon a small table. I picked it up, and found it was a missive from Dr. John Seward to Arthur Holmwood, dated September 6th.

> *My dear Art,*
> *My news today is not so good. Lucy has gone back a bit. There is, however, one good thing which has arisen from it; I*

took advantage of the opportunity, and told her that my old master, Van Helsing, the great specialist, was coming to stay with me, and that I'd put her in his charge conjointly with myself; so now we can come and go without alarming her unduly, for a shock to her, in Lucy's weak condition, might be disastrous. We are hedged in with difficulties, my poor fellow; but, please God, we shall come through them all right. If any need I shall write, so that, if you do not hear from me, take it for granted that I am simply waiting for news.
  In haste, Yours ever,
  Dr. John Seward

  Suddenly I heard footsteps and I set the letter back down.
  "Count Drăcula," Arthur said, coming down the hall, his hand outstretched. I shook his hand smiling, but I was perplexed; he didn't look like a man in mourning. "An unexpected honor, but I'm afraid you've come at a bad time ..."
  "Forgive me if I've intruded," I said to Arthur, holding up my envelope. "I promised to invite you and your fiancée, Miss Westenra, to a dinner party at my house, and I've come to present my invitation in person ..."
  I held up my invitation, offering it, but he didn't take it.
  "My dear count, you must forgive me," Arthur said. "Lucy's very ill, and only the services of a great physician has saved her."

"*Ill ...?*" I asked. *Lucy wasn't dead ...?!?*
"Forgive me, for I'm not skilled in medicine, but if there's anything I can do ...?"

"I thank you, but all that can be done is being accomplished," Arthur said.

"It's inexcusable barging in here at such a time," I said, and I pocketed my invitation. "Poor Lucy! To be so young and beautiful ... and ill? I've never wished anything for her but the best. No, I'll leave you to care for her in peace ..."

"Please stay, Count Drăcula," Arthur said. "Lucy considers you a friend, and she'd be dismayed if I allowed you to leave without refreshment. Come into my study. A friend is there ... and one as wise and learned as you: Dr. Van Helsing."

I staggered: *Dr. Van Helsing! The name on Lucy's note and the telegram!* With alarm tingling my senses, and overwhelming curiosity, I stiffened my shoulders and followed as Arthur led me back to a small, dark-paneled sitting room filled with books, clutter, and two men sitting in chairs before a blazing fireplace. One of them I recognized at once: Quincey P. Morris, the tall, rugged American. Quincey rose as I entered.

"Count Drăcula!" Quincey exclaimed.

"Peace to you, and healing to Miss Lucy," I said, and we shook hands.

"Ah, you are a friend of our dear miss ...?" an old, gray-bearded man asked, holding aside his pipe, his head still wreathed in smoke as he sat before the fire.

"Dr. Van Helsing, may I present Count Drăcula," Arthur said. "He's a dear friend of Lucy's ..."

"Good!" Dr. Van Helsing said, and I noted that his heavy Germanic accent distinguished him as a stranger to these parts, although he was undoubtedly English; he sounded more a foreigner than I. "We have need of all honorable men, if they be strong of heart."

"Forgive me, I'd no idea until I arrived that Miss Westenra was feeling poorly," I said.

"Her condition's prickly as a cactus," Quincey said. "If not for the good doctor here, Lucy would've fallen on the prairie."

"Merciful heavens!" I feigned concern. *So this was why Lucy had warned me of him!* "Forgive me, I'd not meant to intrude ..."

"You could never intrude here, Count Drăcula," Arthur assured me.

"Enough," Dr. Van Helsing stopped us. "You are here. You care for Miss Lucy. We need you."

"For Miss Westenra, anything! How may I help?" I asked.

"We must protect Miss Lucy," Dr. Van Helsing said. "Day and night, but night is the most important."

"I'll make myself available every night," I said.

"Good man!" Quincey said, and Arthur laid a hand on my shoulder.

"Thank you, Count Drăcula," Arthur said. "I ... I don't think I could bear this alone."

"Again, you must beg my pardon, but I don't understand," I said, looking at each of them. "I'm no man of medicine, but ... guards can't stop a sickness. What ails Miss Westenra?"

Arthur and Quincey both looked at Dr. Van Helsing.

"I dare not speak my suspicions," Dr. Van Helsing said, and he broke his pipe against the mantle, then tapped the burning coals down with his bare thumb and puffed on its mouthpiece. "Not yet, for I must be certain. Miss Lucy has fallen under the dire occurrence of a disease so rare and unthinkable I must confirm it before we act, an illness so terrible only the devil himself may be responsible. She needs rest to build up her strength, and her rest must be uninterrupted, or the worst beyond worst may happen. Our first duty is to see she receives all rest, and that I am determined to do. Devil or no devil, or all of the devils at once, it matters not; we fight him all the same."

"*Him ...?*" I asked, but Dr. Van Helsing only shook his head.

"His mouth's tight as a tick," Quincey answered my question.

"Then, how was she saved?" I asked.

"Ah, that was a miracle," Arthur said. "Dr. Van Helsing performed a transfusion ..."

"Transfusion?" I asked, and the look each man gave me told me they'd expected all Englishmen to know this word. "Forgive me, but I've enjoyed excellent health and know little of medicine."

"It's a process of putting the blood of a healthy person, using hollow needles, into the veins of a person needing blood," Arthur said. "Yet we must tread softly; transfusions can kill, and are banned in France, but with Lucy, we had no choice."

I stared at Arthur, amazed; *never had I heard of such an operation!* Living blood, taken not through the mouth, but directly into the inner body! *Could a vampire feed in such a manner? Or would such pure, living, unfiltered blood cause instant death-beyond-death?* I dared not attempt this on myself, but I must learn this method, make another vampire, and test this upon them. Perhaps Renfield ...

"Most ingenious," I said. "I must see this device."

"Hopefully we won't need it again, but I have it standing ready, in case Miss Lucy deteriorates," Dr. Van Helsing said.

"Time," Quincey said suddenly, reaching over to a tall, thin hourglass that stood on a desk. He tapped it as the last of the sands poured through, and then he and Arthur stepped toward the door.

"Time ...?" I asked.

"To check on Lucy," Arthur said. "We'll just be a moment. Would you like to ...?"

"No, the dear thing is probably sleeping," I said. "I'll wait here."

Arthur and Quincey departed, and I looked at the elderly doctor, who waved his pipe, gesturing to the other chair before the fireplace, in which Quincey had been sitting. I took the seat, noting the gray, steely eyes of the doctor focused upon me with intense concentration. He seemed in good physical health for a man his age; doubtless he'd once been strong, but his once-brown hair was thick with white, and his gristly beard completely gray.

"Count Drăcula, where were you made a count?" Dr. Van Helsing asked.

"I was born to the Hungarian imperial family," I said, and then I smiled. "On the morning of my birth, I was 37th in line for the throne, if I remember correctly."

"Hungary ...?" Dr. Van Helsing mused. "That's a very remote birthland; I admit I know it only on maps. Tell me, have you known our dear Miss Lucy long?"

"Several months, I believe," I said. "We met at the opera."

"Which opera?" he asked.

"Le nozze di Teti e di Peleo," I said. "Actually, it was a dismal performance. Being introduced to Lucy and Arthur was the highlight of the evening."

"So, you are new to them ...," Dr. Van Helsing said. "How long have you been in England?"

"Several years now," I said. "Is my accent still so obvious?"

"I am well-traveled and recognize most accents well, even those that have mostly faded," Dr. Van Helsing said. "Why did you come to England?"

"That's no secret," I said. "I've educated myself as far as possible in my homeland, which is far more rugged and medieval than your great empire, and I wished to further my studies ... to bring the edifications of your country to mine. I hope my presence here doesn't distress you."

"I ask not to pry into your private affairs," Dr. Van Helsing said. "It is for the sake of the young lady upstairs I inquire. I must know all things concerning her if I am to treat her illness. Of what afflicts her, I have only suspicions, but if I am correct, then it is something new to England ... and very dangerous."

"Dr. Van Helsing, I give you the inviolate promise of a Drăculeşti: I love our dear Miss Lucy, and for her I wish only for the best. Pray tell me: what afflicts her?"

"Lucy suffers from an illness that endangers both her health ... and her soul," Dr. Van Helsing said, and his pupils followed my eyebrows as they rose. "Come now, my well-travelled friend; we who have seen the wilder parts of this world know there are mysteries for which science cannot account, do we not?"

Dr. Van Helsing leaned closer, his wrinkled, wiry gray brows deepened, and his arresting gaze, staring into me, intensified. I hesitated; he was testing me, and to his eyes I was a man in my thirties, and I dared not divulge any understandings a young visitor to England couldn't possess. I was at least six times his elder, but his mature demeanor was startlingly powerful, almost hypnotic, which implied an impressive intelligence. I was facing a formidable opponent, perhaps even a rival to Mïeta's immortal guile.

"Peasant superstitions thrive in every backward land," I sidestepped his question.

The corners of his lips lowered, and Dr. Van Helsing stared deeper into my eyes, his face radiating determination.

"Count Drăcula, have you ever heard ... of vampires?"

Even I was taken aback by this question, but I shrugged it off.

"No, but English isn't my native tongue," I said.

"I see ...," Dr. Van Helsing said, but he didn't appear convinced.

"So ...," I asked, "what are vampires?"

"Vampires are a curse upon this Earth," Dr. Van Helsing said. "They're a plague upon mankind, and it's the duty of every man of honor to eradicate them."

I waited, but Dr. Van Helsing said no more. I sat, feeling the heat of the fireplace, and momentarily returned his stare, but I was supposed to be younger than he, and so I shrugged first.

"Your words are alarming, but not informative," I said. "Pray tell me more."

Dr. Van Helsing didn't appear to hear me, but he was scrutinizing my every expression, as if he could detect a lie as easily as I.

"I will tell you this," Dr. Van Helsing said at last. "The symptoms of Miss Lucy Westenra's illness have never been seen in this part of the world, but in distant, primitive lands, they are clearly documented. This disease acts within a carrier, a person who is very aware of their infection, and who seeks to spread their infection to others. This makes them very dangerous, for this disease is, by its nature, conscious and aware, and its victims are not chosen by chance, but by choice."

"A disease that thinks ...?" I asked.

"Precisely," Dr. Van Helsing said. "And, as a conscious sickness, it can assume any number of disguises and lurk among us, pretending to be a friend ... while plotting foul murders."

"*Murders?*" I asked. "Have there been murders?"

"Recently, a carriage driver was found on the floor of his own hack ... not a quarter mile from here," Dr. Van Helsing said.

My reaction was horrified, but only I knew its source. *How could I have been so stupid? Despite all my planning, I'd left a body here!*

"Sir, this greatly troubles me," I said. "I came to your England to embroil myself in enlightenment, not in the activities of murderers. I'll do all that I can, but I must keep my family name unsoiled from associations with criminals."

"The throat of this man was bitten, and he was drained of blood," Dr. Van Helsing said.

I assumed an appearance of puzzlement, glad for the sounds of footsteps approaching in the hall.

"Drained of blood ...?" I asked. "This sounds like ... a demon from the Old Testament."

"It does indeed," Dr. Van Helsing said as Arthur and Quincey came back into the room, and he looked up at them. "Speak my friends; how is Lucy?"

"Sleeping soundly," Arthur replied. "Her room is undisturbed."

"Even asleep, she smiles ... her ever-cheerful spirit," Quincey added, glancing at Arthur.

"Excellent, excellent," Dr. Van Helsing said. "The count and I were just discussing Lucy's inexplicable loss of blood ..."

"Yep, that's a shindy," Quincey said.

Dr. Van Helsing tapped his pipe, for it had gone out, and then he drew out his small tobacco pouch, which had sewn into it tiny pockets for tools. One of these was a miniature knife, which heavy pipe smokers used to carve away charred remains inside their pipes. Dr. Van Helsing began scraping at the inside of his pipe, and with a sudden jerk, he slit open a tiny gash across his thumb.

"Ah, speaking of curses!" he exclaimed, and then he held his thumb up to show us. "There, exactly what we are talking about: blood."

The powerful scent of fresh blood filled my senses, yet I restrained myself, merely looking at the glorious red flow as Arthur and Quincey did, with a mixture of interest and sympathy. Yet Dr. Van Helsing held his hand up to my face, holding out his bloody thumb as if expecting me to pounce upon it; he apparently knew more about vampires than I normally allowed mortals to know, but I was Drăcula, not one of my starving brides; *I wouldn't seize his bait.*

His bleeding thumb held out, his eyes stared at mine, until Arthur and Quincey glanced at each other,

Dracula, Deathless Desires

confused by this action. Then Dr. Van Helsing sighed and withdrew his cut thumb.

"Friend Drăcula, you will perhaps forgive me," Dr. Van Helsing said.

"No forgiveness is necessary," I said. "Whatever action you must take to protect Miss Lucy, I support it entirely. This illness which you speak of, it's new to Lucy, as am I, and you must take all precautions. Tomorrow morning I'll speak to my valet and rearrange my busy schedule that I may return each night and offer any assistance I can."

"Count Drăcula, I can't thank you enough," Arthur said, and his took my hand and shook it.

"A fellow of the first water!" Quincey said, and he seized my shoulder and gave it a hardy shake.

"Then we are all united," Dr. Van Helsing said. "Tomorrow our good friend John will join us, and together, we'll find and destroy this infection that torments our sweet Lucy."

I held out my hand, and Dr. Van Helsing warmly shook hands with the very *'infection'* of which he spoke.

Quincey turned the hourglass back over, and its sands began to pour.

I stayed later than usual, and left successful. Dr. Van Helsing had shown me his medical instruments for performing a transfusion, which he named a 'Blundell's Impellor', and he kept stored in a thick mahogany box. It was a complex device consisting of a large funnel, connected by a tube to a circular brass device with a small crank, and more copper tubing, the end of which was connected to a sharp silver needle. The other devices seemed to be a framework for supporting the device.

"I met Dr. James Blundell," Dr. Van Helsing said. "Parts of this device came from his original invention. He was an obstetrician at Guy's Hospital, and Blundell invented his transfusion machine to treat post-partum hemorrhage in 1828 based upon the earlier works of John Henry Leacock, and I have added my own improvements. This large needle and tube goes into the donor and directs the blood into the funnel, and the needle on the larger device goes into the patient. The blood is impelled by turning the crank on this small pump, which Blundell said provides stronger flow than his gravitator."

"An ingenious invention," I said. "I wish I'd met Dr. Blundell."

"My friend, Dr. Blundell died 19 years ago, in 1878," Dr. Van Helsing said. "You would have been a very young boy."

"Of course," I said quickly, hiding my smile.

Arthur gave me the address of Mrs. Effington, and I left about two hours before dawn with the promise to reschedule my dinner party for an evening after Lucy was healthy again, and to invite not only Arthur and Lucy, but Dr. Van Helsing, Quincey, and Dr. John Seward. The best part: *I left with my invitation still in my pocket, unread, my address at Carfax still a secret.*

But my worst suspicions had been confirmed. Dr. Van Helsing knew of my kind, had recognized my handiwork, and had spared my dear Lucy from the death and transformation she wanted and deserved.

Like it or not, I may have to kill them all.

Confidence comes from understanding a difficult situation, even before the problem is resolved. I awoke the next evening weak from my flight back home in the early pre-dawn. The sun had been almost risen before I resumed my human form, and my vampiric resistance did little to spare me the agony of transformation. I'd crawled into my coffin like a cripple. I needed a feeding, but I awoke with the strength of a determined man who knew his intentions.

My mailbox was empty save for newspapers, so I'd no responses to write. My house was only half-cleaned, but Renfield was probably chained up. I'd no other obligations, and so I dressed and departed at once. The dark blue sky was still partly lit, glowing with the last light of day, but I pulled my cloak tight around me and hurried.

As I passed the asylum, I saw Renfield's face in a small, iron-barred, basement window, his hands gripping the bars, staring at me. I glanced to be sure no one was looking, and crossed the lawn to stoop down before him.

"Master, help me!" Renfield begged. "I'm chained!"

"You almost revealed me," I said to his haggard face. "You led guards to my house ..."

"I didn't know they were ...," Renfield began.

"Never lie to Drăcula!" I commanded him, and he fell silent under the power of my anger. "I heard your fist-fight against the guards, and all of your shouts, and the cries of those you led to my door. *Never do that again!* I still have need of you or I'd kill you now. Remain here, silent and respectful, until I come for you. Tell no one of me."

Renfield's face drained of blood, his blood which was now mixed with my own, and would someday arise him as a vampire, if I allowed it. Yet I couldn't; when I'd no further use for him, I'd gladly kill Renfield so he couldn't revive.

I walked away, wasting no more thoughts on Renfield. I'd more important tasks to perform. Soon I'd purchased a large bouquet of flowers, hailed an unfamiliar cab driver, entered his red-painted Victoria, and gave him the address to the home of Mrs. Effington.

The stately home of Mrs. Effington was a palatial estate, lined with marble walkways inside its tall, ivy-overgrown wrought iron fence. Gardens surrounded her mansion, and the entrance was dotted with fountains, splashing cascades into waiting pools reflecting the moonlight.

I knocked, and a young woman answered the door. She appeared to be a maid, and she was quite attractive, but I wasn't looking for an intimate pursuit. She accepted my flowers, promising to take them straight to Mrs. Effington.

My vampiric hearing amused me; less than a minute later, Mrs. Effington's voice squealed with delight, and the pretty maid described me, with a soft tinge of regret in her voice, as a handsome young man who'd asked for a private interview. I could hear them hurry into another room and up some back stairs, calling for other servants. I stood there, alone, looking about at the impressive artistry of her foyer, which was bright, with candles reflecting off white marble walls veined with pink, and a wide stairs of polished oak leading up to an impressive height. A gold chandelier topped everything, of which the precious metal had to be plated over a stronger metal, as it supported a hundred crystal icicles, each shining with light. The few carved and painted faces in the room were angels, each smiling blissfully.

This was a home of the living, of those who delight in brightness and gaiety, the opposite of the dark entryway of Castle Drăculea. I pondered upon the strong impression of the entrance to a building, and how the first impression of a dwelling often affects those who dwell there. When I rebuilt Castle Drăculea, I'd have to plan its entrance carefully.

Twenty minutes later, having changed clothes, her hair brushed, makeup thick upon her face, and reeking of flowery perfumes, Mrs. Effington appeared on the top of a balcony overlooking the entryway, and descended the grand staircase to extend her hand. I kissed it, and she blushed like a schoolgirl.

"Mrs. Effington, so kind of you to see me," I said.

"Count Drăcula, what a delightful surprise," Mrs. Effington said. "You honor my house with your presence."

"I hope you'll forgive me, but I practically pried your address from Arthur Holmwood," I said.

"You should've asked me at the party, silly boy," Mrs. Effington said. "My doors are always open to you."

"I must compliment you on your exquisite taste," I said, again glancing about at the spotless furnishings of the entryway.

"Oh, let me show you my whole house ... and my gardens," Mrs. Effington said. "But first, come into the parlor; you arrived just in time for tea."

As she spoke, a tea kettle began to whistle in a distant room, and urgent whispers too soft for her ears reached mine. Mrs. Effington took my arm in a surprisingly tight grip and pulled me slowly through a series of other rooms, a party room larger than my main library back in Castle Drăculea, a sitting room, and some sort of craft room, all of which were bright and elegant with elaborate furnishings, mostly white edged with gold, many displaying floral patterns. In each room I effused on the grandeur of her styles and taste in the latest fashions. Her house seemed to be less of a home than a showpiece to exhibit her wealth and grandiosity.

    Our final destination was a room intended for a small tea; the pretty maid and two other servants were still setting small plates of treats upon a tiny round table which lay against a wide window overlooking a moonlit garden. Pastoral paintings of young couples picnicking covered the pale-pink walls, and the flowers I'd brought her sat in a crystal vase on the table. The room held only two chairs.

    From my books, I'd learned enough of English customs to hold her chair until she'd seated herself, even if all I did was grasp her chair's back and stand there while she sat. I'd always thought this an odd custom, but the delight espoused by Mrs. Effington at this gesture explained it fully. Finally I took my seat opposite her as she gestured for all of the servants, especially the pretty maid, to depart, which they did so quickly I was impressed.

    Our conversation as she poured our tea was banal, but frequently interrupted with shrill, coy giggles, which quickly became annoying. I was forced to look into her candlelit face, and could easily see the great beauty she must've once been, although age had sunken her cheeks and whitened her pallor, thinned her lips to mere shadows around her mouth, and left wrinkles that looked like cat's claws scratching leather. Yet she had amazingly even and white teeth, even at her age, and her eyes were bright and lively, although her expressions and mannerisms left me with the undoubted opinion that her mind was quite vapid.

The tea was strong, but even the flavors of exotic herbs paled for one accustomed to the rich taste of blood. I excused myself several times as a stranger unused to formal tea, and carefully listened as she offered simple explanations to how one is supposed to sit, not to place your elbows upon the table, and how one should only sip their tea. Despite a barrenness of depth, she did know formal English etiquette, and only a fool doesn't pay rapt attention to an expert in any field.

She frequently thanked me for the beauty of my gift, droning on about her adoration of flowers, and gestured to her garden, insisting I return in the daytime when I could see her blossoms properly. Here I spoke up.

"Oh, Mrs. Effington, nothing you could've said would make me happier," I said. "The joy of your company is such a treat that this one meeting has addicted me!"

Her laughter was like a squealing throng of bats.

"Count Drăcula, I'd be honored if you'd accompany me!" Mrs. Effington said.

I smiled warmly, careful to keep my fangs hidden.

"I must confess, Mrs. Effington ...," I began.

"Oh, Count, please, you must call me Effie," she said.

"As you wish, Effie, but only if you'll call me Vlad," I said.

"Vlad!" Mrs. Effington effused. "I knew I'd heard your name before, but ...!"

"Yes, Miss Westenra, soon to be Mrs. Arthur Holmwood, exclaimed my name at her party," I said.

"I remember now," Mrs. Effington said. "You were going on about terrible things ..."

"Alas, it is for the joyous company of England I remain here," I said. "My life, like my homeland, has been very dark, and portentous of topics too morbid for an English tea ..."

"Oh, we can't discuss dire things here," Mrs. Effington said. "I'll make it my personal duty to show you such delights as will drive the darkness from your soul."

"That would indeed be a blessing," I said, although I had grave suspicions about her meaning. "Yet I mustn't forget propriety; my family is very old and respected, and I must be seen doing nothing to disgrace or demean my ancestral title."

"I wouldn't allow it, save for some trifling matters, of which only you and I will share the secret," Mrs. Effington said in a girlish whisper, her aged smile troublingly mischievous. "After all, we who live at the summit of society can't allow our titles and honors to remove all hopes of pleasurable indulgences ... we're too good for that!"

"Well, forgive me if I must ask, but propriety demands; may I ask ... where your husband is now, and when he'll return?"

The first shadow of displeasure darkened Mrs. Effington's face, and she looked down, and her thin lips seemed to vanish entirely.

"Mr. Effington is currently in Russia, and will return to Frankfort and Belize before he wanders home," Mrs. Effington said.

"Ah, so he is a frequent traveler, and one accustomed to doing business abroad," I said. "Is he often in England?"

"Mr. Effington is always busy, and seldom stays anywhere for long," Mrs. Effington said. "Half the time I never know where he is. His ... secretary ... sends me flowers with a note every time he arrives in a new country, but he flits from city to city so quickly it's almost impossible to get a message to him."

Her entire attitude shifted, as if she'd joined the undead and become as dark as Loritá. While I preferred this change, it would damage my purpose.

"How can any man endure an absence from you?" I asked, eyeing her slyly.

Her smile beamed like the dawn sun, bright and deadly.

"Let's change the subject," Mrs. Effington said.

"Please do, but first, forgive me if I must insist, for proprieties' sake, if we are to ... tea ... often, then I'd like to be introduced to him at the earliest possible opportunity," I said. "For my families' sake ..."

"Yes, yes," Mrs. Effington said huffily, and she seemed to be foundering, seeking another topic, but uncertain which would most edify her purpose.

"Perhaps you could throw a party when he arrives, and invite me," I suggested. "It'd give me the honor of seeing you again ..."

"Oh, I hope we needn't wait that long," Mrs. Effington said.

"Indeed not," I agreed, and I glanced out the window again. "Forgive me, but your gardens are quite lovely, and I have excellent night-vision. Would you honor me with ... a moonlight stroll through your flowers?"

Apparently nothing could've delighted Mrs. Effington more. With a flowing grace reminiscent of Hēlgrēth, Mrs. Effington took my arm tight in hers, and with sparkles in her eyes, she clung to me as we walked into another bright room, down a stair, and out into her garden. Behind me I could hear the whispered giggles of her servants.

An hour we strolled in her starlit garden, and she extolled on the variety of her flowers, of which she was surprisingly knowledgeable.

"These are Evening Primroses," she said, pointing to a pinkish-white flower which was still blooming, for she'd directed our walk to a moon garden filled with night-blooming flowers. Of course, I knew the Evening Primrose, for it was a favorite of Hēlgrēth, as it blossoms at dusk and releases a sweet aroma. Evening Stock produces an even stronger scent, but it's not the prettiest of flowers.

"Quite as lovely as you, Effie," I said.

"Vlad, you naughty boy!" Mrs. Effington exclaimed, pulling tighter on my arm. "And here, see my Moonflowers; how beautiful they are!"

Her Moonflowers were beautiful, and larger than my fist, and their soft, lemony scent suited my tastes more than Primroses. Another patch of the moon garden was filled with Night Phlox, which gives the scent of vanilla, and then we passed between two rows of Night Gladiolus, which blooms all day and evening, but it is to the night it gives off its strong, spicy scent. The entire rest of the moon garden was filled with Angel Trumpet, a flowering vine that grows until it consumes all other plants, and this needed trimming badly, but I only smiled, and Mrs. Effington continued telling me myths and superstitions about these flowers, none of which were new to me.

"Effie, this has been a wonderful walk, but I fear I must be going," I said.

"Oh, Vlad, must you? So early?" Mrs. Effington asked, a desperate misery to her voice.

"I fear I must," I said. "The fiancée of a friend of mine is very ill, and I've promised to attend her vigil, and keep him company as he worries the night away."

"*Lucy ...?*" she asked.

"I fear so, but no one must know ...," I said.

"Oh, you're such a good man," Mrs. Effington said. "I'll be heartbroken, but I can't ask you do forget such a Christian duty."

"I wish you could, Effie," I said. "But let me leave you something to remember me by."

Mrs. Effington's eyes virtually glowed.

With amusement on my lips, I held out my hand, showing her in the moonlight that it was empty, and then I lifted it up, toward a distant row of trees. I reached out with my mind, and as I'd offered to let my precious Lucy witness, I called to the sleeping birds, and summoned them to me. Mrs. Effington looked puzzled, glancing from my hand to my face, and then she gasped as no less than eight birds came flying down from the dark sky, and three of them perched upon my spread fingers while the others fluttered around. I held them for a handful of seconds, and then I waved them off, and they flew back into the night, quickly lost in the darkness.

"*Vlad, how did you do that ...?*" Mrs. Effington asked, her eyes like saucers.

"Oh, it's a simple trick from my homeland, unknown in England," I said.

"It was ... *like magic!*" Mrs. Effington exclaimed.

"Effie, the men of England know sciences unknown in the dark Carpathians," I said. "Yet think not that we're ignorant; my homeland holds secrets unknown to Englishmen. It's to understand our secrets that I came to England, to study the investigative processes of the modern world."

"Vlad, you amaze me, and you must come again soon," Mrs. Effington said.

"I'll come as soon as my other duties allow," I said.

"Do you promise?" Mrs. Effington asked.

There in the moonlight, alone, I drew her to me with one hand, and lifted her hand to my lips with my other.

"Effie, not all the powers of night could keep me from the pleasure of ... your company," I said, and I lowered my lips to her fingers.

Mrs. Effington beamed.

Chapter 13

My escape from Mrs. Effington's was short and quick. She tried to get me to use her drivers and carriage, but I refused; I didn't want local drivers knowing where I'd been. The evening was young, and there was a busy restaurant district nearby. Donning my hat and cloak, and with another distasteful kiss upon her hand, I left 'Effie' at her doorstep and strode her long cobblestone walkway to the street.

Within fifteen minutes I was riding in a coach in sight of the hill near Lucy's house, and twenty minutes later I was standing upon the wooden floor inside her entryway, waiting for the butler to fetch Arthur.

"Count Drăcula, glad yer' here!" Quincey Morris said, approaching me from the hallway.

"Quincey!" I said. "Good to see you!"

"Arthur's upstairs with the docs," Quincey said.

"Docs?" I asked. "Oh, you mean doctors! Is John Seward here?"

"Yes, and you'll be happy to hear Lucy's bloomin'," Quincey said.

"I'm delighted," I said. "I'd hoped to relieve some of you, so you could get some rest."

"Well, I'm grateful for that," Quincey said with a yawn. "I've slept less than a rancher at branding-time."

"Then I've come just in time," I said. "I was able to sleep late this morning, and I just escaped the arms of a woman I feared might never let me go."

Quincey burst into laughter, booming guffaws that thundered through the silent house.

"Aye, men with titles are prized quarry," Quincey said. "Maybe I should buy me a title ...!"

We both laughed, but I insisted he hurry to his rest, and then I sought out the tiny sitting room where we'd sat the previous night. The unattended flames in the fireplace were dying, so I took the poker and pushed the glowing coals against the remains of the charred black logs. I tried to relax, but in this house I was a guest of those who'd thwarted me, and my beloved Lucy was upstairs, being brought further from the rebirth that both of us wanted.

The soft clomps of their footfalls warned me of their approach. As the others joined me, I looked up with a smile.

"Count Drăcula!" Arthur exclaimed.

"At your service, and at the service of your poor fiancée," I said. "Quincey let me in, but he was so tired I sent him to rest."

"Thank you for coming," Arthur said.

"I'm only sorry that I couldn't come sooner," I said. "However, blame me not; one of the young ladies Miss Lucy forced upon me at your dinner party had me for tea this afternoon, and it was all I could do to escape a bachelor."

All chuckled at this, and I noticed Dr. Van Helsing looked relieved by this story.

"Tell me, how is Lucy tonight?" I asked.

"Much improved, but still serious," Dr. Van Helsing said.

"I believe she's recovering fully," Dr. Seward said.

"John, my friend, I only wish you were correct," Dr. Van Helsing said. "She is improved but for the moment, and we must watch her, guard her, and protect her with our very lives."

"You must reveal your diagnosis!" Dr. Seward said to Dr. Van Helsing.

"As I said, my papers should arrive tomorrow, and then I will share with you all I know," Dr. Van Helsing said. "Until then I dare not speak, for fear you may think me mad, and undo the protections I have placed in Miss Lucy's room, and that I cannot allow."

"Papers ...?" I asked. "What papers?"

"Papers from the farthest corners of the world, where modern medicine is considered magic," Dr. Van Helsing said. "There is a tiny description I read, long ago, which describes the exact symptoms our Miss Lucy has evidenced, and I must reread them to assure I am doing all I can for her. When I have confirmed my knowledge, only then will I share it. Until then, I must ask that you all concede to my wishes without proof."

"If you were any other man, I'd refuse," Dr. Seward said, and he yawned loudly. "My brain is beginning to feel the numbness which marks cerebral exhaustion."

"John, Dr. Van Helsing has brought roses back to Lucy's cheeks, and she is eating again," Arthur said.

I struggled not to react while John poured himself some tea; *consuming food fit for the living will slow Lucy's transformation.* I forced a smile, then looked back at the flames, determined to see Lucy tonight.

"Well, I'm here now, and I slept in quite late," I said. "I'll sit here all night and offer what assistance I can. Those of you who've not had sleep should take the opportunity ..."

"I'll stay up with you," Dr. Seward said. "Arthur, Dr. Van Helsing, you've hardly rested at all ... I prescribe bed."

"The family Godalming is forever in debt to you both," Arthur said to us.

"Before I go, I leave this warning," Dr. Van Helsing said. "Do not leave anyone alone with Miss Lucy. Do not let an hour pass without checking on her. Do not open any door or window anywhere in this house and leave it unattended, and do not take a single garlic from Miss Lucy's room ... or allow her to leave it."

"She's sound asleep," Dr. Seward said.

"None the less, I have the only key to her balcony door in my pocket, and it shall stay with me," Dr. Van Helsing said. "I charge you both to watch over her, and hurry to her side if you hear even the slightest disturbance."

"Be off to bed," Dr. Seward insisted. "No harm shall come to Lucy while Count Drăcula and I are here."

Arthur nodded, and took Dr. Van Helsing by the arm, and he reluctantly allowed himself to be led off down the hall. He did look exhausted, and for a living man his age, exhaustion can be insufferable. Dr. Seward and I watched them leave, and then John poured a brandy for me, and we turned the hourglass upside down and sat before the fire.

"Poor Arthur ...!" Dr. Seward exclaimed.

"Arthur ...?" I asked.

"I'm sure he wouldn't want me telling you this, but Arthur's father suffers from consumption," Dr.

Seward said. "Unfortunately, his condition is quite well-known, unlike poor Lucy."

"What is Lucy's condition?" I asked.

"Her symptoms are atypical," Dr. Seward said. "We've tried everything, but our treatments are barely helpful."

"What symptoms?" I asked.

"Shallow breathing, imperceptible pulse, faint heartbeat, and deathly pallor," Dr. Seward said. "Normally these symptoms would be accompanied by a gaping wound causing serious blood-loss, but she has none, save for two little pricks over her jugular vein. Dr. Van Helsing suspects something about those wounds, but Lucy insists she accidentally poked herself while pinning on her cloak, and says they bled very little. Her other vitals seem normal, and we even examined her urine. It ... isn't like her blood is somehow infected ... or malfunctioning, if that were possible. It's like her blood is simply vanishing from her arteries with no cause, no evidence, and no visible vent of escape, yet she evidences no other symptoms of ailment, like fever or vomiting. We even pricked her scalp, where blood would normally spew, and were rewarded with only a slight dribble."

"And modern medicine knows no ... matching condition ...?" I asked.

"Conditions require a cause, and that's what baffles me," Dr. Seward said. "Dr. Van Helsing's treatments, other than his transfusions, are the most unmedical practices I've ever seen."

"What practices?" I asked.

"He fills her room with fresh garlic each day, and has rubbed it over the doors and windows until they're dripping with pungent oils. He sprinkled Holy Water around her bed and upon the very walls of her bedroom, and Lucy sleeps with a wafer of Sacred Host upon her headboard. If I didn't respect the good doctor so much, I'd say he was weaving a spell rather than practicing medicine."

"Was medicine not once considered magic?" I asked.

"Dr. Van Helsing is a metaphysician," Dr. Seward said. "Until now, I would've said he had the sharpest mind on Earth."

"As a fellow physician, this must be a great frustration," I said. "Still, Lucy told me you've been appointed the overship of a large lunatic asylum; surely you've seen much that's strange."

"Too much, but only one baffles me as much as Lucy's condition," Dr. Seward said.

"Tell me," I said.

"It's grim, even for late-night tales ...," Dr. Seward warned me.

"Drăculeştis delight in the grim," I said. "Please ... to expend the dark hours."

"His name is Renfield," Dr. Seward said. "He almost murdered a man, lost in a wild, savage fit, which occasionally returns. Normally calm and quiet, in aboriginal ravings he thrashes like a beast, and bites and snarls, wild and primitive as the most base and untamed creature."

I pretended ignorance as Dr. Seward described my servant in meticulous detail, how he'd caught flies, used them to feed his pet spiders, and then used his spiders to attract and capture small birds, which he ate whole and raw. He even mentioned how Renfield had escaped several times, and was once captured by the door to a chapel on an adjoining residence, which only I knew was mine.

I liked Dr. John Seward. Like my late friend and guest, Jonathan Harker, John Seward was a bright, high-minded, and inquisitive man, completely convinced of his understanding of the universe. Only I knew how little he actually knew.

His tales of insanity filled the eternity as the sands filtered from the upper aperture of the hourglass into the lower. When the sands drained entirely, we rose and wound through the hallways to an ornate stairs, which we ascended to Lucy's room. As we approached, the scent of garlic assailed me, but my nearness to Lucy increased my awareness of her presence; I could feel her dreams.

Lucy's door opened, pouring forth a putrescence unequaled; I gagged and staggered, suddenly dizzy, almost overcome. The poisoned fumes fell upon me like acidic waves cresting over living flesh, or the essence of sacred purity washing over my undead skin. I reeled back and almost retched, and only the strong arm of Dr. Seward steadied me and kept me from falling.

"Noxious, isn't it?" Dr. Seward asked. "I'm amazed Lucy can sleep breathing it."

I felt as if I'd retch, but I drew upon my inner strength. I forced my will over the anguish of the garlic and drove my thoughts into Lucy's mind.

'Awaken ...!'

With a soft, stifled attempt at a scream, Lucy jumped, flinging her covers up into the air to momentarily balloon above her. John released me and rushed into the room, his face turned toward her, and so he didn't see me stagger and almost fall. I seized the doorframe in a grip I feared would crush the wood, but found I was so weak I could scarcely hold on. By willpower alone I righted myself; I'd endured a blood-fast of fifty years in Castle Drăculea ... and I'd be the master of all, especially myself. I couldn't be ruled by a room full of poison vapors. I stiffened my wobbly legs, straightened my shoulders, and with the dignity of a Drăculeşti, I entered Lucy's room.

A light shined blindingly from Lucy's headboard, weakening me further: *the sacred host! The burning power no vampire could withstand!*

I gritted my teeth and pushed into the infernal holy light. The cursed white flowers hovered everywhere, hanging from her every bedpost, laden across each table and chair, and even hanging from her curtain rods. I felt I was entering an invisible acidic fog, burning into me, illuminated by death-beyond-death, but it was only pain; my immortal, undead flesh didn't rot and wither. Yet I felt weak and sick, as if I were on the verge of true-dead, from which even the undead couldn't recover.

Otherwise the room was exactly as I recalled, polished oak furniture, walls of a soft pink with faded paintings of tiny roses, and a spotless white quilt, now askance, with one corner fallen onto the floor.

"Just a dream," John was whispering to Lucy as I stepped up stiffly behind him. "Calm yourself. Count Drăcula and I are here, and ..."

Lucy was sitting straight up in bed, her white quilt haphazardly fallen about her thin waist, her hand laying limply in John's comforting hand. She was as lovely as ever, with perfect porcelain skin, and hair as brightly flaming as an August sunset, and wearing only a nightgown of fine green lace which lay about her tender, desirable flesh. But, as John spoke my name, Lucy's beautiful eyes blazed and she looked at me, startled and afraid.

"At your service, dear Lucy," I said. "I've relieved Arthur, Quincey, and Dr. Van Helsing, so they can get a few hours of sleep."

Her wide eyes and panicked expression told me as much as I could learn with ease, were the smothering, sickly scents of garlic and holy brightness not overwhelming my mental abilities. I forced a relaxed smile and nodded to her, which was as much of a bow as I could manage.

"Vlad ...!" Lucy whispered, horror coloring her voice.

"He's been very helpful," John said. "Without him, I don't know how I'd have stayed awake to check on you. Now, you must go back to sleep. You look much better, but you still need rest."

John quickly felt her pulse, pulled back the lids of her eyes, looked inside her mouth, and proclaimed that she was recovering beautifully. Lucy feigned a smile, but she kept glancing warily at me.

"John," Lucy whispered, "could I ... speak to Count Drăcula ... for a moment ... alone?"

John looked surprised, and glanced quizzically at me.

"Miss Lucy, surely you don't wish to hear about my visits to the young lady you introduced me to at your party ...?" I said.

Lucy looked momentarily puzzled, as if still in the fog of sleep, but she quickly grasped my meaning.

"I ... I'll sleep better ...," Lucy said. "... if I know what ... has passed between you and ... *her.*"

I rolled my eyes as if exasperated, and expelled a heavy sigh.

"Women," I said as I shook my head, and John shrugged as if he agreed with my feelings. "John, you're her doctor; if you disapprove, I'll not tell her a thing."

"Say nothing disturbing," John said, and with a pat of her hand, he stood, half-bowing to her. "I'll give you a minute; sleep is more important than gossip."

John exited, and we both watched in silence until he'd departed.

"Vlad, what are you doing here?" Lucy demanded.

"I had no choice," I whispered to her, sitting in the very spot which John had vacated, and I took her precious hand. "This room is poisoned against our kind, or I'd have made you immortal already. Tomorrow night, at this time, after they've checked upon you, open your windows; I'll be there."

"You still want ... me as your queen?" Lucy asked.

"With all my heart, but you wished to be transformed quietly," I said.

"I do," Lucy said. "But ... *Arthur mustn't suffer.*"

"Your desires are my commands," I said. "Now sleep, and don't fear; neither powers divine nor infernal shall deny us."

"Tomorrow night ...?" Lucy asked.

"I can't abide another delay," I said with a serious smile.

I took her hand, lifted it to my lips, and with a kiss tasted the paradise that would soon be mine.

As John was still in the hallway, I dared not kiss her more, but her hand on my lips strengthened me, as if her scent drove the foul poisons out of my soul. With no small effort, I pulled myself away from her, feeling suddenly empty as her hand dropped from mine. Yet I staggered backwards, unwilling to turn around ... or lose an instant of the sight of her beauty, and to the delight of my soul, before I reached the door, Lucy smiled at me.

I'd not realized how deeply I felt for her. Her beauty was mesmerizing, but her intellect was of the highest, the most prized, such that I had to force myself out of her room, away from the deadly light of the host and poisonous perfume.

John and I descended the stairs together, and John had to hold and assist me, as I was still weak, and I clutched the thick, polished rail like an invalid. I told him the smelly flowers had made me nauseous, and begged his pardon, claiming I'd tried to hold my breath while in her room. John assisted me gladly, and he offered to examine me, but I refused, insisting I just needed a fresh brandy.

I was feeling much better after an hour of banal talk, where I told John stories of the Carpathians that were ancient when I was young. Whenever the sands ran out, we'd ascend the stairs to Lucy's room, but I remained in the hallway and watched while John crept to her bedside, listened to her sleeping breath, and returned to me assurances that she was doing better. So the remainder of the night passed, and an hour before dawn, I reached out with my mind to the fiancé of my precious Lucy, to Arthur, and pressed into his sleeping brain that something was amiss. Moments later, the thunder of his footfalls shook the ceiling, and we dashed upstairs to find Arthur standing in Lucy's open doorway, staring as if disbelieving that she was sleeping quietly.

Assuring Arthur that Lucy was fine, and that we'd been vigilant and attentive all night, Arthur resolved that he must've awoken from a nightmare, and we descended together down the ornate stairs. Three servants in their nightgowns met us at the bottom step, apparently having been awoken by Arthur's mad dash to Lucy's bedroom, and Arthur asked them to provide us with an early breakfast and to stoke up all the fires, for the house had gotten chill. I thanked Arthur, but claimed that I'd a business appointment at noon, and now that he and John could continue guarding Lucy, it was past time I departed. Arthur offered to have a servant run to fetch me a cab, but I refused, claiming that a brisk walk before dawn was just what I needed, and after accepting their many thanks, I departed.

It was late, and the sky was no longer deep black, now displaying only a portion of the stars. *I couldn't wait;* as soon as their door closed behind me, I glanced around to assure myself that no one was watching, and then I raised my arms to the night.

Be the bat!

"Vlad, you must tell me how you did that!" Mrs. Effington said, her eyes drilling into mine.

"Of what you are speaking ...?" I asked with a smile.

"How you called wild birds to come to you!" Mrs. Effington said. "That was amazing!"

"Oh, I wish I could tell you, Effie," I said. "These things are dark and dire, and I shouldn't have exposed you to practices that even in my lands are considered unchristian."

"I must know ...!" Mrs. Effington's eyes virtually glowed as she pressed herself against me.

I feigned a delighted smile, but Mrs. Effington reeked of too much floral perfume, she had over-powdered her heavily-painted face, and her breath smelled of fish and wine. Still, I didn't return or repel her overly-familiar touches. She was dressed all in pinks and reds tonight, and her lips were caked in red paste. She'd again drawn me into her large parlor, which was overgrown with paintings of flowers. She gestured for me to join her on her couch, but I remained standing, and so she did, too.

"It's a simple trick, nothing more," I assured her. "All the boys of my land do it."

"Only the boys ...?" Mrs. Effington asked coyly.

"Certainly," I said, pretending to speak casually. "Girls aren't interested in summoning birds or making fish jump ..."

"You can make fish jump ...?" Mrs. Effington asked suddenly.

"Oh, it's much the same trick, with birds or fish," I said. "Boys like doing that. Girls ... well, girls are more interested in other tricks ..."

"Are there magics just for girls?" Mrs. Effington asked.

"Well, boys could do girl magic, but boys don't care about smooth, young skin or ..."

"Smooth ...?" Mrs. Effington asked. " *Young ...?*"

"Yes, girls of my homeland are very meticulous about their vanity," I said.

"Does it work?" Mrs. Effington asked desperately.

"Does what work?" I asked, trying to appear curious.

"Youth and smoothness ...?" Mrs. Effington demanded.

"I ... believe so," I said. "Very few women of my land appear aged, even after half a century ..."

"You must teach me this magic!" Mrs. Effington almost shouted.

"Me ...?" I asked. "Teach girl magic ...?"

"You must know something about it," Mrs. Effington sounded desperate.

"A little, I suppose," I said. "I could ... but it would take some time ..."

"Take all the time you need," Mrs. Effington said. "I'm your eager student!"

"Please, Effie, I'll be glad to teach you all I know," I said. "I can't start tonight, for it'd take too long. It'll take you months to master."

"This is your home," Mrs. Effington said. "From now on, you must live here and teach me ..."

"Oh, Effie, if only I could!" I said. "But ... I have my studies ... and I told you of Arthur; Lucy is deathly ill ... I fear she has only a few nights left."

"Oh, poor Lucy ...!" Mrs. Effington said.

"I must soon leave to help Arthur," I said. "I may not be able to return for a day or two. But ... I promise, if you'll be patient, I'll come as soon as I may ... and teach you everything I know."

Our lips met; *it was rather disgusting.* Now I knew how Miëta, Hēlgrēth, and Loritá must have felt when I kissed them during my fast of blood, at the height of my decrepitude.

I got away from Mrs. Effington sooner than I expected, so quickly I slowed my pace once I was out of sight of her windows, walking along the pebbled path outside the overgrown wall that shielded passersby from the full view of her front door. I was hungry, but this was no place to feed, lest my plans for Mrs. Effington be ruined. I shuddered slightly as I remembered her touches and foul kiss.

Why was I doing this? I could just slay to get anything I wanted, take it from the corpses of my feasts, and walk away unbothered. But there'd be questions, investigations, and I needed to keep my identity and residence secret. However, as I walked, I had to admit the truth to myself: my youth-restored body was enjoying the game, the thrill of the sport, playing with mortals whose desperate, self-serving motives were as obvious as the cries of hungry children. *I was enjoying my new life ... and toying with those easily deceived.*

As time allowed, I bought a newspaper and pretended to drink a beer in a local tavern. To my amusement, there was a story about my local pet.

18 September
The Pall Mall Gazette
THE ESCAPED WOLF
*Interview with the Keeper
in the Zoölogical Gardens.*

After many inquiries and almost as many refusals, and perpetually using the words "Pall Mall Gazette" as a sort of talisman, I managed to find the keeper of the section of the Zoölogical Gardens in which the wolf department is included. Thomas Bilder lives in one of the cottages in the enclosure behind the elephant-house, and was just sitting down to his tea when I found him. Thomas and his wife are hospitable folk, elderly, without children, and if the specimen I enjoyed of their hospitality be of the average kind, their lives must be pretty comfortable. The keeper wouldn't enter onto what he called 'business' until the supper was over. Then, when the table was cleared, and he had lit his pipe, he said:

"That 'ere wolf what we called Bersicker was one of three dark grey ones that came from Norway to Jamrach's, which we bought off him four years ago. He was a nice, well-behaved wolf, that never gave no trouble to talk of. I'm more surprised at 'im for wantin' to get out nor any other animile in the place. But, there, you can't trust wolves no more nor women."

"Don't you mind him, sir!" broke in Mrs. Tom, with a cheery laugh. "E's got mindin' the animiles so long that blest if he ain't like a old wolf 'isself! But there ain't no 'arm in 'im."

"Well, sir, it was about two hours after feedin' yesterday when I first hear my disturbance. I was makin' up a litter in the monkey-house for a young puma which is ill; but when I heard the yelpin' and 'owlin' I kem away straight. There was Bersicker a-tearin' like a mad thing at the bars as if he wanted to get out. There wasn't much people about that day, and close at hand was only one man, a tall, thin chap, with a 'ook nose and a pointed beard, with a few white hairs runnin' through it. He had a 'ard, cold look and red eyes, and I took a sort of mislike to him, for it seemed as if it was 'im as the wolf was hirritated at. He pointed out the animiles to me and says:

"Keeper, this wolf seems upset at something."

"Maybe it's you,' says I, for I didn't like the airs as he give 'isself. He didn't git angry, as I 'oped he would, but he smiled a kind of insolent smile, with a mouth full of white, sharp teeth.

"Oh no, wolves like me," 'e says.

"Ow yes, they would," says I, a-imitatin' of him. "They always likes a bone or two to clean their teeth on about tea-time, which you 'as a bagful."

"Well, it was a odd thing, but when the animiles see us a-talkin' they lay down, and when I went over to Bersicker he let me stroke his ears same as ever. That there man kem over, and blessed but if he didn't put in his hand and stroke the old wolf's ears, too!"

"Tyke care," says I. "Bersicker is quick."

"Never mind," he says. "I'm used to 'em!"

"Are you in the business yourself?" I says, tyking off my 'at, for a man what trades in wolves, anceterer, is a good friend to keepers.

"No," says he, "not exactly in the business, but I 'ave made pets of several."

"And with that he lifts his 'at as perlite as a lord, and walks away. Old Bersicker kep' a-lookin' arter 'im till 'e was out of sight, and then went and lay down in a corner and wouldn't come out the 'ole evening. Well, larst night, so soon as the moon was hup, the wolves here all began a-'owling. There warn't nothing for them to 'owl at. There warn't no one near, except some one that was evidently a-callin' a dog somewheres out back of the gardings in the Park road. Once or twice I went out to see that all was right, and it was, and then the 'owling stopped. Just before twelve o'clock I just took a look round afore turnin' in, an', bust me, but when I kem opposite to old Bersicker's cage I see the rails broken and twisted about and the cage empty. And that's all I know for certing."

"Did anyone else see anything?"

"One of our gard'ners was a-comin' 'ome about that time from a 'armony, when he sees a big grey dog comin' out through the garding 'edges. At least, so he says, but I don't give much for it myself, for if he did 'e never said a word about it to his missis when 'e got 'ome, and it was only after the escape of the wolf was made known, and we had been up all night-a-huntin' of the Park for Bersicker, that he remembered seein' anything. My own belief was that the 'armony 'ad got into his 'ead."

"Now, Mr. Bilder, can you account in any way for the escape of the wolf?"

"Well, sir," he said, with a suspicious sort of modesty, "I think I can; but I don't know as 'ow you'd be satisfied with the theory."

"Certainly I shall. If a man like you, who knows the animals from experience, can't hazard a good guess at any rate, who is even to try?"

"Well then, sir, I accounts for it this way; it seems to me that 'ere wolf escaped ... simply 'cause he wanted to get out."

From the hearty way that both Thomas and his wife laughed at the joke, I could see the whole explanation was simply an elaborate sell. I couldn't cope in badinage with the worthy Thomas, but I knew a surer way to his heart, so I said:

"Now, Mr. Bilder, we'll consider that first half-sovereign worked off, and this brother of his is waiting to be claimed when you've told me what you think will happen."

"Right y'are, sir," he said briskly. "Ye'll excoose me, I know, for a-chaffin' of ye, but the old woman here winked at me, which was as much as telling me to go on."

"Well, I never!" said the old lady.

"Wolves is fine things in a storybook, and I dessay when they gets in packs and does be chivyin' somethin' that's more afeared than they is."

I was handing him the half-sovereign, when something came bobbing up against the window, and Mr. Bilder's face doubled its natural length with surprise.

"God bless me!" he said. "If there ain't old Bersicker come back by 'isself!"

The whole scene was an unutterable mixture of comedy and pathos. The wicked wolf that for half a day had paralyzed London and set all the children in the town shivering in their shoes, stood there in a sort of penitent mood, and was received and petted like a sort of vulpine prodigal son.

He took the wolf and locked him up in his cage, with a big piece of meat to satisfy him, in quantity at any rate. Thus was the beast returned, although the mystery unsolved.

The article went on for some length about previous sightings of the wolf, the missing farm animals many suspected the wolf had eaten, and the local constables and hunters attempts to corner and slay the beast, but the wolf seemed to always be able to trick them.

I smiled, for my friend must've decided to return to his confinement. Clearly it retained a trace of human intellect.

An hour before Lucy had agreed to open her doors and windows, I entered a growler and ordered the driver to her street. I was hungry, such that the blood of the driver was tempting, but if things worked right, then soon I'd be filled with the blood of my Lucy, and I was loathe to mix her precious, high-born elixir with the fluids of lesser mortals. We drove noisily through the darkness, for the sky above was thick with clouds, leaving only ghosts of starlight where they thinned. I sat hungry, but determined; *this time Lucy herself would be helping me.*

I jumped from the growler and handed up my payment to the driver just a few feet past the low white wall around Lucy's house, and the loud noise of his growler continued as he drove away.

"Drăcula ...?" asked a voice.

I startled. John and Quincey were walking toward me out of the shadows of trees shading the starlit road.

"Friends!" I said, disconcerted. "What're you doing here?"

"We've been soaking at the Oxtail Tavern," Quincey said, and I noticed he swayed slightly as he walked, and John was carrying a small leather satchel. "Lucy's much better tonight, and Arthur felt he was taxing our friendship, so he sent us to bend our elbows."

"Not that we minded!" John insisted. "It's my sacred duty to heal the sick, and for our dear Lucy, there's nowhere I'd rather ply my skills."

"Why're you here?" Quincey asked. "You've driven past their bunkhouse."

"I shouted to the driver as we drove past," I said. "I think he might've been drinking."

"Well, if he hasn't, we have!" John said, and Quincey burst out laughing.

"What's in the satchel?" I asked John.

"The ghastly paraphernalia of my beneficial trade," John chuckled.

I'd intended to arrive unseen, and wait in the white gazebo for Lucy to open her doors, but Quincey and John seized my arms and drug me along to the dark road, through the front gate, and inside the door of the brightly-lit foyer, to see Arthur and Dr. Van Helsing just coming down the stairs.

"Where did you find Count Drăcula?" Arthur asked. "At the Oxtail?"

"No, he was absconded by a chiseler hack-driver," Quincey said, grinning.

"Well, we welcome his company," Dr. Van Helsing said. "Lucy looks better ..."

As they descended to the lowest step, both Arthur and Dr. Van Helsing suddenly stopped and stared at me, their eyes bulging.

"Ummm ..., Count Drăcula ...," Arthur chuckled. "Unless you want Lucy enquiring about your romantic activities ... you may wish to wash off that lipstick ...!"

All four men broke into deep guffaws, laughing at me, and I stood embarrassed, drawing a white handkerchief and quickly wiping my face, horrified to see thick smears of red paste stain my handkerchief. Nearly hysterical, John and Quincey leaned close to see the unwanted red caked on my face, which the darkness of night had hidden. I silently cursed my 'Effie'. It took numerous hard scrapes to get all of it off, and I was glad I was young; during my fast, my brittle, cracked skin would have come off with the lipstick.

For five minutes I was pressed to reveal the name of the young lady whose affections for me were undeniable, but I squeezed my lips closed, and then appealed to Dr. Van Helsing to silence their adolescent prodding, but he brushed my concerns aside.

"The day will come when memories of sweet kisses will be all that warms your heart," Dr. Van Helsing said. "Arthur is lucky, for although Miss Lucy is recovering quickly, there were times I feared the only kisses he'd long for would be from lips of the past. Take it from an old widower: ignore not the camaraderie of your peers, nor let it dim the delights of the lucky young woman you favor, for someday both will be precious."

I thanked him, and we went into the drawing room. I learned that John and Quincey had been awake and watching Lucy since dawn while Arthur and Dr. Van Helsing slept, and John and Quincey were both expected to retire to their guest rooms soon.

I insisted I needed to visit the privy and slipped out. Two servants were in the hallway, so I went into the privy for a few moments, carefully washed my face, and I then ascended the stairs quietly, snuck to Lucy's room, and opened her door. I found her wide awake, standing before her open door, with her thin curtains blowing around her opened windows.

She was looking out into the darkness, searching for me.

I closed and locked her door behind me. She heard the click, turned to face me, and rushed toward me smiling.

"Vlad ...!" she said, and she threw herself into my arms.

I held her tightly, overjoyed. The wind blowing in from the door thinned the foulness of the garlic-stench, but it did nothing to affect the glaring sacred host. I glanced around the elegant bedroom at all of the holy-illuminated poisonous white garlands, proud, as if I were defying both of their potencies.

"They know I'm here," I said.

"I was expecting ...," Lucy began.

"They saw me arrive," I said. "John and Quincey. I couldn't get away."

"Is it still real?" Lucy asked. "Will I live forever?"

"Yes, but the question is, will you live forever ... with me?"

We kissed, and paradise cascaded. Heaven, if God ever allows me to glimpse it, must look like Lucy's kisses made me feel. I kissed her back with equal fervor, but I silently made a mental note to wipe my lips before the men saw me again.

"What should we do?" Lucy whispered as our lips slid to cheeks. "Can you take me now?"

"If you wish, but they'll suspect ...," I said.

"I don't care," Lucy said. "Vlad, make me yours."

I didn't hesitate. I lifted her chin with my thumb, and then I bit into her delicious throat. Blood flowed thick and strong into my mouth, her own blood, so tasty I almost gasped, but I couldn't afford to waste a moment. I sucked hard, deeply, swallowed, and pulled the life from her body into mine as quickly as I could. I felt her weaken; soon she'd pass out. I needed to drain her so deeply no transfusion could save her.

Suddenly the doorknob shook and a woman's voice screamed.

"Mistress ...!"

The whole door shook, and a fist pounded on the opposite side of the door. A servant was in the hallway, screaming: the men were probably already running toward the stairs.

"Let them come," I said. *"I'll kill them ...!"*

"No!" Lucy said weakly. *"Go!"*

I grimaced; *not another delay!* Yet I couldn't deny my love, and heavy footfalls were tramping up the stairs; pushing Lucy aside, I ran out the open door to her balcony, and sprinted toward the stair just as I heard her locked door crash inwards; *Arthur, John, and Quincey must've forced it together.*

I'd escaped just in time, but there was still a chance to maintain my secrecy. I ran all the way around to the front, found the main door unlocked, and slipped in while the servants were gathered at the foot of the stairs, looking upwards. I dashed down a hallway, wiped off my face, and then ran back, straight into the crowd of servants.

"Where are they?" I demanded, and they all pointed upstairs.

The door to Lucy's room was broken open, John, Arthur, and Dr. Van Helsing were gathered around Lucy, who looked to have fainted, and Quincey was forcibly closing the windows and the door to her balcony. Luckily the open windows had thinned the garlic-stink.

"What happened ...?" I demanded.

"It is terrible!" Dr. Van Helsing said. "Her pulse is weak. We must begin again. Arthur, John, and I have already bled for her; who now will open their veins?"

"What's the matter with me?" Quincey said.

"Good man!" Dr. Van Helsing said. "Roll up your sleeve."

"I'm here, too, if she needs me," I added, for I suspected they trusted Quincey more than I.

"I pray we need no more donors," Dr. Van Helsing said. "John, get my instruments. We dare not delay a second."

As I watched, they began the amazing process. John fetched his satchel and Dr. Van Helsing's mahogany box. They drew out the funnel, the copper tube with its tiny faucets, the small pump, and the thin silver needles. John stabbed one needle into Quincey's arm, and directed its flow through a tube to fill the funnel. The first faucet under the bloody funnel was opened, and then the second, and Dr. Van Helsing slowly turned the crank. Blood flowed out of the other silver needle into a small drip pan John was holding under it, and then Dr. Van Helsing closed the lowest faucet, near the needle, and the flow of blood ceased. He stabbed the second needle into the unconscious Lucy's flesh, seeking a strong vein. Satisfied, Dr. Van Helsing opened the last faucet, and as he spun the crank, Quincey's blood streamed from the funnel into Lucy through the copper tube.

The color of her veins darkened with the potency of his strong blood near the site of her needle-puncture.

The scent of Quincey's blood was strong and heady, with an animalistic musk, and no drink could be as rich or fulfilling. Yet I stared, delighted to witness the process men of science had developed; I wanted Lucy with me, but the chance to see this latest technical innovation was fascinating, and I broke the worried tension only once to quip:

"So ... this will be the last time I go to the privy ... unless all four of you are up here."

My humor fell flat; Arthur was holding Lucy's hand and begging her to awaken. John was wiping the

Dracula, Deathless Desires

little trails of blood leaking from their needle-wounds. Dr. Van Helsing kept cranking, his eyes fixed on Lucy's arm where the needle penetrated her flesh, and he watched the tiny color changes of her skin with unwavering attentiveness.

Little else was said. I saw the color of Lucy's skin flush as the blood of Quincey filled her, and soon her eyes fluttered, but she didn't regain consciousness. Arthur was anxious, Quincey stalwart, and John seemed more frustrated than anything else, but the outside door and windows were now shut tight, and I couldn't long bear the thickening stench of garlic.

"Five of us here, awake, and still she's attacked," I said.

"She had an attack," John corrected me. "We don't know what happened."

"Who opened them doors and windows?" Quincey demanded.

"I fear ... forgive me, but I've already talked to Arthur about this," Dr. Van Helsing said. "What is most likely is ... Lucy is doing this to herself."

"She's lost a tremendous amount of blood four times," John said. "She's bleeding from her neck, but only a tiny amount. If she did this, where's the blood ...?"

"I can't just stand here," I said. "Whoever did this isn't here now; I should go outside and seek them."

"No, friend Drăcula," Dr. Van Helsing said. "It would be very dangerous, and we must all protect Lucy. Even Quincey will be weak after this."

"At least let me get each of us a brandy," I said.

With everyone's approval, I escaped just as the cloying stink was starting to make me feel ill. *A disaster;*

again I'd almost sired Lucy, only to have her life restored.

Chapter 14

I awoke in my coffin at dusk on September the 19th thinking *'Tonight I'll claim my Lucy'*. I'd said that before, but every possible form of bad luck had delayed us, from Jonathan Harker's interfering Mina to Dr. Van Helsing filling Lucy's room with garlic. Yet this time I was determined; as soon as my fangs pierced her throat, I'd empty her veins until her heart stopped, so completely no transfusion would avail her.

I needed help again.

I arose from my coffin with grim determination. I had to take every possible precaution, every advantage to insure I wouldn't fail. I descended from my mound and crossed my basement, then ascended the stairs to my chapel.

To my surprise, Renfield was sitting on a wooden pew, the door to my garden slightly ajar.

"Master!" Renfield cried excitedly.

Instantly I judged that he was lost in his mania again. I was glad, but I'd no time to waste with him.

"Welcome, Renfield," I said.

"Master, when ...?" Renfield jumped up and faced me, his eyes alight. "*When can I be like you? Strong ...! Wise ...!*"

"When I say so ... and not a moment sooner," I said.

"Why?" Renfield demanded. "Why not now? *Right now!*"

"Renfield!" I shouted, for he was practically salivating. "Calm yourself! You know what you'll suffer if you risk my wrath again!"

"Forgive me, Master, but I must know!" Renfield said, although he absently rubbed his still-bandaged hand. "How soon? Tonight? Tomorrow? I can't wait ...!"

"Clean," I said. "Clean my house as you've never cleaned before. Clean my house well, and I'll answer you when I return."

"Oh, thank you, Master!" Renfield said. "Thank you!"

"I'll return before dawn to inspect your cleaning ...," I said.

"Everything will be spotless, I swear!" Renfield promised.

With Renfield panting like a salivating dog, I hurried into my main rooms and found my hat hanging by the front door. I placed it on my head, fastened my cloak about my shoulders, walked to a window, and flung it open. Renfield was standing in the doorway behind me, watching, but I didn't care; if Renfield cleaned my house for Lucy, then I'd be glad, and my need for him would lessen. Witnessing my transformation again would only instill his dedication to me. If not for his insanity, I might consider keeping my promise to him.

The stars were weak, but visible. The sky was black in the east and gray in the west. It was early for flying, but I'd much to do and no time to waste.

Be the bat!

My flight was taxing. I staggered against a wrought iron fence and clung for support until the pain and weariness of transformation passed. When my strength returned, I looked up and smiled: the sign nearest to me read 'Zoo'.
I needed my other set of eyes again.
Listening, I heard footfalls within the zoo, and so I waited patiently until they walked away. Then I walked into the shadows of two trees, and with relative ease I squeezed through a gap in the fence, and entered the empty little streets of the zoo. Ahead of me, I saw a guard sauntering slowly toward my brother, and I had to slow my pace and wait, ignoring a bear that growled softly at me as I slipped past his cage. Finally the guard wandered into another section, and as I approached, my scent arrived before I did. Sensing me, the huge gray wolf jumped to his feet, his tongue hanging and tail wagging back and forth. I smiled and reached into his cage to greet him, and he licked and rubbed against my hand.

"Greetings again, my chosen friend," I said.

The wolf looked up at me and our eyes met, I reached out with my mind and joined with the wolf.

His thoughts greeted me with wildly eager but fearful reverence, as befits any creature communicating with its god. He reveled, sharing my human thoughts, so above his abilities. My awareness of his praise was muted by my knowledge of the minimal reach of his weaker mind, but his wave of joy washed over me like love.

"Be calm, my friend, for your rightful lord and master has returned to you, and together we shall journey again," I said.

The wolf raised his eyes to me, and only I could read the effusive wonder in his face. My presence was another universe to him, and every contact with my mind elevated his abilities.

Moments later, his cage was open and he was trotting by my side. The guard was elsewhere, and we strode to the gap in the gate with ease, and soon we were out on the street, a young man and his tame pet, walking calmly under the stars.

"Nothing must go wrong, for tonight I kill my bride," I said to my faithful follower.

Joy effused between us.

An hour later, less than two hours after sunset, I gave my pet orders, and he obediently loped off into the woods behind their house, while I approached the front door. I'd scarcely finished knocking before a servant opened the door, and I was admitted at once, and led to a small, ornate dining room, not as grand or opulent as Arthur and Lucy used for their extravagant dinner party, but richly darker, more appealing to my tastes. The walls were rowan from the floors to the ceiling, and each boasted an austere painting of a man who was undoubtedly an ancestor of Lucy's family, with grim painted eyes staring at descendants they never really saw. The furniture was mahogany, stained dark and fashionably carved, the table just big enough to serve the eight chairs around it. Only half of those chairs were occupied; Arthur Holmwood, Quincey, Dr. John Seward, and Dr. Van Helsing greeted me as I entered.

"What's this?" I asked. "No one's sleeping?"

"We just finished supper, but we've plenty left," Arthur said, gesturing to an empty chair.

"No, please, if I eat another bite ...," I said, patting my stomach, "although I must admit, your dinner looks more appetizing than anything cooked by Miss ..."

I froze, and slapped my hand over my mouth as if I needed to silence myself.

"Yes ...?" Arthur grinned slyly. "Miss ... *who* ...?"

"Ah, gentlemen, not for the known world!" I said. "I've given my promise to keep our ... association ... secret, especially from her father!"

Laughter exploded from the table, Quincey's deep guffaws drowning out the others. I sat while they laughed, pretending embarrassment.

"Dear friends, I'd trust each of you, but the promise of a Drăculeşti is inviolate," I said when their chuckling lessened. "However, I'm beginning to find the whole affair ..."

"*Affair ...?*" Quincey interrupted me, and the chuckling at my expense resumed.

"Upon my honor, gentlemen, I haven't allowed familiarities to extend that far," I said. "Is marriage all women of England discuss?"

"Certainly not!" Dr. John Seward said. "Many women never speak of it ... but that doesn't mean it isn't constantly haunting their psyches."

More laughter ensued.

"I'm beginning to find the subject tiresome," I said. "Royal blood flows in my veins, and any bride I claim must be worthy of my birthright."

"That's very wise," Dr. Van Helsing said. "Too many people your age treat marriage as a goal, a prize to be won, instead of the bittersweet responsibility it is."

"Bitter fer' certain," Quincey chuckled.

"Ah, but there is sweetness!" Arthur said.

"You only say that because Lucy accepted your proposal," John Seward said to Arthur. "Had she accepted mine, I might think the same."

"You proposed to Miss Lucy?" I asked Dr. Seward.

"We all did," Quincey said. "Arthur, John, and I. Learning that the lot of us were boonswaggled by the same filly, we swore a friendship bond to let her decide ... rather than shoot it out."

"I'm the most respected and accomplished of us three," John Seward said. "Quincey is the richest and most successful. Yet Arthur has noble blood in his veins, born to the uppercrust of society ..."

"Alas, this does not bode well for Count Drăcula," Dr. Van Helsing raised his glass to me. "Young women must stay up nights plotting routes to your altar."

"Heed my words, gentlemen," I spoke firmly over their raucous laughter. "The pledge of a Drăculeşti isn't given lightly: to no woman but the greatest in England shall Drăcula give vows of marriage, and even then, I will choose her."

Even Dr. Van Helsing nodded and joined in the brief applause the others gave to my speech. I acknowledged their approval with a pretense to drink the red wine I'd been provided by a servant.

"I'm sure she'll be as perfect as my Lucy," Arthur said to me.

I couldn't prevent the wry smile upturning my lips.

"No lady exists as perfect as your Lucy," I raised my glass to Arthur, and the others joined in my toast.

"We must celebrate two-fold tonight," John Seward said. "The notes Dr. Van Helsing's been waiting for arrived this afternoon."

"You should've awakened me," Dr. Van Helsing said. "I may not be as young as you four, but I'm not so old that I can forsake my duty."

"You and Quincey were awake all night and most of the morning," Arthur said. "After dinner, you'll have all evening to read."

"Dr. Van Helsing, it'd be my great honor to assist you ...," I said, and all of the young men rolled their eyes.

"As I told your fellows, I must refuse," Dr. Van Helsing said. "My papers and journals are quite extensive, and I must quickly find the essential passages."

"Some of them are diaries ... from his younger days," John Seward said. "He fears we'll learn he wasn't always so dignified ..."

"Ah, friend John, were it only so simple," Dr. Van Helsing said. "I was once young ... and entertained much the same thoughts you four enjoy. But I've traveled pointless roads and chased threads of thought that led to nowhere, and we haven't time to pollute our sacred purpose with inconsequentials."

"Sacred purpose ...?" Quincey asked.

"As our friend Count Drăcula knows, some things exist in defiance of God," Dr. Van Helsing said. "Such a monster is the cause of Miss Lucy's affliction, and it's our sacred duty to defy it ... and, if possible, to destroy it. And with that, I retire to my papers."

Words, and even thoughts, failed me. My entire plan, from coming to England to arising as King of the Earth, was poised on a stack of journals one old man was about to read. As the others wished Dr. Van Helsing goodnight, I sat stunned, unable to reply. *What could I do?* How could I insure my secrets would remain undiscovered and continue with my plan? *I'd sworn to kill Lucy tonight!* I couldn't stomach another delay that kept her from my arms! Yet, to keep my secrets, would I have to surrender my disguise? *Or ... would I have to kill Dr. Van Helsing?*

"Count Drăcula?" Arthur asked. "Are you unwell?"

I startled from my reverie. "Oh, forgive me; my mind was elsewhere."

"You looked dogged," Quincey said with a grin. "Women; nothing distracts a man so, not even his favorite horse."

"Alas, I'm transparent," I said truthfully.

"We've all shimmied up that pole," Quincey said.

"All except Arthur," John corrected.

"Oh, I've chased many a skirt that fled from me," Arthur smiled. "Of course, I was only thirteen ..."

We all laughed, and I pushed aside my doubts ... and reached out with my mind. Hiding in the shadows, in the woods, waited my loyal wolf-friend, watching the house from the outside. I told him to be patient, but to come fast when I called.

Hours passed, and Arthur and John marked the passage of every hour by going up and checking on Lucy. I suggested several times that some of them should get some rest, but with the inclusion of Dr. Van Helsing, we were now five protectors, and each felt confident that Lucy was in no danger. I bided my time, making careful plans while we discoursed on countless subjects. I was enjoying the companionship of these men. Friendship was a luxury I'd forgotten, and one I'd miss once Lucy was undead.

Finally the appointed hour came, and when Arthur and John ascended the stairs, I called out to my wolf. I gave him instructions and ordered him into action. Quincey was telling an exciting tale of herding cows and shooting rattlesnakes, and the footfalls of Arthur and John had just reached the top of the stairs when the *crash!* of shattered glass filled the silent house. Quincey leapt to his feet, and I chased him out into the main hallway to the foot of the stairs which Arthur and John were running down.

"*What was that ...?*" Arthur shouted.

"*Where did it come from ...?*" John demanded at the same time.

"*It weren't us!*" Quincey said, his deep voice growling, and he glanced about as if invaders were about to charge in.

Suddenly a high-pitched, piercing scream filled the house; downstairs, not upstairs. John and Quincey dashed off in the direction of the scream, but I seized Arthur's arm.

"Lucy!" I shouted. "She must be protected!"

Sheer terror whitened Arthur's face, and seconds later he and I were racing upstairs. To Lucy's door we ran, and she screamed as we burst through her door.

"Darling!" Arthur cried, and he ran to her.

"Be not concerned," I said to Lucy, whose eyes had widened when she saw me. "Something alarmed one of the servants; Quincey and John went to investigate."

"What alarmed ...?" Lucy asked.

"We don't know," Arthur said. "Hush, you're still weak. John will quickly solve this mystery, and few can out-muscle Quincey."

"Yes, don't be distressed," I said, fighting to resist the evil aroma and holy light.

Another scream echoed from below; a man's cry of horror, and again the sound of breaking glass.

"What can it be?" Arthur asked me as he held Lucy protectively.

"I'll look," I said, and I ran into the hall just in time to see Dr. Van Helsing reach the top of the stairs.

"Lucy ...!" Dr. Van Helsing cried.

"We have her," I said. "She's protected."

Dr. Van Helsing ran to my side and peered into Lucy's room, but he didn't look relieved until he saw Lucy safe in Arthur's arms. Then the howl of a wolf echoed loudly through the house, and no one looked relieved anymore.

"Doctor, what is it?" Arthur demanded.

"A wolf ... as my papers described!" Dr. Van Helsing said. "It's a distraction ... to draw us from Lucy!"

To my surprise, Arthur reached inside his jacket and drew a loaded pistol.

"Nothing will harm Lucy!" Arthur promised.

Standing in the hallway, outside of Lucy's poisoned room, I felt my strength return. I reached out with my mind and saw dark bushes sliding past my sight as I ran on all fours, felt their leaves brush against my fur, and saw windows which I jumped toward and smashed into, hearing their fragile glass shatter right in my ears, and felt their sharp fragments rain onto my pointed ears, before I jumped back outside. Then I called my wolf to me, directed him again up the narrow stair to Lucy's balcony, and soon the glass of Lucy's door pane shattered. Instantly I ordered the wolf to flee, and scarcely was it drawn back when the thunder of Arthur's pistol blasted a projectile at the broken window. I flinched as the ball tore through thick fur; I could feel its burning passage, but only my fur was singed; my wolf ran off, unhurt, as Arthur ran to the door and shouldered it open, breaking its lock and more of its panes, and knocking aside the strands of garlic hanging over it.

"*I see it ...!*" Arthur shouted, his hands rapidly reloading his pistol.

"*Arthur, no ...!*" Dr. Van Helsing shouted, but Arthur ignored him.

"*This ends now!*" Arthur said, and he ran after it.

No human could match pace with a running wolf, so I directed my friend back to the front of the house. This took a full minute, and footsteps pounding up the stairs told me John and Quincey were running to join us.

With a final command to my wolf-friend, I ordered him to enter the building again. With another resounding *crash!*, my wolf leapt in through a downstairs window, and several servants cried out. Hearing them, John and Quincey halted at the top of the stairs, saw Dr. Van Helsing and I guarding Lucy, and when I nodded to them, they turned and ran back down the stairs.

At my command, my wolf jumped back out the window and ran away from the house. A distant pistol shot informed me that Arthur was still chasing it, but I felt no stinging pain, which told me my wolf-friend was unhurt.

The time had come. I glanced inside Lucy's room; Dr. Van Helsing was standing in the ruin of Lucy's door to the balcony, looking outside for any trace of Arthur. John and Quincey were doubtlessly joining Arthur on his hunt. The servants were probably hiding in corners, comforting each other and cringing in fear.

I entered Lucy's polluted room, my face resolute. Lucy gasped to see me so determined, and drew back, but Dr. Van Helsing, looking outside, never saw me coming. I seized upon a tall statue of white marble and swung hard, not with my full vampiric strength, but with sufficient force to subdue any human. My blow struck Dr. Van Helsing across the back of his head, and he collapsed in a pile on the doorstep.

Lucy let out a stifled scream, but I turned to face her.

"We have only moments," I said.

I rushed to her. Servants could arrive at any time, and Arthur, Quincey, and John wouldn't be gone long. I took Lucy in my arms, staring into her beautiful, wise eyes. She met my stare undaunted, as adamant as I. Fearlessly she raised her chin, exposing her precious throat, and I didn't hesitate. With ravenous lust, I bit into her neck hard, deeply, my lips pressed over her wound.

Her most-delicious blood streamed into my mouth, and I gulped and sucked for more. Thousands I'd consumed; I could drink very fast when pressed, and I swallowed as a wild beast, faster than any human, and filled my dead arteries with her perfection. The wash of her tantalizing warmth swelled my senses like an euphoric drug, but I couldn't be distracted. I drained Lucy until I sensed her heart failing, until I was certain no healing could save her. Lucy swooned and fell unconscious in my arms. Then I heard the front door bang open and shouts echo up as three sets of footfalls stomped up the wooden stairs.

Quickly I wiped my bloody lips with my hand and smeared Lucy's blood across my forehead, and then I picked up the white marble statue with which I'd knocked Dr. Van Helsing unconscious ... and slammed the marble statue into my own head.

When Arthur, Quincey, and John burst into Lucy's room, they found three unconscious bodies dripping blood.

They went to Lucy first, and soon I felt Quincey try to rouse me, but I pretended to be unconscious. He left me to check on Dr. Van Helsing, while Arthur was shouting at Lucy to rouse her, and John was studiously examining her.

After Lucy, John went to Dr. Van Helsing, and slowly managed to bring him around with some massage of his skull, gentle shakes, and several passes of some vile-smelling vial under his nose. Dr. Van Helsing awoke slowly, grunting and gasping, but as soon as he came to his senses, he pushed John aside and rushed to Lucy's side, ignoring the blood still trickling from the back of his head.

"Gott in Himmel!" Dr. Van Helsing shouted, examining Lucy's neck-wound. *"Beeile dich! Fetch brandy!"*

Quincey flew out the door, but soon he returned with the decanter. Dr. Van Helsing wetted her poor white lips with it, and together they rubbed her palms, wrists, and heart. Dr. Van Helsing listened for her heartbeat, and after a few moments of agonizing suspense, he opened his satchel and began pulling out his tools.

"It's not too late," he said. "Her heart beats, but feebly. All our work is undone; we must begin again."

I pretended to revive, lest John search for my pulse and find none. As I opened my eyes, I let out a cry, and I pushed against John as if fighting him. To my surprise, Quincey seized and pinned my arms to my side with relative ease; *his strength was impressive!*

"Stop wrastlin'! It's us!" Quincey shouted at me.

"I ... I ...!" I stammered. "*I saw him ...!*"

"Keep his image in your mind," Dr. Van Helsing shouted at me. "I must know all you remember, but first we must treat Lucy. Arthur, Quincey, John, and I have aided Miss Lucy; who now will open his veins for her?"

"It's my turn," I said, and I pulled up my sleeve.

As I watched, the good doctors began their medical practice, and I stood memorizing their every action, and the meticulous adjustments of their instruments. They drew out their funnel and long tubes of copper, and blew through them to insure their hollows were clear. Then I allowed them to pierce my flesh, and soon Drăculeşti blood, mixed with her own, flowed back into the arm of my beloved Lucy; *if she hadn't been infected with vampirism before, surely this would empower her.*

"Lucy ...!" Arthur called.

"Do not stir her," Dr. Van Helsing said. "She is so weak waking may only drain her, and that would make danger, oh, so much danger. I must make a precaution: I'll give her a hypodermic injection of morphia."

I'd seen morphine smoked by sailors, but this morphine was liquid, and he proceeded to fill a small device he called a hypodermic, a small siphon topped with a needle, and he stabbed it into her arm, then pressed the morphine directly into her veins. I stared amazed; *how did I fail to learn of this, another medical marvel? Was I illiterate in the sciences of modern men?* The effect on Lucy was instantaneous: her skin tone evened, and her faint seemed to merge subtly into the narcotic sleep of morphine. Yet not even a faint tinge of color stole back into her pallid cheeks and lips.

"She's not responding," Dr. Van Helsing said at last, and Arthur paled at his words.

"Already ...?" John asked. "Perhaps more blood; you took longer with Arthur."

"He is her lover and her fiancé," Dr. Van Helsing said, and he turned the lower faucet, stopping the flow. "Only half of Dr. Blundell's patients survived this procedure. We must end this, lest Lucy's condition worsen. We've done all science can, for the present. Pray our efforts suffice."

The strong night breeze blowing in the shattered door slowly helped clear the room of the garlic's foulness, yet I still had my part to play; as I was disconnected from the silver needle, I stiffened myself and walked back toward the door to the hall.

"I should've stopped him," I complained. "This's my fault."

"*Drăcula!*" Arthur shouted, and he released Lucy's hand and caught up with me just outside her door, seizing my arm. "Drăcula, you're no more to blame than the rest of us. We all should've stayed here ... surrounding her."

"You didn't see him," I said. "His eyes ... like looking into wells of a depth no mortal mind could possess. He was ... a force of nature ... as if God himself had empowered him."

"*You must ...!*" Arthur began, but I cut him off.

"I saw him ... materialize ... *out of thin air!*" I said. "No mortal could do that! He lifted that statue and took out Dr. Van Helsing before I could cry an alarm. I rushed him, but he moved with the speed of a great warrior ... I couldn't stop him."

"You're not to blame," Arthur said. "We need you. We'll hunt and kill this thing together."

"I've disgraced my family," I whispered, keeping my eyes from meeting his.

I shrugged free of Arthur's grip as the servants reached the top of the stairs and peeked around the corner at us. Ignoring them, I stomped resolutely past and down the stairs. At the foot of the banister I found four more servants, all looking terrified, clutching shawls over their nightshirts, and staring at the blood on my forehead. I gestured for them to hurry upstairs, and at my command, they obeyed. I stepped into the foyer, hearing them ascend behind me.

With a glance back, I reversed my course, and headed down a hallway. Most of the doors were opened, and I ran to each, glancing inside every room. Finally I found what I sought: beside a brightly-glowing oil lamp on a small table stood a stack of journals: *the papers and diaries of Dr. Van Helsing*, sitting where he'd left them to rush to Lucy's aid.

With a delighted smile, I lifted the lamp, and tilted it slowly. The flammable oil poured out, dripping upon the papers containing my secrets of vampirism. With these burned to a cinder, my secrets would be safe forever. I poured oil all over the papers, and then I lowered the flame of the lamp, closer and closer, until it ignited.

As flames rose upon the papers of Dr. Van Helsing, I opened his window and looked up at the night's sky. *Everything I'd wanted to accomplish tonight I'd attained.*

Be the bat!

Enriched by the blood of my Lucy, despite the return of some of her blood by transfusion, even my transformation back to my human form seemed to hurt less. I felt elated: *not even the modern medical transfusions of Dr. Van Helsing could save Lucy; my blood had defeated them! My bride would soon arise! We'd finally be together!*

Voices disturbed me, but it was only a group of young people on the other side of my stone fence. I paused to listen, fearful they'd seen my transformation, but they were complaining about the sprinkles falling from the sky and their hate of rain. I waited in the shadows of my garden until they passed out of hearing, and then I strode toward my house.

Inside, I swept off my hat and cloak, and before I could even hang them on their pegs by my door, Renfield rushed into the room, his hands filled with a small bucket of water and a damp rag.

"Master! You're back early!"

"I return triumphant!" I said. "Tonight Drăcula was victorious!"

"Excellent, Master!" Renfield said. "I'm deeply happy for you!"

"Thank you, faithful one," I said. "Soon there'll a guest coming, and your duties will not have been in vain."

"Company ...?" Renfield asked.

"Yes, and you mustn't be here when she arrives," I said.

"*She ...?*" Renfield asked.

"She ... she whom Drăcula has chosen," I said.

"You ... you have made her ... like you, Master?" Renfield asked.

"The process has begun," I said. "It won't be quick, for she wasn't prepared. Two nights at the soonest, more likely three nights, and she'll arise to a new life!"

"But ... Master, I beg you ... *when can I ...?"* Renfield began.

I smiled, knowingly, and assumed a friendly, fatherly tone.

"Renfield, as soon as you're ready ...," I began.

"I'm ready now ... tonight!" Renfield said.

"Where will you live?" I asked Renfield. "Where will you sleep your days away where no one will find you? Upon whom will you feed ... and how will you leave no traces for authorities to find? They'll look for you, if they find your victims, and constables are neither fools nor do they tire of searching. How will you face eternity? What is your long-term goal? What will you do to take up your time, not for hours, but for centuries? Others have slain themselves rather than endure eternal boredom. Renfield, I see you as a child, unready to answer these simplest of questions ..."

"This house is big ...," Renfield said.

"Do you think I intend to reside here forever?" I asked. "No, and you'll no longer be Renfield, my slave, but a Master of the Night; you can't rely upon others for upkeep. That's why you're not ready, my child; you barely grasp forever. You need to plan, to prepare, to be ready to embrace your glorious future before it comes.

"Besides, as all of our kind, you'll need to feed, and I've taken great precautions to insure that those I feast upon leave no trail constables can trace to my estate. I can't trust your feedings will be equally untraceable, especially if you dwell in my house, where your beginner fumblings could lead others to me."

I placed my arm around Renfield's shoulders in a fatherly, reassuring way.

"Trust me, my mortal servant," I said. "I've no desire to lose your services ... and you've already been seeded with the gift of immortality. Yet you mustn't access this gift until you're ready ... because my secrecy is worth more than your eternal life ... and you don't want me to hunt you, do you?"

Renfield looked up at me, his face askew with contradictory expressions. Obviously he'd never thought of any of these things.

"I ... I could ...," Renfield began.

"Yes!" I said. "That's what you must do: think about it! Think long and hard. Plan! Choose the future you want to arise to, the glory you'll seek. Think about it for a month ... or a year! What is a year when you shall walk through eternity as another man walks down a garden path? Plan, and when time allows, come and tell me what you've planned; then we'll discuss if you're ready.

"Now, return to your cleaning, and come back tomorrow night and clean again. Focus on the main rooms, for they'll be what she sees first."

"Will she live with you, Master?"

"Not at first," I said. "Even if I wished her to live here, she couldn't. See what I mean? Being sired is a sacred time, and each ariser must acclimate to the consecrated ground on which they were first interred."

Renfield wished to talk more, but I refused, and sent him to finish his cleaning and return to his asylum before dawn. Renfield assured me he could resume his cell without his absence being detected, and slunk off with his bucket and rags.

I wandered out to my mailbox and retrieved my newspapers. I had at least two evenings free in which to set my plan in motion, and then I'd have money aplenty.

I left my house early, while the sun still shined. I arrived at Lucy's house less than half an hour after sunset. I apologized for being late, blaming my business requirements for taking so long. I was ushered straight up to Lucy's room, where all the men were gathered in silence.

"Gentlemen, who will stay up with me tonight if none of you have slept?" I asked.

To my surprise, Quincey gestured to me to follow, and he and I walked out, past the railing of the stairs.

"It's not working," Quincey told me. "Lucy ain't responding to your blood like she did to ours ..."

"Perhaps a different man ...," I suggested.

"Dr. Van Helsing and John said no," Quincey said. "She's got plenty of blood in her veins, but she's suffered too much, too often. The color she gained last night faded with the sunrise. Apparently there's ... no more they can do; it's all Lucy's toss now."

"Has she gained consciousness?" I asked.

"A few times, but she passes out quick as a possum," Quincey said. "Draw up a chair, partner. We may not bide long now."

I struggled to hide my excitement; *their modern medical knowledge was failing! Lucy's life was ending! Soon she'd be mine!*

As we walked back, Arthur came out and started descending the stairs.

"I'll find the servants ... and get them to make us some food," Arthur said, and he stumbled down the stairs like a man unaware of where he was.

"Lucky if he does," Quincey said, and as we walked back to Lucy's room, he added: "Servants mostly quit last night. They said this house is cursed."

"I'll wait here, by the door," I said. "I hate the smell of garlic."

"No, come inside," Dr. Van Helsing called to us, and we obliged. "My friends, it won't be long now. Lucy is dying. I sent Arthur away so we could talk. I know her enemy and ours, and we must face it together. But first, we must be strong for our good friend Arthur."

We all nodded in silent agreement.

In silence, Dr. Van Helsing kept examining Lucy. I entered behind Quincey, but the room still held everything I hated.

"Someone go and get Arthur," Dr. Van Helsing said. "Now. She's fading, and he should be here for the end."

"I'll do it," I said, and I fled the evil vapors and holy light.

In the large kitchen, Arthur was pulling human food out and stacking it on a white counter.

"Can't find a single servant," he mumbled.

"Forget the food," I said. "Dr. Van Helsing says you must come at once."

The bowl Arthur was holding fell toward the floor, and Arthur was walking toward me before it broke. I stepped aside, let him proceed, and followed in respectful silence.

When we reached the now-familiar bedroom, which was no longer neat or clean, Dr. Van Helsing stood up to face Arthur.

"My friend, I am sorry," Dr. Van Helsing said. "I can bring her to consciousness one last time, but I fear the effort will drain her last strengths. Her poor body has endured too much to hold out much longer. If you wish to say good-bye, now is the only time you'll have."

"Is there no hope?" Arthur asked, his voice flat and lifeless.

"With God, there's always hope, but only a miracle will prevail," Dr. Van Helsing said. "Come, Arthur; you must be strong."

I stayed at the door, conflicted. *I'd done all of this. I was the cause of Arthur's suffering, and like it or not, as I sat with him, pretending to protect Lucy from myself, I'd come to like Arthur and his friends. I even liked Dr. Van Helsing, and was more impressed with him than by all the others combined. I regretted hurting them.*

"I will awaken her," Dr. Van Helsing said. "Yet I warn you; we must all be very careful now."

With medical skills I didn't know, slowly Dr. Van Helsing gave Lucy another shot, and then squeezed her hand until Lucy's eyes fluttered, then opened.

"...*Where ...?*" Lucy whispered.

"Here, my love," Arthur said, and he knelt before her and took her hand.

Lucy and Arthur exchanged glances, hers frail and soft, his fighting back tears.

"*I will love you forever,*" Arthur said.

Suddenly a change came over Lucy. I suspected only I saw it, but her eyes grew intensely hard, and a wicked grin raised the edges of her lips.

"*Arthur, my love,*" Lucy said, an unexpected soft, underlining power to her voice. "*Come to me, Arthur, my love. Kiss me.*"

Arthur leaned forward, but suddenly Dr. Van Helsing pulled him back and shoved into Lucy's face, of all things, a large silver crucifix. She winced, scowled, and hissed angrily, and I drew back, worried.

Dr. Van Helsing knew about crosses!

"No!" Dr. Van Helsing shouted at Lucy. "*Not for all the world! Not for your soul or his!*"

Lucy recoiled before the crucifix as Arthur, John, and Quincey gaped confused, but slowly Lucy's eyes softened, and she reached out her other hand to Dr. Van Helsing.

"*My true friend,*" Lucy whispered weakly to Dr. Van Helsing. "*You are my true friend.*"

Arthur started to speak, but Dr. Van Helsing waved him silent. He set his crucifix in his lap, took Lucy's hand from his, and placed it atop her other hand that Arthur was already holding. Arthur and Lucy looked once at each other, one long, eternal glance, and then her eyes closed, she slumped back upon the pillows piled behind her, and her hands fell from Arthur's grasp.

"It is over," Dr. Van Helsing said gently. "Her pain is ended. Lucy ... is with the angels."

Arthur began to weep. Slowly John and Quincey came forward, and their hands joined Dr. Van Helsing's aged grip on Arthur's shoulders. I was again torn; *this room was poison to me, but Arthur had offered me real friendship, and I'd not known welcomed kindness for centuries; it was a strangely powerful influence.* I stepped forward, into the poisoned air, and my hand joined the hands of the others, offering what support I could.

Amazingly, I'd thought I was playing a game, but I truly felt sorry for Arthur. However, an elation grew deep inside of me: *Lucy was finally dead!*

The rest of the evening was one of those times that binds men. We spoke softly, and slowly, each word carefully chosen to avoid suffering and promote sympathy. During the long hours, every one of us voiced a suggestion that Lucy's demise was our fault ... based on some action we should've done but didn't ... and every time the others denied that self-blame. The last servant, a scullery maid, appeared like a ghost and vanished just as quickly after every glass was filled and every empty bottle removed. We ate nothing, which was lucky for me, as even the little I drank was too much and would have to be purged later, before I transformed and flew home.

For the first time in a century I regretted being a vampire. Among the frightened peasants of my homeland, I was undeniably a superior being. Yet I knew, as I'd once written in my diary, that this was a fancy of my own creation. I was the reason why my homeland was backwards; no one came to Transylvania seeking wisdom or knowledge ... because I'd murdered and drained every Transylvanian who was wise, knowledgeable, or brave, as those were the only ones who'd dared to fight me. When rumors of my existence first spread, then those with the brains and ability fled the region my family had once ruled, and the cream of society that had once graced Castle Drăculea became extinct, leaving only the dregs of humanity to repopulate each new generation.

In my silent heart ... I knew ... I'd caused my people's downfall.

Yet here, sharing this sad, solemn moment, were four great men. Arthur was a young nobleman, and never did any nobility shine as brightly as his in the wake of his fiancée's death. He carried himself as proudly and with all the dignity of a Hungarian prince, without a word or nuance of recrimination. Dr. John Seward was the best speaker, a wise and gentle man, whose soft words comforted us all even in the most trying of times. Quincey Morris stood like a silent mountain of strength, a pillar that supported us, when all words failed. With his sturdy hand gripping our shoulders and, when needed, with a manly hug when eyes moistened on the verge of tears, Quincey kept us whole. Only Dr. Van Helsing actually wept, a brief fit of sobs for the loss of the beautiful young lady he'd failed to save. Yet, in his mourning, he proved to be the most manly of all of us. Dr. Van Helsing was unafraid of anything, not even of showing his weaker side, and his soft-spoken wisdom, muttered in his thick, old-world accent, proved to me he was a most-educated man, and all he shared suffused us with courage and humility, as if his mortal life had gifted him with immortal wisdom.

I stood proudly among them, one of them, but separate. I wasn't a man, but a mortal-born gifted with immortality and filled with wisdom greater than any living human could possess, but at a terrible price. I wasn't a god, for gods required no blood to exist, and I'd never be free of my endless appetite, unless in some distant, unforeseeable future when I become even greater.

I sat sated; my joy of Lucy's demise was overwhelming, and I felt light and energized, as if I could dance were the circumstances not so grim. However, the thought that kept me frowning wasn't about Lucy, or of my future with her at my side, but that her loving friends and fiancé could be no part of my life. After all my centuries, traveling the world or haunting my family castle, I was no longer lonely. I was welcomed in the company of men. And now ... I'd have to say good-bye to the only friends I'd known since God had cursed me.

Chapter 15

"Mrs. Effington ...," I started.

"Effie!" she insisted.

"Effie," I corrected myself. "You must understand: in the backwards lands of this world, where scientific learning hasn't penetrated, magics are still practiced."

"Oh, Vlad, those are ... peasant superstitions and ignorance!" Mrs. Effington said.

We descended the narrow stairs to a room exactly as I'd requested. The room was separate from the main areas of the house, a sort of basement lounge of dark colors, mostly reds, that stank of cigars long reduced to ashes. I carried the candelabra in and set out to light all the candles and sconces in the room, for I desired brightness. Then I examined the room again; no windows and only one door existed. *It was perfect.*

Thick cobwebs and dust lay untouched; this room hadn't been cleaned in months. Its ill state reminded me of Castle Drăculea.

"You're certain your servants won't bother us here?" I asked.

"Absolutely," Mrs. Effington smiled mischievously, and she approached me coyly. "We're completely alone. Not a whisper of what we do here ... will ever leave this room."

Mrs. Effington came close to me, reached out her arms, drew me into a tight embrace, and kissed me passionately.

I didn't resist, but allowed her to press her lips against mine as long as she wanted. Obviously she'd assumed I had a completely different motive for asking her to the most remote, secluded part of her huge mansion, a place where activities could proceed witnessed only by eyes divine. It was no easy struggle; Mrs. Effington was repugnant. Her age, weight, manner of dress, and personality were the least of her drawbacks; she was a woman of great pride but small intellect, grasping at momentary pleasures, with no care for tomorrow nor goal other than to retain the social position her marriage provided. Her husband, I expected, was a man who prided himself only on his wealth, which explained his long absences for business on the mainland. Yet I couldn't let this continue.

When Mrs. Effington drew away, she leaned back deeply, as if in the throes of ecstasy, which lifted her huge breasts, which were supported by reinforced undergarments until they bulged, right into my vision. Doubtlessly she thought this view would please me.

"I've something to show you," I whispered.

The devil lived in her smile. She looked at me hungrily, as if she bore the curse of my thirst.

"I wish ... I wish to give you that which you want most," I said.

"And ... what is that?" she grinned wickedly.

"What we spoke of before," I said. "Youth."

"Oh, Vlad, I knew you were teasing me," Mrs. Effington said.

"But I wasn't," I said. "That's why I insisted we come here; what would your servants say if they witnessed ... magic?"

"*Magic ...?*" Mrs. Effington laughed.

"I don't jest," I said. "Scientific thought promotes itself by teaching the modern world that magic doesn't exist. You saw me summon the birds. Tonight I'll show you ... more."

"*More ...?*" Mrs. Effington asked, and she looked sober and thoughtful for the first time since I'd arrived.

"Only if you wish it," I said. "The magic I'll show you'll be ... quite startling."

Mrs. Effington considered, then pulled me in close, tight against her breasts.

"Vlad, you need no excuse for wanting us to be alone," she said.

"I ... fear that your servants might come running ... if you scream," I said.

She purred like a cat in my arms.

"Go ahead," she said. "*Make me scream.*"

"Look," I nodded my head to the table. "Look at the candelabra."

With a doubtful glance, Mrs. Effington appeased me and glanced at the seven glowing candles set in the brass arms of the candelabra, which stood on the dark, dusty surface of the table. She shook her head with impatience.

"Wait," I said. "You'll see it soon."

As one, a dozen spiders slowly descended from the ceiling. They were small spiders, brown, and no threat, but Mrs. Effington gasped when she spied them. Then her eyes widened. The twelve spiders were descending from the ceiling in perfect unison, forming a perfect circle around the candelabra. I held Mrs. Effington firmly to keep her from turning away, and she was too shocked to resist. The spiders descended so perfectly all of them touched the surface of the table at the same instant.

"Don't be alarmed," I whispered to Mrs. Effington. "These small creatures are completely obedient to me. I could have them weave their webs in any shape you desire, or crawl away from here and never return. They obey me ... by the very magics science told you don't exist."

As we watched, I extended my hand and issued the simplest command. Each spider abandoned its web, crawled on its eight limbs clockwise to the web adjacent to it, and began to ascend as they'd descended ... in unison.

"I ... don't like spiders," Mrs. Effington whispered through short, rapid breaths.

"Really?" I asked, amused. "There're many spiders hiding in your house. If you wish, I'll send them all outside."

I gestured again, and the spiders ceased their ascent, and leaped in so sudden a movement Mrs. Effington let out a brief, stifled scream, but I gripped her tightly to restrain her. All of the spiders started to creep across the dusty table toward the back of the room.

"Where ...?" she began.

"Effie, the spiders in your house know every crack they can squeeze through," I said. "They're headed as I commanded: outside ... by the quickest route they can take. And these spiders aren't alone ..."

I gestured to the ceiling, where other spiders had emerged, moving upside down or sideways along the walls. Every spider was crawling in the same direction.

A distant scream echoed from upstairs.

"Your servants have seen them," I whispered. "Don't worry; in fifteen minutes every spider in your house will have departed."

"How ... *how's this possible?*" Mrs. Effington gasped, looking incredulous.

"Don't be alarmed," I grinned. "Accepting that magic is more than science-not-understood takes time. Effie, I want to share this with you ... and I don't have much time ..."

"Time ...?" Mrs. Effington asked. "What do you mean?"

I bowed my head and tried to look displeased.

"Effie, my parents sent me a letter," I said. "I'm commanded to return to Hungary. I can only be here a few more days."

Her hands gripped me tightly.

"Vlad, no ...!" she said.

"I must," I said. "My visit here is expensive, and my family's finances are suffering. I can't ask my entire family to suffer for my sake."

"I have money," Mrs. Effington said. "Millions ...!"

"Your husband wouldn't approve ...," I said.

"I long ago gave up caring what he approves," Mrs. Effington said. "*Vlad, you can't leave me ...!*"

"I can't take you home, not as you are," I said.

"As I ...?" she began.

"Old," I said bluntly. "If I could stay, I'd make you young again, and then we ..."

"*Young ...?*" Mrs. Effington asked, her eyes astounded. "You ... *could really make me young ...?*"

"No, but I could teach you to make yourself young," I said. "However, it would take months, and I must leave in a few days ..."

"*I'll give you money!*" Mrs. Effington said. "*All you want ...! More than you ever dreamed of ...!*"

I hesitated as if this idea was new to me.

"Effie, if I could cable enough money home, then I needn't leave!" I said. "I've no desire to go ... to leave you ...!"

"*I'll make you rich!*" Mrs. Effington promised, and I pulled her into the tightest of embraces. We clung to each other long, but then I squirmed to be free.

"Effie, you've seen but simple tricks," I said. "You've been indoctrinated by science all your life. If you'd do this, then I need to show you how powerful my magics are ... the magics I'll have to teach you."

At this, Mrs. Effington released me and stepped back, silent and amazed.

"Don't scream," I warned her. "This magic ... will be quite unbelievable."

Mrs. Effington steadied herself as best she could.

I stepped back and opened my arms to display myself fully in the candlelight. This was very difficult magic; I didn't want her to miss it.

I concentrated, forgetting Mrs. Effington. My will had to be resolute, and irrefutable, even more than reality ... as it had been the first time I'd transformed like this ... when desperation drove me to find a skill I'd never known.

Once, more than a century ago, I was captured in a cage. My conqueror was an African prince from a tribe in the deepest part of the escarpment, central to their continent. One of the earliest vampires I'd ever sired had fled to that region, and there she was worshiped as a goddess. All of the local tribes knelt before the powers she showed them, and brought her victims as tribute. In my global search, I'd found her, and her acceptance of me as her sire, and her intellect, and the fact that she'd never sired another vampire impressed me. I stayed with her for weeks, and we departed as friends. But this African prince had grown weary of the obedience she demanded, and fashioned a great, unbreakable cage woven so tightly she couldn't escape it, not even as a bat. He wished her to make him a god, but she refused, remaining true to her promise to me. In his anger, he ordered her cage to be carried out into the relentless African sunlight at the height of day ... and she was burned to a crisp in less than a minute.

Furious that he'd failed to become a god, he recalled the legends of my visit, and so he plotted to seek me out, and from me acquire the godhood he desired. I'd grown incautious, surrounded only by frightened peasants, and one night, while seeking sustenance, I stumbled into his trap. He demanded of me the same thing he'd demanded of her, but I knew my undead existence would end as hers did if I complied. Fortunately, I was older and more powerful; while the tiny gaps in his cage could restrain a bat, I was capable of assuming many other forms. I'd concentrated ... and drawn upon all of my strength ... and spoke the command:

Be the dust!

When I finally coalesced to my human form, the African prince and his helpers became unwilling feasts for my hungers, and I mounted their heads on spears outside my castle as a warning to any who dared challenge me.

I smiled, and looked at Mrs. Effington, who was watching me intently. I concentrated ... drew upon all of my strength ... and spoke my command aloud:
"Be the dust!"

No awareness of time exists for elemental particles dancing in the air. Finally I became aware of pain, of intense strain, and slowly my consciousness restored itself as my human form reclaimed its natural state. It was agonizing, as I'd known it would be, but this was my most-powerful magic, and it couldn't fail to impress.

Mrs. Effington stared as if I were Satan himself. I steadied myself, wearied from the exertion. Not even a feast of Lucy's blood could sustain such magics twice.

"Did ... did you scream?" I asked hesitantly.

Long moments passed before she answered.

"I ... don't think so," she whispered.

"This is my most powerful magic," I said. "When I ... came back, I could've come back at any age, my own ... as an old man ... or even as a child."

"Was ... that ... *real?*" Mrs. Effington asked.

"What did you see?" I asked.

"You ... became ... dust," Mrs. Effington said, her words coming slowly, as if each utterance threatened her sanity. "You ... swirled around ... like a whirlwind ... filling this room. I was ... too stunned to move. I just watched ... recoiled as you brushed against me, and then ... then you came back."

"*Back to you, my Effie,*" I said.

I held out my hand and approached her cautiously. Hesitantly she reached out and touched my fingers, as if testing to see if I was real.

"This is why I couldn't allow your servants to watch us," I said. "This is what you must learn to do ... as women of my homeland do ... to make yourself young again."

"*Teach me ...!*" Mrs. Effington said breathlessly. "Teach me ... *and I'm yours!*"

"Bring me money that I can stay in your country ...," I said.

"You'll have all I can get ... tomorrow!" Mrs. Effington promised.

The next day, September the 22nd, I felt greatly wearied. Becoming elemental particles was difficult, but I felt certain becoming a bat wouldn't have endeared Mrs. Effington to agree to my plan. Explaining my exhaustion, I'd left her shortly after my demonstration and flagged a hack, amid a gentle, misty rain, to carry me to my very doorstep, as I hadn't the strength to transform again. A whole day in my coffin helped restore me, but I needed to feed again.

All day I'd thought about Lucy, shifting from living to undead, wherever she was. Doubtlessly she was on display, and I couldn't arrive on Arthur's doorstep late at night anymore; without Lucy's illness and Dr. Van Helsing's insistence she be protected, they had no reason to remain awake all night. Yet I arose early from my coffin, while the sun was still high; I had much to do today. Before I returned to Mrs. Effington's unwanted amorous fancies, I had to check on my Lucy ... and I'd have to do it during the early evening.

Rain spattered the windows of the main rooms of my house. Renfield wasn't there, but I could see nothing that needed cleaning; he'd done his chores well. The sun was still up, but the sky was dark with low, gray clouds, and so I donned my hat and cloak and braved the daylight. I took the longer route to avoid being seen, as Dr. John Seward might've returned to his asylum, and I'd no desire for him to realize I was his neighbor. When I arrived at the shopping district, I hailed a cab and rode it to another populous district, where in daylight I switched hacks, and rode to the door of my late Lucy Westenra.

A servant let me right inside, and went ahead to announce me. I waited in respectful silence, for there's no excuse for failing social customs in a house of mourning. When I was summoned, it was Dr. Van Helsing himself who came to escort me.

"Friend Drăcula, thank you for coming," Dr. Van Helsing said to me. "Arthur will be greatly comforted by your company."

"Thank you," I said. "I thought to come yesterday, but I feared it would be ... too soon."

"Alas!" Dr. Van Helsing said. "It was a sad day. You would've been welcomed, but I think you were wise to avoid this house yesterday. Yet I'm glad you are here now ... especially at this hour."

"At this hour ...?" I asked.

Dr. Van Helsing glanced at the bright windows and almost chuckled.

"Forgive the suspicions of an old man," Dr. Van Helsing said. "This is the first time I have seen you in daylight. Our enemy cannot travel under the sun, so I feared, for a while, that you were he."

"*Me ...?*" I asked, unable to keep the grin from my lips. "*Count Drăcula ...? A vampire ...?*"

"I ask your forgiveness, but we can't be too careful," Dr. Van Helsing said. "Our foe has unholy powers, greater cunning than any mortal man, and the wisdom of the ages."

I tried to suppress my mirth but I failed.

"Dr. Van Helsing, you're a man of science!" I chuckled softly.

"Perhaps," Dr. Van Helsing said. "But I'm also a man of God's will, and thus my duty is to remain stalwart against all threats to His world. Still, let's delay this conversation; Arthur's upset enough for now."

"Indeed," I said. "However, before I leave, you must tell me all about vampires."

With Dr. Van Helsing's assurances, I approached Arthur and offered my condolences. He thanked me for coming and hugged me, claiming I was a close friend, and that my every visit to his house was an honor. Lucy's body was on display in a parlor, and I was relieved to learn, upon enquiry, that the shutters and drapes around her were tightly closed. I also learned, from Arthur's soft voice, that our friends were absent; Quincey was attending to duties he'd been neglecting due to protecting Lucy, and John was busy with his patients in the asylum.

Other than this, little was said. We sipped at brandies and spoke in whispers of how beautiful and lively Lucy was, and then changed the subject to banal topics which no one cared to discuss, yet remained all we could voice.

Two hours passed in frustrated impatience. We spoke of Lucy very little, but obviously all our thoughts were on her. I learned that Lucy's late father had given her this grand house, and Lucy had left it to Arthur in her will. It was difficult for me to see my good friend in such pain ... while silently knowing I was the source of his misery.

I asked Arthur about his father, and he hung his head even further.

"I fear my father may not last much longer," Arthur said. "He seldom wakes, and when he does, he doesn't recognize me. I should be with him now ..."

"If you can't help him, he'd insist you help yourself," I said.

Arthur thanked me, and then he fell into an exhausted silence.

Eventually Quincey arrived, and Dr. John Seward came in a short while later, and our greetings were a welcomed distraction from our solemnity. I excused myself and begged pardon for abandoning them so early, and prepared to depart. My last act before I left, I told them, would be to pay my respects to Lucy, and pray over her, for I feared I'd be poor company afterwards.

"We've all shed tears; that's no disgrace," John said.

"No disgrace in England, perhaps, but I must honor the customs of my homeland," I said. "Therefore, good friends, I wish each of you the very best a man may wish at such a moment. Good-night, and may sleep help us all."

"Count Drăcula, allow me to walk with you," Dr. Van Helsing said, and I nodded.

Dr. Van Helsing and I walked slowly into the entryway and down a hallway toward the parlor where my beloved Lucy's remains lay on display.

"Before you leave, I must tell you what I've spoken to the others," Dr. Van Helsing said.

"Ah, yes; the secrets of your books," I said.

"Of what is left of my books," Dr. Van Helsing said. "The night Lucy was slain, our enemy attempted to destroy all that might reveal his weaknesses. A fire was started in my room, right atop my papers; if not for Quincey's courage, the whole house might have burned to the ground."

"How terrible!" I said, but my alarm wasn't for the house. "So, not all of your papers were lost?"

"I'd already found the book I needed before Lucy screamed, and I pocketed it before I ran to her side," Dr. Van Helsing said. "The fire consumed all the rest, but by the grace of God, the knowledge we need was spared."

"God's grace indeed," I frowned, wondering if God was again interfering in my life. "What've you learned?"

"It is as I remembered," Dr. Van Helsing said. "Our enemy is the summit of evil, a scourge that must be eliminated at any cost."

"That's a bold claim," I said.

"Tell me, Count Drăcula; what do you think our young Miss Lucy died of?"

"Oh, surely you or Dr. Seward are better qualified to render medical opinions," I said.

"John and I have spoken extensively," Dr. Van Helsing said. "We are agreed that Lucy perished of extreme loss of blood. But the question is: what caused her loss of blood? She had no great wounds. How did the blood exit her body ... and where did it go?"

I didn't answer, but I shrugged my shoulders, pretending ignorance.

"There is such a thing as vampires," Dr. Van Helsing said. "They are as real as the infernals you described to Arthur, John, and Quincey. They don't live as we do, for they are neither alive nor dead; they are undead. They don't eat any food, but exist solely upon the blood of their victims."

"Do you truly believe this?" I asked.

"Count Drăcula, I say to you that vampires are fact," Dr. Van Helsing said. "They are ageless, and thus gain wisdom beyond mortal years. They have unnatural cunning and the arts of necromancy. They walk in a human shape, but they can take the form of a bat, a wolf, or even elemental dust."

"A wolf ...?" I asked. "John and Quincey chased a wolf outside the house the night Lucy died."

"I saw him also, but it wasn't a wolf," Dr. Van Helsing said. "It was our enemy, and a powerful foe he is. But remember this: for all his powers, he is not free of weaknesses. He can't walk while the sun is up, and he recoils before holy objects, such as the crucifix and sacred wafer. Garlic repels him ..."

"Ah, that's why you filled Lucy's room with those smelly flowers," I said.

"Indeed, but there my notes were wrong, for he killed Lucy and her mother in that room," Dr. Van Helsing said.

"Then we must take extra care, for we know not what other of your notes may be wrong," I said.

"Count Drăcula, your wisdom shall help us kill this vampire," Dr. Van Helsing said.

"Can he be killed?" I asked.

"Yes," Dr. Van Helsing said. "A wooden stake through his dead heart will end his existence, as will beheading or burning him."

"A creature of power and wisdom will be difficult to hunt," I said.

"That's why I must ask that you help me avenge Lucy ... and allow no other duty to interfere," Dr. Van Helsing said.

"Ah, Dr. Van Helsing, here I must make a personal confession to you," I said. "My daylight hours haven't been spent in business, as I've told you, but in study. My homeland doesn't have the educational opportunities readily available in England. I spend my days with private tutors, trying to catch up with men as learned as you and your companions. But perhaps I am wrong and selfish; I should've spent my time here ... helping protect Lucy."

"You were here when you were most needed," Dr. Van Helsing said. "I can't fault any man for seeking to educate himself, but there may be more evil nights; we must gather to seek out and eradicate our foe."

"I'm at your disposal," I said stalwartly.

"Good!" Dr. Van Helsing said. "We've agreed to postpone our pursuit until after Lucy and her mother's funeral, out of respect for the dead, but ..."

"I may be away until then, but I'll be at your side that night," I promised.

"And that day," Dr. Van Helsing said. "The funeral mass is at noon, and from there we shall inter our poor lost love."

"Count on me," I said, and we embraced as true friends. "Now, forgive me, but before I leave, I must pray over Lucy."

Dr. Van Helsing patted my shoulder with his firm hand, and then he turned and walked back to the others. I frowned as he walked away; *he knew more about me than I wanted known in England, and he'd told Arthur, John, and Quincey all he'd told me. I should kill all four of them, to insure the secrecy of my plan, but their deaths would spoil Lucy's rebirth, and eventually transform her into another Miëta.*

I entered the parlor alone. Lucy and her long-dead mother lay side-by-side in matching black coffins of such style and grandeur I was instantly jealous. Candles lit the parlor, for the heavy drapes were tightly closed. I checked every direction to insure no one was watching, and then laid my head on Lucy's chest, listening. Her heart was silent, but there were soft sounds no mortals could hear, subtle churnings; *Lucy was transforming.* Tomorrow night she'd arise, and I'd have to be here to awaken my new bride.

I departed from Arthur's house in silence and started walking toward the nearest shop, but I managed to wave down an empty cab passing by. It was a rare barouche, a fashionable, four-wheeled, shallow vehicle suspended on metal springs, with two double seats inside, arranged vis-à-vis, so the sitters on the front seat faced those on the back seat. It had a soft collapsible half-hood folding like a bellows over the back seat and a high, outside box seat in front for the driver. I gave him directions to a populated area near Mrs. Effington's house, had him drop me off on the far side of her property, and walked from there.

"*Vlad ...!*" Mrs. Effington exuded repressed enthusiasm as I followed her butler inside. She was wearing several colors of green silk, a stunning dress even for one of her age and figure. She stood apart, as was proper for a wife entertaining a male guest ... while others were watching.

"Forgive me, Effie; I was delayed," I said. "I had to console my friends."

"You're so kind and thoughtful," Mrs. Effington said.

"Yet seeing you brightens my mood," I said.

"May you be brightened every day!" Mrs. Effington said, and she dismissed the butler. After he'd departed, Mrs. Effington ran into my arms and kissed me long and hard. "Oh, Vlad, I was afraid you weren't coming ..."

"The promises of a Drăculești are never broken," I said. "My dearest Effie, believe me: as long as you're alive, I'll keep every promise I made to you."

"Even ... *to make me young?*" Mrs. Effington asked.

"Effie, please!" I whispered, glancing about. "No one must hear that!"

"My servants don't spy upon me," Mrs. Effington said. "I sent them to their rooms after dinner with orders not to emerge into the main house tonight."

I smiled; *that would make my tasks more difficult, but still doable.*

"Did you bring what you promised?" I asked.

"Yes," Mrs. Effington said. "Come and see."

Mrs. Effington led me to the parlor we'd often visited, and there she lifted a silk tablecloth that draped to the rug beneath it, and pulled from under the table a large, heavy satchel. Ever the gentleman, I rushed to take the heavy load from her and set it on the table.

"Thank you," Mrs. Effington said, hugging me and pressing her huge breasts against me again. "This is for you ... *for us.* One hundred and eighty thousand pounds, in notes, and two hundred shillings in coin, and I'll get more; you're worth every farthing."

"You're too generous, my love," I said, and I opened the bag; stacked bills filled the clinking satchel. I knew well the accounting of British currency, as it had begun with the Emperor Charlemagne, who ruled in 768 A.D. The values had changed, but today four farthings were equal to one penny, twelve pence equaled one shilling, and twenty shillings equaled one pound of sterling silver. Inside this bag was a fortune, more than I could earn in years, which would free me from monetary worries during my honeymoon with Lucy, and would seed the unequaled fortune which my plan required. Even if I'd have preferred to gain it through other means, with this wealth my plan to rule the world was greatly advanced.

"My love, with this, I can stay in England ... with you," I said. "Lead me somewhere where I can demonstrate my affections ... we've waited long enough."

Mrs. Effington shivered with anticipation, took my hand, and led me toward a back staircase, up a dark hallway, and into a bedroom as opulent as a palace. Everything in it was yellow, matching the countless daffodils in ornate vases. The flowers were all fresh; *Mrs. Effington had staged this room for this moment.*

As soon as we closed her door behind us, Mrs. Effington threw herself against me.

"*Oh, Vlad!*" she gasped. "*I'm yours!*"

"Effie, let us devour each other," I said.

We embraced tightly, kissing fervently, and my young body surprised me by reacting to her lustful desperation with unexpected arousal. I considered fulfilling her desires as a last reward, a final service, to my most generous benefactress. Yet time was pressing, the servants retiring, and I couldn't wait. I kissed Mrs. Effington deeply, ardently, filling her hungry mouth, and then I kissed her chin, her jaw, her throat ...

My hand smothered her mouth as I bit, expecting a scream, but only a moan of fervent ecstasy issued from her, and then her blood filled my mouth. Her taste was bland and bitter; Mrs. Effington was no socialite of generations of careful breeding; she was as common as a Transylvanian peasant. She'd lied to everyone, and as she gasped in carnal abandon, I drank her in huge gulps. She began to sway, as some victims do when the sudden loss of blood makes them lightheaded, but still she clung to me tightly, her fingernails digging into my flesh.

Finally Mrs. Effington swooned, having never cried out or resisted. Indeed, I think her languid passing was never perceived while she writhed, lost in her frantic erotic cravings. She slipped into endless oblivion with a smile upon her lips ... which was perhaps the nicest gift I could've given her. I lifted and carried her to the bed she'd fancied to share with me, and listened at her chest until her old, desperate heart beat its last.

I carried my new satchel of money downstairs, set it by the back door, and went to the parlor where her bell sat. I wiped my lips clean, took her bell, and rang it loudly. Within a minute I heard several sets of footsteps approaching, and the butler and the young maid appeared, him still in his jacket, her dressed for sleeping in a nightgown of white cotton from America.

"Mrs. Effington asked me to give something to each of you," I said, and I extended both my arms, pretending to conceal something in my hands.

Puzzled but unwary, they both came forward. With the agility of a Hungarian soldier, and the new strength flowing throughout me, I seized their heads and slammed them together. Both fell with nary a scream, and I wasted no time. Tonight would be a feast such as I'd not indulged in for a century; *I could leave no one alive who knew I'd been visiting Mrs. Effington.*

As I rose from their side-by-side corpses, I couldn't help but smile; both her attractive maid and her aged butler were more pureblood than Mrs. Effington; their tastes cleaned her bitter tang from my palate. Yet I wasn't done. Servants gossip, and I proceeded through the house, knocking on, and then opening every door. I found two other servants, a middle-aged cook with two young children, and a stableman who was so drunk he barely noticed my entering his room, which was just to the right of her carriage stable. All of their blood filled me, and I felt so alive warmth radiated from my flesh. I was so full I'd barely tasted the last two, finally killing them by breaking their necks. I trembled as I poured brandy upon several elegant couches, and lit them to hide my murders. As the flames rose, I felt equally energized, drunk on blood, especially from the children, whose innocent intensity radiated from my countenance, enough to frighten any who saw me. I stood as I'd not stood in a century, as God had intended, the true and greatest power on Earth, the conqueror of all who resisted me, the slayer of lesser mortals: *the rightful King of Humanity!*

Jay Palmer

Chapter 16

The next evening, the three cab rides I took in the last hour of daylight helped me to pass unnoticed through the crowds of lesser peoples. I was still glutted from my feeding, and the ride home with my heavy satchel of coins and British bank notes, my sleep of the victorious, and my awakening as an owner of undisputed wealth hadn't calmed the excitement and vigor which surged in me. On my three rides, everything I saw delighted me, even the newspaper I purchased and read in my second cab ride, which described the bloody carnage of the terrible house-fire which consumed a local wealthy woman and her servants while her husband was abroad. Regretfully, any clues to the cause was hopelessly lost in the fire that 'consumed one of the finest homes in England'. The reporter chastised all Englishmen who leave their wives unprotected while they travel alone, which made me smile. Had I not killed her, Mrs. Effington would've surely attacked me, surrendering to her most humble, primitive lusts.

I'd succeeded completely. Yet I felt no self-adulation; I'd murdered thousands in my four centuries of undeath, and these pitiful few were no challenge. Killing didn't excite me anymore, but to perform the magics I needed, and brave the daylight, I needed to feed daily ... just like any mortal. My goal wasn't to increase the dying but to conquer the living. Yet even that goal paled before my greatest accomplishment to date.

I had to arrive in time!

Hearing my offer of additional coinage, my last driver whipped his stallions into speeds matching my need, and so I arrived at the church near Lucy's house before sunset. The day had been clear, the sunlight bright, so I was bundled under my heavy cloak and broad hat, and still I felt discomfort at the garish glare of day. I'd hidden in shadows as much as I could, and I'd chosen only covered hacks, and so I arrived before sunset well and strong. A priest was outside the church, chopping firewood; summer was over and the nights getting cooler. He asked me if I wished to enter the church to pray, and I declined, yet I offered him a silver sovereign for his blessing, and walked away as he greedily examined my coin.

Soon I arrived at my old haunt, the white gazebo behind Lucy's house, and there I halted. People were gathered on the patio, in clear view, and if the sun had been any higher and I not so bundled in black, then they would've seen me. I counted at least eight people. Arthur was among them, but Quincey, John, and Dr. Van Helsing were nowhere to be seen. I waited impatiently; the sun was setting fast.

As the shadows extended and joined into a single darkness, I hurried from my hiding place. Slipping through the garden like a wolf unseen, I approached the house, glad that the party on the patio were intent only on their drinks and each other, and I hurried up the outer stair to the balcony. Treading quietly across the boards, I reached the broken doors of Lucy's bedroom, which had been closed, bound on the inside with a tight cord, but were otherwise unrepaired. Through the jagged glass of a broken pane I reached in, removed the cord, and opened the door. Lucy's bedroom still stank of garlic, but the maids had cleaned it thoroughly, and no trace of my attacks remained but the broken door and the stinking residues of oils around the windows.

I crept into her bedroom and crossed to her door, glad that the sacred wafer was gone, and found her door to the hall locked. However, my newly-enhanced strength thwarted their lock with ease; with a hard click of bending metal I forced the door open, and then I glanced out to insure the hallway was clear.

From the top of the balcony, I heard the busy servants rushing food and drinks to Arthur and his guests; probably relatives come to share sympathy over Lucy's death. I snuck down the stairs, across the foyer unseen, and found the front parlor empty save for the two resting in their coffins: Lucy and her mother. With unequaled anticipation, I lifted the lid of Lucy's coffin and saw her resting in angelic beauty such as I'd never before seen. Lucy's transformation had enhanced each of her already-perfect features, and now she glowed with a beauty only the undead possess. Her skin was soft as fresh cream and twice as smooth, and the sight of her filled me with luxurious longings. I bent over and softly kissed her cold lips; anything I could do to make her first awakening pleasant. At first she didn't respond, but then a slight movement of her jaw alerted me that her awakening was at hand. I kissed her again, then gently brushed her cheek with my fingers.

"Awaken, my lovely Lucy," I whispered. "You're young, beautiful, and immortal ... and we're one at last!"

The first awakening of a vampire is a powerful experience. A dread anticipation seemed to silence all the world, and a chill breeze suddenly gusted around the room from no source. No other physical signs manifested, and I'd often speculated on the cause of the wind: human souls were only sent to Earth at the birth of a child and the rebirth of a vampire, and of the two, the rebirth of a vampire was undeniably more powerful. A soul united with an infant was a new soul, empty, unmarked by life. The soul of a vampire was a powerful soul, experienced, full of passion and desire; a soul flown to Heaven and returned to Earth, cementing a permanent bond, capable of enduring to infinity. Only the eyes of the wise could see and appreciate the holy sanctification as a mortal arises undead.

Slowly Lucy's eyes fluttered, her pupils focused on mine, and a contented smile arced her lips.

"It's done," I leaned over and whispered to her. "We're the same. Now we must avoid upsetting Arthur and his guests; say nothing, but come with me."

"I ... feel strange," Lucy said.

"The strangeness will pass, but we mustn't be seen."

Lucy slowly sat up, with all the grace of the undead, but she startled as she glanced about, not recognizing she was in a coffin. I slid my arms under her and lifted her from it, carefully set her upon her feet, and gave her the most sincere kiss I'd ever given a woman. *My bride had awakened!* Lucy wasn't just another woman for my pleasure, or my hunger, nor even one of my many brides; *Lucy was my queen, and I truly loved her.*

As our lips parted, I reached out and lowered the lid of her coffin, and for the first time Lucy spied the other coffin beside it.

"I'll explain later," I said to her. "We must flee ... before Arthur sees you!"

Lucy offered no resistance as I pulled her to a window, drew the heavy curtain aside, and opened it. With my enhanced strength, I lifted and gently set her down among the trimmed bushes, and then I climbed out after her, pulling the drapes closed and window shut behind me. Taking her hand, we walked off together under the starlight, calmly, leisurely, holding as tightly as the bonds that would unite us for all eternity. My plan was at hand, but even greater to me was the touch of Lucy's hand holding mine; *my true and devoted love!*

I stayed away from strangers walking their dogs in the evening; Lucy was well-known by the cream of London society, and it boded ill for her neighbors to see her strolling about with a strange man only days after her death.

"I can't believe it!" Lucy whispered to me. "Are you sure ... I'm dead?"

"You've no pulse," I told her.

Lucy stopped, placed her bare hand upon her chest, and remained still.

"No heartbeat!" Lucy gasped.

"Immortals don't need heartbeats," I said.

Lucy glanced at me worriedly. "We can ... love, can't we?"

I took her in my arms and kissed her.

"Lucy, I'm learned, and I know no name for my feelings but love. My only hope is that you're feeling love as deeply as I."

"What happened to Arthur?" Lucy asked.

"He's entertaining your mourners on the patio," I said.

"Then ... who was in ... the other coffin?" Lucy asked.

"That's the only sadness I have to report," I said. "They decided to hide it from you until you were well again. Its occupant was someone you loved, but she wasn't killed on purpose; her heart gave out. Even Dr. Van Helsing couldn't save her."

"Mother ...?" Lucy gasped.

"I'm sorry," I said. "It wasn't of anyone's plan ..."

Lucy burst into tears, and I held her tightly. Even as she mourned her mother, I feared, for I'd hoped that Lucy's awakening would come without regrets, to spare me the betrayal of my other brides. Yet I was also impressed; she didn't need to be told whose heart had given out, or collapsed in horror when she discovered her heart was no longer beating. Lucy was an amazing woman, but awakening didn't complete her transformation; she'd spend the next few days building a new strength she'd need, and the next century developing even a fraction of the powers I possessed.

"Come, my love," I said. "Your condition is fragile, and we've much to do before dawn. Nothing can help your mother now, but your health needs tending; the strength you feel will soon fail."

With hesitant steps, Lucy let me lead her. We walked very slowly, and she was still crying, when we reached the next road and saw an elderly couple approaching us. I turned our path abruptly, veering away from them, up a side street. Even with her eyes filled with tears, Lucy glanced up at me questioningly.

"Your picture's been in the newspaper ... and you can't afford to be recognized," I said.

Lucy nodded, and wordlessly pointed at an overgrown gate in the stone wall beside the road. I directed our steps toward it, and opened it with no small effort, tearing down many thin vines that held it closed.

The iron gate enclosed a fence around the Hampstead Heath, a wooded area, mostly young trees, thickly overgrown. Even with my eyesight it was difficult to find a path, yet Lucy kept pointing, and I led as she directed. Our thin route wound up a tall hill, evenly sloped, which took us a long time to climb, and was so steep I feared for Lucy's health at this tender stage. We reached the top and kept walking. On the other side, the hill opened out into tall grasslands dotted with large yew trees and, in the distance, a sight that I hadn't expected: a large, ancient graveyard.

"Lucy, is this your family's ...?" I asked.

Lucy nodded.

"You'll be interred here?" I asked.

Again she nodded.

"Lucy, you'll have all eternity to mourn your mother, but your future health requires you to feed tonight ... soon," I said.

Lucy didn't stop walking. The moon rose as we watched it, and I grew worried, watching it rise as we clung to each other, silent save for the occasional escaped sob as Lucy wept for her mother. Then, as night deepened and we reached the graveyard, another sound, soft and distant, reached my ears: *childish laughter.*

"Come," Lucy said.

We walked half a mile past the graveyard, which was small and surrounded by a short stone wall topped with a wrought iron fence, more for decoration than to keep out the deer. The white and grey tombstones inside were straight and even: this was once a well-tended graveyard, slowly falling into disarray. Yet we left it behind, crowning the hill it covered, as I sought the source of the laughter.

Then I spied it; a long ways away, at the foot of the next hill, where a wide stream split upon a huge stone outcropping, behind which was a small shelf of wooded ground before the two sections of stream reunited, making this small patch an island; around this island in the stream were a dozen children of various young ages, laughing and playing.

"You ... knew they'd be here?" I asked Lucy.

"When I was young, on summer nights, I'd sneak out here after I was put to bed," Lucy whispered to me.

"So, these are the miscreant children of your neighbors," I said.

"Children have been playing here for generations," Lucy said. "Vlad: remember, I'll not kill."

"As you wish, my love," I said. "But you must feed."

"What will ... blood ... taste like?" Lucy asked.

"All bloodlines have specific tastes," I replied.

"Vlad, I ... hunger, I think," Lucy said.

"That's to be expected," I said. "Show me your teeth."

Lucy looked at me carefully, then opened her mouth, and her pearly gems shone in the moonlight. She had perfect teeth, and her incisors had grown longer and pointed, although still less than what they'd become.

"Let me go to them alone," Lucy said.

"My love, are you strong enough?" I asked.

Lucy let go of my hand, and I freed her. With vampiric ease, she floated down the long slope, moving slowly, away from me. I stepped into the shadows of a tall, widely-branching oak, and watched. At first, the children didn't seem to notice her, but as she approached, some kids stopped playing and seemed to draw back. A few ran off, but Lucy moved toward the others, gently flowing down the grassy hill.

When she reached them, she stopped and spoke to them. Even I couldn't hear their words, but the children seemed to grow less afraid of her. Finally she took one of them with her hand, and to my amazement, she led them in a merry line, each child holding the hand of the child before it, and I thought I heard Lucy's voice singing. She was playing with them, making them less afraid of her. I watched astounded; most vampires arose as little more than animals, starving for their first meal. Others arose terrified of themselves, too frightened to feed, and they became weak, unable to ever gain their full strength. Lucy had planned this, I realized. Lucy had grasped the basics of vampirism before she'd died.

Truly a superior woman ...!

Lucy played with the children as if she were one of them. They seemed to accept her, and soon I could hear their high-pitched laughter, mixed with hers, rolling up the hill.

Next, Lucy led the children to a place where the small stream was narrowest, between the little island and the bank, and she watched and clapped as the children jumped across. She even took the hands of the littlest children to help them jump safely, and they laughed with delight.

Eventually she let them go, and they ran about, playing their infantile games, comfortable as she watched. Lucy seemed content to just stand while they ran about her, laughing shrilly, but finally she took one by the hand and knelt to whisper in its ear. When she slowly stood, she walked back up the hill, leading the child toward me, and once they were apart from the others, she lowered to her knees on the grass and hugged the little child. As she held it, she gestured to me, and then pointed to the child. I reached out with my mind, touched the child's thoughts, and with ease I put it to sleep.

Lucy never let the child fall, but she looked up at me and smiled, and then, with her eyes alight, Lucy bared her fangs like an expert and descended her lips to the throat of the babe in her arms. Spellbound by my will, it never awoke or cried out, and several minutes passed as I watched and smiled. As she lifted her head and wiped her lips, I released the child, and with a gentle shake from Lucy's hands, the child awoke, unaware it'd been bitten. Lucy hugged the child again, and kissed its forehead, and the child wandered back down toward the others, stopping only to turn and wave at Lucy several times.

As Lucy approached me, I stood speechless.

"That was ... incredible," Lucy said. "As sweet as syrup, as rich as a hearty soup; I've never tasted the like!"

"You're a queen worthy of eternity," I said to Lucy. "Never in my death have I seen any arise as magnificently as you."

"You told me what to expect," Lucy said.

"Yes, but you grasped it, while alive, better than many who've been undead for months," I said.

"Vlad, what else must I do?" she asked.

"We've ten hours of night remaining," I said. "Lucy, if you agree, I'd like to show you my home ... our home, if you wish it."

"Gladly," Lucy agreed.

"We don't have all night," I warned. "For the first cycle of the moon, you must sleep in your own coffin, your first coffin, to complete your transformation. Then, in order to retain your full strength, we'll transport several cartloads of dirt from your graveyard to my home, and place your casket upon it. For your first year, resting atop dirt from your own burial ground is essential; even I, the first vampire, require dirt from my homeland to rest upon, to maintain my full strength."

"Can we not rest together?" Lucy asked.

"Not yet," I said. "Not during the daytime. As you learn the limits of your strength, you'll feel when you're ready to share your days with me. Until then, you can't stir in the daytime, nor sleep anywhere but in your own coffin. That coffin lies in your ... I mean, in Arthur's house, and you must be inside it before the dawn."

"Vlad, take me home," Lucy smiled.

She extended her hand, and I took her delicate fingers and kissed them.

"I've never loved any as I love you," I said to Lucy.

She smiled, and flames of angels danced in her green eyes. Lucy was perfect; she'd make my plan succeed greater than I'd imagined. Arm-in-arm we walked to the populated district I'd come to know. It was late now, and only coaches with passengers passed us on the road.

"Vlad, many here know me," Lucy whispered.

I glanced about, then noticed the wide rings of lace circling the skirt of her funeral dress.

"Are you sentimental about this dress?" I asked.

"This ...?" Lucy asked, and she shook her head. "I can't believe they were going to bury me in this."

"I'll buy you many more," I said, and with a sudden gesture, I reached down and tore a wide section of lace off her skirt, which I then laid gently over her head, veiling much of her face.

"Now I need a new dress," Lucy smiled, and she tied the lace veil lightly under her chin and lowered it over her eyes.

I ignored two open cabs and hailed a fully-covered calèche, and then assisted Lucy to enter. Gladly I ordered him to drive directly to my home in Carfax. I no longer feared my nightly transports; Lucy was dead as far as Arthur and the others were concerned, and unless they opened her coffin in the middle of the night and found her missing, there was nothing left for the police to investigate.

All the while we rode, Lucy and I held hands and talked, confident that the horse's hooves would hide our conversation.

"What else have I to learn?" Lucy asked.

"Answer me first," I countered her question. "Lucy, do you love me?"

Lucy paused, and then she leaned close and kissed me, long and softly.

"Vlad, we barely know each other," Lucy said as our lips parted. "I'll be your queen, a loyal and faithful companion, but ... *love?* Wealthy women seldom marry for love ... although we pray it comes later. How can you know me well enough to love me?"

"Lucy, you're so beautiful I can't help myself," I said.

"Beauty fades," Lucy said.

"Vampiric beauty is ageless," I smiled at her.

"To new eyes," Lucy said. "Yet even a masterpiece can only be appreciated so many times before the sculptor sees past his artistry and notices only his mistakes."

"Ah, but a statue is never changing, while you're a daily amazement," I said. "Tonight you arose understanding concepts other undead take decades to grasp. Your outer beauty equals your inner brilliance, and of no man or woman could I say better."

"Now answer my question," Lucy said.

"You'll learn to bend yourself to shapes of your will, but not quickly," I said. "Even if your willpower allows it, these things take time, and true transformation to our kind takes months ... if you'd do it right. Your new body must learn as your old one began, with baby steps, and if you proceed slowly, you'll advance faster in the end. You must acclimate to your new diet, your new habits, and control your new instincts; vampires who can't rein in their first impulses quickly become ashes."

"How long before I can become a bat?" Lucy asked.

"Seven decades passed before I began conscious transformation," I said.

"Conscious ...?" Lucy asked.

"Lucy, we've an eternity to learn about abilities," I said. "Is this really the first conversation you wish to have with your husband?"

"Are we married?" Lucy asked.

"If you wish it, for we're bound by ties thicker than blood," I said. "We could have a ceremony ..."

"I told you I'd be your wife and queen," Lucy said. "I'll hold to that promise, but I never said when ..."

"Beside the pledge of a Drăculeşti, ceremonies are meaningless," I said. "I may or may not be your husband now, but you have my promise of protection and fidelity, the pledges of a husband ..."

"And I give to you my pledges as a wife," Lucy said.

"You're my bride tonight and always," I said, and we kissed again, long and passionately.

When finally Lucy drew back, she looked away.

"There's more I need to know," Lucy said.

"I'll teach you all I ...," I began.

"We come from different worlds," Lucy said. "I'm nineteen. Our manners are separated by four centuries and thousands of miles. Our customs aren't the same ..."

"Lucy, my sweet," I smiled and pulled her close. "You're not confined by customs, moral or otherwise. From this day on, you're free of any barrier. Customs dictate not to you; you dictate customs."

"And what if our customs differ?" Lucy asked.

I raised one finger, traced it through the thin locks of her flaming red hair hanging onto her perfect forehead, slowly followed the softness of her porcelain cheek to her exquisite jaw, down her neck to her round bosoms, and meticulously dragged my fingertip across the delicious curve of her breast, right overtop her nipple. Lucy stiffened; English customs dictated no unmarried woman should ever be touched so, and after marriage only by her husband.

"Not even God may dictate what true lovers may or may not do," I said. "True love has no limits."

We kissed again, and my soul swelled as if her blood was filling me again.

As we disembarked, Lucy was unaware of our location, but as she spied Dr. John Seward's huge asylum, her eyes widened.

"I didn't plan to be his neighbor," I said as we passed under the shadows of several elm trees, glowing in the starlight. "We must be careful, for John would recognize either of us."

"Is it safe?" Lucy asked, eyeing the asylum.

"I've lived here for months, and never once have we seen each other," I said. "Now, here is my Carfax estate, your new home. I've left it undecorated, for I thought you would enjoy choosing its furnishings."

My huge house rose in the darkness, looking stark and ominous.

"It ... looks like ... it was once a castle," Lucy said.

"It shares many points of its architecture with castles, but it's only a home," I said. "It's not our permanent dwelling, for that won't be built for many years."

I braved the street once we were past the asylum, for I wished Lucy to first enter through the main doors into my furnished rooms, not the aged, rotten-wooded dilapidation of my chapel, where the pews might break if you sat in them. Lucy insisted I carry her over the doorstep, a quaint English custom I readily agreed to, and then she closed our door and kissed me.

My partial tour of our house was quickly done; the night was passing and would be gone too soon. Lighting a candelabra of twelve tapers, I showed her the main rooms, and we peered down a few hallways Lucy left unexplored; I told her where my mound of dirt lay under the chapel, and she desired to see it. I led her through the ruinous chapel and down the stairs. When she saw my coffin atop the dirt, she stopped, looking stunned for the first time.

"We're undead," I reminded her. "Coffins to us are but furniture, like a bed ..."

"How long ... must I sleep in a coffin?" Lucy asked.

"Several months," I said. "Then you may sleep as you wish. I've slept in beds, although you may not find them as comfortable and secure as a coffin when the daytime steals your strength."

"Could we not share a coffin ... big enough to hold a bed?" Lucy asked.

"In time, we'll share everything you can imagine," I said. "Anything that pleases you ..."

I thought this would delight her, but Lucy turned to face the bare wall, her back to me.

"Vlad, you're my husband, but I'm no wife," Lucy said. "My education ... fails me here."

"A good wife is obedient," I smiled, and I reached out and took her hand. "Trust me, and I'll reveal every mystery."

Lucy turned to me, and I drew her into an ardent kiss. As I hugged her, my fingers found her laces, and I gently undid their bows. I moved slowly, cautiously, noting her every reaction; it was the first time I'd ever seen anything close to real fear in her eyes. Yet slowly her garments loosened, and I draped them over my wardrobe. Lucy struggled to remain passive, but I could see the straining effort in her posture and her subtle flinches. With each layer she showed resistance, so I stopped and slowly kissed her ... until she calmed enough for me to continue.

When only one last layer of cloth covered her, I removed my coat and began laying my clothes beside hers. I lifted her fingers to the white buttons of my shirt, and waited patiently while she fumbled them free. Finally my shirt and trousers lay beside her dress. Lucy looked like a small, hunted fox surrounded by hounds, but I progressed as gently as I could. Her English training forbid what we were beginning, yet this was an important part of her new life. Slowly I blew out every candle but the topmost, which I left glowing, and then I reached out to her.

"All I am is yours," I said to her. "Feast yourself upon any part of me you desire."

Taking her last shred of covering in my grasp, I paused and nodded to her. Lucy didn't need to breathe, but she was stifling gasps. Finally she grasped my meaning, and repeated my words.

"All I am ... is yours," Lucy said to me. "Feast ... yourself ... upon any part of me ... you desire."

Softly I lifted off her last garment, and her perfect form revealed itself in dazzling splendor. Lucy was flawlessness worthy of a Drăculeşti. No woman could more fulfill a man's desire. I took her in my arms and embraced her fully, feeling her tremble with reservations. When at last I stepped back and unbound my drawstring, I let my underdrawers fall unchecked. Lucy's eyes flashed down and then fixated upon my eyes, as if unwilling to view me again.

"You're unbound," I reminded her in a whisper. "Manners bow to you."

Lucy's breathing changed; she understood, and accepted, but remained trepidatious. I took her hand and drew her from the candlelight toward my mound, barefoot up the stone steps of my packed hill of dirt, and to the raised edge of my coffin. Naked, we hugged and kissed, and then I lifted her chin with my finger, and lowered my lips to her magnificent breasts. I moved as slowly as a clock's hands, watching her all the time, and sensing into her mind to undo her panic, to ease her into her wifely duties. The least I could do was share with her as much pleasure as her new body could stand, and no living man had more experience at pleasuring women than I.

As I kissed her, I lightly took her wrist, and pressed her palm against my raised weapon against her virginity. Lucy neither grasped me nor recoiled, but accepted this as best any woman could endure a new experience which her restrictive society forbade.

"I'll teach you desire, my love," I whispered. "But it's you who must embrace it."

In both arms I lifted her into the air, against my chest. With our gazes locked, I lowered her into my coffin, and then I kissed her forehead, her lips, her chest, her nipples, stomach, legs, and finally her knees. Lucy quivered from fear and anticipation, and I climbed in and laid down atop her so gently she knew not what was happening until it began in earnest.

Our lovemaking was hot and sensual, pounding so hard our hearts began to beat on their own, although I knew it wouldn't last. Lucy gasped, writhed, and squeezed her eyes shut as if to block out the explosions of fleshly delights coursing through her body, sensations as enhanced as her undead beauty and my unbound strength. She gnashed her teeth and bit back moans and screams of ecstasy, and trembled at my filling her with all the passions I possessed. Flashes of heat poured through us, making our bodies feel as alive as any mortal's, and pleasures cascaded over our conscious thoughts, fogged by sensations too powerful to contain.

We continued for hours. I grew aroused anew each time I looked at her, squeezed her curves or explored her crevices, and slowly her tutor-taught inhibitions faded behind elevations of lust only the King of Vampires could titillate to their fullest.

Long afterwards I held her tightly, side-by-side, squeezed together in languid etherealness. Our hearts were still beating, but to a calmer, more relaxed rhythm.

"*Now we're one ... for eternity,*" I whispered.

"*My Vlad,*" Lucy whispered softly, barely a breath. "*I love you.*"

I waited as long as I dared, and then I rose and lifted Lucy from my coffin ... our coffin. The beating of my heart continued, longer than I could recall. Even as I set her down, upon her feet, I longed to hold on, to never release her, to always be one with her. Not one of my many former brides, experts after decades of lovemaking, had ever inspired me to desires such as I felt for my young, lovely Lucy.

Never had I loved anyone or anything as I loved her.

As we toweled before dressing, Lucy asked if I had a bath, but I could only promise to purchase her any washing tub she desired. This seemed to content her, and soon we were pulling on our clothes over our dried sweat.

"As time passes, deeper pleasures we'll explore," I promised her. "In time, we'll withhold no secrets ... or desires."

The whole ride back we sat together, holding hands. For the first time, we spoke no words; *we needed none.*

The next day was definitely cooler, less cloudy, and bright, yet I braved the evening sun without hesitation. Under my wide hat and cloak, all danger was insignificant; *I was going to see my Lucy!*

I chided myself all the way there; I was too old to feel giddy, too proud and too mature, yet my anticipation at seeing my bride overwhelmed even my dignity.

I was glad to be a different man. In my mind I counted off the stages of my long life: child-prince, youthful lover, Hungarian soldier, warrior captain, defeater of the Turks, hero, Savior of the West, sickly victim of an unknown curse, kin-slayer, horror of Transylvania, monster of the Carpathians, sire of legions, general of death, hunter of the undead, scholar, world-traveler, philosopher, architect of a new world order, love-struck suitor of Lucy Westenra, and finally: master of my own destiny. Through each of my previous incarnations, my persona had adapted to new perceptions, and there was no reason to doubt falling in love wouldn't have a profound effect upon me. I should've anticipated it.

All of these stages were leading to my final stage: Emperor of Earth. Doubtlessly, sitting upon my future throne would eventually change me yet again, but I'd have my Lucy with me, to help mold me into the leader I should be.

I'd not planned on becoming a different man, but no matter; *to Hell with my plans! It was time I embraced my victory!*

As the sun was setting, I arrived at Arthur's house and rode past; *I didn't want to be seen tonight!* Finally I called for the driver to halt, paid my fare, and discretely slipped into the shadows to insure Quincey and John didn't spy me. The front window to the parlor was still unlocked, and I listened intently, then peeked in to find both coffins unwatched. Quietly I opened the window and glided in. After checking to make sure the hallway was empty, I tapped on Lucy's coffin.

"I'm here, my love!"

Minutes later we'd escaped again, and were wandering holding hands toward the graveyard where Lucy's coffin would be interred. We took a path right through it, and she pointed out her family crypt, a small building of white marble with a locked iron gate fashioned in the likeness of roses on swirling, thorny vines over the door. I was looking forward to her internment; no lock could prevent a vampire from returning to its coffin, and it would be much easier to escort Lucy from her crypt than from her former fiancé's house.

Again we proceeded to the Hampstead Heath where the local children came to play after dark, and again I allowed Lucy to approach them alone. They were less afraid tonight, and some ran to her, laughing with delight. While I watched, Lucy played with them, dancing upon the grass as lightly and freely as they, and when she finally drew one child apart from the others, I rendered it unconscious so she could drink. I smiled as she bit the sleeping child; *the blood of children was the most energetic of all.* With this diet, my Lucy would quickly grow strong.

Still in her funeral dress, wearing the torn lace as her veil, we wandered back toward the local shopping district, where Lucy lamented over the 'closed' sign in the window of a dress shop. I reminded her she couldn't shop so close to her house, where she'd certainly be recognized, and she pouted while I hailed a covered hack.

Inside, hidden by the shaking curtains, her kisses warmed my mouth.

"I wish to be properly married," Lucy whispered in my ear.

"I live to fulfill your desires," I whispered back.

"Soon," Lucy added.

"As soon as possible," I said. "This must be planned carefully. The nearness of a cross can weaken our powers, and the taste of a communion wafer would burn our tongues forever ... and possibly kill us."

"Are we so unclean ...?" Lucy asked as a shadow of worry darkened her features.

"Not at all," I said. "God himself endowed me with abilities greater than many ancient gods, but He cursed me with constant reminders that my superiority exists only by His will."

"How do you know this?" Lucy asked.

"It took me centuries to understand this, and it'll take months to explain fully," I said.

"I'm a quick learner," Lucy chided.

"Yes, but understanding God requires knowing all the lore of the greatest philosophers," I said.

"You understand God?" Lucy asked doubtfully.

"Not perfectly, but I've studied His followers longer than any man alive," I said.

We arrived at my house – our house – only three hours after sunset, and our love-making excelled my wildest imaginings. Our ritual proceeded much as before, as Lucy was still recreant, wary of the unfamiliarity of touches which once would've been violations. Yet this time she seemed slightly anticipatory, as if secretly eager to repeat the novel pleasures of our first mating, and delighted when it was accompanied by no pain of her virginal defeat. We remained in the positions of ecstasy far longer, yet I was careful not to introduce her to variations of pleasure too soon; we'd have all eternity to explore passion's heat. I'd no need to hurry; someday her carnal desires would equal my own, and on that day we'd finally be equals.

When at last we fell to cuddling tightly, I was sated more than blood could accomplish. My mind reeled; for the first time in centuries, I was overcome with passion beyond my ability to vocalize, more than even Loritá could evoke. My former brides had each trembled upon learning the burden of my blessing/curse, but Lucy understood and accepted; I loved her with an immortal lust, not only for the pleasures of her angelic body but the intricacies of her superior mind. She was truly the supreme woman, the rightful queen for the future king of the world.

And I told her so.
And she smiled at me.

Cleaned and dressed, I showed Lucy more of my home than she'd seen before, and she made a few suggestions as to how she'd like to decorate it. I promised her she'd have all she desired, and that my house was equally hers.

As we strolled the late-night streets of my local Purfleet marketplace, Lucy suggested we enter one of the few open taverns where musicians were playing, but I advised against it.

"My love, once you attain your full strength, you may choose to sip tea with no ill effects," I said. "Eating and alcohol is less palatable, but that must wait or your full strength might never manifest."

"What about daylight?" Lucy asked. "All the dress shops close before dusk."

"Even my skin can't endure direct sunlight for long," I said. "When you fully mature, you may brave the daylight, but only on dark and rainy days ... until you grow used to it."

"I hope I don't have to wait that long for a dress ... and a real veil," Lucy said.

We rode back to her house cuddling, but talking intently.

"What's it like ... to transform?" Lucy asked.

"It appears more impressive than it feels," I said. "As a wolf, or a bat, your thoughts are strangled by the limitations of your form's mind. Intentions must dominate your mind before you transform, so your lesser intellect's shape obeys, as if your will were its instinct. After restoration, memories of flapping wings or running four-footed remain like ... intense dreams. Shapes of wolves and bats revert on command, or with the sunrise, but one shape, elemental dust, is the most difficult to attain and the most difficult from which to return. Weeks ... or years may pass before one recovers, if the mind isn't strong."

"Dust ...?" Lucy asked.

"Elemental particles," I said. "It took me centuries to learn."

"You learned by trial and error," Lucy said. "With you to teach me, I should learn faster."

"I'll hold no secrets from you," I said. "In this, you must reciprocate ..."

"A good wife hides nothing from her husband," Lucy said.

"Someday we'll truly be one," I said. "As your physical powers mature, your mental powers will grow. The day will come when we'll think as one mind. Upon that day, we'll have no secrets."

Lucy smiled and took my hand.

"I look forward to that day," Lucy said. "But there is one other ..."

"Name your desire," I said.

"Vlad, in your ... in our ... new world, must you ... we ... kill?" Lucy asked.

"We must feed ...," I said, for I'd not anticipated this question.

"Millions of people will be our subjects," Lucy said. "A thimbleful from a hundred could feed both of us each night."

I smiled, and then I kissed her.

"Lucy, my plans for our future must be revised to include yours," I said.

Lucy smiled and kissed me.

As the dawn approached, with great regret I ended the most perfect night of my life. Lucy slipped inside the window of Arthur's darkened house, turned to blow me a farewell kiss, and then vanished behind the heavy drapes. I waited a minute until I was confident she was safely inside her coffin, and then I strode across the lawn as proud as I'd ever been. Everything was better than I'd planned, and I couldn't have been happier.

I arose in the late afternoon, determined to brave the sun again. I dressed heavily, glad a misty rain was spitting from the dark clouds. I walked past the asylum to the district, past passengerless hacks, to the local dress shop. The two women working there startled as I entered their shop, but I took off my hat, bowed respectfully to them, and enquired if they would assist me in picking out a present for my wife.

We spent over an hour shopping, and I ended up purchasing three gowns and other necessities which women required. I excused my requirement by insisting that my wife had been traveling, and my cigar had ignited half of her wardrobe, and I wished to replace everything before she returned. Both women thought this was a wonderful testament to a husband's devotion, and they promised to have my purchases delivered to my house immediately, as it was so near to their shop. I instructed them on where to leave my packages, paid generously, and thanked them for their assistance.

To celebrate my success, I purchased a newspaper and stopped in at the local tavern to read it. Pretending to nurse an ale, I scanned through the pages, but only one article caught my eye.

25 September
The Westminster Gazette
A HAMPSTEAD MYSTERY

The neighborhood of Hampstead is at present exercised with a series of events which seem to run on lines parallel to "The Kensington Horror" or "The Stabbing Woman". During the past two or three days, several cases have occurred of young children straying home late from playing on the Heath. In all these cases, the children were too young to give any intelligible account of themselves, but their consensus is that they'd been with a "bloofer lady." It has always been late in the evening when they've been missed, and on two occasions the children haven't been found until early in the following morning. It is generally supposed in the neighborhood that, as the first child gave as her reason that a "bloofer lady" had asked her to come for a walk, the others had picked up the phrase.

There is, however, possibly a serious side to the question, for some of the children have been slightly wounded in the throat. The wounds seem such as might be made by a rat or a small dog, and would tend to show that whatever animal inflicts them has a system or method of its own. The police have been instructed to keep a sharp look-out for straying children, especially when very young, in and around Hampstead Heath, and for any stray dogs which may be about.

I folded my paper and mused that we'd have to find a different childish haunt. Surmising that I'd given the good ladies at the dress shop ample time to have my packages delivered, I rose and proceeded to return home and prepare my surprise before I departed to awaken Lucy for our third night together. My hunger was growing; my gorging of Mrs. Effington and her servants was wearing off, and I'd need to feed soon.

I strode out of the tavern, delighted to find the rain had ceased, but dark clouds remained, blocking out most of the sunlight. Bareheaded I stepped out, looking up as if challenging the sun itself to thwart the utter happiness of my current existence, when a comely young woman walked past me. Instinctively my eyes followed her, for although I was devoted to my lovely Lucy, I still needed to feed, and this young lady walked with a grace and bearing that implied she might have tasty blood.

Then I heard an odd sound, a distant breaking of glass, as if someone had dropped their drink. I scanned the busy street, and suddenly my dead heart froze:

Jonathan Harker ...?!?

I stared at him ... *Jonathan Harker* ... and he at me. I couldn't mistake his familiar features: across the street, a restaurant had opened its wide windows, such that its many diners could enjoy the fresh air, and there by the windows sat a face I'd first seen on the doorstep of Castle Drăculea, my young visitor that'd come to explain the purchase of my new estate at Carfax.

But it couldn't be him!

I'd left him to be feasted upon by my brides!

Then my startled eyes strayed to the lady seated beside him: *Mina Murray, Lucy's friend ... Jonathan Harker's fiancée!*

Despite my restored youth, and the smoothness of my new face, Jonathan's eyes were wide with recognition, his mouth agape in horror. He paled as if he'd pass out.

I didn't wait to see if he swooned; *Jonathan knew about me, my place of origin, and he'd seen me with*

Loritá, Miëta, and Hēlgrēth! I hailed the first cab I saw, an open hack with only a flat canvas roof, and jumped into it, ordering the driver to whip his horses.

"But, sir, the pedestrians ...!" he tried to argue.

"Drive!" I shouted. *"Half a crown if you get me home quickly!"*

The lurch of the carriage threw me back, but it also shook the wet cloth roof, making droplets fall upon me. I slapped on my hat and pulled up my cloak to hide my face; Jonathan had seen me, but if I vanished quickly enough, perhaps he'd convince himself he'd been mistaken.

I decided against giving this driver my address, lest he be questioned, so I had him drive me up my street, intending to disembark past my house. Cautiously I glanced behind, to make sure we weren't being followed, when a familiar voice terrified me.

"Drăcula ...! Count Drăcula ...!"

Turning, I stared at another face I knew well, looking right at me. Dr. John Seward was standing by the road in front of his asylum, beside two other men, and he waved excitedly at me. *I was riding right past his asylum in daylight, looking out of a half-covered hack, my face clearly visible to all of my neighbors!*

"Faster, driver!" I urged him desperately. *"Faster ...!"*

As we raced past, John ran out into the street right behind us, still calling my name. There was no point in pretending; I waved to him, our eyes met, but my driver cracked his whip, and his horses drug us onward down the cobblestones, bouncing like madmen. John called out to me again, then stood in the center of the road and watched, with a bewildered expression, as I rode away from him.

I couldn't stop anytime soon, for I couldn't afford for anyone to see this hack return to its starting point, so I let him drive for some time while I considered my options.

How had Jonathan Harker escaped Loritá, Miëta, and Hēlgrēth ... and returned to England ...?

I marveled at this, but then I frowned; *this was a violation of my plan!* For fifty years I'd purposed that no man in England should know about my nature, and now all my plans were ruined. First, the remarkable Dr. Van Helsing knew more about vampires than I'd expected any man of England to know, and he'd told Arthur, John, and Quincey. Now Jonathan Harker had somehow ... *inexplicably!* ... returned to England.

No man had ever escaped my former brides! How had he done it ...?

Jonathan Harker knew my address, and his wife Mina knew Lucy, and therefore Arthur, John, and Quincey! *All my plans were unravelling!*

When a man who seldom makes mistakes does so, he reproaches himself dreadfully, and I reprimanded myself thoroughly. I'd deviated from my plan, seduced by the forgotten pleasures of intelligent conversation and companionship, however false they may be. I was so busy enjoying my new life I'd allowed every distraction I'd intended to avoid.

How could Jonathan Harker still be alive ...?

Eventually I calmed enough to realize we'd ridden far from my house. I called for the driver to slow down, then directed him to a nearby house, where I disembarked and paid him a whole crown, suggesting he find water and rest his tired mounts before taking on another fare. Amazed, but greedily seizing the crown, and checking to make sure it was real, he thanked me most eloquently for a man of his station, and then he rode off. I watched him go, then turned to look for a wooded area under whose shadows I could hide.

I had no choice but to wait all day for sunset, as irritating as it was. I didn't dare attempt to return home, in case either Jonathan Harker or Dr. John Seward had hailed a cab to pursue me. It began to rain again, softly at first, but as the sun lowered, it became a downpour, and I was forced to stand helplessly under the tree limbs as the water dripped down on me.

I wouldn't be there when Lucy awoke. What would she do ...?

Finally the sun set.

Be the bat!

Jay Palmer

Chapter 17

An eternity seemed to pass before I resumed my human form. I was in the white gazebo again; apparently my winged form seemed to think this was my second home. I reached out with my mind, and scanned Arthur's house; *Lucy wasn't there!*

With dread, I ran toward the Hampstead Heath. *Everything had gone wrong!* Asleep, Lucy couldn't have read the newspaper article ... *about the bitten children!* There could be policemen watching the site of her attacks. *I had to get there in time!*

My transformation had drained my strength, but I pushed myself to keep running, knowing every second counted. Finally I saw the hilltop graveyard of Lucy's family, and I dashed toward it, heedless of my weariness. Past the overgrown crypts and headstones I ran, and finally I came within view of the sight I feared: *Lucy was drawing back from the frightened children ... and three uniformed constables were converging upon her!*

I couldn't allow this to continue. *I was still Drăcula, Prince, Count, and vampire!* I ran out into view, and then halted, staring down at everyone downhill of me. *I had to do this!*

Reaching out with my superior mind, I broke into the minds of everyone I saw ... *and commanded them all to swoon!*

Instantly every form I saw, even Lucy, collapsed onto the tall, wet grasses. I cursed myself for not absenting her, but desperation had ruled me. Dazed by the effort, I recovered my strength, for I was greatly weakened. Yet I was secretly proud; *I'd rendered them all unconscious with a single thought!*

Only my love for Lucy had given me the strength!

When I could, I walked down and knelt beside Lucy. I was too weak to reach into her mind, but I took her hand and patted her face, and slowly Lucy awakened.

"Vlad!" Lucy smiled, looking up at me.

"Forgive me, my love; I was detained," I said.

"I was hungry ...," Lucy said.

"You needn't explain hunger to me," I said. "Come, my love, the grass is wet."

"What happened?" Lucy asked.

"Later," I said. "First, you must feast, and I should imbibe as well ..."

"Must you kill ...?" Lucy asked.

"If you wish it, I won't," I promised, and I helped her to stand.

Lucy chose several of the sleeping children, drinking briefly from each, and I elected to drink deeply from each of the three constables, not enough to kill them, yet more than enough to sustain me. Their blood was common, a little dry for my taste, but I rose sated and refreshed. I took Lucy's hand, and together we fled from the scene before any of our victims woke.

In a covered carriage to my house, I explained about all of the disasters that had occurred that day, and my consternation that I'd not prevented any of it. Lucy listened silently, intently, and finally she smiled. I loved her smile, but I didn't understand it, and my confusion must've been evident upon my face.

"You were mistaken," Lucy smiled. "Vlad, what I've feared most is that we'd marry only to find we've nothing in common. Compared to you, I'm a child ..."

"A mature man may marry a girl twenty years his junior, but eventually both will be adults," I said.

"As the centuries pass, the differences between us will lessen?" Lucy asked.

"It's I who should be afraid," I smiled back at her. "You grasp concepts so quickly you may eventually surpass me."

This observation earned me a sweet kiss.

"So you knew ... even before you left your homelands, that Jonathan and Mina Harker were friends of mine," Lucy smiled as she drew back.

"They ... they're married ...?" I asked.

"They got married in Budapest, where Mina traveled to find him," Lucy explained.

"Back then, your and Mina's names were only scribblings in a letter," I said. "My former brides were cunning and relentless; I don't see how Jonathan could've evaded them. Perhaps he murdered them before they awoke. But ... we're discovered ... at least, I am. Lucy, perhaps we should flee England ..."

"What ...?" Lucy gasped.

"You're well-known here, and I'm discovered." I said. "We can go anywhere ... and rethink our plan ..."

"Vlad, what're you afraid of?" Lucy asked. "Jonathan, Mina, Arthur; my friends would never harm me."

"Lucy, here you must bow to my superior experience," I said. "Humans hate vampires, and will destroy us at any cost."

"Didn't you say I must remain here ... if I'd someday gain the same strengths as you?" Lucy asked.

"Yes: I'm asking a great sacrifice of you ...," I said.

"The Queen of Earth can't be a second-rate vampire," Lucy said. "I left Arthur to become your queen; I won't be anything less."

My arguments fell flat, and eventually I gave up. No other person on Earth could deny my will; that's both the power and weakness of love. But, for the first time, I began to doubt my plan.

We arrived at my house amid a misty rain, and for the first time since I'd seen Jonathan Harker in England, luck shined upon me. Lucy's new dresses were stacked under my small porch awning and hadn't gotten wet. Lucy examined each one, exclaiming over my thoughtfulness, although I sensed a little reservation in her voice. I'd tried to become an expert at every facet of life in England, but when it came to women's fashions, apparently my education had shortcomings.

However, even the little smile on Lucy's face faded when I pointed out she couldn't wear them yet. Her funeral would precede her burial, and it'd raise uncomfortable questions to have Lucy's dress change colors while she lay sealed inside her coffin. Yet my effort pleased her, such that she approached a subject she found troubling.

"Vlad, what we do ... in your coffin," Lucy stammered, and with the fresh blood of children coursing through her, she actually blushed. "Well, we're not married ..."

"Enough," I waved her silent. "Lucy, let me prove my love to you; if you're uncomfortable, we'll delay our physical mergings until we're wedded."

"Oh, Vlad, thank you!" Lucy exclaimed.

"However, this is no small request, for at no time do we feel as alive as when our bodies are united," I said. "That also means we must enter a church, and you're not yet strong, but I'll do so, if you wish it."

"You're a worthy fiancé," Lucy said. "Make the arrangements, and I promise you, afterwards I'll do all you ... *desire.*"

I smiled at her choice of words.

"I know this is all new to you, but I hope you, too, find pleasure from our joinings," I said.

"It's improper for an unmarried woman to speak of such pleasures," Lucy said determinedly.

"Propriety is yours to set, my queen," I said.

This comment earned me another kiss, albeit reluctantly.

"Ours will be a good marriage," Lucy said.

"Indeed," I said. "Death has joined us ... and we'll never part."

It'd be October soon, and Lucy informed me there'd soon be many lavish fancy-dress parties. Costumes, including masks, would be required, and Lucy suggested we could attend them without being recognized. My request that we attend only parties where her former fiancé and closest friends absented themselves earned a frown, but I contented her with the news that I could easily manage attendance, as I'd invaded her and Arthur's engagement party with almost no effort.

This earned me several kisses, but I respected my promise and restrained my hands from her most precious areas.

The next evening I arrived in time for Lucy's awakening, and for the last time I snuck her from Arthur's house. Lucy's funeral was scheduled for noon the next day, and after her burial, I'd be awakening her inside her crypt. No one would be watching us, and our need to crawl through windows would be over.

My descriptions of the arrangements I'd made with a local priest placated Lucy, although she would've preferred a full-blown ceremony inside a large church with a bishop to wed us. Yet I quickly undid those regrets. Lucy needed to gain her strength, but she also needed to understand our weaknesses. With many apologies, I led Lucy along the path behind her house, past her white gazebo, and all the way up the hill to the church.

"There," I said, and I pointed upwards at the church. "Look upon that, if you can."

Lucy lifted her chin with all of the confidence of a child, and her eyes rose to see the great wooden cross atop the steeple. At first, she seemed unperturbed, disdainful of my warnings, but then her slight sneer became a frown, and her poise faltered, and she looked afraid. I seized her arms to keep her from falling, and she staggered as if she'd collapse.

"Come, let's be away," I said.

We passed by four mansions, and reached the base of the hill, almost a quarter of a mile away, before Lucy's illness faded. She glanced at me warily.

"What ... what have you made me ...?" Lucy asked.

"That same thought tormented me four centuries ago," I said, still holding her protectively. "It was the wrong question, and trying to answer the wrong question cost me countless sufferings. The right question is: *why did God choose holy symbols to prove His power over me?* When you understand that, then you'll understand His purpose."

"Why?" Lucy asked, almost gasping.

"You're weak ... or you'd have guessed it," I said. "You must feed soon, and from a different place, or we'll be discovered. The answer is simple: God is the master, and He set this limitation on me so I'd no choice but to accept His rule."

"But ...," Lucy said, "that would make you ..."

"God's student," I answered. "Yes, I've learned lessons from immortality only God could know, and He must've known I'd learn them."

"So ... your relationship with God is ... *master and student?"* Lucy asked.

"There can be no other conclusion," I said.

"Why you?" Lucy asked.

"Without me, much of God's church would've fallen," I said. "I stopped the invasion of Western Europe that might've conquered all the lands from the Middle-East to the Atlantic Ocean."

"So ... vampirism ... was your reward ...?" Lucy asked.

"I don't think so," I said. "I think it was more a ... a recognition. I think vampirism is a ... transitional phase, a way of letting one man experience and accumulate the wisdom of ages."

"To what purpose?" Lucy asked.

"Only God knows," I said. "Perhaps to do exactly as I am: bring all the world under one rulership, under a leader who must forever recognize his subordination to God due to an intrinsic weakness to holy objects."

"That may not be the only reason," Lucy said.

"We can speculate on that for centuries, but your opinions will change as the ages pass," I said.

"How do you know that?" Lucy asked.

"Personal experience," I smiled.

Lucy grinned, and spoke no more until we were far away from the cross atop the church's steeple. Her strength slowly returned, and we sought out another park where, after a brief moonlit walk, a group of five teenage boys quietly converged upon us. I grinned again as I saw them, swarthy youths wearing clothes bought for them by their parents, boys whose entire lives had sheltered and weakened them, now trying to prove they were tough. I'd seen tens of thousands like them and knew their intent.

"Now see the Warlord of Transylvania," I said to Lucy.

These pampered pups drew closer, but I moved first. With a speed they'd never seen, and strength they'd never experienced, and dexterity they'd never dreamed of, I hurled myself at the first, and soon I was surrounded by pathetic pummeling fists. One I rendered unconscious with my fist, two I flung headfirst into nearby trees, and when the remaining pair attempted to flee, I seized them and pulled them helplessly backwards, and then tossed them to the ground.

"Time to pay for your foolishness ... in blood!" I warned them.

One tried to rise, and I kicked his most vulnerable parts, leaving him writhing on the ground. Cowering in fear, his companion recoiled from me, but I yanked him to his feet with ease and drew him to Lucy.

"Harm her, and all the powers of Hell shall torment you!" I said, and then I held him out to her.

He watched her approach as an insect might perceive an angel. He had no concept of what she was, other than beautiful, but the mischievous smile on her face belied her anticipation of feeding. I grinned as she drew his head back, exposing his neck; only a week before Lucy would've hesitated before harming a fly. Yet I understood her newfound thirst. As she bit into him, he shuddered, yet I held him firm and didn't let him pull away.

She drank upon him longer than I expected, but I knew the effect that first exposure to a cross had.

"He'll die soon ... if you don't stop," I warned her.

Still drinking, her eye's flashed to meet mine, and slowly she drew back, as if she wanted to continue.

With a single hammering of my fist, the wide, frightened eyes of the boy rolled back in his head and he collapsed to the ground. Then I turned; the boy that I'd kicked was still there, staring up at us disbelievingly, and his three other companions were lying unconscious beside him.

"Why devour only one food at a feast?" I asked.

Lucy smiled.

Half an hour later, we hailed a cab and rode into London. As I'd promised to delay our sexual encounters until Lucy and I were formally married, we had no reason to return to my house. Instead, we invaded a section of London where nightlife teemed, but not one where elite celebrities frequented, as in her former environs Lucy might be recognized.

Lights shined from bohemian theaters, taverns, and barely-disguised whorehouses, which bore signs offering massages and other delights, and we joined in the throng of humanity. Lucy was delighted, and the undead walked among the living unmolested, enjoying the revelry as amused spectators. Our recent feast had fully refreshed us, and we'd both be resting in our coffins before any of those boys awoke.

Life was a party, an endless celebration, and all you had to do was go where the celebration was happening. Walking beside my Lucy, surrounded by happy people, I could only look back with regret upon the centuries I'd spent alone. *Never again!* With my beloved at my side, I'd remake this world into one grand party, and every night would be a walk through paradise. Lucy had a wonderful time, and confessed to me she'd feared our existence would be bleak and dark, but I assured her I'd experienced enough darkness for a hundred lifetimes, and under our rulership even the night would be joyous.

I'd brought a pocketful of wealth from Mrs. Effington's hoard, and we were welcomed into every tavern we attempted to enter. I bought us the best drinks, but I could only sip, and I couldn't let Lucy do any more than wet her lips; *she wasn't yet strong enough to endure a mortal diet.*

When at last I returned Lucy to Arthur's house, I kissed her long. Dawn was an hour away, yet I had many chores to do, and doubted if I'd even get to sleep the next day. In the morning I had to make final arrangements for our wedding, and at noon I was expected at Lucy's funeral; *it would be a busy day!*

A deposit and the promise of a generous tip secured a tiny but very nice chapel near the waterfront with a tipsy old priest who stank of rum and seemed to make his living marrying local prostitutes to drunken sailors. I invented a tale of young lovers defying their parents, and the old priest only raised his price by two crowns ... and assured me he had no objections ... for payment in advance. I'd promised to bring the amount he required and more. Then I sought out a local jeweler of unquestioned reputation, and from him I purchased a beautiful ring: gold with a blood-red ruby.

Having a few hours to kill, I found a new tailor's shop near the waterfront, displaying a new black suit of the most fashionable style, along with a silver vest, a black silk cloak, a matching top hat, and a silver-topped cane, which would look wonderful at Lucy's funeral. I also purchased a spotless white shirt to accompany my new attire, as my shirt of the former night now bore rather large stains smeared on its collar. The shopkeeper gaped astounded as I jerked away, when he held an oval mirror up for me to view myself, but he gave me a generous discount for my former clothes, as I'd no way to carry them and no desire to give him my address, in case someone chose to speculate on the bloody shirt. Then I rode a phaéton to the district near

Arthur's house, bought a newspaper, and hid from the sun inside a tea shop until the appointed hour.

At noon, a short britzka ride deposited me at the church behind Lucy's house, where many carriages stood waiting. I hurried into the shade to stiffen my resolve, for I'd need all of it. I waited a full minute, and then I reached out and took the wide wooden handle in my hand, pulled the door open, and entered the church.

The needling power of the cross atop the steeple was insignificant beside the overpowering stabbing I felt inside the House of God. My form seemed to resume the dry, crackling existence I'd endured before leaving Castle Drăculea; my stomach tightened, my strength drained, and a surge of nausea crested over me. Every movement became painful. *How had I survived this for fifty years?* I resisted my instinct to flee and pushed forward, feeling deluges of divinity crash overtop me, increasing with each step, as if I were wading naked into a stormy sea of stinging jellyfish. The glaring brilliance of the holy altar made me wince, and the tabernacle behind it shone like the brightest sun, searing into my eyes like flaming brands. God Himself faced me, determined to prove His superiority, which only inflamed my determination; *why would God need to prove His superiority unless I was a threat to Him?*

Boldly I stared into the blinding light, for I'd expected it, and I struggled to retain even a vestige of my former imperiousness as the torments of holiness cascaded over me. Inside that tabernacle lay the consecrated sacred host, the ultimate gift of life, and the deadliest poison to the undead. Yet I was no mere coffin-hanger; *I was Drăcula, the first and father of all vampires, and my will was adamant even before He whose curse I bore.* I resisted the nausea, the burning, and my sudden weakness, and turned my gaze away from the blinding holy of holies to examine the unfamiliar church's interior and those mourners already seated in pews.

My eyes fell upon Lucy first. The holy altar was surrounded by brilliant blooms of many flowers, especially pink roses and white gardenias, which didn't normally bloom this late in the year. Lucy would've loved to see them, but she was still an infant vampire, in her deep, dreamless sleep during the daytime ... although the idea of her rising from her coffin to look at the flowers, and the pandemonium it would engender, brought a brief grin to my lips. Her coffin was displayed before the altar, its lid closed and covered with more flowers, and the rows of pews were filled with whimpering and whispering mourners.

Another coffin lay beside hers: Lucy's mother, whose death had marred Lucy's rebirth.

"Welcome, sir," said a familiar voice. "Please come in and ... *Count Drăcula!*"

To my amazement, I looked upon the usher, and was startled to recognize the features I'd assumed I'd never see nose-to-nose again: *Jonathan Harker!*

Panic seized me, but I was too mature to be dominated by the unexpected.

"A sad day indeed," I said to him.

Jonathan's eyes rounded as his expression paled, and he took a step backward.

"It ... it really is you!" Jonathan whispered. "But ... but Count: *you're ... young ...!*"

"Age is no mystery to me," I said softly. "Mortality holds no secrets to those beyond it; *you know this.*"

"What ... are you doing ... *here?*" Jonathan asked.

"I'd ask the same of one whom I left in the arms of my brides," I said. "To escape their hungers is an amazing feat; I've underestimated the men of England."

"Count Drăcula," said a deep familiar voice, and its strong accent identified Dr. Van Helsing.

From behind Jonathan Harker, four men stepped up, all with grim, determined faces. I stared into the faces of Dr. Van Helsing, Arthur Holmwood, Dr. John Seward, Quincey Morris, and Jonathan Harker, all allied against me.

For a moment I feared, for I stood at my weakest, in a church in the daytime, facing the five wisest and most-worthy men in England, and their expressions bore no trace of the friendships I'd once seen on them. My wisest choice would be a speedy retreat, but they knew not how shaky and sickly I felt, and I had to trust that my vaunted self-control would allow no evidence.

"So, daylight doesn't deter evil," Dr. Van Helsing frowned.

"Your understanding of evil is primitive and naïve," I said to Dr. Van Helsing, but addressing all of them.

"To you alone I concede a greater understanding of evil," Dr. Van Helsing snarled, bristling with an anger I'd never seen on his aged face.

"A greater understanding of all things," I corrected him.

"Superiority is not measured by knowledge, but by how one applies knowledge," Dr. John Seward said.

"You're the wisest men I've ever met," I said to them all. "Trust me, my friends. Allow me to show you how I'd use my knowledge."

"*Murderer ...!*" Arthur hissed, and only the strong hand of Quincey landing on his shoulder restrained him.

"We mustn't disgrace Lucy's ceremony with a confrontation," Dr. Van Helsing said. "However, after this, Count Drăcula, you have the promise of a Van Helsing; your long career is ended. We know all your secrets ... and have sworn to vanquish you."

His depth of hatred suffused them all, and their combined glares screamed determination. Filled with regret , I stared at each of their faces; *these five were the first friends I'd known in four centuries.*

"I'll take no joy ending your lives," I said, looking at each of them in turn. "You're the most worthy men I've known. It's been an honor to be your friend."

"Sneaky rattler, this ain't your hitch no more," Quincey said, his tone bristling. "We'll have us a real shoot out ... *soon 'nuff!*"

"Don't set yourselves against me, my dear friends," I said. "No enemy of Drăcula prevails ... or endures."

With a nod to all of them, and a last glance at the blinding glare of the tabernacle, I turned to depart. *My plan was ruined;* I couldn't accompany them to the graveyard and watch as Lucy was interred. I walked back to the main door and pushed my way out of the church, waving to the closest covered wagon awaiting passengers.

In the hack, I pulled the curtains closed to block the sunlight. My invasion of God's house had greatly weakened me, but I had much to do. Jonathan had sold me my house, and they'd surely invade it: *I could sleep there no more.*

"Driver!" I called. "Take me to Colchester, to the office of Carter, Paterson & Co."

"Colchester ...?" the driver asked. "That's a long ways from here."

"Colchester!" I shouted, and he questioned me no more.

I sat in the rickety hack and worried; I'd never met Mr. Carter or Mr. Paterson, but Mr. Peter Hawkins, Jonathan Harker's employer, was the only other estate solicitor I knew, and he lived in Exeter, over a hundred miles west of London. I needed a new residence, and I needed it quickly.

Away from the church, my strength slowly returned, but my pain and nausea remained. It was still daylight, and I hadn't slept at all. *I'd need a lot of blood to restore me.*

It was foolish of me to attend Lucy's funeral. She was wholly mine, a creature of the night, and I'd no business consorting with those who could no longer be a part of my life. Yet, if I hadn't gone to her funeral, I wouldn't know Jonathan Harker had allied himself with my former friends, or about their determination to confront me. *Foolish as it'd been, I was better off knowing ...*

Mr. Carter was a short, balding man in an immaculate gray suit with white lace peeking out of the cuffs and collars, which was either his attempt to appear to be of the highest class or he was wearing a fashion tailors claimed was long out of style. His hair was peppery sprinkled over snow, and he seemed delighted by my urgency. Like Mr. Peter Hawkins, Mr. Carter couldn't walk, as his foot was heavily bandaged and resting on a thickly-cushioned chair, and I wondered how many solicitors suffered from gout. I introduced myself with a false name, Mr. John Carding, and I told him my hated brother-in-law had returned to England unexpectedly, expecting to lodge with me.

"I assume you've no desire to share anything with him ...?" Mr. Carter asked with a knowing grin.

"Nothing," I replied. "I'd have him carted aboard a ship sailing to China, but ... other members of my family would be displeased."

"I sympathize," Mr. Carter said.

"I need a house, not too far from here, of the poorest condition," I said. "I hope to make it as temporary a residence as possible."

"You could rent a house ...," Mr. Carter offered.

"No, I must be his sole landlord," I said. "Another landlord could be appealed to in the hopes of improving the residence."

"You're a devious man, Mr. John Carding," Mr. Carter said. "I believe I have several choices ..."

"My only preference is that it has a large basement," I said.

A troubled shadow crossed Mr. Carter's face.

"You ... aren't hoping to do anything ... illegal, I pray," Mr. Carter said.

"Certainly not," I smiled. "Yet I may choose to allow other relatives to reside in the same domicile ... and force him to live in the basement."

We both laughed wickedly at that.

Mr. Carter and I quickly agreed upon a ramshackle house nearly falling down in the district of Piccadilly, and from his description it was indeed a ruinous abode. Its former residents had been renting it out until the roof began to leak, and due to its age, they saw no benefit in paying to have it repaired. I promised Mr. Carter I'd observe it tomorrow morning and return within a few days with a full first-payment. He asked only a crown for a down-payment, and gave to me the key and address, and after the signing of a few documents, I thanked him.

Of course, by the time Mr. Carter came looking for more payments, I'll have secured a dwelling closer to Lucy, and need his residence no longer.

The burning of the noontime sun exacerbated my already taxed state, weakening me even inside the covered carriage I flagged to take me home. I was exhausted, possessed no strength, and needed rest. *I needed to be inside her crypt, beside Lucy, when she awoke.*

My coffin was a welcomed comfort, yet I couldn't afford a deep sleep. I laid unmoving, recovering my strength for hours.

When I could delay no longer, I forced my limbs back into motion with a mental effort I hadn't needed since Jonathan Harker had been my guest in Castle Drăculea. The pain recalled my decades of meticulous planning, which I'd cast aside for the foolishness of youth. Previously I'd have reviled myself for taking the chances I had since coming to England. Now I was paying the price that all young men suffer for presumptuousness.

I seriously considered returning to Transylvania and beginning again, having learned the errors in my plan. Yet I couldn't leave without Lucy: *love was another power I'd deeply underestimated.*

As I was still weak, I hailed and directed my driver to steer me to the closest street corner to Lucy's crypt, and then I had him circle the block until sunset. In the last light of day, I paid him enough to wait for my return and struggled along the path and up the hill to where my sleeping Lucy lay.

Many fresh flowers were piled about her crypt, and my lips smiled as I picked one. No one was about, and I'd long ago mastered the art of picking locks; within moments, I was inside, holding a stolen pink rose.

Unsealing her coffin for the last time, I threw back the lid and observed my beloved Lucy in all her beauty. My desires rose at the sight of her; I'd truly chosen well, and tonight we'd be joined in God's eyes.

Kissing her cold lips, I touched the pink rose to her forehead, and brushed its soft petals down her face with infinite slowness. Below her chin, I slid the pink petals down her perfect throat, across her lovely chest, and between her luscious breasts.

Lucy's lips grinned, and I bent and kissed her again. Slowly she began to kiss me back. Silently I chided myself; we had to hurry, but I couldn't resist Lucy's soft, delicate kiss.

Finally I took her in my arms, lifted her from her coffin, and set her beside me.

"Come, my love," I said. "We've far to go and much to discuss."

My hack had departed. In silence I led Lucy through the woods to the popular district of Hillingham. She needed to feed, but we couldn't risk the playground where the constables were probably still watching, and we'd no time to search for other children. Lucy objected, but I promised her answers while we rode to the waterfront.

In a hack, I told Lucy everything. I left out nothing, not even my threat to kill her former fiancé and his friends.

"You can't kill them!" Lucy insisted.

"I won't ... unless I've no choice," I said. "I know it'd hurt you, and I'd rather lose everything than make you suffer. But we must be careful! I've underestimated these men of England ... and their technologies ... too many times."

"As soon as my full strength is assured, we'll leave England," Lucy said.

"That may take months," I said. "The abode I purchased, which I still haven't seen, is a temporary arrangement. Soon I'll find a new house near to you, so we won't have to travel, but we'll still need to be careful."

"I know that staying in England's a risk," Lucy said. "I'll make it worthwhile ..."

"Lucy, I must love you," I said. "I can deny you nothing."

Lucy rewarded my devotion with another delicious kiss.

At the waterfront I convinced Lucy we both needed to feed, and we couldn't wait for a child. Within minutes I identified a drunken prostitute, and with a sight of the shilling in my hand, she followed as I gestured her into a dark alley. She seemed surprised when I led her to Lucy, but she assured us that she'd welcome the kisses of a woman ... for double her usual charge ... in advance. I placed the shilling in her hand, which she buried in her blatantly exposed cleavage, and instantly I cupped her mouth and bit.

"Remember, Vlad: don't kill," Lucy whispered.

A second later, Lucy bit, and we shared the prostitute, whose struggles quickly weakened as she succumbed to unconsciousness. Her blood tasted vile, but I needed it desperately, and the expression of distaste on Lucy's face soon mirrored mine.

"Common blood," I explained. "Come, let's hurry away ... before she awakens."

Depositing her behind an empty crate, we fled quickly, and soon arrived at the tiny chapel I'd reserved. There stood the old priest, bottle in hand, awaiting our arrival.

"Is ... this to be our ...?" Lucy asked, a shadow of disgust on her face.

I chose not to answer; *Lucy understood our situation almost as well as I.* Instead, I drew out the gold ring and showed it to her, the large ruby flashing in the lantern light.

"Vlad, it's beautiful," Lucy said.

"You're beautiful," I said to her.

"This isn't the wedding I'd hoped for," Lucy said sadly, looking askance at the drunken priest.

"This is a blessed night," I said. "If you'd like, we can be married on this night every year. We'll make it a national holiday."

"Really ...?" Lucy asked.

"It'll be the first fashion we set," I assured her.

Lucy squeezed my hand in hers.

"What a wonderful world we'll make," Lucy smiled. "Every husband and wife must repeat their wedding vows every year ...!"

"I'll make this world ours," I promised her. "You'll make it perfect."

We kissed, softly but long, and the priest hiccupped.

Inside the chapel, the only cross was large, painted white, and nailed to the wall over a rickety altar holding a worn bible. Normally I'd have barely noticed, but my recent confronting of the holiest was still affecting me. Lucy staggered, and she had to grit her teeth to resist the effect of the white cross. The rest of the chapel's walls were covered with deep red and bright gold curtains, with three rows of splintery pews crammed too close together for people to sit on them comfortably.

"We're in a hurry," I said to the old priest, supporting Lucy with one arm as I handed him the remainder of his payment.

Our ceremony was brief and plain, the customary words badly-recited with many slurred and unintelligible mutterings. We both spoke a hurried "I do", I slid the ring on Lucy's finger, and after a quick kiss, I hurried her out of that cursed, unworthy house of God.

Despite our appeased appetites, Lucy was wearied and had to rest. I waved down an open-air hack, too distressed to wait for a better ride, and practically lifted her onto the starlit seat. We rode straight to my house, and I carried her inside.

"I don't understand," Lucy gasped. "*Why ...?*"

"Here, sit down," I helped her into a comfortable chair, and I knelt before her and held her hands in mine. "Lucy, we discussed this ..."

"But ... *you sleep ... below a chapel,*" Lucy said.

"A holy object is empowered by the faith of those who worship it," I said. "The stone cross in my chapel has hung unworshipped for decades. The power of God lies not in any object, but in the reverence His people give to it."

"*Reverence ...?*" Lucy asked.

"Vampiric powers aren't inhuman," I said. "All humans have it, equal to the strength of their will. Those of great will, who live long enough, can learn to harness many of our powers. As immortals, vampires have great advantages, but not all vampires are equal; I've never met my match ... until you."

Lucy paused and looked down at me.

"You really do love me, don't you?" Lucy asked me.

"My beloved wife, let me share with you the greatest wisdom of the ages," I said, looking up into her beautiful eyes. "Only the strongest can walk through eternity. I've known many pains, but loneliness has always been my worst curse. Every plan I've ever imagined included one paramount requirement: a woman with whom I could share a deep, eternal, romantic love. Let me give you all my heart, and accept it; you'll find even the powers of vampiric perfection pale before equals sharing love."

Lucy's smile shined brighter than any tabernacle. Despite her weariness, Lucy leaned forward and kissed me.

"Take me downstairs," Lucy said. "I wish to ... *please my husband.*"

Our lovemaking surpassed Loritá's savage, carnal appetites, Miëta's endless desire for sensory aberration, and Hēlgrēth's writhing, sensual passivity. Lucy thrilled me to aspired lasciviousness, an ecstasy of sensuous merging. Unable to resist, I drew her to a sitting position, her thighs overtop mine, her perfect breasts pressed against my chest, and I bit and drank from her throat, and felt her fangs penetrate mine, and our juices flowed as one, joining us forever. In this perfect circle, consuming and consumed, vampires become one, our newly-beating hearts pounding; *no greater pleasure exists for our kind.*

In that moment, or eternity, I knew I was on the path that God had chosen for me, for by no power but the will of the Utmost could I experience such paradise. Lucy was made for me, and I for her, and no power on Earth would ever separate us. Our minds and thoughts merged, and I sensed all of her desires in lockstep with mine, and never had I been so certain I'd chosen the perfect bride ... *my perfect wife.*

Hours of wondrous luxuriating slid past, sometimes ardent with pounding passion, othertimes frozen in warm, clinging embraces. Yet time was passing, and the requirements of life seldom care for the desires of the living ... or the undead.

"Dawn isn't far off," I said. "I've much to do, and we're both weakened. You need your sleep ..."

"We have all eternity," Lucy agreed.

Dressed, we walked arm-in-arm, unable to cease smiling, past the asylum. With casual ease, I reached my mind out to Renfield and summoned him, and sensed his agreement. Then I forgot him, intent only upon my new wife.

We spoke little, but conversed in smiles and kisses the whole carriage ride back to her crypt. Our horses were old and slow; our ride was comfortably smooth, but it took longer than I'd expected. The sky was already growing light as we approached Lucy's resting place.

"You look as tired as I," Lucy said. "Let's say goodnight here. I can walk home, and you have much to do."

"Indeed," I said, "but we say *'good-day'.*"

Lucy grinned.

"Good-day, my husband," she said.

"I love you, Lucy," I said.

With a last kiss, Lucy disembarked, and she ordered our driver to return me to Carfax. I sat back against the cushions, delighted. *I had the perfect wife, and now all I had to do was conquer the world.*

Jay Palmer

Chapter 18

Returning back home as the sun rose, I staggered, even under my wide hat and long cloak, to reach my doors, glad to close them behind me. Renfield stood there, a bottle in hand, his eyes wide.

"I saw her ... with you," Renfield said.

"Her name is Lucy, and she's my wife," I said. "You will show her all honor, and obey her as you obey me. However, today, you must find and rent a sturdy horse and cart. We're moving to another house."

"Moving ...?" Renfield asked.

"This house is discovered ... and no longer safe," I said. "My coffin and personal effects must be transferred today; my mound of dirt you must transport, one box at a time, to my new residence. In this, you mustn't be seen, and I'll give you a false address, which you'll give if any asks for the secret of my new residence."

"Yes, master," Renfield said.

Hours later we arrived at my new house, which was little more than an abandoned ruin, its roof thick with moss. From under a heavy, protective carpet, I arose from my coffin, and Renfield assisted me off the cart. The few holes in the roof matched the spots of sunlight on the warped living room floor, yet the basement was completely dark, free of solar invasion. We carried my new coffin inside, filled only with Mrs. Effington's generous donation, my new diary, and the portrait of me, down the steps onto the filthy wooden floor of the basement, and there I paused to rest while Renfield fetched the rest of my belongings, including my traveling coffin and all of my clothes. A few rats scampered past my feet as I waited, but I ignored them; rats could be a watchful guard, my eyes in the daylight, if I melded with them at night. When the cart was empty, I promised Renfield I'd have brandy awaiting his return, and sent him to start transferring my dirt ... with a warning of unbearable pain if he should be caught.

  I laid down in my coffin for a brief rest, but without my native soil, my strength wouldn't return quickly.

  My eyes opened, but there was no light to see. I knew something was wrong. Then I sensed it: *the sun was setting. I was late.*

  I pushed open the lid to my coffin; *how had I allowed this? Lucy was awakening, and I was over an hour's hack ride away!*

  I calmed myself; *I was too mature to panic.* I had to get to Lucy; *I'd have to fly.*

  The unfamiliar surroundings of my new house disgusted me. My former residence had been perfect for my tastes, but I still owned it; *someday I could return.* Tomorrow morning, after I put Lucy to sleep, I'd have to seek out another real estate agent and use part of Mrs. Effington's wealth to purchase a dwelling near her crypt.

I dusted off my clothes and smoothed its creases of sleep. I shouldn't have slept late, but despite a brief feeding, I was exhausted by two visits to churches, confronting Arthur and his friends, and by braving the daylight to finish my deal with Mr. Carter, transferring my necessities to this temporary dwelling, and my few hours of sleep had done little to revive me. Beside my coffin, I found a small mound of dirt, barely a coffin-full; Renfield must've deposited it while I slept. Two bottles of brandy were missing from the supply I'd purchased on the way here.

Where was Renfield? Had he been captured again?

I needed more Transylvanian dirt to enjoy my full vampiric rest!

Ascending the stairs into the bare and grimy main room, I ignored my new residence and strode straight to the nearest window, opened it, and saw the dim sunlight diminishing from the sky. It was barely night, and I was weak, but Lucy was still new to vampirism, and needed me to guide and protect her. Despite my exhaustion, I was still Drăcula, and my will remained adamant.

Be the bat!

My next thoughts were of granite; I was leaning against a huge block of stone topped with a statue of a guardian angel. Trees with bare branches and many tombstones surrounded me. Exhausted, I looked up at the chiseled angel's face and saw its look of peace, a slight smile on its cherub lips. I wished I felt the peace of the angels, but existence was a series of impediments for both the living and the undead.

"*Lucy ...?*" I called weakly, looking about the graveyard.

The tiny hairs on the back of my neck rose; the iron gate to Lucy's crypt was closed ... *and a rosary was tied to its bars.* I stepped back, and then noticed many recent footprints in the leaves and grasses before her gate; *someone had been here.*

Desperately, heedless of the burning glare of the crucifix on the rosary, I ran forward and seized the iron gate, only to find it locked. Despite my fatigue, and my weakness in the presence of a crucifix, my fear rose so desperately I yanked the gate open ... and broke both the lock and iron hinges. The heavy gate fell with a crashing clang, and I dashed inside. In three strides I reached Lucy's coffin and flung open its lid ...

God, no ...!!!
Haven't you tortured me enough ...?!?

My beautiful Lucy ... lay in her eternal slumber ... never to awaken again. Her throat had been completely severed, her mouth stuffed with garlic, and a bloody wooden stake protruded from between her once-luscious breasts.

My Lucy ... my perfect wife ... was true-dead.
Murdered ...!

Exhaustion and shock overtook me; I stumbled back and fell against another coffin, and then I slid to the leaf-littered marble floor.

It was over.
All my plans.
All my dreams.
Everything was ruined.

How long I laid there, too stunned to think, consumed by sadness, I couldn't say, but one thought awoke me and rekindled the fire of my brain: Arthur, Quincey, John, Dr. Van Helsing, and Jonathan Harker: *these men had murdered my Lucy!*

Hours passed. Finally I rose to shaky feet and approached the remains of my perfect queen. Drăcula had opened his heart, given it fully ... for the first time in centuries, and now it would never open again. My mortal enemies hadn't slain my beloved alone; I'd taken stupid chances, when there was no need ... for the fun of it. I'd succumbed to the foolishness of youth, I who'd seen four centuries pass and learned to be more careful than a spider traversing its web. I'd become friends with those I should've slain on sight. I'd tried to be what I no longer was, forgotten myself and what I needed to focus on, all for joys that were nothing but a dead memory in Castle Drăculea.

I'd forgotten myself ... *I bore part of the blame for Lucy's death.*

I stared at my fallen beloved. To remove beauty such as hers from the world, for any reason, was the ultimate crime. To slay intelligence and wit such as hers, innocent and bubbly, was a monumental travesty. Tears of blood came to my eyes and dripped down my pale cheeks; *I'd mourn her forever!*

But first ... I'd avenge her!

Those who'd done this must pay!

I bent and kissed her smooth, soft forehead, and traced the curve of her cheek with my longing fingers, and then I could bear the suffering no more. For the last time, I closed the lid of Lucy's coffin, never to open it again.

My Lucy ...!
How can I continue without you ...?

Bereft of conscious thought, I staggered to the doorway and walked atop the fallen iron gate. My thoughts spun, confused. I looked out upon a serene landscape with hazy eyes. *Immortality expounded my misery, now with a new curse of loneliness I'd feel forever.*

I'd nowhere to go. I'd nothing to do. I cared nothing for wealth or power or world domination. Lucy had been my whole future, the bedrock of all my plans, and now I had nothing.

Death, I've longed for you so many times!
Couldn't you have taken me instead?

I fell to the ground, too weak to stand. More bloody tears flowed, unrestrained. I wept like a mortal child.

The hand of God was tormenting me ... again!

I lifted my face to the stars and cursed God with every fiber of my being.

The night passed. I wandered in circles about the tombstones, their sleeping inhabitants mocking me. Twice I re-entered Lucy's crypt, yet I hadn't the resolve to reopen her coffin and look upon her again. The very thought of her blighted perfection tortured my eyes no matter where I looked. I couldn't bear to view her ruin again.

Wild thoughts filled my mind, as affects even mortals. I considered chasing down Dr. Van Helsing, Arthur, and the others, and slaying them, tearing their heads from their bodies, but I didn't have the strength. I was weak and they knew my secrets. I considered picking them off one-by-one, slowly torturing them, with the cruel delights of Miëta, and then returning their insane, dying forms to the others so they could witness the doom Drăcula had decreed for each of them. I even considered laying before the door to Lucy's crypt, naked, to await the sun, and join Lucy in her dreamless oblivion.

I wept not only for Lucy ... but for our lost future together, and the love I'd never know again.

When the dawn finally threatened, I conceded to the inevitable. I had to return to my rancid, decrepit new home, as much a grave as her crypt.

Be the bat!

Lucy ...!
My perfect queen ...!
Nightmares worthy of the prince of darkness tormented my day-sleep, horrors of eternal torments incomprehensible to mortals who know not the realities of endlessness. I awoke in a blood-sweat, trembling from secret fears to threaten even the sanity of Drăcula.

Revenge ...!

Imagined terrors gave way to ultimate despair. My still heart crushed, I felt a pressing weight of mourning another four centuries couldn't hope to avail. *I was ruined, cheated of my greatest triumph!* My plan lay shredded, murdered by the mortal instruments of an unjust God endlessly laughing at my failures. As much as I now hated my former friends, those whose hands had slain my beautiful wife, I recognized God's unique cruelty; no mortals could so completely defy the will of Drăcula.

I must avenge my beloved ...!
Yet doubts compounded. I'd pretended to be human, for the love of longed-for companionship. I'd allowed the murder of Lucy. I'd enjoyed my momentary fun of deception to cultivate friendships. I'd allowed myself to be swayed by Lucy's beauty and her desire to keep Arthur from knowing of her escape from their pledges. Now I was alone, after a marriage that lasted less than one night.
Alone for all eternity ...!
I needed to leave England. I'd miss the modern liveliness of civilization, but that was irrelevant; it was time I was alone again. I needed to be Drăculeşti again, and abandoned foolish temptations for assured victory. I'd underestimated the sciences of modern men, their formidable tenacity, their broadness of knowledge, and the immortal contempt God had always held toward me. My underestimations had cost me my perfect prize. Now my plans were impossible. These men knew both my nature and weaknesses, and they'd track me like a wild animal.
I could stay here no longer.
A wise man knows when to withdraw and repurpose: *I'd begin again.* I'd return to Castle Drăculea, to learn and prepare even longer. Secretly I'd send invitations to men of great wisdom, and guest them long, learning all they knew, before I finally drank them dry. When next I came forth to conquer the world, I'd understand every science known to man, and I'd be merciless. No more chances would I take, nor delays allow, with a plan so masterfully-crafted even God would be powerless to stop me.

But I couldn't rest until those who'd harmed Lucy had suffered as much as I ...!

With slow determinedness, I lifted my lid and rose from my coffin. Renfield hadn't returned, so I'd arranged my coffin on the small pile of dirt he'd transported, and my sleep had been slightly restorative. Yet I'd soon refresh myself with the blood of my enemies ... *and any other I chose.* Now I was no man's friend, nor a gentle suitor; *now I'd be all my enemies feared ... the monster they made!*

I needed passage back to Transylvania. Without hesitation, I filled my pockets with fistfuls of the wealth of Mrs. Effington, recriminating myself for not having treated everyone in England like her; a tool to be slain once my needs were met. With bulging pockets, I departed. I rode a hack to the waterfront, and as I arrived, I called for the driver to help me down. Grumbling, he climbed down from the gotza and opened the door, and with my vampiric strength, I yanked him inside his own carriage, hammered my fist into his face until he collapsed unconscious, and then I drank him dry, and left him dead upon his cushions, his curtains hiding him from passersby. As I exited, I almost smiled, the first grin to upturn my lips since I'd found Lucy murdered.

I was Drăcula again, killing wherever I willed, with no concern for my victims.

Men make first that which destroys them. Arthur, John, Quincey, Jonathan Harker, and mostly that cursed Dr. Van Helsing had doomed themselves by making me vengeful.

At the purser's office, I learned that a great vessel, the Czarina Catherine, was scheduled to depart England in three days, on October 4th, sailing for

Hungary. I arranged for a cabin of my own and the transport of a great chest I'd bring to the docks an hour before sailing. The clerk took my payment and delivered a receipt for boarding and passage, and although his blood smelled tempting, I allowed him to live, to insure my paperwork was properly handled.

However, it was still early in the dark, cloudy evening, and many sailors were about, walking the docks and navigating their routes to taverns. I took the opportunity to board a ship with only one guard, and as I pretended to be drunk and have boarded the wrong ship, he grabbed my arm to force me back to the gangplank. I responded by taking him by the throat, and I gorged myself for the second time in an hour.

His blood was uncommon, of several mixed races, which I recognized from having tasted each, yet I was unconcerned about discriminations. A glut of fresh blood was exactly what I needed, more strengthening than any amount of rest. I rose from him strong, sated, and determined.

It was time.
Be the bat!

Pangs of longing filled me as I recognized my favorite white gazebo, where I'd courted and won the heart of my precious Lucy. Her loss burned within my breast, and I lifted my eyes to view her former residence with a glare of hatred so powerful the mansion appeared red, as if it'd burst aflame from my hateful intensity.

When my strength returned, I considered searching Arthur's house with my mind, but I was too angry, too overwhelmed with grief to concentrate so deeply. Thus I strode the shadows, a furtive predator on the hunt. Every sight to remind me of my happiest days spent among the very companions who were now my quarry. I steeled my resolve and pushed past the countless pleasant memories; *this time I'd act like a Drăculeşti!*

I spied inside the windows. A maid I recognized was carrying blankets; once she'd served me brandy, and I wouldn't mind drinking her dry, yet her death would inflict little anguish among my foes. *The deaths I sought must be more painful!* I spied John and Arthur talking in the very living room where I'd once been introduced to many of the fashionable dilettantes of England. My first instinct was to burst in and slay them both, but I noticed a hated brilliance shining from the table; a container of sacred host, atop three large crosses on chains ... beside long strands of garlic cloves, a large mallet, and a sharp wooden stake.

I hesitated, wondering what I should do, when my delicate hearing perceived a name I'd not expected.

"His name is Renfield," John said. "He's a very troubled patient I've been working with for months. Very dangerous ..."

"You let Mina talk to a madman?" Arthur asked, alarm in his voice.

"She wished it," John said. "He's not always dangerous, but he suffers from phases of lunacy bordering on homicidal. Believe me, I brought my two strongest orderlies, and I was prepared to take any action to protect her."

"What did she say to him?" Arthur asked.

"She asked him about Count Drăcula," John said casually.

"What ...?!?" Arthur demanded. "*How could he know ...?*"

"We suspect he's been visiting him," John said. "Several times we've chased him onto the Count's property, not knowing he owned the property next door, and we always found him pressed against one of the Count's doors, the back entrance to his chapel."

"Why would Count Drăcula have a chapel?" Arthur asked.

"We'll ask him tomorrow, if we can," John said. "Dr. Van Helsing and Jonathan will be back before noon tomorrow, with Mina Harker, and then we'll take the battle to Drăcula's doorstep."

"He must know Jonathan told us his address," Arthur said.

"Yes, but we need to investigate it, just in case," John said. "I won't rest easy until I know that infernal is no longer my neighbor."

"So, what did this ... Renfield ... say about Count Drăcula?" Arthur asked.

"He tried to avoid her questions, but badly," John said. "He accidentally referred to Drăcula only once; he said: '*The Master is at hand*'."

"*Master ...?*" Arthur asked.

"Yes," John said. "We found him driving a cart to Drăcula's house yesterday, and he fought us like a madman; I suspect he's been serving Drăcula since he came to England. However, we caught him today in an unusually lucid moment. His one request to Mrs. Mina Harker was ... he prayed he'd never again see her pretty face ... ever."

"I pray his prayer comes true," Arthur said. "I lost my fiancée to that monster; now that they're married, we must do all we can to protect Mina; Jonathan Harker mustn't suffer my fate."

A servant entered, and lest I be seen, I ducked out of sight, and then I quit my hiding place altogether. These murderers were no fools, and heavily armed against me; *no vengeance of mine would be served by walking into their trap.*

Yet the words of Arthur Holmwood made me smile. Why kill my enemies when I could make them live in agony and regret all the days of their lives? *Mrs. Mina Harker, Jonathan's wife, would be the perfect tool of my vengeance! I could kill her, and the others would live in suffering rather than sleep in peace!*

Why only kill her ...? I could make her a vampire ... *and force them to kill her!*

What a glorious revenge! Jonathan, Arthur, John, Quincey, and Dr. Van Helsing would never forgive themselves for allowing her to come to harm, let alone causing her death themselves!

It was perfect!

The *crack!* of a breaking twig alerted me; *I wasn't alone.* I turned and saw a moonlit shape behind me, walking amid the flowery garden. Quincey's huge form loomed, stepping as stealthily as his weighty bulk could manage, and he was peering between each row of blossoms, examining every shadow, and then moving to the next. *He was looking for me!*

My devilish grin widened, and my fangs ached for his flesh. Yes, to pick off one of them, especially their giant, would send a clear message to the others that I wasn't done with them. They'd be incensed by his death, and rush to avenge him, leaving Mina Harker alone and undefended.

How I'd take advantage of their mortal foolishness by taking as my bride she whom they most-desired to protect!

I crouched down, into the bushes, and waited patiently. Quincey was being very thorough, searching each clump of flora before advancing to the next. My silence was matched only by the grave, and when he came close, I pounced.

Quincey tried to cry out, yet I seized his throat in a crushing grip, undaunted by the stout tendons of his muscular neck. Quincey fell backwards with a crashing, meaty *thud!*, and lay on his back helpless as I bared my fangs.

Suddenly a fist like a juggernaut slammed into me, and I fell back; my hold on his throat failed. I feared he'd cry for his friends, but his hand reached inside his coat and brought out a radiance brighter than any lantern: Quincey drew out a huge yellow cross hanging from a long chain around his neck, and he pressed it against my chest.

Pain, such as his fist could never aspire to, suffused me. I jumped back in agony, and with a dexterity I doubted he possessed, Quincey jumped to his feet. He held his cross before him, forcing me back.

"Now you'll pay, you murderin' snake!" Quincey snarled.

"You're more a murderer than I," I snapped back at him. "*I gave Lucy what she wanted most: immortality!*"

"*Liar!*" Quincey growled.

"Drăcula doesn't lie," I said. "I swear upon the grave of my father, Lucy chose to end her mortal engagement with Arthur ... and live with me forever."

"You ... *you tricked her!*" Quincey said.

"No, I told her everything," I said. "Her intelligence was renowned; Lucy wasn't one to swim in untested waters."

"You ... you're saying ... *she wanted to leave Arthur ...?*" Quincey asked. "To become ... *like you ...?*"

"What could Arthur give her but a few decades of ever-increasing decrepitude?" I asked. "I offered her immortality and eternal beauty, a God-like husband worthy of her, and I transformed her perfection into a goddess of the night! She would've lived forever! You murdered her ... *and you slew a thousand lifetimes when you ended her innocence!*"

Quincey hesitated, and a look of doubt mingled with his suspicious expression, but then his brows knit; *I was too experienced not to recognize a silent decision.*

"Tell them all," I said, a sneering grin on my face. "Watch Arthur's face as he learns the one he loved most was willing to undergo death to escape him!"

Quincey frowned, his square jaw set, and he reached inside his coat pocket and drew out a pistol. For the first time, worry tensed my muscles; *guns were still a novelty to me.* His glowing yellow cross was withdrawn slightly, as if he trusted his gun more than divine power; *this was my chance to escape!*

"Them words ain't for Arthur's ears," Quincey said, and he lowered his cross and aimed his pistol at me.

I didn't know what effect gunfire would have upon me, and I had no desire to learn right now. Quincey aimed his pistol right at my heart ...

Be the bat!

The blast of his pistol echoed in the sensitive hearing of my winged shape so loudly even I couldn't help but notice and remember. Then the branches of Arthur's trees were whipping past me, and I flew away unharmed.

If not for the strength of fresh blood I wouldn't have managed my last transformation, but even with a double-feeding, I slowly became aware of my surroundings through a haze of weariness. Doubtless my desperation had given me the impetus I needed.

I looked about; I was in the overgrown garden of my old abode, near the gate in the wall; through the gate I could see the asylum managed by Dr. John Seward, who was probably being lied to by Quincey. For an American, Quincey was infallibly honest and straightforward; his last words to me would doubtlessly dominate what he revealed to Arthur, but his deceitfulness to his friends would torment him forever.

I rested against the wall. *I needed to see Renfield, and I had no idea where he was.*

I'd underestimated Lucy's killers far too often. They knew too much, and their ability to discover secrets I wished to keep from them was infuriating. I couldn't trust they wouldn't soon find my new residence. I had to prepare for that possibility, at least until my revenge was completed.

When the sun rose, despite an aching weakness in my limbs, I braved the morning to find two new, local real estate solicitors. Introducing myself differently to each of them, I related the same story I'd given to Mr. Carter, and purchased two new ruined estates for small down-payments, the remainder to never be paid, their bills weren't due until after I'd departed for my homeland. Their addresses were 197 Chicksand Street, Mile End New Town, and Jamaica Lane, Bermondsey. I took the keys and thanked each solicitor, and then I left them alive ... to leave false clues for my enemies.

My last task, before I headed home, was to ask for a common laborer with a cart and a strong back, and I was directed to Mr. Thomas Snelling, who lived at Bethnal Green. His assistant was Mr. Joseph Smollet, and I gave them keys to my new residences and the key to my main estate. My instructions were to find my old home, enter my chapel, take twelve of the large wooden boxes they'd find still filled with dirt, and deliver six boxes to the basements of each of my new houses. I paid them well, enough that Mr. Thomas Snelling boasted that, after all twelve boxes were moved, he'd be visiting his favorite tavern and not leaving until he was stumbling drunk. I helped them with their first load, and then I was too weary to continue. I hailed a hack to my new house in Piccadilly and the restful comfort of my coffin.

I awoke very late, still tired from my exertions, but mostly aching from the emptiness in my heart.

Lucy, having loved you once, how will I exist throughout eternity?

I'd never get Lucy out of my system. I didn't want her out of my system, but only God could restore her to me, and since He'd been the one to take her away, His cooperation seemed unlikely. My hatred for Him grew, and I vowed to somehow avenge myself upon God. Many times I'd contemplated suicide; God had obviously wanted my suffering to endure forever; *why else would He have made me immortal?* To kill myself would end my suffering, and if I thought my death would harm God, then I'd gladly slay myself. Yet I'd decided to live too many times; *someday my chance to hurt God would come, and then I'd be as merciless as He!*

But to murder Lucy, His most-exquisite creation, was a mystery beyond explanation. I had be patient; *each century I grew wiser, and someday I'd understand His plan ... and find a way to avenge my suffering ... and Lucy's death, upon He who bore ultimate blame!*

Yet I was so weak that I could barely rise from my coffin. My ship would be departing England in less than three days; before then, I had to nurse back my full strength and avenge Lucy.

Forcing myself to arise strained my will, which it hadn't done since I'd ended my fast of blood. My body was young again, yet I was sleeping on only a thin layer of my homeland over English soil; I needed more of my dirt, but first, I needed to feed.

After I dressed and climbed the stairs, I saw rain was falling again; *curse this England! Must it rain so often?* I also noticed it was after nine in the evening; a quarter of the night had already passed. I must've been exceptionally tired from my escape of Quincey's pistol. *What would it have done to me? Perhaps I should raise another vampire and test the effects of pistols upon the undead ...*

Donning my hat and cloak, I stepped out into the rain and started toward the central district of Piccadilly to hail a hack. However, only three blocks from my house, I came upon an old woman under a voluminous brolly walking three decoratively-groomed poodles. I tipped my hat to her as we approached, and she acknowledged me with a brief smile, but as we passed by I seized her throat in a crushing grip. Her dogs barked loudly, aggressively, baring tiny sharp teeth, but at a glare from me they cowered.

The old lady fainted and collapsed onto the soggy ground. I considered drinking from her wrist, but that would take too long, and others might happen by, on foot or in a carriage. Resting my knees upon her midsection to keep from kneeling on the wet grass, I pushed back my hat, sank my fangs into her throat, and drank every drop while her dogs whined.

She tasted awful!

An hour later, brimming with a newfound strength, I emerged from a covered hack to stand before my destination: Dr. John Seward's asylum. I raised the ballooning brolly of the dog-lady and stepped into the shadows, lest I be seen. With the new blood surging through me, I focused my mental strengths and reached out:

'Renfield ...!'

At once, a distant call entered my mind.

'Master ...!'

'Come to me, Renfield ...!'

'Master, I can't! I'm chained!'

'Chained ...?'

'To the wall! I tried to escape again ... to come find you ...!'

I cursed and broke my connection. Renfield was a threat to me. I'd allowed him to drink of my blood, and now he'd become a vampire when he died, but he wasn't worthy. He'd be caught and killed, and perhaps reveal even more of my secrets before his execution. Dr. Van Helsing already knew too much; *I couldn't afford to give him a weak, insane vampire to experiment upon.* Before I left England, I'd have to kill Renfield.

I walked away, wondering what to do. *Should I enter the asylum and risk myself?* If Renfield couldn't come outside, I'd have no choice. Yet Dr. John Seward was a compassionate man, and he knew Renfield's madness, however repetitive, was always temporary. If I left him alone, perhaps Renfield would yet escape again ... *his last escape.*

Walking through the wet grass, I crossed the grounds of the asylum and came to the tall gate to my property. The gate was closed, but it bore no lock, so I entered with ease. A few minutes later I was in my chapel, shaking off the rain water.

Quickly I opened the inner door to the rest of my house, listening intently. Humans are invariably noisy, but my enhanced perceptions quickly resolved I was alone. With a glad sigh, I descended to my basement to find my remaining belongings had been rifled, and many small items were missing. At first I suspected Arthur and his companions, but men of science and honor wouldn't steal ties or shirts from my wardrobe; it had to be the laborers I'd sent to ship my dirt to other houses. I considered tracking them down and punishing them, but they were unimportant. I counted the remaining crates, to be surprised: out of the fifty crates I'd brought here, twenty-nine chests remained. One was in my new house in Piccadilly. Six were moved to each of my other two houses. That left eight crates unaccounted for. *Had the laborers stolen eight of my empty wooden crates? Why would they want them?*

Again, it didn't matter. I'd need only one for my journey back home.

I stepped onto the remains of my mound of dirt upon which I'd once rested my coffin. Strength and calmness flowed into me; *how restorative homeland dirt was to my kind!* I stood there long, soaking it in ...

Suddenly I heard a small dog's bark and footsteps above me.

"This is it: Drăcula's chapel!" a whisper exclaimed.

"Quiet!" hissed another voice. *"If the count is here, we don't want to warn him!"*

I glanced about; there was only one exit from my underground chamber. Alarmed, I fled to a back corner of my catacomb, wondering how I could escape without being noticed. *I needed a diversion!*

With a moment's hesitation, I reached out and summoned help.

"Here's the stairs!" came another whisper, which I recognized as Quincey.

"Hold your crosses high and ready!" replied the harsh whisper of Dr. Van Helsing.

The first tiny squeak coincided with the first creak of a wooden step, but as more creaks followed, the scratches of tiny feet multiplied. Lantern-light illuminated the last few steps; *they were coming!* I stepped back into a shadowed alcove; *they weren't the only ones coming!*

As my pursuers arrived at the bottom step, their lamps shone from the eyes of a hundred rats, arrived from my summoning, which were scampering all over my basement. I peeked to see the invaders draw back, but then they came on, kicking and shouting at my vermin, and driving them backwards. Arthur had four small dogs on leashes, and they barked madly at the rats, chasing them back, their barks echoing deafeningly in the wide basement. I considered linking with my rats ... and having them attack my enemies and their dogs, but such pitiful threats would only convince them I was there. Instead, I let them drive back my little friends, who scurried away from the glare of the lanterns, the barks of the small dogs, and the hard shoes that stomped several of them to death.

Once the rats had fled or cowered into the corners, my enemies grew bolder.

"It looks like no one's home," Arthur said.

"But see what we've found!" Dr. Van Helsing said. "This must be the dirt he brought to rest upon; dirt from his original grave! See? There are the crates he must've shipped it in. John, count them quickly, while the rest of you search the corners. Keep your crosses ready!"

I leaned back; *I was soon to be discovered! Then I'd have no choice but to fight!*

Yet ... against five educated men with crosses and guns ... would I have a chance?

Footsteps came close, and I recognized the scent I'd hosted in Castle Drăculea. *I had to act before I was discovered!*

'Jonathan Harker, stop!'

My unvoiced command was strong, penetrating right into his mind.

'Lower your cross; you don't need it!'

A second later, Jonathan rounded the corner and saw me, but his face was gaunt, his expression devoid of emotion. His cross hung loosely in his hand, still a threat, but not brandished against me.

'What do your fellows know of my other houses?' I demanded.

'We ... Dr. Seward ... sent an enquiry to every real estate solicitor near Purfleet,' Jonathan's thoughts flashed through his mind. *'We've identified eleven*

recent purchases, and we're trying to eliminate the ones that aren't our enemy.'

'Is that all?' I demanded, glad that I'd first used a real estate solicitor from Colchester.

'Several rumors of people moving large boxes of dirt are circulating; we're trying to find the laborers.'

'Where's your wife, Mrs. Mina Harker?'

'Mina is in Arthur's house. We're all staying there.'

"You've seen nothing,' I commanded him. 'Return to the others now ... and remember nothing of these moments.'

I fell back, exhausted, as Jonathan Harker walked back toward the others. Mental connections over the strong-willed were taxing, and despite the bad-tasting dog-lady, I'd struggled to control Jonathan. I was lucky he'd found me; Quincey was an American, with thoughts that were powerful, if not deep. Arthur was a deep thinker, if not a powerful one, and both of them would've been hard to control; *possibly too hard.* Dr. John Seward thought deeply and powerfully; even my powers were unlikely to prevail over his mental acuity, and against Dr. Van Helsing even the will of the father of vampires held no hope.

"Twenty nine," Dr. John Seward announced.

"Ah, only twenty-nine chests left out of the fifty transported from Hungary," Dr. Van Helsing said. "Our enemy has been busy ... he may have countless lairs by now."

"That makes our task ... *Harker! What is it?*"

I seized up, fearing, but I'd no choice. Transforming in here would be dangerous, in case I couldn't get out. *Had they closed the door at the top of the stairs?* I tensed my muscles, preparing to run, if I had to.

"Somewhere, looking out from the shadow, I seemed to see ... the count's ... evil face," Jonathan said.

"Where ...?" the others asked.

"It was only shadows," Jonathan said. "Perhaps I shouldn't have come. Those months in Castle Drăculea still haunt my dreams. I see him everywhere, his appalling face: the ridge of his nose, those red eyes, horrid lips, and awful pallor."

"We missed the pole-cat ... again!" Quincey scowled.

"Yet we've purged his main lair," John said.

"We've failed to avenge Lucy!" Arthur sneered.

"So far, our night has been eminently successful," Dr. Van Helsing said. "No harm has come to us, such as I feared, and we have ascertained how many boxes are missing. I rejoice that this, our first intrusion, and perhaps our most difficult and dangerous step, has been accomplished without bringing into danger our most sweet Madam Mina. One lesson, too, we have learned, if it be allowed to argue a particular: those tiny beasts, which yield to the count's command, are yet themselves, not amenable to his spiritual power; for see, the rats obeyed his command, just as from his castle he summoned wolves to silence that poor mother's cry. Yet they ran pell-mell from the so-little dogs of Arthur; Count Drăcula is not here.

"We have other matters before us, other dangers, and other fears. He's gone elsewhere. Good! He's given us opportunity to cry 'check' in this chess game, which we play for the sake of human souls. Now, let's go home. Dawn is close at hand, and we have reason to be content with our first night's work. We may have many nights and days to follow, full of peril, but we must be brave, and from no danger shrink."

"Fancy speech, but I don't need it," Quincey said. "When Quincey Morris hunts, prey never escapes!"

"Let's search the rest of the house," John suggested. "We may find more clues."

With general agreement, they ascended the stairs, and I watched their lamp-light recede. Then, with a soft sigh of relief, I stepped out of hiding and hurried to my mound of dirt, hoping to restore myself, but as I approached it, needles stabbed through me and a bright light blinded me; I fell back in agony, clenching my teeth to keep from crying out.

Dr. Van Helsing had sprinkled crumbs of sacred wafer upon my dirt!

The soil that could restore me was now poisoned!

I staggered back, weakened, and growing weaker. I fell against a wall and clung to keep from collapsing, blinded by the holy glow. In its radiance I was diminished, and none of my powers would work.

For hours I was forced to lay, stabbed by holiness, before I was convinced they'd departed. When I could, I crawled up the creaky stairs, too tired to stand.

How was I going to avenge Lucy against men such as these?

Yet I'd gained several victories: *I knew they were looking for my other homes. They would probably find my two newest purchases. They were searching for my hired laborers. I knew where Mina Harker was!*

Dawn was still hours away, yet I couldn't flee and hope to recover from resting. Seeing no one, I staggered toward the nearest tavern, and outside it, I spied an old man stumbling toward me. He looked ragged; doubtlessly he'd been evicted from a tavern and was seeking a place to sleep.

I gave him no opportunity to flee. Before he was aware of my presence, I pounced like a wolf and my fangs sank deep. He struggled, and he was stronger than he looked, but I was furious and determined.

This was how I was supposed to live, as the unrepentant murderer God made me!

I ignored the vile taste of his blood and sucked him dry in minutes. Then I dropped his corpse to lay where it'd died, and moved on to find another.

God had made me a killer, and if I needed to, I'd kill every follower He had!

Chapter 19

I awoke long after sunset, feeling barely rested. I'd gorged myself on three right before dawn, that old man and two ugly prostitutes headed home in the twilight before dawn, and I was full and sated. Yet my coffin was stacked upon only one box-load of Transylvanian dirt; *it wasn't enough. I needed more blood, yet my time in England was ended.*

I arose determined. Tonight I'd invade the asylum of Dr. John Seward.

Despite a slight rain, I strode the much-longer walk to arrive at the popular area of Piccadilly, from where only a short ride deposited me just outside my former residence. I glanced at its huge, shadowy outline and wondered if I'd ever be able to return there. I didn't stand long in the rain; I headed up the front steps and pulled open the front doors of Dr. John Seward's asylum.

Attempting to appear casual, I entered the asylum foyer, which was starkly elegant, with maple trim and a marble fireplace; doubtless a residual of its owner before it became an asylum. A thin young man in a white outfit was sitting behind a desk covered with papers, and he looked up at me. I took my time shaking the water from my hat and cloak, and then I approached him directly.

"Good evening, sir," he said. "How may I help you?"

"Is Dr. John Seward in residence this evening?" I asked.

"Not yet, but he's expected," the thin man said. "He's helping another physician with an important case."

I smiled widely at him, and his eyes widened to their fullest as my fangs shined brightly. This man was startled, which left most minds open to easy penetration. With only a moderate effort, I entered his thoughts and left him speechless. He sat entranced, stunned, and I noticed a door behind him that could only be a closet.

Glancing about to insure no one else was nearby, I circled his desk and opened the closet door, and then I scized and lifted the young man inside, his eyes wavering, unable to focus on anything. I bit deeply into his neck and drank my fill. His blood was common but left a pleasant aftertaste, which I only noticed after his heart had stopped beating forever. I lowered his corpse to the closet floor and closed the door; *I'd be gone before he was discovered.*

Cautiously I penetrated deeper into the asylum. A wide, empty hallway led to a closed door, which was heavily barred, and two burly guards sat on chairs before it. These guards weren't young and scrawny like the young man in the closet, but older, with bulging muscles, bigger than Cromwick; doubtless these were the orderlies of whom John had spoken.

I sucked air as if I needed breath. *This wasn't a job for Drăcula, or any vampire; this was a test worthy of Vlad, the Warlord of Transylvania, who'd led his men from the shieldwall against invaders and killers.* I needed no distraction or deception; *it was time to be the man I really was!*

I stepped into their view silently, and their eyes rose in surprise. I didn't hide my intention from my expression or my posture, and clearly these men saw the blood on my lips. I hesitated only a moment, just long enough for them to recoil in surprise. Then I charged.

These giants weren't intimidated; they tended madmen and violent maniacs. They rose as I hurled myself forward, leaning forward to intercept my attack with professional determination. The closest raised both hands as if to seize me, and I leapt into the air, seized his thick wrists, and flipped my whole body over his head. *He was prepared for my attack, and attacks are best inflicted upon those unprepared.* My hard shoes slammed into the face of the second orderly, who hadn't expected the suddenness of my assault, and I hammered him back against the solid door behind him with a crashing *Boom!* that shook the hall and left him stunned. The first orderly seemed equally surprised by my athletics, but a second later I rebounded upon him, while his dazed partner crumpled to the floor.

We grappled and thrashed, and I kneed his rocky stomach, but the impact trembled my whole leg more than his midsection. He only winced, and then he grabbed my forearms and slammed me back against the wall. A sneering smile evidenced on his face, as if he expected my resistance to end, but I wasn't done. I struggled, strength against strength, muscle and willpower unwilling to yield. He was stronger than me. He was heavier than me. Yet no beast stands defeated while fight remained within them.

I was Drăcula, fed only moments before upon young blood, and I never surrender!

Forcing my muscles harder, I pressed until my arms, pushing against his, pulled free of the wall, and I inched him backwards, one step, and then another. Yet he pushed harder, and we strove as opposing juggernauts, poised in strife until only one remained. His smile vanished, and he pressed his hardest, and my limbs inched backwards, toward the wall.

Then I smiled, not a sneer, but the wicked grin of Vlad Drăcula. I opened my mouth fully and hissed like a cornered wildcat, and his eyes locked on my fangs; his certainty of victory paled in the light of my true face.

I was no mortal! I was no living man! I was superior to every creature that walked this Earth, and failure held no grip upon me!

The fear on his face fueled me, and I pressed him backwards with every muscle I owned and a will-power no muscle-bound goon could match.

A foot from the wall at my back, I reversed my straining, and with both his strength and mine, I pulled him toward me. Thinking my strength has given out, he hurtled forward, pushing with all his might. Suddenly I dropped low, my back striking the wall a second before my butt hit the floor: his face slammed into the wooden wall above me, and his head broke through, shattering the thick boards. Instantly I slipped behind him as he tried to pull himself out of the shattered wood, and I helped by pulling him out, then flinging his momentum backwards, repeating his face-first crash into one side of the hallway by slamming the back of his head into the stout timbers of the opposite wall. These boards only cracked, yet my foe staggered, dazed and limp, and I seized his head and twisted; his neck bones crackled as they separated, and he fell trembling at my feet.

Only a fighter with my centuries of practice could snap a neck so to render the limbs useless without killing the man. I yearned for his blood, but the second orderly was rising, shaking his head and wincing, and reaching for a rope hanging from a bell, which hung in a corner. I threw myself against him, knocked him away from the bell-rope, and then snagged his head in both my hands, which were trembling with the strength of my squeeze. His fists punched me furiously, stomach, ribs, stomach, harder than the heaviest blacksmith's hammer. I staggered, but forced myself to hold on. However, his skull was strong, and I couldn't endure the pounding of his fists. Unable to bear the punishment, I stabbed my thumbs into his eyes, digging in with my hard nails, and his fists ceased punching to seize my wrists, attempting to pull away my hands before sight left him forever.

I answered with my knee to his chin, again, and again, and he fell back against the shaking door, breaking it open and falling to the floor, me atop him. Beyond that door was a horror to match any vampiric nightmare: madmen, and madwomen, ragged, unkempt, screaming in terror as I fought the mountain that'd chained them to walls and locked them in cages.

Normally I didn't like having an audience, but this lot was no danger to me. My blood was pounding so hard my heart beat, and I yanked the muscled-fool's head to the side and sank my fangs into his neck. He screamed as every onlooker screamed, and I drank blood of such mighty supremacy my vitals soared, my energies escalating above any strength I'd ever felt. The shock of my bite seemed to startle my victim; his struggle altered, confused rather than focused. I sucked him into me, his métier, his authority, his overpowering dominance, and added his indomitability to mine. My muscles swelled and bulged, filled with vigor, a robustness I'd never had, surely enough to defeat any mortal foe. My mind reeled, and I expanded into an ever-greater superiority of man over beast.

My foe's struggles failed as his blood flowed into me. Soon I released him; his head lolled to the side and his eyes rolled up into his head, yet I left him alive.

Why should I kill a feast I might want again?

I went back to his companion, determined to indulge in a new feast. Other workers at the asylum ran up, smaller men, but seeing their fallen champions, they froze in disbelief, and then they fled screaming. Those of the insane who could fled with them, and the others could only pull at their chains or wrench upon their iron bars as if Death sought them. Yet they were small and weak, and I was Death.

The eyes of the paralyzed orderly blazed as I knelt upon his chest, bared my fangs, and repeated my orgy of blood. His fluids energized me no less than his fellow, and I supped fully. He was another powerhouse, his blood vital and hefty, rich and brawny. I'd left his companion alive, barely, out of respect for a fellow warrior. Yet this man would never regain use of his limbs; *to leave him alive would be no mercy.* So I drained him, glutting myself until I'd swallowed all of his strength and his heart failed.

I rose immaculate, glowing, my potency resonating like an infinite gong resounding out across the countryside. I walked down the corridor like a god, every figure I passed hurling itself down to cringe before my magnificence, averting their eyes for fear of attracting my disfavor. I felt swollen, developed, evolved beyond anything I'd ever felt before. I stood as godly as any man could be, determined to accomplish my will.

'Renfield ...!'

My call needed no reply; instantly I knew where he was. Past fools and lunatics flinging hay and excrement at each other, yet cringing before me, I strode with majesty unparalleled. The thick wooden door with its iron lock broke in half at my slightest push, and there, in the cell, was Renfield, a steel ring around his neck, chained to a wall.

"Master ...!" Renfield shouted joyously.

I stared directly into his mind, and his elation changed to a final scream to echo in the souls of the fearful. At a foolish whim I'd allowed this cretin a taste of my blood, and now I must insure that, before I left England, nothing of him remained to arise as an unworthy undead. I stormed to him, seized his head, and pulled, curious if he or his iron collar would give first.

The iron collar won, and his blood splashed, drenching me. I hurled his torn and severed head to the floor.

"Drăcula ...!"

I spun, ready for any attack. In the doorway stood Dr. John Seward, staring at me. Fear filled his eyes, and he paled, looking upon my carnage.

"John!" I accused. *"You dare face me, murderer of Lucy?"*

"Look at yourself!" John Seward shouted. "You stand ... covered in blood ... and call me a murderer?"

"Renfield had to die ... and you know why," I said. "He was unworthy of immortality."

"All men are unworthy of immortality," John said. "Look what it's done to you!"

I hesitated, intently feeling the wet gore plastered all over me.

"You're wise, John Seward," I said. "You're observant and keen, without the blind fanaticism of Dr. Van Helsing. Yet your knowledge and experience pale before mine. As hungry as I am for your blood, I'll spare you, for my final vengeance, my justice for Lucy, shall harm you far worse than death."

"I know Lucy chose you," John Seward said. "Doubtless you felt you were helping her, but men ... and women ... aren't made to be gods!"

"So ... you believed Quincey, yet you deny truth when it stands before you," I said. "Always are there losses for gain. Surgeons sacrifice a leg to save a body. Farmers clear an overgrown field that it can be replanted. Perhaps it's you, doctor, who can't reach beyond your fears."

"A man who sacrifices his humanity has nothing," John said.

"Only the unworthy limit their destiny," I said.

"Destiny is an assumption," John said.

"Destiny is a choice," I said.

"Choices have costs," John said. "You can choose your destiny, and strive for it, but consider the cost, not just to yourself, but to mankind!"

"What better service to mankind could the great offer than for those who can to rise above all others, to brave, discover, and share enlightenments no man could learn in a single lifetime?"

"Who, and how many, must pay the cost of those enlightenments?" John asked. "How many thousands have ended up like Renfield? Or like Lucy?"

"You started this war," I said. "I came here to learn, and elevated Lucy to join me ... at her request. *You murdered her ... the woman I loved ...!*"

"*We all loved her ...!*" John shouted.

A brief silence passed as we glared at each other.

"You're right," I said. "John, although they're good men, you alone surpass your fellows. Come with me, and learn all I can teach. I'll share with you all I know."

John hesitated. "I'll not join you."

"I didn't offer vampirism," I said. "Come; learn from an ... infernal. I'll insure your safety."

"What must I do?" John asked.

"You must keep my secrets, and swear to never act against me," I said. "For knowledge such as I offer, that's a small price."

"I'll never side with you," John said.

"I ask no man to deny his principals," I said. "I offer learning, my accumulated knowledge of centuries, experiences only immortals can offer. Come with me, not as a friend or an enemy, but as a student. I'll give you wisdom no mortal possesses, secrets you can bring back to England and increase the enlightenment your lands already enjoy."

"Why should I trust ...?" John began.

"It is my trust that matters," I said. "You know my weaknesses; each of us will have the power to slay the other, but the knowledge we may mingle, your New World sciences and my Old World understandings, could combine to create a basis for technologies to recreate both of our worlds. You know learning is the foundation of all improvements. I ask you to join me, not for your sake or mine, but for the betterment of everyone."

"You would take me with you ... and share with me ... everything ...?" John asked.

"I know more than any living man," I said. "I'll share everything I know."

"Why me ...?" John asked.

"Be not deceived," I said. "I desire the wisdom you possess, but more important, I require a man whom I believe to be fair ... smart and honest ... to learn all I know. Lucy was exceptionally intelligent, and plied me with a hundred questions, and wouldn't consent to vampirism until she knew everything about it. Once she knew all, she made her choice. I never forced her, nor did I lie to her. I give you her choice. Come with me, John Seward. Learn all, and then judge."

John hesitated, his eyes losing focus as he considered my offer. For a moment I was hopeful that my visit to England wouldn't be a complete failure, but then he shook his head.

"Thus does the devil ensnare the unwary," John said. "I can't be friends with her murderer."

"You're her murderer!" I shouted. "I cherished our friendship, and will abide by it, even though you murdered ... the one we both loved."

"You tricked us into accepting you, disguising your true nature, so you could steal Arthur's fiancée," John said. "Our friendship was your lie."

"You keep a journal, do you not?" I asked. "Read it; doubtless your own entries describe our friendship."

"No written record of our friendship will survive," John said. "I swear that."

"I, too, keep journals, my testimony of a life lasting four and a half centuries," I said. "They're the greatest almanac of human thought ever written: you'll never destroy those."

"If they make soulless killers, infernals like you, then I will destroy them," John said.

"You're a fool ... and a hypocrite!" I snarled. "You seek enlightenment, but reject it if its messenger has been cursed by God."

"I trust to God in all judgements," John said.

"A man who doesn't trust himself first can never hope to comprehend God, for he'll grovel in the dirt rather than raise his face to look ... and judge what he sees," I said. "Farewell, Dr. John Seward. You'll regret this night."

"Farewell, Count Drăcula," John said. "I pray you never see another night."

I stepped to the window, smashed its glass, and bent apart its iron bars like they were soft clay. Then I gave one last glance to John, hating him now more than ever.

Be the bat!

The sun set with imperial glory as I stood and watched, undaunted by the purity of its warm, golden rays, which could no longer harm me. The power radiating from my chest, containing my strongly-beating heart, warmed a body coursing with the blood of two mighty contenders. I stood victorious, unbeatable, ready for my last challenge in England: the eternal corruption of the heart of my enemies: *Mina Harker!*

The bright daystar, turning crimson, descended to the horizon as I watched, then beamed its last radiance to the sky as it slipped over. Night came again, and the wash of superhuman senses and powers crescendoed as the nocturnal strengths of my nature infused my enhanced form. I rivaled the ancient gods of forgotten mythologies. I felt invulnerable, and glanced skyward, seeing the emerging stars twinkling against the deepening twilight; *someday I'd evolve even greater than this, and on that day God himself will tremble before my revenge!*

But my ship, the Czarnia Catherine, sailed with the morning tide, and I must be on it. Until I was equal to God, and ready to challenge Him, I had to bide my time ... and leave England. When next I return, I'll already be England's conqueror.

I had only one task to finish, my final revenge, and that wouldn't happen until later, in the dark hours approaching midnight.

Wasted time is the eternal foe of the immortal. Waiting was an endless and infuriating frustration, which even my supreme patience couldn't thwart. Yet I'd nothing to gain by leaving my hovel, nor any reason to remain. With a shake of my head, I re-entered my second house and descended to my basement. There I lifted my crate and placed it on its edge beside the pitiful mound Renfield had made. Moving my coffin aside, I shoveled with my hands until as much of the Transylvanian dirt as I could move without a broom was transferred, and slowly filled the bottom quarter of my box. As the dirt settled, I lifted my travelling coffin and set it to rest upon the small layer of dirt from my homeland; *when next I slept, it would be aboard ship, travelling to my princedom.*

With careful deliberation, I picked up my two remaining treasures, the sketch of me I'd purchased from the street artist, and my Diary of England. Of my adventures in this modern world, these were all I wished to keep, save for the remaining wealth of Mrs. Effington's foolish infatuation, which was already in my coffin.

Gently, I removed my portrait from its frame, rolled the sketch, set it inside my coffin beside my diary and money, and closed its lid.

I placed the wooden top onto my crate, and with no small satisfaction, I drove the steel nails into the wood with the sheer strength in my hands. Then, with little physical effort, but an awkwardness caused by my crate's bulk and the narrowness of my staircase, I carried my heavy crate of dirt and coffin upstairs and set it in my living room. When I returned, I'd be driving a horse-driven cart, the taste of its owner still on my lips, to carry my box to the waterfront, where I'd see it loaded in preparation for my return to Castle Drăculea.

I brushed the dirt from my hands, and failing to clean them, proceeded to a water-barrel standing in the weeds outside my back door. I washed my hands properly. I'd already scrubbed off the gore of Renfield and those who'd worked in the asylum, and dressed in my best suit. These would be my last hours as a proper English gentleman, perhaps for another century, and it was improper for me to walk about its cobblestone avenues like an urchin soaked in blood.

Fog filled the air but it wasn't raining. After several hours passed, walking the streets, I bought and scanned a newspaper, yet I didn't feel like sitting and reading every article, and so I discarded it. I was tired of waiting. Many carriages were about, and I summoned one, a fancy Victoria with the top lowered, to carry me to Lucy's former residence, the home of Arthur Holmwood, where I'd find my delectable victim.

With a wide, devilish smile I rode exposed all the way. I held my head high, letting everyone I passed see my face. *What did it matter, as all of these fools would die of old age before I returned?* I could begin my second rise to ultimate royalty anywhere, in Alexandria, or Taiwan, or perhaps in one of those new cities in America. *When next I planned, I'd choose a city where my nature would never be suspected.*

I emerged from the carriage, paid and tipped the driver well, and then I waited until he drove away. Finally I turned to face the mansion. This time I wouldn't be delayed or thwarted by medical sciences. If my enemies attempted to stop me, then I'd unleash what a Drăculeşti should do to any enemy.

Nothing would upset my plan, not even if I had to kill every Englander on this accused island!

After entering the gate, I stepped into a deep shadow beneath a tree. There was no point in making this any more difficult than necessary. I needed to be aboard my ship by dawn. I chose not to use my mental powers to search for Mina, as I feared Dr. Van Helsing might sense my mind, even if the others lived in mental peasantry. So I circled the house, glancing inside the lit windows, and chanced to see my mortal adversaries, John, Quincey, Arthur, and Van Helsing, drinking and speaking, probably about my whereabouts, wreathed in the blue-gray wisps of cigar smoke. I paused there, but with a pang of disgust, I forced myself away; *my love of their companionship had made me incautious, which had left them free to murder my bride.*

At length I found what I sought, which was easy enough. I'd walked this balcony many times and knew where the bedrooms lay. Mina sat in a room not far from where I'd bitten Lucy. Now I'd repeat my generosity, although I doubted if the dignified Mrs. Harker would appreciate it any more than her husband or his friends.

I watched her through the window; she was dressed in her night-clothes, ready for bed, but sitting at a small table pecking at the keys of a typewriter. The *clack-clack* of her activity would serve me well, for it masked any sounds that might warn her of my presence. She was lovely in a youthful, very prim fashion; not a rival for the beauty of my Lucy but definitely attractive, if not overly-proper, even in her lacy white robe and negligee. No door offered entrance to her room from the balcony, and her window was locked, yet I could feel night air stealing into her room through the tiny cracks about the window jams, and no room I wished to enter could prevent me. Now I was glad I'd chosen to ride here rather than fly, for this transformation was my most-difficult.

Be the dust!

Moments later, I was seeping like vapor through passages few insects could traverse, and then I was inside, securely and fully entered. Silently, I passed as a thin mist to flow behind Mina Harker, who never looked up, intent on her typing. There I coalesced, returning to my human form, glad I was wearing a new suit of the most-impressive fashion. I stood beside her bed, not three feet from the back of Mina Harker, who was blissfully unaware of my presence.

I glanced over her shoulder, glad I cast no shadow. I read a few lines of what she was typing: a record of the visits of my foemen to my other houses, which she was transcribing from a handwritten diary.

Then Mina stopped typing and yawned deeply.

"Oh, that sleeping draught Dr. Van Helsing gave me is finally starting to work," Mina said loudly.

"Don't fret, my dear," came the voice of Jonathan Harker from an adjacent room, in which the door was partially closed. "You must be brave and strong, and help me through this horrible task. If you only knew how I regret telling you of this fearful thing, you'd understand how much we need your help."

I'd not expected Jonathan to be in an adjacent room, as he clearly was, while his young wife worked. I couldn't allow him to interfere; with silent treads, I slipped to the partially-opened door and stepped behind it.

"Well, I must help the medicine work, I guess," Mina said, and she spun the carriage and slid the paper from her machine, setting it down atop the others.

At this moment, Jonathan emerged in his nightclothes, looking so much like the friend I'd hosted in Castle Drăculea that I hesitated, yet only for a second. With my vampiric strength, I seized him by his throat so he couldn't cry out, and delved into the depths of his mind as I'd penetrated Renfield's. I rendered him asleep ... not dead, as he deserved. Jonathan instantly succumbed, and with a gentle push, I dropped him onto his bed and rushed to seize Mina.

"Jonathan ...?" she asked as she turned, and then she startled to see me rushing her. Mina tried to scream, but my hand struck like an angry snake, closing over her throat and choking her attempt to cry out.

"Silence!" I hissed malevolently. *"If you make a sound I'll dash your husband's brains out before your eyes."*

Mina cowered, stunned and frightened, but she didn't faint; *she was like Lucy, a strong-willed woman.*

With a mocking smile, I placed one hand upon her thin shoulder, and then slid it down to brush across the soft tops of her breasts exposed by her nightgown.

Mina jerked back with such fury that, had I not held her inviolate, she might've broken my grip.

"Patience, my lovely," I said to her. "Whom Drăcula claims belongs to him ... and Drăcula claims you. If you summon help, all who come to your aid shall die. However, if you don't resist, I'll allow those you love to live."

Her struggles lessened, but her eyes flashed a glare worthy of my three brides. I examined her freely with my caressing hand, and she made no effort to repel my invasions, although revulsion blazed in her eyes. On another night I might take my full pleasure upon her, but I'd made too many mistakes; *my goal was to finish and depart.*

"First, a little refreshment to reward my exertions," I said. "You may as well be quiet; it isn't the first time veins in his house have appeased my thirst!"

I bared my fangs, and her eyes widened with horror, but I tilted her head and bit deeply. Her blood was marvelous, exquisite, and as flavorful as my memory of Lucy's blood, but thicker, with a remarkable piquant and an unexpected zestiness. I drank deeply, thrilled by her flavor, yet I wasn't there to feed. Quickly I drew back; *I needed her conscious.*

I glanced at the many papers she'd typed; a record of my activities.

"So, like those who murdered my Lucy, you would pit your mortal brain against mine. You've helped frustrate my designs. Know now, as they know already, and will soon know even more, what it means to cross Drăcula. Whilst they plied their wits against me, I was countermanding them. And you, their best beloved one, shall now be to me flesh of my flesh, blood of my blood, kin of my kin; my bountiful wine-press. None of them shall minister to your needs, so in the end, they must slay you, their beloved, as they slew my Lucy."

With quick gestures, I unbuttoned my vest and white shirt, exposing my bare chest. With a hard fingernail, I scratched deeply across my dead flesh until the vital blood I'd so recently drunk dribbled from my wound. Mina stared aghast, confused by this, but I didn't hesitate. With a grin worthy of Satan, I forced her head down and pressed her face to my chest, her mouth smothered against my wound. Mina struggled, such that her supple hip struck the small table upon which her typewriter sat, and both toppled and crashed to the floor. Yet I couldn't stop: I pressed Mina's face into my flesh until she had no choice but to open her mouth to breathe, and then I held her firmly over my wound so drops of my blood entered her mouth.

However, the fall of her typewriter hadn't gone unnoticed; footsteps thundered up the stairs, exactly as I'd heard them before, and urgent voices spoke in the hallway.

"May it not frighten her terribly ...?" Arthur said.

"This is life and death," said Dr. Van Helsing. "Put your shoulders down and shove. *Now!*"

The door to the hall burst open, and there stood Dr. Van Helsing, Arthur, John, and Quincey, all staring in horror as I held Mina Harker pressed to my naked flesh, her husband unconscious upon their bed.

I laughed coldly at them, and I pulled Mina from my chest and turned her blood-stained face toward them, so they could all see my red filling her mouth, smeared upon her lips. Then I flung her, with little effort, onto her bed, where she fainted and lay unmoving beside her husband's still form.

"You think to baffle me ...!" I chuckled at their faces, alight with fear. "You four ... with your pale skins, face me like sheep in a butcher's shop. You'll be sorry, each of you! My revenge is just! I'll continue over centuries ... while you slowly die. Your precious Mina is already mine, a Queen of the Night, and I leave you to care for her ... *with all the cruelty you used to murder Lucy!*"

My revenge was complete!

With one last glare at them, but without another word, I chose to depart.

Be the dust!

October the 4th dawned clear and bright, with a strong ocean breeze. I was glad, for a rising yellow sun predicted a smooth sea, and I stood upon the bridge, watching as the mighty Czarina Catherine sailed eastward upon the Thames River toward the coast, away from the London waterfront where I'd drained the blood of so many. Above, sailors unfurling sails shouted commands and warnings to each other. Behind, England was already separate, its soil no longer under my feet. I stood upon the deck, rocking with the swells of the distant breakers, and looked back at the glorious island where I'd hoped to build my New World Order. Now I'd have to begin planning all over, and start somewhere else, but this adventure hadn't been a waste; I'd learned valuable lessons here which my future plans would circumvent.

But I was also leaving the birthland of my beloved Lucy. My heart was heavy, for never had I so regretted any death, not even that of my father. Lucy had proven to me there were women as worthy of immorality as I, and she'd taught me a lesson I'd not expected: *even Drăcula wasn't immune to love.* I'd have given anything to save her, even my death-beyond-death; I loved her more deeply than I'd ever loved anyone.

I'd miss her unto the last day of eternity.

The sun's rays stung my exposed flesh; *the invigorating effects of the blood of Dr. John Seward's strong orderlies was fading, protecting me no longer.*

With a last glance at the sea, I told the first mate I was going to my cabin to sleep, and instructed him to see that no one disturbed me. Then, while the sailors were busy making ready to enter the English Channel, and thence south to the Atlantic Ocean, I slipped down into the hull, made my way through the dark cargo bay, and pried the lid of my crate open. I slipped into my coffin, and there I fell into an exhausted sleep.

Chapter 20

Something unusual awoke me. *Had I been discovered?* I lay silent, hearing only the rush of heavy waters and the creaks of the ship. I sensed no one nearby. *What had awakened me?*

I'd planned to sleep for the entire voyage home. I'd not intended to awaken. Yet, as the sun set, something odd bothered me, a feeling I'd never known before ... subtle and strange. It lasted only a minute, and then it was gone.

I lay unmoving, wondering what had disturbed me. I could feel my vampiric powers newly arisen; twelve hours had passed since dawn. The sounds and rocking of the ship told me we were on the wide sea, and I doubted if anyone had ventured into the cargo hold.

Finally I gave up and went back to sleep, determined to be more observant if it happened again.

On October the 6th, less than an hour after sunset, the feeling returned. I was instantly awake, and I expanded my mind, but found no one near me, no living humans in the cargo hold, only a few rats scurrying about. I reached out my thoughts, yet none of the crew seemed alarmed or agitated, so I could only assume I hadn't been discovered.

Again, the strange feeling vanished after only a minute, and I was left wondering what was happening.

It was something, I was sure, and tomorrow night I'd be prepared, if it came again.

October the 7th was a long day, and I slept poorly, anticipating the sunset and the return of the unexplained sensation. When the dusk finally came, I laid as still and calm as I could, waiting for the feeling to return.

Finally the sensation began again, and this time I surrendered to it. A strange warmth seemed to wash over me, accompanied by the rise and fall of my ... *breasts* ...? I felt a youthful beating heart, although mine was still, and a vision came to my closed eyes ...

Dr. Van Helsing ...?

Dimly, his candlelit face swam before me, his deep, focused eyes staring into my absent, vacant expression. I recognized his short, thick beard, his strong forehead, and his thin, worried lips. He was looking right at me, at my soft, beautiful face ...!

Mina!

I was Mrs. Mina Harker ...!

Somehow Dr. Van Helsing was using Mina Harker to track my movements! She could sense me, feel the rocking waves, and hear the rush of the ocean! They knew I was on a ship!

Our connection broke. The feeling vanished as quickly as it'd come.

How was Dr. Van Helsing influencing Mina Harker? He was mentally-superior to most, but he was still mortal. *Had Englishmen unlocked the secrets of mesmerism?* Mina wasn't even undead; her heart was beating! *How else could Mina be connecting with me?*

I dwelt on this long, but no reached conclusions. *What were they trying to do? Was Dr. Van Helsing experimenting with Mina, perhaps seeking a way to undo God's curse?*

What would I do ... if the good doctor found a cure?

My sleep came troubled, and the sun set on October 8th with annoying slowness as I lay still and calm ... *awaiting Mina Harker.*

The feelings of her living body, her warmth, her beating heart and breathing lungs, stole over me gently. I lay relaxed, open to all perceptions. Again the face of Dr. Van Helsing filled my mind, and I detected others: Jonathan Harker, his expression worried, and Quincey, his brows lowered, his frown rigid. I made no attempt to communicate with them, although I was certain I could speak through Mina, if I tried.

Then Mina's voice spoke, softly but clearly:

"*Nothing,*" she said hesitantly, her tone lacking the passion it usually held. "*All is dark.*"

I wondered what she meant, as candle flames reflected off the faces staring at her, but then she continued.

"*I hear waves lapping ... against the hull, and water rushes by. Canvas and cordage strain ... and masts and yards creak. The wind is high. I hear it in the shrouds, and the bow throws back foam."*

"Do you know where he's going?" Dr. Van Helsing asked.

Our connection broke as I startled, jumping so hard I banged my head on the lid of my coffin.

Me ...!

They were using Mina to track me ... to my home!

The next dusk deepened and I laid awake, eager to begin. As it began, I allowed myself to become fully overwhelmed, wondering where it might lead.

"Where are you?" Dr. Van Helsing asked.

"I don't know," Mina said. "All is dark ... but I feel motion. I'm swaying, and I hear a ... creaking. Ropes strain, and the wind blows amid the rain."

"Still aboard ship," said Dr. John Seward's voice.

A hand rested upon my shoulder, a familiar hand, but Dr. Van Helsing gestured a sharp, quick wave, and the touch lifted. Somehow I knew it was Jonathan Harker, my husband's comforting grip.

Quincey came into view, stepping up beside Dr. Van Helsing, and he leaned over and looked into my eyes.

"Do we know he's on the Czarina Catherine?" Quincey asked.

"We know too little, but the purser on the dock described him exactly," Dr. Van Helsing said. "Now, Mina, I'm going to awaken you. When I count to three, you will awaken ... one ... two ..."

I frowned, but then relaxed. *What did it matter if they were tracking my movements?* They were in England, hundreds of miles away, and many days had passed. *I'd never see them again.* I was certain I could break and block our weak mental connection. I toyed with the idea of taking over Mina and making her attack them, but my evening connection was a pleasant distraction, and perhaps I'd learn more, if I kept watching in silence.

October the 12th arrived and passed; my connection with Mina never came. I wondered if they'd given up tracking my movements and discovered I was disappointed. I was starting to enjoy our brief intimacies, however distant. Yet the next evening, her connection came, a little stronger, yet our connection was broken and stuttering, as if troubled by distractions.

My mental image of Dr. Van Helsing trembled, and a loud noise filled my ears, and behind Dr. Van Helsing I saw a strange window, as of a thin-walled compartment, with shaking curtains showing Asian designs. Outside the windows, the landscape was moving past rapidly, hills covered with scrub brush, flashing by at great speed. The jostling and tumult hid Mina's words from my mind, but a rumbling filled my ears, loud ... and mechanical. I saw Arthur sitting beside Dr. Van Helsing, and his lips moved, yet I could hear nothing. Then Mina awoke ... and I was alone in my coffin.

Only after our connection broke did I realize its import: I'd seen pictures of this device in books.

They were on a train: The Orient Express!

They'd crossed the channel. They must've missed communicating the night before because they were in a carriage hurrying toward Paris. Only there could they catch The Orient Express.

But why? Where were they going?

The realization startled me. *Varna ...! They were taking The Orient Express to catch up with the Czarina Catherine ... at Varna!*

They were chasing me ...!

If nothing else, the determination of Englishmen never failed to astound me. They were fearless and single-minded ... and ultimately foolish.

Did they think to surprise the Master of Mesmerism, who's been eavesdropping on them every sunset?

They'd regret their insolence.

I was Drăcula, the Hunter, not to be hunted by puny mortals! I wasn't entering their lands; *they were entering mine!*

However, a quick calculation warned me they'd arrive at Varna two days before my ship docked there. With their connections and that much time, they could board and search the Czarina Catherine by daylight with crosses and stakes.

I couldn't sleep away the rest of my voyage. *They'd find my crate, open it, and murder me as they killed Lucy.*

In the darkness I pushed open my coffin lid, reached out, and shoved the wooden lid off my crate. Yet, before I climbed out of my coffin, I filled my pockets with coins from my stash. Then I went to find the captain.

The sea was smooth, the waves gentle in the starlight, and a new yellow moon hung in the brisk sea air. The first sailor I saw jumped at my sudden appearance, and my demand that he take me to his captain led to an introduction to their purser, an Italian, who introduced me to the first mate, and after a stout refusal to answer his questions, I was finally escorted to the captain of the Czarina Catherine.

"I want you ... to miss your stop at Varna," I said.

The captain, a swarthy, dark-skinned giant who looked like a shaved bear, stared at me.

"This ship will dock on time, where we're scheduled, and nothing ...!"

I tossed a gold coin at him, and he caught it, his eyes alight with surprise. He stammered a reply, but I tossed two more.

"But ... I'll miss my connections ...!" the captain argued. "I have contracts ... obligations ...!"

Beside him was a small desk; I dropped seven more gold coins upon it.

"My needs require me at Dardanelles," I said. "You'll sail straight there ... and not even come in sight of Varna."

"How can I explain ...?" the captain asked.

"Navigational error; a broken sextant," I suggested. "Any excuse for missing Varna ... or return my gold."

Asking if I was mad, but pocketing my gold sovereigns, he called his officers and changed the route. He'd get in trouble, he grumbled as he patted my pocketed bribe, but his return route would dock him to

Varna only five days later, and then he'd apologize for missing his stop.

Delighted, I returned to my coffin. My enemies would arrive at Varna awaiting a ship that wouldn't arrive. Once in Castle Drăculea, surrounded by the Szgany, my beloved wolf-pack, and countless other allies, I'd be invulnerable.

The Czarina Catherine would arrive at Dardanelles in eleven days, and from there I'd wire my cousins with instructions to return to my lands, collect my crate when we docked in Wallachia, and transport it to Castle Drăculea.

My chasers arrived in Varna late, on October 14th, but well in time to await my ship. My communion with Mina came exactly on time; they were in an elegant hotel room, still and quiet, and Mina repeated her descriptions of the sounds and feelings of being aboard ship.

"Waves, splashing," Mina said. *"I hear it clearly. Canvas cracks. I'm on a ship."*

"More clearly than last night?" Dr. Van Helsing asked.

"Yes," Mina said.

"Perhaps he's on deck," Arthur said.

"Can you see anything?" Dr. Van Helsing asked.

"Darkness," Mina said.

I grinned, fighting the urge to play with their minds further, but certain they'd cease their mesmeric connections if they knew I was aware of them.

Yet ... what did that matter? Jonathan Harker knew the route ... to and from Castle Drăculea. No man walked in my homeland I wasn't aware of; I'd have two nights warning before they approached the Borgo Pass.

"*Are you hungry?*" *Dr. Van Helsing asked.*

"*No,*" *Mina said.* "*Yes. I'm ... fasting.*"

"*The varmint's wearing his hat low,*" *I heard Quincey's voice.*

"*Are you sure he can't sense Mina ... or harm her?*" *Jonathan asked.*

"*Can you sense us?*" *Dr. Van Helsing asked.*

With a single wish, I broke our connection.

On October the 15th, our connection lasted longer.

"*Creaking, waves, and strong wind,*" *Mina said.* "*Sloshing water.*"

"*They could have been blown off course,*" *John Seward said.* "*That sailor said a storm was brewing.*"

"*If Drăcula killed the crew, he could be sailing anywhere,*" *Jonathan said.*

"*The Czarina Catherine is a big ship for one man to manage, even Drăcula,*" *Arthur said.*

"*What do you see?*" *Dr. Van Helsing asked.*

"*Darkness,*" *Mina said.*

"*If he was sailing the ship himself, he wouldn't be in his coffin at night,*" *John Seward said.*

"*Do we wait ... or press on?*" *Jonathan asked.*

"*We need to know more,*" *Dr. Van Helsing said.* "*Let's wait until tomorrow.*"

I smiled; my foes were puzzling over the failure of the Czarina Catherine to dock at Varna. Dr. Van Helsing looked especially unhappy, but I resisted laughing lest Mina break out in demonic chuckles.

I'd triumphed over them again!
But ... would they turn back, defeated?

That night I arose and sought out the captain again. I urged him to push his vessel to its top-speed, and another handful of gold gained me his assurance he'd do his best. I suspected my enemies would soon realize their mistake and come after me again, as I'd seen no evidence of Englishmen surrendering to the inevitable.

We were in a race, and the first to arrive at Castle Drăculea would be the winner.

My hunger was rising, yet I was determined not to feed aboard the Czarina Catherine.

I couldn't sail this giant ship alone.

On October 18th my communication didn't come, and I assumed that they were traveling again. No trains followed the coast now, so their roads would be more rugged, assuming they didn't board a ship to continue the chase. Yet ... *would they not be able to mesmerize Mina in her cabin?* Her failure to connect suggested they were traveling overland.

On October the 24th we docked at Dardanelles an hour before sunset, and despite the sun, I disembarked with the other passengers. I took the opportunity to send a telegram to my cousins with detailed instructions to collect me. However, before I sent the telegram, I overheard that another ship was about to depart from Dardanelles headed to Vervesti, a destination even closer to my home than Galatz.

I hurried to board the other ship, and met a crew I considered pirates, yet their captain was a small, older Slovak with greasy hair and skin. This ship was smaller, its crew less than ten, but their reaction to my offer of gold was astounding. Their captain smiled with his few remaining teeth and quickly agreed to my conditions.

Returning to the Czarina Catherine, I arranged for my crate to be immediately transferred to this ship. If my pursuers traveled fast, they'd arrive at Galatz on October 29th, the day the Czarina Catherine docked there. Then they could search for my crate all night. By the time they realized their error, I'd be far ahead of them again.

I'd missed my connection with Mina that evening. In my absence, they'd know something was different, but what would they do?

I enjoyed the diversion of the chase. I felt Mina only once before October 30th; they were in a hotel room again, this time more rustic than elegant, and Dr. Van Helsing and the men looked exhausted and frustrated.

"Darkness, loud splashes, and rushing wind," Mina said. *"We are shaking ... harder."*

"Are you in a storm?" Dr. Van Helsing asked.

"I can't tell," Mina said.

John Seward was sitting beside Dr. Van Helsing, with Jonathan on his other side. Behind them, Quincey was pacing back and forth. John Seward leaned over and whispered in Van Helsing's ear.

"Is Drăcula asleep ... or awake?" Jonathan asked.

"Awake," Mina said.

"Is he in his coffin?" Jonathan asked.

"Yes," Mina said.

"The Czarina Catherine has left its scheduled route," Arthur's voice came from behind me. "It could sail anywhere: China ... or South America."

"We must keep connecting Mina to Drăcula," Dr. Van Helsing said. "Eventually, he must land."

"I still say a snake always slithers toward its hole," Quincey said.

"Drăcula chose the Czarina Catherine because it was headed back to his home," John said. "Until we learn otherwise, we should assume that's his destination."

"Drăcula didn't live alone," Jonathan said. "If we follow him to Transylvania, when we meet, he'll be reinforced."

We sailed onwards on my new ship, but a new sense of urgency pressed me. I gave the captain more gold to sail faster. I'd been foolish, I realized, during my whole stay in England. Gold moved men more readily than fear. I should've secured my wealth first, then used gold to accommodate my wishes, rather than transforming every other night, which required me to frequently feed. If I'd used wealth, rather than vampiric powers, fewer bodies would have marked my presence.

But then I might have missed meeting Lucy ...!

That evening, shortly before dawn, my new ship arrived at Veresti, docked briefly, and then departed with the dawn. The next day we stopped while the sun was high at Fundu, and then sailed on, past Galatz, to my final destination: Bistritza.

My arrival at Bistritza came shortly after dawn, but as I'd well-bribed the Slovak captain upon boarding his ship, and my crate was unloaded first. I listened carefully, glad to hear the accents of my native land again. Voices of my cousins filled my ears as soon as my crate was set upon my native Hungary.

I'd beaten my chasers home!

I was loaded aboard a small boat that rocked violently, a skiff of my cousins, and we pushed off at once. The sounds of the water changed, from the deep rush of the ocean to the shrill splashing of river-waters, and I considered refusing any more connections, if they came, but they were too late: *not even the determination of Englishmen could stop me now!*

"Water rushing," Mina said. *"I hear an engine chugging. I'm on a ship ... a small ship."*

"A steam launch?" John asked.

"Most likely," Quincey said. *"He's not on the ocean anymore."*

I was slightly shaking, softly bouncing; I was in a carriage, moving slowly against chill air. The scent of horses filled my nose, and I breathed the dusty air of a road. My connection was stronger, more intense. I felt dry, my stiff undergarments tight, and my dress crumpled and unwashed. I could feel my heart pound, strongly, and I was horribly cold. I was seated between Jonathan and John, facing Quincey, Arthur, and Dr. Van Helsing.

I broke our connection. My enemies had abandoned their chase of ships and were heading straight over the Carpathian Mountains to Bistritz, not far from Castle Drăculea.

It was they, not I, who'd arrive first!

That night I arose and helped my cousins pole. At first, they crossed themselves and put out two fingers towards me, to ward off the evil eye, but I commanded them to hurry. Our skiff had a steam engine, but it was slow, and every minute counted. I couldn't eat my cousins or they'd abandon me, yet I was dreadfully hungry. I ignored my communications with Mina the next night, busy helping to pole, but I had to return to my coffin before dawn. I was weak and could afford no errors. Yet I'd increased our speed.

Who would arrive first?

On November the 5th, around midday, we beached on some rocky sand, and I heard the whinny of horses; *we were on the last leg.* Despite the bright sunlight, which burned me terribly, I helped lift my crate onto the wagon, and as my driver mounted the gotza and cracked his whip, I crawled back inside my coffin, exhausted but determined. By sunset tomorrow we'd arrive at the Borgo Pass, and as soon as the sunlight failed, I'd be close enough to transform and fly back to

Castle Drăculea. Once there, not even my enemies could threaten me.

Our horses raced, and we changed mounts three times, but every minute we had to stop to water and rest the tired beasts ate at my soul. I could sense Mina now, not behind me, but ahead of me; *we'd meet again soon!*

Yet, when we met, would I have the strength to resist them?

A small group of Szgany arrived to accompany me on horseback, but these were woodsmen, not warriors. *Would they risk their lives to defend me?*

Sunset was nearing as we rode through the Mittel into the rugged, boulder-strewn Borgo Pass. Soon my victory would be assured, and then those who'd slain my Lucy would pay the ultimate price.

I'd murder them slowly, with tortures to madden any god or mortal ... and they'd beg me for death!

Then, to my utter horror, my driver stopped my wagon so abruptly I was hurled into the top of my coffin. A loud voice shouted in anger; *Quincey Morris, his deep American accent unmistakable in the heart of Transylvania.*

I hesitated; the sun would be down in minutes, and then my full vampiric powers would arise.

Crack! Crack! Crack!

Gunfire blasted out in the Borgo Pass, mixed with the screams of my cousins. My Szgany were armed with swords, spears, and bows; they couldn't defy modern weaponry.

Wild gallops of two more horses assailed my ears, and then the voice of Dr. John Seward cried out.

"Arthur ...! Jonathan ...! Hold them at bay!"

The sun was still up, but I reached out with my mind to my closest brothers.

'Wolves! Hear my call, and come to your master! Kill all strangers in our land!'

In daylight I couldn't sense them. I could only hope they heard me. My Szgany warriors cried out, and I listened with disgust to their fearful mutters. *What cowards they were!* But doubts gnawed; *hadn't I been the one who'd taught them fear?*

"Halt ...!" Jonathan Harker shouted, his voice heightened with passion, and the *Crack!* of another gunshot rang out, followed by more Szgany cries.

"Hurry!" shouted the aged voice of Dr. Van Helsing. "*The sun is almost set!*"

A great scuffling broke out, and many shouts from the Szgany, followed by curses and *Cracks!*

Screams sounded out, mixed with shouts of anger and clashes of steel; *my Szgany were fighting!*

Should I emerge to help them ... or wait until the sunset, when I'd arise all-powerful?

One cry delighted me: Quincey Morris bellowed, a guttural scream of pain and fury, and I decided I could wait no more. Yet my decision was too late; a metal tool stabbed into the top of my crate with loud *chunk!*

My decision was instantaneous. *I wouldn't be taken like a fox in a trap!* With all of my daylight strength, I pushed hard, slammed back the lid of my coffin, and pushed open the top of my crate.

Over me stood Jonathan Harker, the first modern Englishman I'd ever seen, holding a great Kukri knife in one hand, a spent pistol in the other. His eyes blazed with alarm as I rose before him, for of all my foes, Jonathan had been the youngest, the longest in my company, and the most fearful of me. He attacked with his knife, but I was a true warrior. With deft agility, I dodged his slice and seized his wrist with one hand, his throat with my other. *Even in the daytime, I was still Drăcula, the mightiest warrior since Alexander the Great! No minor English businessman could defy me, especially not this frightened youth!*

Crack ...!

The gunshot blasted into my ears even as I staggered back. With horror, I looked down to see a ragged vent torn through my coat, vest, and shirt, a gaping hole in my chest, from which no blood spilled. The pain was staggering, and I followed its origin to see Mrs. Mina Harker, her face awestruck, holding a smoking pistol.

Mina Harker had shot me ...!

The fighting suddenly ceased as I fell back, releasing Jonathan, and reeling in agony. The gunshot hadn't killed me, but the pain was colossal, such that my mind blanked, overcoming immortal reasoning. Yet, at that second, the stinging sunlight left my face, and the last light of the daystar rose above the trees.

Sunset had come, and with it, my vampiric powers returned!

Jonathan saw the look of triumph on my face, and stepped back in fear, but the ever-avenging angel, Quincey Morris, dripping with blood from many knife-wounds in his flesh, leaped up onto the cart and stabbed his thick bowie knife right into my heart!

Our cart was too small; I fell back, tripped against my crate, and fell onto it, landing upon the hard insides of my coffin. Quincey stood over me, gritting his teeth against his own pains, still gripping the handle of the bowie knife he'd embedded in my chest. *The agony was unparalleled!* Then Jonathan Harker appeared at his side, holding his Kukri knife, and he raised it over my throat.

I gasped; *decapitation could kill a vampire ...!*
Even as Jonathan's blade descended, I knew I must act or die. *But I was weak and badly injured! Would I have enough strength?* His blade struck my throat and cut deep; *the agony was indescribable!*
Be the dust ...!!!

Midnight, May the 22nd; I'd no idea what year it was. In the empty, lonely hollows of the moonlit Borgo Pass, only silence dwelt. No signs of disturbance marred the deep, empty ruts of the road. Long winter snows and hard spring rains had long destroyed all the footprints and hoof-marks that told a tragic story. Dim traces of blood remained, as did the nearby graves of the Szgany that'd died here, fighting a losing battle for a lord who'd ruled over them for four centuries.

The moonlight shone ghostly white, with a soft hue of blue, upon dirt once moistened with human blood, mixed with memories best forgotten by this land's fearful inhabitants. Yet the wind still rose here, often, swirling around the dust of this ancient land amid the tall, lonely rocks and aged trees where once ruled a mighty king.

The wind blew again, silently, and swirled the dust into a shape, a figure, which slowly pieced itself together, and formed a weak, quivering substance out of the nothingness it'd become. Pain, intense strain ... and slowly consciousness grew.
I'd returned ...!
I recognized the Borgo Pass.
I'd won ...! God hadn't defeated me ...!
Time to begin again ...

Weakness crushed my slowly gathering form. I collapsed onto the dry, summer dirt. The heaviness of my limbs pressed upon me like countless iron chains, squeezing agonies from every fiber. Long I lay, helpless as a legless centipede, barely able to move muscles that rebelled against my every effort. Finally I rolled onto my back, stabbed by needles only my immortal will could overpower. Never had I awoken so famished, maddened by starvation, yet unable to feed.

Above me, the silent, vast, endless cosmos of eternity stung my eyes, tormenting me with its starry endlessness, its summit of peaceful serenity. Yet I stared up at the sadistic, twinkling entirety of creation, angered and undaunted.

"Do your ... worst, Great Teacher," I whispered, with barely a breath eking from my lips. "Enjoy my suffering ... while you can. With each castigation ... I arise farther from them ... and closer to you. Your day of reckoning ... will dawn. In the end, there ... will be ... only ... Drăcula."

NEVER THE END

All Books by Jay Palmer

The VIKINGS! Trilogy:
    DeathQuest
    The Mourning Trail
    Quest for Valhalla

The EGYPTIANS! Trilogy:
    SoulQuest
    Song of the Sphinx
    Quest for Osiris

The Magic of Play
The Heart of Play
The Grotesquerie Games
The Grotesquerie Gambit
Souls of Steam
The Seneschal
Jeremy Wrecker - Pirate of Land and Sea
Viking Son
Viking Daughter
Dracula - Deathless Desire

ABOUT THE AUTHOR

Born in Tripler Army Medical Center, Honolulu, Hawaii, Jay Palmer works as a technical writer in the software industry in Seattle, Washington. Jay enjoys parties, reading everything in sight, woodworking, obscure board games, and riding his Kawasaki Vulcan. Jay is a knight in the SCA, frequently attends writer conferences, SciFi Conventions, and he and Karen are both avid ballroom dancers. But most of all, Jay enjoys writing.

Jay Palmer

JayPalmerBooks.com

Made in the USA
Monee, IL
06 February 2024